Beyond the Border Forest

INTO THE PRAWDZIWY LAS

THE IMMORTAL SEASONS CYCLE
BOOK ONE

MOLLY HANISZEWSKI

QUILLS & COSMOS PRESS

ISBN (paperback): 978-1-965790-03-8

ISBN (hardback): 978-1-965790-04-5

ISBN (ebook): 978-1-965790-05-2

Library of Congress Control Number: 2025939825

CONTENT WARNINGS IN BACK.

For Alva and Billy.
This book would never have been written without the two of you.

Prologue

I n the old days, the magic of the seasons ran rampant through the forest. Storms of ice and snow battled fires and blistering waves of heat. The turmoil spilled from the forest into the surrounding land, causing mayhem. The creatures of the forest looked to their ruler, the Bear Maiden, to save them from the chaos.

The Bear Maiden carefully gathered up the feral magic and bided her time, waiting for the right person to come along.

As luck would have it, there were two.

Two men, young travelers seeking knowledge and greatness, came to the forest one day, and the Bear Maiden offered them the wild magic. They accepted, and they each took half of the power she had collected. The younger, handsomer one took the magic of warmth and growth and fire and became the Oak King. And the older, more serious one took the magic of cold and ice and death, becoming the Holly King. And so it was that the Oak King ruled the forest for the months of Spring and Summer, while the Holly King ruled in the months of Autumn and Winter. The seasons fell into place, blending seamlessly into the year. The Kings told the plants when to grow and when to die, told the animals when to mate and when to birth, and told the people when to plant and when to harvest.

So it has been for generations.

It is said that, during the Holly King's rule, the Oak King leaves the *forest and travels the world. During the Oak King's rule, the Holly King withdraws into his mountain fortress and forsakes all company.*

And while they do, on occasion, reveal themselves to mortals, entry into their forest is forbidden. Those who trespass will find themselves at the Kings' mercy.

Yet, countless mortals have risked their lives and entered the forest in order to reach the mountains. For it is said that if one meets the Bear Maiden as she descends from her Winter cave upon the first day of Spring, she will grant that person the dearest wish of their heart.

And wishes are powerful things indeed.

CHAPTER 1

Rowan

WINTER SOLSTICE

"What husband is going to want to see this mess first thing in the morning?" Elzbieta asked, her eyes roving over Rowan's hastily braided crown. "I taught you better than this. Go fix it."

Rowan's mother had been prodding a bowlful of dough when Rowan entered the kitchen, deftly pressing a finger into the wheat-flecked mass and watching how quickly it sprang back from the indentation. But when she saw Rowan in the doorway, she had let the cloth fall back over the bowl and stuck her hands on her hips, scowling at her second eldest daughter.

Rowan's shoulders slumped. She had dressed in the dark, hurrying so she could get downstairs and help her mother prepare the food for the Winter Solstice. She had pulled on a pale green dress, laced up her russet *kamizelka* over it, and wrapped a hasty braid around her head. But of course, it wasn't good enough for her mother.

Wilting under her mother's glare, she hurried to the mirror in the sitting room. She redid the braids more tightly this time and pinned them up with care. She didn't know why it mattered what she looked like while she was preparing breakfast, but of late, her parents had been particularly picky about her appearance.

When Rowan reentered the kitchen and showed her mother her work, Elzbieta grunted.

"Better," was all she said. While Rowan tied on an apron and poured herself a cup of coffee, her mother listed off the morning's tasks.

"The dough is ready for twisting. You'll need to make the spice mixture yourself first, I haven't had time—you should have been down here helping me at least half an hour ago. Once you've set the knots to rise, chop me carrots and onions, in separate bowls. And don't forget to skim the stock."

An unnecessary reminder—Elzbieta had trained all her children to frequently peek into the giant stock pot simmering on the stove all day and skim off any unpleasantness that had bubbled up from the bones and vegetable scraps within.

Rowan took a sip of her coffee, then set to work, grinding spices and rolling out the pillowy, egg-rich dough out onto the floury counter. She pressed it into a huge rectangle and sprinkled it with the spice mixture. After cutting the rectangle into long strips, she took each piece and twisted, wrapping it into an intricate knot, which she set in a buttered tin. They needed a lot of spice-knots, both for their own breakfast and to give to any friends and family who came to call that day.

"Was that sister of yours showing any signs of life?" Elzbieta asked curtly as she braided ropes of dough into a large loaf.

"I think Celine went back to sleep—she seemed tired," Rowan said as she lay the cloth over the spice-knots. She had dressed in the hallway to avoid waking her sister, who always grouched at her if she made too much noise.

"She'd better get up soon if she really means to catch us something for dinner." Elzbieta's voice had that odd, tight quality it always had when she spoke about her eldest daughter.

Rowan knew her mother wanted Celine here with them in the kitchen, learning to keep house from her mother. But Rowan's father had been weakened years ago by a wasting sickness, which left him unable to hunt or cut wood to earn the family's income. Rowan's brother Ademun was still too young to take up his trade, so they were forced to rely on Celine to bring in the wood and catch food for the table.

And now, as if summoned by the mention of her name, Celine stomped into the kitchen, already dressed and wearing her good, thick-soled boots.

"The bold hunter, out of bed at last," her mother said, hands on her hips. "You still think it's a good idea to go out? It's cold, and there's a fresh blanket of snow waiting for you."

Rowan quickly passed Celine a mug of coffee, wishing her mother would stop talking.

"I'll be fine," Celine mumbled into her coffee.

She looked as though she'd yet to fully open her eyes. Without a word, Rowan began to pack a bag with dried meat and cheese.

"Why don't you put that pretty face to good use and go ask Piotr Kowal's son for a leg of venison instead?" Elzbieta raised her eyebrows at Celine. "He's a fine looking man, and he'd keep you in meat and furs aplenty."

"I said I'll be fine," Celine snapped. "I said I would go and I mean to keep my word. A bit of snow is nothing. Besides," she said more evenly, "Irys is going out with me."

Elzbieta scooped the braided loaf off the counter and gently placed it on a pan, covering it with a towel to rise. "Hoping to get something big?"

Celine shrugged. "I've seen some tracks in the forest in the past few days—should prove interesting. And if that doesn't lead anywhere, there are always doves and rabbits."

Rowan grimaced. "Leave the doves. They're so small, plucking them makes my hands cramp up."

Elzbieta opened her mouth—surely to tell Rowan her hands cramped only because she just wasn't doing it right—but before she could speak, Celine downed her coffee, grabbed the bag of food from the counter, and slunk out the door with a wide yawn.

Rowan caught the brief look of hurt on her mother's face as she watched her oldest child leave without a word of goodbye. But Elzbieta was Elzbieta, and when there wasn't time for something, she pushed onward.

She cleared away Celine's coffee cup and rolled up her sleeves with renewed vigor. She began grinding meat using the hefty cast-iron grinder that Rowan could barely lift by herself.

"Rowan, mince me half an onion for the *frikadelle*," her mother ordered. "I don't know why you're standing around—you know there's work to do."

Please, Rowan added in her mind. She set aside a portion of the onion she was chopping and went over it again and again with her knife, until the pieces were small as slivers of wood. She slid the onion from the blade of her knife into the bowl of ground meat. Elzbieta tossed in pinches of this spice and that herb—fennel, sage, paprika, nutmeg.

A rustling came from the doorway. Rowan looked up as Ademun shuffled in, yawning and rubbing sleep from his eyes.

"Happy Solstice," she told him as she cleaned off the knife.

"It smells good in here already," he mumbled, climbing onto the stool near the fire. It was the warmest spot in the whole house.

"If you wanted to get up so early, you should have gone out with Celine," Elzbieta chided, frowning at her only son. "And you know the kitchen's no place for a boy. Go sit in the other room."

"But it's so cold in there!" Ademun protested, wrapping his skinny arms around himself.

He and Celine had inherited their father's slight frame, where Rowan had their mother's plump, sturdy build and wide hips. Danica and Kestrel had yet to hit their growth.

"What kind of man complains of the cold?" Elzbieta retorted, pointing toward the door. "Out."

Rowan gave her brother an apologetic smile as he shambled out of the kitchen. She didn't know why her parents forbade Ademun from helping with the cooking or even spending time in the kitchen. If Celine could go out and do "men's" work, why couldn't Ademun do "women's" work?

"And tell your sisters to get themselves out of bed!" Elzbieta called after him. "They're not too young to help with the Solstice meal."

Rowan heard Ademun calling up the stairs, and minutes later, Kestrel wandered in, her hair disheveled and her skirt so wrinkled that Rowan wondered if she had slept in it last night.

Elzbieta took one look at her third eldest daughter and her face turned furious. "*Niechlujny!*" she cried, shooing Kestrel back out the door, "What a mess you are! Haven't I taught you all better than this? We will never find husbands for any of you at this rate! Go put on a different skirt, and I swear, if that one is as wrinkled as this one..."

"Mother," Rowan began as Kestrel scurried back out the door.

"Don't *you* start anything!" Her mother shook her wooden spoon at Rowan. "She's picked up all of *your* bad habits—don't think your father and I don't know it!"

Rowan shut her mouth. When her mother got worked up like this, she often went to complain to Rowan's father. Once Lodin got involved, it meant the end of all merrymaking for the day.

When Kestrel returned, Danica was with her. They were dressed in matching red vests and green skirts, and Rowan suspected Danica had helped Kestrel with her hair. Though she was the youngest, Danica was better than any of them at avoiding their parents' ire.

"Finally." Elzbieta directed the girls to put on aprons. "Go and set the table, then start cooking the eggs."

"But, Mother," Danica protested. "I haven't finished making my Solstice gifts yet."

Danica loved painting. Rowan knew, despite her sister's attempt at secrecy, that her gifts this year were little portraits of each family member.

"And I need to check on the pigs!" Kestrel added.

One of their two sows had developed an infection in her ear. Kestrel had taken it upon herself to care for the sick pig.

"Your little craft projects do not matter as much as getting breakfast on the table," Elzbieta replied without missing a beat. "And you will have plenty of time to grub around with the pigs later. Now, for the love of the gods, do something *useful*. I've got to get this frikadelle mixture chilling soon."

Rowan's stomach growled at the very thought of the frikadelle to come—little meatballs, fried until brown, then cooked for a long time in a rich gravy. The intensely savory dish was always served with an orange-spiked currant jam, and as you cut a bit of frikadelle, you scooped a little jam with it and ate the two together. Ademun liked his separate, but it was considered bad manners not to combine them. Regardless, it was always served for Solstice dinner.

Her mother began folding the flavorings into the ground meat, kneading with a lighter hand than she used for kneading dough. Rowan poked at the spice-knots. The dough sprang back a little, but the impression of her finger remained. They were ready. The heat of the busy kitchen always helped speed along the rise.

Rowan brushed the tops of the knots with beaten egg, sprinkled a little sugar over them, and slid the pans into the oven. Now she needed to remember to constantly sniff at the air—as soon as she could smell them, they were close to being done. And for some reason, her mother could always smell them before Rowan could.

Sure enough, just as Rowan tipped the last of the chopped carrots into a bowl, her mother called, "Check the spice-knots," without even looking up.

Rowan peeked at the baking treats. She pressed lightly on the tops of the few paler ones at the front, gave the pans a turn, and left them for just another minute or two to deepen in color.

"Done," she called to her mother, and she brought a pan over for her the check.

Elzbieta scrutinized the pan, simultaneously stirring a pan of sizzling sausages on the stove.

"Eh, good enough," she said at last, "Let's just get this breakfast on the table quickly."

Rowan's face fell. She thought the spice-knots were baked to perfection. But her mother always found fault with her bakes. She tried not to think about it as she pried each spice-knot from the tin, setting them on a serving plate.

As soon as the plate was full, all work in the kitchen stopped. Rowan and her mother carried the plates of spice-knots, little apple-sage sausages, sliced oranges, eggs, and dishes of jam, butter, and cream into the family hall. Rowan's father was already up and seated in an armchair before the fire.

"Did you go down the stairs by yourself, Lodin?" Elzbieta asked, her voice sharp with worry. He hadn't managed to make that trip alone in years.

He waved a hand dismissively. "Celine helped me down ages ago. Don't fuss, *kochanie*. You've been working so hard all morning."

He frowned at Rowan and her sisters, as if to say that they were the cause of all their mother's hardships.

Everyone took their place at the table as Rowan settled her father in his chair and poured him coffee. Elzbieta reached for a spice-knot and tore it in half, setting the steaming hot pastry on Celine's plate.

"For the hunter," she murmured grudgingly. It was half ceremony, half superstition, the notion that no plate should be empty on the Solstice, even if the family member in question could not come to the table.

Lodin smirked and reached for a spice-knot. Rather than being grateful that Celine worked so hard to feed her family, he acted as though it was a hobby for her—something he tolerated but would not take seriously.

As for the rest of the village, some folk raised their eyebrows at an eldest daughter out doing men's work, and Elzbieta raised her eyebrows right back at them.

"With her father ill and her brother too young to swing an axe on his own, we'd starve if Celine didn't go out for us. Besides, she's already out woodcutting—she might as well bring dinner home to boot. She'll still make a fine wife someday."

And most folk knew to leave them alone about it. At least the family had one daughter—Rowan—who had spent her teenage years the way all daughters were supposed to: preparing for her betrothal.

The family tucked into their breakfast. Rowan couldn't help but grin as she watched her father slyly scoot the jar of blackberry jam over to his plate. For some reason, he only liked the spice-knots dipped in jam —said it brought out the best in their flavor. Rowan's mother was horrified at the thought of her favorite baked good needing a condiment, so he stayed surreptitious about his use of jam.

Rowan herself loved the spice-knots with just a little butter melting over them. She pulled off a sugar-coated strip and watched with satisfaction as the tender bread stretched and broke with a little burst of steam. The dough was enriched with buttermilk, egg yolks, and a great deal of butter, resulting in a rich, tangy flavor bread balanced well with warm, comforting spices. Rowan ate three spice-knots before even looking at the other food on the table.

Once finished with breakfast, Danica threw her napkin on the table and jumped to her feet.

"Come on, let's go gather holly in *las graniczny!*"

Ademun and Kestrel promptly abandoned their food. Danica might have been the youngest, but the older two always followed her lead—even into mischief.

Ademun dashed out the door to the hallway after Danica, but Kestrel came around the table and tugged at Rowan's arm.

"Come out with us," she begged. "You haven't helped us gather holly for *years!*"

Rowan bit back a smile. She glanced at her mother, who was already piling up dirty dishes to take back to the kitchen, then her father, who was frowning faintly at her. He shook his head.

"I'm sorry, Kes," she told her little sister. "Mother and I have too much to do today."

Kestrel's face fell, but when Danica called to her she dropped Rowan's arm and ran after the others. The pack of them squawked and screeched their way upstairs to change into their outdoor clothes. Tradition stated that the children of the family must contribute pine boughs and holly to decorate the home, as well as firewood to warm the house through the night. Celine had already provided the firewood, so they scampered out of the house wrapped in their fur-lined coats and went to the edge of the *las graniczny*, the Border Forest, to look for kindling and decorations. Elzbieta called after them to bring her some wintergreen, if they could find it.

Rowan stared after them, wistfully aware of the biting chill in her face. Much as she loved working in the kitchens, her favorite Solstice tradition was tromping around the Border Forest looking for holly. She had happy memories of untangling long strands of mistletoe from a tree with Celine. The two of them would dare each other to step across the Border lining the Oak King's forest. On the last occasion, Celine had boldly placed a whole foot on the other side of the Border. Not to be outdone, Rowan had simply walked across entirely.

Celine's eyes had widened, and she yanked her back, hissing, "You can't go all the way in! The Oak King will make trees sprout in your stomach!"

Rowan had shrugged, pretending she wasn't scared in the least. "It's the Holly King's season—the Oak King is weak right now."

Celine had grumbled. "I don't even think they're separate people. I think it's the same man, and his power changes with the seasons."

Rowan didn't like that idea one bit. She liked the stories of the two Kings—the Holly King high in his mountain, and the Oak King in his palace of trees. On the first day of Autumn, the Holly King came down from his mountain. As he passed, birds flew off to warmer climes. Trees changed the color of their leaves and dropped them. Animals found themselves warm burrows and readied themselves to sleep, or else hunted and fattened themselves in anticipation of the lean months.

These signs told folk in the villages it was time to harvest. In the forest, the Holly King would call on the Oak King in his palace. The two Kings were old friends and would greet each other warmly. Then the Oak King would take his leave, and the Holly King would rule the forest until the first day of Spring.

Rowan loved the fairy tales her grandmother told, and she liked to think about what the Kings might be doing at any given time. In some stories, the Holly King was stern and fierce, coming down from his mountain to punish and kill those who refused him proper tribute. In her grandmother's stories, he was benevolent and kind, easing suffering into death, while the Oak King played the more frivolous, carefree part.

Rowan believed the Holly King was far too busy to pay attention to a young girl stepping into the Winter Forest in play. Besides, everyone knew the Forest belonged more to the Oak King, and the tales of *his* punishment for trespassers chilled Rowan to the bone. Even so, after that day with Celine, she stepped across the Border, on her own, many times.

Elzbieta must have noticed Rowan staring sadly after her siblings as they played in the snow, for she sighed and softened a little. "Oh, go on out with the others. You're still young enough to go holly gathering. Just be back in time to help me with the frikadelle."

"Are you sure?" Rowan asked, unable to believe her own luck. Her mother never let her skip chores these days. And, of course, she wouldn't have any idea what opportunity she was offering her second eldest.

"Well, you don't quite have the knack for rolling the frikadelle out properly yet, but I still need the help," her mother said with a straight face.

Rowan's face fell a little. She thought she'd done well with her lessons in the kitchen.

"I'm only joking, you goose!" Her mother gave her a little shove. "Try to have a little faith in yourself, Rowan, or I'll never feel right sending you off to a husband."

Rowan nearly burst with joy. At last, a break from all the work and a few moments of the Solstice she could have for herself! She ran upstairs and pulled on her woolen underwear, thick socks, and the warmest dress she owned, woven of rich blue wool. Elzbieta handed her an old scarlet scarf of her father's, which she wound around her head. Once her boots and coat were on, her mother passed her a basket.

"Keep away from the Border," she warned as Rowan stepped gingerly down the icy steps.

That was her warning to all of her children each time they visited the Border Forest, but still Rowan's stomach lurched with guilt. She shook it off. It was only a superstition, after all; she'd gone into the *prawdziwy las*, the True Forest, countless times, and nothing had ever happened to her. Clearly, no one cared.

CHAPTER 2

Rowan

Rowan trudged through the powdery white banks of snow with her basket tucked tight against her side. At the top of a small rise, just where the trees began to thicken, she paused, looking over her shoulder.

Not a soul. Good.

Entry into the Oak King's forest was forbidden. No one—not the village folk, not even the king of Belagrod himself—was permitted inside without the Oak King's invitation.

And I've never heard of anyone *being invited.*

She could faintly hear the cries of Danica, Kestrel, and Ademun, off somewhere combing the *las graniczny* for its pitiful offerings of holly and wintergreen.

Only Rowan knew where to find a decent patch this time of year, and she didn't mind breaking a rule or two to do so.

The air was crisp and cold, spiked with the citrus-sharp smell of broken pine needles and crushed wintergreen. But as Rowan neared the Border, a different smell took over—the smell of snow and moss and bark, mixed with the musk of a deer.

The *las graniczny* and the *prawdziwy las* were separated almost by a line. Here were the Border trees—normal, average-sized trees surrounded by a good foot of snow. A few of them held tangles of mistletoe and ivy, interspersed with a few short, delicate holly trees. But across the Border, there was a change.

Huge trees, and a wider variety of shapes—some with twisting, gnarled limbs tangling with each other, some straight as arrows shooting toward the sky. And from where Rowan stood, she could see dense clusters of holly trees and clumps of wintergreen beneath them, all dotted with bright red berries. There was mistletoe here, too, its frosty green bright amidst all the white.

Her stomach gave a little quaver as she stepped over the Border. As always, the shift was unmistakable. It was discernibly colder in the *prawdziwy las*, a more intense Winter; icicles hung from tree limbs, and almost every twig and leaf was coated in hoarfrost.

Even the sounds were different. On the village side of the Border, you could hear the faint cries of the children out holly gathering, or a cow lowing in the distance. Here was thick silence, broken only by a raven taking off from a branch with a loud cry.

Rowan watched the bird flap away. There were a great many animals in the *prawdziwy las*, but usually she saw the same old animals that lived in the *las graniczny*—deer, birds, rabbits, badgers.

Once in a while, she caught sight of something magical—a pair of tiny feet in minuscule red shoes disappearing behind a tree, a rabbit with horns like a ram contentedly munching on water hemlock, a blackbird with a jewel-encrusted beak flitting from tree to tree.

Rowan carefully snapped a sprig of holly off a branch and shook off the snow, laying it in her basket.

"Forgive me, Lord Holly, but this *is* in your honor," she murmured as she worked.

Though she didn't believe the Holly King would care if a village girl took a decorative branch or two, she didn't want to damage his trees just on the off chance that he *did* stop by and catch her.

Once she had a good pile of holly, she began pulling mistletoe from a nearby tree, taking the pieces with the whitest berries. The younglings never bothered with mistletoe, but Rowan liked the way it looked on the evergreen.

Her basket was already dangerously full, but still she knelt and began picking sprigs of wintergreen, popping a few of the bright red berries into her mouth as she worked. They'd been warned, of course, never to eat anything that came from the *prawdziwy las*, but Rowan knew the deer and rabbits her sister brought home lived equally on both sides of the Border. The villagers had eaten those animals their entire lives; there was nothing in them to poison or enchant. Rowan assumed it was the same with the plants.

She stood and leaned against a tree for a moment, watching her breath spiral through the air before her. She liked being in the *prawdziwy las*. The *las graniczny* felt small and loose and out of place, as though someone had dropped it there by mistake and never remembered to gather it up again. The True Forest felt different, though she couldn't say how.

It really was the only time she was alone. Gone were the days when Celine would come out with her to climb trees, look for mushrooms, or peek daringly across the Border.

In fact, it had been Celine refusing to go out with her all those years ago that had prompted Rowan to burst out of the house, stomp her way through the *las graniczny*, and step right over the Border, glaring at the trees in challenge as she did so. But the trees didn't care, and neither did anyone else, it seemed. It became Rowan's hideaway—an entire forest, where the rest of Gramylka village was too afraid to set foot. She knew she could count on not seeing another soul as long as she stayed there.

Rowan knew she didn't have long before her mother started calling for her, so she picked a few more branches of holly, then trudged back up the hill toward the Border. But even as she resigned herself to returning home and adding her findings to the decorations, she let her feet turn and take her to the hazelnut bush that grew a little further north. The squirrels of the Oak King's forest had left this bush largely untouched, and Rowan thought her mother might forgive her tardiness if she came back with an unexpected present. She set to picking.

But when she stopped to count how many she had picked, she froze. The sound of feet crunching in the snow, the murmur of a conversation —it was coming from deeper inside the forest, and it was getting louder.

Rowan nearly upended her basket as she scrambled up the nearest tree, hauling herself as high as she could. She dearly hoped she wasn't making enough noise to be noticed. She found a sturdy branch to stand on and nestled her basket by her feet. Then she wrapped her arms around the tree trunk, hoping her brown coat made her look like part of the tree.

And then, looking down, she realized with a jolt that the area below was covered in her footprints. She stamped on the branch. Snow cascaded down from the limb, and, as if the rest of the tree had taken note, the rest of the branches shed their snow. To Rowan's surprise, several of the other trees near her chose that moment to do exactly the same thing. Snow dumped from their crowns, covering the trail she'd made to the holly grove.

That was lucky, but that was all she had time to think. Two figures came trudging up the hill, dragging something behind them on a blanket. Rowan's heart plunged. The axes strapped to Celine's back and leg were unmistakable, as were the two black braids wound around Irys's head. And behind them on the blanket, tusks glinting, lay a wild boar.

"The snow's not starting up again, is it?" Irys asked, watching flakes drift down from the tree nearest her, which fortunately did not contain Rowan. Rowan prayed to the Holly King that Irys wouldn't look up at her tree next.

A snowflake landed on Irys's cheek, stark white against her dark skin. Celine reached out and brushed the flake away, grinning. Rowan was startled—she hadn't seen Celine smile like that in a long time.

"No, the trees are just shedding their snow," Celine was saying. "Careful not to get caught under one—I'd have to dig you out."

Irys gave her a devious smile and opened her mouth to reply, but then she caught sight of something.

"Look! Hazelnuts!" she cried, dropping her end of the blanket and running to the bush Rowan had just left.

If it had been any other person, Celine would have scowled, picked up the other end of the blanket, and left the woods without them. But this was Irys, and Rowan watched as her sister let the blanket drop and followed Irys to the hazelnut bush.

"There's still lots," Irys exclaimed happily, showing a handful to Celine. Celine pulled out an empty game bag and held it open for her to fill.

"What do you think Elzbieta will make with these?" Irys asked, tipping the nuts into the game bag.

"Some cake or other," Celine shrugged, turning sullen. "Doesn't matter. The more I bring back from these trips, the fewer questions my mother asks."

Irys's face fell a little. "Have they been talking again?"

Celine scowled, her most common expression at home. "They're always talking. I'm twenty years old and out woodcutting and hunting instead of embroidering my wedding dress and letting old men pinch me in the streets." She turned and kicked the base of the hazelnut bush, spooking a chickadee that had landed on the other side. "The older Ademun gets, the more they look at me in that awful way, start saying 'it's only a matter of time.'"

Rowan knew exactly what she was talking about. Every village girl began working on her wedding chest the day she turned twelve, and she would continue to do so until someone made her parents a good offer. Rowan's own chest was nearly complete.

Celine, however, had worked on hers for just a year but ceased when their father fell ill. He lost his position keeping horses for the *burmistrz* and their family would have starved or frozen to death in the Winter if it hadn't been for Celine.

"I don't understand it," Irys said, shaking her head. "You *saved* your family by taking up your trades—and you're better at it than Ademun will ever be. Why are they so determined to marry you off?"

Celine had disappeared with the family's horse Charly for two whole days, then returned with a cart full of wood, a deer, and three fox pelts. The deer filled her family's bellies, while the wood and pelts brought in much needed coin. Their parents didn't like it, but a tentative agreement was reached: Celine would hunt and cut wood until Ademun, the only boy, was old enough to take up the work himself. She was now twenty and unmarried—a state almost unheard of in Gramylka.

Rowan dearly wished she had run for it instead of hiding in a tree. She wasn't eavesdropping on purpose, but it still felt wrong. And if one of them just happened to glance up, she would be caught.

Irys let go of the branch she held and went to Celine, taking the game bag from her and setting it on the ground. Then she took both of Celine's hands and looked into her face.

"This time next year, everything will be different," she said quietly. "You and I will celebrate the Solstice together as a family, and no one will stop us. I mean that."

And just when Rowan thought her eyes couldn't get any wider, Irys leaned forward and kissed Celine.

Rowan gaped for a second, then screwed her eyes shut. This was an extremely private moment that she should not have witnessed, and especially now, she knew Celine would be furious if she saw her.

Rowan kept her eyes shut, willing the pair to go away.

"Come on, it's getting colder," she heard Irys murmur, and they moved away from her tree.

Once the crunch of their feet in the snow had faded into the distance, she finally opened her eyes again and let herself drop from the branch into the snow below.

She landed with a *WHUMP* and didn't move for a long time.

What in the world just happened? She tried to make sense of what she had witnessed. Celine and Irys had been the closest of friends since childhood. Their parents had promised that each girl would carry flowers at the other's wedding. But clearly, they had feelings for each other far beyond friendship. And though Rowan had heard rumors about relationships between two women or two men, mainly in stories about the great city, Javsbor, the village folk believed those stories only confirmed the depravity of the urban region and forbade their children from ever going there.

Rowan had always secretly hoped that Celine would somehow convince their parents that it would be better for everyone if she remained unmarried, so that she could continue to hunt and keep the family in meat and warm clothes. Or that Lodin would somehow manage to pick someone she wouldn't detest as her betrothed—something Rowan dearly hoped would be the case for herself as well.

Rowan, at age eighteen, was dangerously close to the same scandalous state as Celine, but not for long. Her mother hinted frequently that Rowan's father had met with several men to discuss an offer for

Rowan. Rowan, of course, would not know who they were until her betrothal was announced.

Rowan had promised herself that if she was ever forced into an engagement she didn't want, she would run away and go to Javsbor to start a new life. She hadn't realized she wasn't the only one in her family who might want to escape. Rowan had assumed Celine didn't want to get married at all; she'd had no idea that her sister might have a very specific person who she *did* want to marry.

Rowan gathered everything that had fallen out of her basket and began to walk home. She was too distracted to pay attention to the icicles and hoarfrost, though she did notice a fine black raven quirking its head at her as she passed under its tree. The ravens never left, even in the heart of Winter. Rowan dropped a hazelnut in the snow beneath the tree, an offering to the raven in honor of Winter. Or maybe a bribe to keep it from telling its lord that she had entered the forest on his holiday.

Just as she was about to step back across the Border, a branch snapped behind her, making her yelp. She spun around, scattering snow with her boots.

A boy dressed head to toe in fur was standing in the footprints she'd just made, his arms folded. The little she could see of his face looked stern.

"What were you doing in the *prawdziwy las?*" he asked, a steely edge to his voice.

Rowan tried her best to look innocent.

"Do I know you, *nieznajomy?*" she asked, with the air of someone who has done absolutely nothing wrong. She used the polite word for "stranger," even though she would just as soon call him a *plotkarz*—a busybody.

The boy rolled his eyes. Most of his face was covered with a scarf, but a shock of dark hair was just visible under his hat, and his eyes were startling—bright brown with copper flecks.

"Look. I know your sister hunts and cuts wood here, too—I've already tried to warn her, and she won't listen. But there's no reason for you to be a fool as well. It isn't safe here." He gestured to the *prawdziwy las* around them.

Rowan's nose itched. How dare this *stranger* try to tell her what to do?

"I'm *grateful* for your concern," she said, her voice dripping with sarcasm. "But it's entirely unnecessary. I wasn't paying attention and must have stepped across the Border by mistake."

The stranger's eyes narrowed. Rowan was sure he didn't believe a word she said, not that it mattered.

"And in any case," she continued, gesturing to where he stood. "Isn't there an old saying about pots and kettles? Seems like it might apply to this situation."

Briefly, amusement flickered in those copper eyes of his.

"Tell your sister to tread carefully," he said finally. "The *las graniczny* may hold fewer animals of interest, but it's a good sight safer than other hunting grounds."

He turned and tromped off through the snow, going *deeper* into the *prawdziwy las.*

"Not one to follow your own advice, are you?" Rowan called after him, but he had already vanished into the trees.

Feeling annoyed, she crossed back into the *las graniczny.*

I thought I had the whole prawdziwy las *to myself, then twice in one day someone else invades it!*

Then she froze, her breath caught in her throat.

Could that have been the Oak King, or the Holly King?

She turned around and stared back the way she had come, her mind racing.

No, she decided, forcing herself to keep going. *I'm sure such a rude boy couldn't possibly be the ruler of Summer or Winter.*

The Kings were ancient, after all, and they had never shown themselves to anyone in Rowan's lifetime. The rude boy was just a rude boy. Nothing more.

CHAPTER 3

Nash

I was born in the rising tide. My mother told me the story when I was twelve years old. It was custom for women to give birth in the ocean —the warm water helped ease the struggles of labor, helped to soothe their aching bodies. Some said the salt kept the birth clean and aided with healing afterward, though I am no doctor and don't know if there is truth in this.

But my mother's pregnancy had not been a joyful one, and it had been with a heavy heart that she struggled to the water, alone, without the usual attendants for a birth.

But at her first cries, folk came running. They would not let her suffer through it on her own, would not let her be swept away with the tide when she tired from labor. They came and held her in the shallows and scooped me from the water when I was born. They sat with us in the hot sand and welcomed me to my new home.

My mother confessed to me what she had feared—that she would not be able to love me, because of the circumstances under which I had been conceived. And she wept when she first held me, for she had found her fears to be baseless. She loved me. I was made of her, and I knew her. She saw no trace of the cruel man who had abandoned her to bear their child alone, but even if she had, she told me, she wanted me.

"And make no mistake," she told me seriously, as we wound reeds into *baskets. "I have no qualms about encouraging girls to rid themselves of unwanted babies. No one should carry a child if they do not want to."*

But she had wanted to. And so she didn't end the pregnancy, and she didn't give me away afterward. And of course I felt guilty for it. The man who fathered me should have stayed to support her, but he had gone away, forever in search of magic.

"He was looking for me," she told me, her voice growing a little softer, smaller, as it always did when she spoke of the man who had fathered me. "He had heard tales of my magic from the fishing ships that pass by."

It was strange, the way she talked about him, as if she both loved and hated him.

"He was charming at first, and fascinated by my magic—and I was young and reckless enough to be excited by his attention. But afterward, I realized I knew next to nothing about him. He was manipulative, full of secrets. Once he knew I was pregnant with his child, he left."

"At first he tried to convince me to go with him, to his forest in a faraway land. But our island would not permit him to take me away. He left, saying he would come back for you someday."

She looked at me, her eyes as smooth and sparkling as the surface of the ocean on a calm day.

"He will not take you, Nash. I will not let him."

And I believed her.

My mother was a good woman, a good leader to her people, as her father was before her. Blessed with the magic of the ocean and the rains, she ruled our island as the best rulers do—caring for her people and taking nothing from them for herself. We didn't need to. There was always plenty to eat—fish, fruit, seaweed that we dried and threw into stews or ate in strips—and there weren't really any riches to hoard. We worked together, because everyone benefited when everyone did well.

She was good woman. She deserved someone to stand by her.

"It was so strange, the way he talked about you. He never thought you might be a boy—he insisted that you would be a girl."

I said nothing to this. When I was born, my body was like my moth-er's, and so they called me a girl. But things were not so strict in our village as they are in other places. I knew of a handful of people who did not feel that their bodies made them men or women. They were free to be themselves.

But for some reason, my body bothered me. I knew I was a boy—that was who I was. But my body would do the things a girl's body would do. I sobbed the day I realized breasts were swelling on my chest, and I kept bandages and a dish of water on hand at all times, unable to sleep at night for fear that my first blood would come. It terrified me, not because any of these things were bad, but because I didn't want them to happen to me. They weren't part of me.

I knew others accepted that it was just the way it was. But for me, it was unacceptable. I knew the way my body was supposed to be. I hated the idea that if I went to lie with a woman, my body would be like hers. I didn't want that. It felt wrong to me, wrong in a way I couldn't explain.

But I tried to explain it to my mother. She listened. She let me cry and beat my fists on the wall in frustration at not having the right words. And when I could find nothing more to say, only then did she speak.

"I believe I understand, Nash. In any case, I would like to understand. And I would like to help you."

My mother ran her hand over the shells strung around her throat.

"I have heard of a wish-granter, far away in a distant, treacherous land. If you can make the journey there, she will grant you whatever you ask for."

I straightened, wiping the tears from my cheeks.

"Do you think she would grant my wish? For my body to match how I know it should be?"

She nodded. "Perhaps, someday, when you are old enough to make that journey, we could find her together. Though the journey is said to be a difficult one, Nash, fraught with danger."

I swallowed. I had never left the island, and I did not yet have my mother's skill with water magic.

"Do you think I'll be able to reach her?" I asked, tears smarting once more in my eyes.

"Of course I do, Nash. Have faith in yourself, my love. You are capable of anything you wish."

I ducked my head, willing myself to stop crying. "Aunt Alizeh says I must accept life the way it is."

"Sometimes that is true, but not in this case," she told me. "This matters, Nash. I don't want you to hate the body you live in. I would wish you peace. If a change is the only way to achieve it, then we shall find a way."

What a good woman. And I know that she would have made good on her promise, given the chance.

But he came. He stayed away so long, I had thought he forgot about us, but he was only waiting, skulking about his forest while he counted the years until I was thirteen.

CHAPTER 4

Rowan

TWO WEEKS BEFORE THE SPRING EQUINOX

Rowan sniffed the air, catching the scent of hot spiced cider from a cauldron across the market. She caught her mother's eye and nodded hopefully at the stall.

Elzbieta rolled her eyes and dug a coin from her pocket. "I swear, it's not enough that we clothe and feed you all—you always want more and more. No dawdling—I need your help today. I never remember which animal any of *these* came from." With a grimace, she gestured to the piles of pelts that took up half their table.

Celine had trapped and hunted every one of those animals, but come market day, she could not be convinced to help sell them. So it fell to Rowan to describe the qualities of each piece to would-be buyers.

Rowan pocketed the coin and wove merrily through the crowd to the cider cauldron, clutching two mugs she'd brought along just in case her mother was feeling generous. She waved to Oliwia, who stood stirring the cauldron with a wooden spoon, sending up a curtain of spiced steam into the faces of passersby.

The hot amber drink swirled around the pot, bobbing with orange peel, strips of cinnamon, little clove pinpricks, and a handful of cranberries, which one by one burst from the heat. The cider family sweetened their brew with honey, and, on special occasions, they sometimes added a whole bottle of their family's blackberry and plum wine.

Oliwia ladled cider into Rowan's mug but waved away the coin.

"Set aside a pie for me and we'll call it even," she said, nodding her head at the row of cranberry pies lining half of Rowan's mother's table.

Rowan walked slowly back to the stall, balancing the mugs of scalding cider carefully so they didn't slosh on her. She told her mother what the girl had said and held out the coin, intending to return it.

Her mother closed her hand back over the coin. "Keep it. I suppose we can afford a little pocket money these days."

Rowan sipped her cider and daydreamed about what she would buy with her coin as she helped her mother with the stall. They sold more pastries than anything else, but slowly the pile of pelts grew smaller.

She drained the last dregs of her cider and helped her mother wrap up a large order of pelts for a family from the hills who had come in for their twice-a-year restock. Rowan was always glad to see these folk, as their arrival meant the snow was melting in the hills. Much as she loved Winter, she missed the fresh fruits and vegetables that would come with Spring, and she eagerly anticipated that particular change of the year.

Celine would soon go out in search of Spring turkeys, and their mother would plant the first peas and the hardy, bitter mustard greens her eldest daughter liked so much—all the plants that loved the cool days with their slight bursts of warmth.

Once their wares had depleted a good amount, Elzbieta released Rowan to the market. She wasn't completely at liberty—she had to shop for the items her mother listed off as she left, but she could amble at her own pace and pick out a thing or two for herself.

She passed Celine and Irys, who both munched on pasties from another stall. Celine ignored Rowan and kept her eyes trained ahead of her. Irys, however, offered a smile as they went in the opposite direction.

Rowan watched them meander through the crowd. Sometimes she wanted to tell Celine she knew her secret—both that she poached the Oak King's game and forest, and that she was in love with her best friend—just to get her sister to appreciate all the work she had done to help them conceal their relationship and Celine's real hunting grounds. But she didn't think Celine would see it that way.

She could hear her sister's response perfectly in her head. *"So you've been spying on me? I never asked you for help, and I never wanted you getting involved in my business. Go help mother bake a cake or something."*

At this point, Rowan only felt sorrier for herself, and that really wasn't worth anything. She tried to brush off the snub and went to choose a turnover from Widow Bergmeier's table. The widow hoarded fruit like a hungry dragon so that she could bake her famous turnovers throughout Winter. Even when she had been reduced to apples, dried plums, and preserved cherries, Rowan still loved her baked goods best of all.

Rowan quickly found most of the items her mother wanted and returned to her family's stall laden with wrapped parcels. They didn't rely on many supplies from other folk, but spices and medicines were among the things they always needed.

Once the last pelt sold, they wrapped up the few remaining pastries, broke down the awning and the table, and loaded up the wood cart. Celine was nowhere to be found, so Rowan went and fetched their cart horse, Charly, from the market stables. Everyone made much of the horse's attachment to Celine, but the horse snuffled Rowan's hand the same way the little calves did in Summertime, and Charly let her hitch him to the cart without pulling away.

Elzbieta climbed into the cart and peered around one last time for her eldest daughter. "Off with Irys somewhere, no doubt," she said, rolling her eyes. "Then she can walk home, if she cares to come at all. And I suppose if she stays at their house for dinner tonight, there'll be one less mouth for me to worry about." And she sat down and flicked the reins.

Charly drew them out of the market bustle, where most of the other vendors were also breaking down their stalls for the day, rubbing their hands in anticipation of their warm homes and hot dinners.

Rowan said nothing. She knew that if *she* had gone and disappeared like that on market day, her mother would have the whole town looking for her, and then she'd get a tongue-lashing and be punished for at least a week. And there was no question of *her* spending an evening at a friend's house, not when dinner needed making and the younglings needed watching and the kitchen needed cleaning.

They reached home, and Ademun rushed out to meet them,

helping Rowan unload the day's purchases. Together they put the awning and the folded table in the shed, where they would sit until the next market day.

Then, while Ademun begged her for details about the market and what she had seen, they went inside and put away the supplies they had bought. Elzbieta went to give Lodin his medicine, while Rowan started preparing for dinner.

Rowan smiled inwardly as Ademun accompanied her into the kitchen and seated himself by the fire so he could keep asking her questions. She knew in just a few minutes time, when he ran out of questions, he'd ask to help make dinner.

Sure enough, while Rowan told him about the mysterious trapper who had been so interested in Celine's pelts, Ademun went to the bowl of potatoes on the counter and started to peel them with a paring knife.

Elzbieta came in moments later and threw her hands in the air.

"So this is what my children think is right? My eldest daughter roams the forest like a man while my only son hangs about the kitchen like a girl?"

Ademun's face crumpled, and he set down the paring knife.

"I just wanted to help, since there's so much to do," he mumbled.

"If you really want to help, go with your sister the next time she's hunting," Elzbieta snapped as she bustled around the kitchen, putting away the various herbs she'd used to brew Lodin's medicine.

"Mother," Rowan said, knowing it would be wiser to keep her mouth shut. "There is a lot to do to prepare for dinner. Why don't you go rest while Ademun and I take care of it? You've been working since dawn getting ready for the market."

Rowan could see the conflict in her mother's face. She wanted to raise her children right, doing the things girls and boys were supposed to do, but she also worked tirelessly every single day cooking, cleaning, and keeping house.

"Just this once." She raised a warning finger at Ademun.

He bobbed his head vigorously. "Yes, Mother."

She sighed and left the room.

Ademun beamed at Rowan. He sat on his stool by the fire and peeled the potatoes, slicing the entire skin off in one long, spiraling cut.

He had become quite an adept peeler, though Rowan knew he longed to take part in the actual cooking and baking.

Rowan sighed, stirring the gravy on the stove. When she was younger, things had seemed so simple, much more pleasant. Now that she approached adulthood, stress bubbled at the edge of every thought, every idea. There was tension in her family, dissatisfaction. It seemed each of the five children wanted something different, and their parents spent all their time explaining why it just couldn't be that way. And none of their explanations were very good.

Danica loved to paint and draw. Kestrel loved tending the animals and could already handle a mother sow at her meanest. But these things were considered supplemental, hobbies they could spend time on in the Winter or skills that would help run a farm—not ways for them to make a living. They were girls—their living was to be marriage and nothing else.

There were times the idea of her own future made Rowan panicked, breathless, and she wanted to run, to dive into the forest and never come back to the wedding chest that sat upstairs, gradually filling with frippery.

But where would she go? And she couldn't fathom leaving her family and never seeing them again, no more than she could fathom resigning herself to the fate they insisted upon. She didn't know what she'd do when the time came, when a man's family approached their doorstep and he asked her father's permission to take her as his wife. It was all so completely out of her hands, and she hated the thought of it.

And so, as she did every time her mind took her down this troubling trail of thoughts, she pushed it from her mind and focused on the meal she was making: roast chicken stuffed with onions, herbs, and half a lemon; mashed rutabaga sprinkled with nutmeg; potatoes cooked in pork fat and sprigs of rosemary from the plant her mother kept in a pot by the door; sharp, spicy pickles swimming in a brine laced with bright-red cherry peppers.

It wasn't until they were all seated at the dinner table, ladling gravy and selecting pieces of chicken, that they heard the door open. The conversation dropped a little as they all listened to Celine stomp snow off her boots, hang up her coat and scarf, then make her way up the stairs without poking her head in the dining hall to say hello. Rowan would bet good money, too, that by the time she finished helping her mother clean up after dinner, Celine would already be deep asleep.

And then she'll still be in bed when I get up to start breakfast, and then she'll come down, grab food, and leave again. Despite Celine's moodiness and unwillingness to be around her, Rowan missed her sister. They had been great friends once, but now it seemed she couldn't stand to spend time with her family.

Rowan's mother seemed to be thinking along the same lines, and Rowan's heart sank as Elzbieta folded up her napkin, rose, and followed her eldest child upstairs. The sound of a door opening, muffled voices drifting down the stairs, then rising in volume, then the sounds of stomping, bumping, and other sounds Rowan couldn't quite identify.

And finally, Celine's voice came quite clearly down the stairs—Elzbieta must have tried to pull her back down the hallway.

"After all the work I do all week for this family, I'm not allowed any rest or time to myself? I don't need any dinner—I ate at Irys's!"

"You've hardly seen your family since you got back—it would do you good to see what real life is like once in a while!"

Their voices sounded so very much alike when raised. Celine truly was the spitting image of her mother, even though the two of them lived such drastically different lives.

Celine laughed at her mother's words. "And just what am I doing out there in the forest? Playing make-believe? I think I deserve a little more respect than that—you'd all be starving without what I do."

A slap rang out, echoing through the stairwell.

"You may not be a child any longer, but you are *my* daughter. You will do what you are told. I will have no more talk of *respect* from you. Your father and I gave you life. It is your *duty*—"

There was a strange scuffling sound and a muffled *thud*. Rowan ran to the doorway just in time to see Celine storming down the stairs, her cheek bright red where her mother had struck her. Celine met her eyes for one furious second, and then, grabbing her coat, she left, slamming the door behind her.

Elzbieta came down the stairs a few moments later, looking shaken. She passed Rowan in the doorway and looked to her husband.

"She *pushed* me. Pushed right past me. And now who knows where she's gone."

"You slapped her!" Rowan burst out, glaring at her mother. "You hit her right in the face, but you're upset she got you out of her way? She didn't even hurt you!"

"You will not speak to your mother in that manner," her father said darkly. Everyone at the table had lain down their silverware, appetites diminished with the rising discord.

"I will not have impertinence from *you* as well," her mother hissed, grabbing her by the arm and pulling her up the stairs.

"Are you going to hit me, too, then?" Rowan asked, angry tears spilling down her cheeks. Her mother had rarely struck her, but with the mood she was in now, she was almost certainly to that point.

Her mother didn't answer. She opened the door to Rowan and Celine's room and pushed her inside.

"I will not have this from you, Rowan. Your sister marches to the beat of her own drum, but I had thought I had at least one daughter I could count on," Elzbieta hissed, as though she was afraid of being overheard.

"Elzbieta."

Rowan's mother turned to look over her shoulder, as though surprised to see her husband standing there. Ademun had helped him up the stairs.

"Let me talk to her."

Rowan's stomach clenched as her mother helped her father into the chair in her room. Ademun shrank back against the wall outside the door, his wide eyes fixed on Rowan. Then her mother left and shut the door behind her, looking pale.

Rowan's father sat quietly for a time, as though lost in thought.

"I'm disappointed in you, Rowan," he said finally, his voice heavy with exhaustion. "I like to think of you as such a help to your mother and your siblings, not a burden like Celine."

"How is she a burden?" Rowan snapped. "She's the only reason our family isn't in the streets."

"That's one good thing to come of it, but surely you know by now how unnatural your sister is," Lodin answered mildly.

Rowan said nothing. She hated the way he talked about Celine, as though she wasn't even his daughter.

"Fortunately for Celine, she's pretty enough that I've had men clamoring at the door for me to give them her hand. That will more than make up for the trouble she's caused. You, on the other hand..." His mouth twisted sourly and he shook his head. "You are neither pretty enough nor interesting enough to attract that kind of attention. And so your best hopes lie in following your mother's example—be dutiful, obedient, helpful. You need to earn your place, because no one will ever want you if you earn the reputation for being contrary as well as plain."

Rowan felt sick. Tears welled in her eyes, even though she screwed up her face against them.

"I'm only being honest with you, my dear," he said gently. "This is the way our world works—I certainly didn't make it this way. I'm lenient compared with most men in this village. In any other household, you and Celine would be married off by now. Be grateful that I haven't decided that is necessary yet. Soon you will be married, and if you do not obey your husband the way we have tried to teach you to obey us, life will be very hard for you."

He watched her for a moment. She clenched her fists, digging her nails into her palms to try and stay composed.

"Are you prepared to apologize, or shall I have your mother come in and whip you?" he asked, as though inquiring if she wanted dessert.

"I'm sorry, father," Rowan mumbled, her voice hoarse.

"Louder, please. I will be respected," Lodin said curtly.

"I'm sorry, father," Rowan said again, knowing she did not sound particularly sorry.

He sighed. "You'll stay in your room until morning. No meals until dinner tomorrow, but I expect you to be up bright and early to help your mother, as usual."

He pushed himself up using the back of the chair and made it to the door, holding onto its edge for support. Before he closed it, he leaned toward Rowan.

"I want you to think about the choices you make, Rowan. You are my daughter. I need you on my side, not your sister's." He closed the door, latching it behind him.

Once his footsteps faded down the hallway, Rowan threw herself down on the bed and beat her fists into the mattress. She was too angry to cry, too angry to think. She flung a pillow across the room, wishing she could break something, shatter something against the worn walls. It wasn't right. It wasn't fair. The wrongness of her father's words echoed in her head. His punishments scared her more than beatings from her mother—his words worked like poison, even when she tried not to listen to him.

Her mother was no better. Elzbieta had hit Celine, but she had the gall to be angry when her daughters just tried to stand up for themselves.

She didn't even hurt her. But Rowan knew that didn't matter to her parents. Children were things to be used, not people with their own thoughts and ideas and lives. They were to be sculpted into whatever was needed, regardless of their feelings. And, with few exceptions, all children in the villages had much the same treatment.

And now, for standing up for her sister even the tiniest bit, she was confined to her room and sentenced to starve for a day, even though she had worked all day at the market and in the kitchen. One small glimmer of disobedience was enough to warrant punishment.

She must have dozed off, for she suddenly started. There was a tapping at the window. She leaped up from her bed, her head dizzy at the sudden movement, and she crept to the window, carefully treading where she knew the floorboards wouldn't creak.

Celine's face, framed by her white-blond hair, glowered at her from the other side of the glass. She gestured for Rowan to raise the window. Rowan obliged and helped pull her sister into their room.

"Where were you?" she whispered as Celine went about pulling clothes and other items from her drawers and the chest at the foot of her bed.

"Where do you think?" Celine hissed back. She still looked upset. "Did you all have a nice meal together, or did I manage to ruin the evening for you?"

Rowan glared at her sister's back. "I was sent to bed for talking back to mother. And father came by for a chat."

Celine paused, her hand extended to pick up her boots. Her shoulders sagged a little. "I'm sorry. I should have just come down."

"It's not your fault," Rowan said at once. "You were tired. And she shouldn't have hit you."

Celine turned around, and, to Rowan's surprise, her sister's eyes filled with tears.

"I can't *do* this anymore, Ro," she said finally, her voice breaking. "All they do is take from us. We're their children—why can't they love us for who we are instead of hurting us for who we're not?"

Rowan found her own eyes welling, but she screwed up her mouth, determined not to cry. She'd be no help if she, too, gave in to how sad she felt.

"We won't be here forever," she offered, hoping what she had to say would make Celine feel better. "You're already of age, and I'm almost—"

"Of age to be married off to some groping pighead, you mean," Celine scoffed, her face turning angry again. "Thanks, Rowan, but that's really not a solution for me, even if it's one for you."

"That's not what I meant," Rowan snapped, unable to keep her tone from turning ugly.

"Then what did you mean?"

Celine's particular brand of sarcasm stung, and Rowan almost refused to keep talking to her. But she was worried about her sister, and she felt a glimmer of hope that, if she shared her own small plan of escape, they could work together to get away.

"Javsbor," she said in a rush, her voice dropping low. "I have a map from Grandmother's peddler friend, and he's offered me a job if I ever make it to the city. And there are shops and bakeries there—and probably places to sell pelts and wood, too. It's far enough away that mother and father couldn't find us, even if they tried."

Celine stared at her for a moment. "But what about the younglings?" she said at last. "I didn't think you'd ever want to leave them."

"We could take them with us," Rowan said hurriedly, knowing how desperate she sounded. "Irys could come too," she added, hoping that would make Celine listen to her. "We could find someplace to live together, and the younglings could do whatever they wanted. They could apprentice to be artists, or bakers, or farmers, or—"

"Rowan, I don't want to live in Javsbor," Celine looked so tired as she spoke.

"Then on the outskirts of the city—they border the forest, too, and you could hunt and—"

"Just stop," Celine said, closing her eyes and rubbing her temples. "I shouldn't have to leave the land where I live to be allowed to be myself. I shouldn't have to go learn to live somewhere else. I know *this* place, these hills and trees and animals. Who even knows what it's like near the city?"

Rowan's answers died on her tongue. She wanted to say their Grandmother would help them, the peddler would help them, she, Rowan, would work tirelessly to make sure they were all right, but Celine had already stopped listening. She was stuffing her things in her knapsack again.

"Things are going to happen the way they've always been going to happen. I'm going to do what I've always meant to do, and that's that."

"Where are you going?" Rowan asked, alarmed at the sudden notion that her sister might run away without her.

"Stop fretting. I'm leaving early for my next cutting trip. I'll be gone a week." She stood up and breathed out a deep breath. "If mother and father ask where I am, just tell them that, alright? I'll stay at Irys's when I come back. After that..." She glanced at Rowan, then shook her head and cinched her knapsack shut.

"But... but," Rowan stammered, wanting her sister to stay. "You don't have any food."

Celine smacked the purse tied to her belt. "The benefit of earning all the family income—it's my income, too. If I hold some back from Father, he never knows it exists. Goodbye, Ro."

She heaved the window open again and slung her pack out onto the top of the shed just below. Then she climbed out after it and was gone.

Rowan pushed the window shut and watched her sister disappear through the farmyard. Intense jealousy came over her. How nice, to have the skills and the means to just leave, just walk away from this stupid house with all its rules and requirements and spend a week in the forest.

Rowan lay back down on the bed, thinking over how poorly that conversation had gone. She really meant what she had said—she wanted to take the younglings far away, to someplace where they would be free of the expectations the village held for them. Her grandmother's stories of the city and its freedom called to her. Of course, she didn't want to leave the hills and the forest either—this was her *home*. But in the same way she loved her parents despite their unfairness, she could love the village while recognizing that it was strangling her.

We could always come back, she thought, *once we've all learned a trade and earned money. We could come back and show them how successful we've been, and that we didn't need to get married to make good lives for ourselves.*

But that wouldn't solve their problems and she knew it. Her parents had the expectation of a return. They viewed investing in their children as a means to fund their own futures. More than that, they saw marrying off their daughters to rich men as a way to regain the stature in the village they had lost when Rowan's father fell ill. Their talk of the girl's dowries, Ademun's future bride and her family wealth, the grand-children they demanded they all produce—it all came back to them securing their place in the village, not their children's welfare.

Rowan couldn't imagine looking at her own child that way—as something meant to benefit herself rather than a growing human destined for a life of their own. And she couldn't for the life of her understand how her grandmother, so much more open-minded than either of Rowan's parents, had managed to raise a daughter who shared so few of her own values.

Rowan wished she could live with her grandmother. She wished a good many things were different. She felt guilty for thinking so badly of her parents, but there was no way around it. She needed to get away someday. They all did. And, since Celine was already breaking off by herself, it fell to Rowan to rescue her younger siblings from the colorless life ahead of them. And she had no idea how to do it.

To help herself sleep, she told herself one of her grandmother's fairy tales—the story of the Underworlde and all the vicious beasts that crept from that dark abyss into people's nightmares. It was a chilling story, but Rowan found it comforting, for some reason. Maybe because its horrors were all made up, while the unpleasantness in her life was all too real.

She woke the next morning with a pounding headache, as though she'd had too much wine at the dinner she hadn't eaten the night before. She found the door unlatched. Celine's bed sat empty.

So Rowan washed and dressed and went downstairs and wordlessly helped her mother prepare porridge, sausage, and stewed fruit. Rowan's father made her sit at the table with the rest of the family while they ate. He even made her set an empty plate for herself, just as a reminder.

She went through the motions of the day. Everything that happened was normal, entirely normal, but Rowan felt sick and on the verge of tears through all of it. The younglings, too, seemed unusually somber. She wondered if they'd received a talking-to after she'd been sent to bed, warned that if they showed the tiniest bit of defiance toward their parents, they could expect the same treatment.

The next three days passed in similar fashion. Only once did Celine come up, and Rowan dutifully told her mother that Celine had gone out early on her woodcutting trip.

Elzbieta, her face stony, looked over Rowan's head at her husband. "We will be having a discussion when she gets back. It's time this nonsense ended. Ademun will begin apprenticing when Spring starts, and Celine will take up her wedding chest again."

Rowan said nothing. She would not tell them that Celine planned to stay with Irys when she returned, and she hoped they wouldn't find out some other way. She didn't know what was going to happen, and she was surprised that one little burst of conflict had prompted her parents to change their plans so drastically.

But she heard them talking later that night, through a crack in the wall above her bed.

"Marriage will fix her," her father murmured. Rowan heard the sound of paper scraping and knew he was looking through one of his ledgers. "She needs to learn her place, and a husband will teach it to her."

"But *we* should have taught Celine her place," her mother said. She was pacing their room, by the sound of it. "What man will take a wife used to so much independence? He'll send her right back to us the day after the wedding, and no one will believe in her chastity then."

"She's pretty," her father said, his voice staying calm and even. "Men will forgive anything with a pretty wife to bed."

Elzbieta laughed a cold bark of a laugh, humorless. "You really think she'll let a *man* bed her without putting up a fight?"

Rowan sat up in bed. They knew. Her parents knew.

"Some men like that kind of thing," her father responded. The way they were talking made Rowan's stomach turn. "And if they treat her right and discipline her properly--"

"The way *we* should have been doing all along," Elzbieta interjected.

"Then she'll soon forget the mistakes she's made and learn to be a good wife."

A moment of silence.

"I hope you're right," was all Elzbieta said.

Rowan pulled her blanket over her head to block out their conversation, unwilling to listen to them anymore.

CHAPTER 5

Celine

Celine drew back her arrow. The deer shifted again, stepping behind some brush. She waited.

By some stroke of luck, this deer had all but walked into her camp, and she'd gotten her bow into position with painful slowness, praying it wouldn't cross the river. It grazed leisurely, stripping bark from trees and nipping up tiny shoots of young grass growing in patches newly freed from snow.

She'd been watching it here, where the river was low enough for it to cross, for some time. It wouldn't turn and give her a good shot at its broad side, and she hated using more than one arrow for a kill.

Besides, Irys's father had always told her, "If you can't take a good shot, don't shoot." Prolonged pain and suffering were always avoidable.

When she'd asked him why it mattered if a deer suffered, he'd sat quiet for a good long while.

Then he'd said, "It takes something from you, to cause another creature pain. Makes you into something less than human. Many folk start down that sick road, and I don't care for who they become along that way."

She'd later learned the meaning of the word "demoralizing" from her grandmother, and she thought that's what Irys's father had been trying to tell her. And later, the way she felt when she saw that some village boys had pinned live squirrels to a tree with arrowheads had been enough to show she didn't tolerate cruelty; not toward animals, and not toward people either. That was why she and Irys had to leave.

The deer abruptly lifted its head, staring off into the bushes in front of it. Celine raised her bow and loosed the arrow—but the deer sprang into the river in a flash, kicking up water as it sprinted away and into the trees on the other side.

"What a pity. That meat will be sorely missed by your family, I'm sure." A melodic male voice came from the trees behind her.

Celine scrambled around, fumbling for the axe on her back. Then she froze at the sight of the speaker.

"It's all right," said the golden man, stepping from the shadows of an elm. He held his empty hands palm up at his sides. "I haven't got a weapon. Just want to talk."

His clothes were fine—a strong green wool shirt with copper-colored buttons, velvety brown trousers, rich black leather boots—and he looked as though he'd never known a day of cold or hunger or uncertainty in his life. His hair was luxurious, blond, and curly—true gold, not like Celine's pale, almost white hair—and his face was completely clean-shaven. He couldn't be from the villages. Any man there of marriageable age took great pains to keep a beard on his face.

He seemed to be appraising her, taking note of her axes and quiver. "So. You're the young poacher of the last few years. It has taken me some time to track you down."

He tutted, shaking his head. "So little respect in the villages these days. I was recently told that your sister has also been sneaking about my forest. What a bad example to set. I did wonder if she would follow in your footsteps, but she seems content with mushrooms and berries. Not so keen to steal my beasts and cut down my trees."

If Celine had hackles, they'd have risen. This man knew who she was, who Rowan was?

He smiled warmly. It was hard not to like the look of someone so beautiful, but everything in Celine screamed that this conversation was wrong and she ought to flee like the deer.

"In any case, I'm not interested in your little sister. I am, however, interested in why you think you have the right to hunt my creatures. Is your family truly that poor? Does your father not know how to keep his house and home?"

Celine frowned. "'Your' creatures?"

The man's smile widened. "Or did you think I wasn't real? Just a tale made up to keep young children out of the woods—is that it?"

Celine felt cold now, despite the warm sun filtering through the trees. She gripped the handle of the axe strapped to her leg.

The man—the Oak King—shook his head at her. "Oh, I don't think so. You see—"

He flicked a finger, almost lazily. The axe shot out of her hand, pulled by some invisible force.

"The trees, they belong to me. They do what I say. And something made of wood? Well."

The axe sank its handle into the ground. The handle shifted, darkened, and a coating of black bark crusted over it. Heat flowed across Celine's face, melting the remaining patches of snow in the little clearing where she'd set up camp. But more was happening to her axe. Little twigs sprang out, unfurling leaves right before Celine's eyes. A delicate white blossom burst open at the tip of a small branch.

"It still remembers where it came from, as you see."

Celine swallowed, looking at the axe-headed tree that had just seconds ago sat lifeless in her hand.

"Still nothing to say? I thought that was impressive, if I do say so myself." The Oak King sounded disappointed, as if he'd been hoping for applause.

"I'm not sure what to say," Celine managed, finally. "Or why you're talking to me at all. Shall I leave?"

The Oak King looked completely surprised, and it took Celine a moment to realize that his tone had turned mocking. "Leave? Oh, no, no, no, certainly not! This matter needs to be settled. You have been trespassing in my forest, taking what isn't rightfully yours. I'd call that unfair. Wouldn't you?"

Celine said nothing. She wished he would just get to the point. She knew exactly what she'd do—flip her other axe from her side strap and throw it, just as a distraction. Then she'd grab her hunting knife. If he came at her, she'd cut him up and run for it.

Something in his smile had shifted. His look had somehow become icy cold, though his features were still fixed in that pleasant expression.

"I don't know if you appreciate the gravity of this situation. You see." He took a step toward her. "There's something different about you. I thought there might be, and now I see it's true." He took another step. "You have cut down trees here, too, haven't you?" He didn't wait for her answer. "Now, you shouldn't have been able to do that, not without the trees attacking you. Not without me finding out immediately. That indicates to me that *my* forest..." He spread his hands, indicating the trees around him. "... *accepts* you, for some reason. They think you have the authority to cut them down, to hunt my animals, all without alerting me to your presence."

"Then how did you know I was here?" Celine asked. She needed to stall him, keep him from coming closer. She did not want him near her, especially not with that awful smile.

He paused. "I have many loyal subjects, all of whom protect the forest on my behalf. They recently let me know about your... excursions. And your sister's, too, but like I said, a village girl picking flowers isn't my concern. Someone meddling with my trees? Now that's another matter." He stepped closer again. He was only a few feet away now.

"The trees are *mine*," he hissed, "and this is *my* kingdom. No human has the right to come in here and disrupt the order of things."

"Then I won't," Celine said, trying to keep her voice calm "I won't come back to this forest ever again."

The Oak King shook his head slowly.

"I'm afraid the opposite is true. You will never leave my forest again. You see, I haven't been able to travel in recent years, and I find myself in need of magic. And this rapport you seem to have with my trees is most certainly rooted in magic. Therefore..." he said, with a flick of his wrist, "a little harvesting will make it mine."

Behind her came a groaning, creaking sound, like a tree falling. And before she could turn to see what it was, something clubbed Celine on the side of the head and she fell to the ground. Her world went dark.

CHAPTER 6

Rowan

ONE WEEK BEFORE THE SPRING
EQUINOX

Rowan brought that axe down with a satisfying THUD, neatly splitting the log in two. When Celine was around, Rowan didn't often get to do many of the outdoor chores, but when her sister was off on a cutting or hunting trip, it often fell to her to take over Celine's duties.

And I'd rather split firewood than muck out the pig's stall, she thought with a shudder. At least in Winter the stall didn't stink as much, but she could feel the weather warming. It brought out some melancholy in her, to watch the snow thin and melt. She loved Spring, of course—the scent of flowers in the air, the promise of fresh strawberries and peas, the birthing of the little lambs on the neighboring farms. But she missed the colder months and the coziness that came with them all the same.

Celine, however, couldn't stand staying cooped up; each year, at the slightest hint of warmth, she always went off on another long expedition. Usually that fell on or after the first day of Spring, but that was still a week away. Rowan wondered if her sister was enjoying the first real warmth of the year, or if she was still upset about the circumstances under which she'd departed.

Probably not, if she's off with Irys, Rowan thought ruefully. She didn't know exactly how she felt about their relationship. While most of the villagers believed love could only happen between a man and a woman, Rowan wasn't so sure. More than that, she didn't think it really mattered how *she* felt about it—the relationship between two other people had nothing to do with her. But it was hard to get the voices of the townsfolk, preaching hellfire and damnation to those who went against the natural ways, out of her head.

Oh, what does it matter? Rowan thought, sending bits of wood flying with her next chop. *How does it hurt anyone if they're together?*

Her cut hadn't quite gone through the log, and she raised the axe again to finish the job. Then a flicker of red startled her, and the axe nearly flew out of her hands. Irys had come around the corner of the house, her face drawn with worry.

"Rowan, I'm so glad I found you!" she said, breathless. She puffed like she'd run a mile to get there.

"What's happened? I thought you were out with Celine," Rowan said, setting the axe in the chopping block with a THUNK. She felt nervous for some reason, like it wasn't right for her to speak with Irys while Celine wasn't present.

"That's just it—I can't find her anywhere. We were supposed to meet at... well, a spot where we've met before. But she wasn't there. I waited all morning and she never showed up." Irys nervously twisted the cuff of her coat.

"Did she go on ahead?" Rowan suggested.

Irys shook her head. "There was no sign of her. And I went the way she should have come—nothing. Did she say anything to you? Or did she have an unexpected errand come up?"

Rowan shook her head. "Where was your meeting place? Maybe she got lost." Even as she said it, she knew it couldn't be the case; Celine never got lost.

Irys looked uncomfortable. "Er, it was further down that way." She gestured to the south. "Close to the Border. But we've both been there many times—she couldn't have lost her way."

Rowan looked at the other girl for a moment. "Irys," she said gently, "I know you two go into the *prawdziwy las*. It's all right—I go there, too, sometimes."

Irys blanched. "You've seen us?" Her voice shook, and Rowan immediately regretted saying anything.

"I—yes. I did, on the Solstice. It's all right, I won't tell anyone, don't worry. I would never—I didn't say anything." She stumbled over her words, cursing herself for scaring Irys so badly.

Irys's lips trembled as she spoke. "You won't tell anyone about us going to the Forest? Or about..." She didn't finish the sentence, but Rowan knew what she meant.

"Celine is my sister," she said, as firmly as she could. "And you make her very happy. That's all I care about."

Irys made a choking sound and threw her arms around Rowan. Startled, Rowan patted her back, feeling extremely awkward as the older girl sobbed onto her shoulder.

Finally, Irys pushed herself back up, wiping tears from her eyes.

"I can't tell you—" she choked out, half smiling, half crying. "How —how much that means. We've both been so scared, so worried, if any of you—I can't describe how it's been."

"Yes, well..." Rowan couldn't think of what to say. She felt horrible that Celine and Irys had been so terrified of even her finding out about their relationship. *Did they really think I would tell someone?* she wondered, watching Irys dry her eyes on a handkerchief.

"When was the last time you saw Celine?" she asked, trying to focus on the matter at hand. Celine was very prompt and would certainly have kept her word to meet at a certain time at a certain place, especially if it involved Irys.

"She—she came to dinner at our house three days ago. She was going to get her work done ahead of time so we could... well, we go to the Forest together, where we know no one will see us," she said, awkwardly skirting something she clearly didn't want to tell Rowan.

"What is it?" Rowan asked pointedly.

Irys anxiously twisted the ends of her braids. "Celine built us a cabin —in *las graniczny*, not the Oak King's forest. We... we sent off for a certifi-cate of marriage—with just our initials, so they won't know we're both women—and we were planning to leave the village this year, to live there."

Rowan's mouth fell open.

"You were going to get married? And just leave?" She was stunned. Celine had been planning to leave her family forever, leave *her* forever, without ever telling her why?

Irys looked miserable. "It's the only way we can be together. We want a life with each other—that can't happen here." She gestured at the houses around them.

"But you've had a relationship here," Rowan burst out. She couldn't help herself—she felt so hurt by the revelation. "Couldn't you just keep..." She trailed off, realizing how it sounded.

"Just keep hiding ourselves?" Irys's voice turned bitter. Her eyes were still glassy but her face was angry now. "Just keep waiting for someone to find us out and hang us for perversion? Or marry us off to make us right again? You've seen what happens to people like us here. You'd ask us to stay, just so you can have your sister with you?"

The harsh words echoed across the snow. A swirl of flakes drifted off the roof and blew across the woodpile.

"No," Rowan said finally, her voice very quiet, "of course not. I just wish it could be different. I'm sorry."

Irys sniffed and wiped at her eyes again. "I need to find her. I don't want to live without her. If anything's happened..."

"Nothing's happened to her." Rowan hoped she sounded convincing. "It's Celine—she knows how to take care of herself. But..." She tried to sound less worried than she felt. "Maybe we could find the trail she took into the forest and see where it leads. Maybe something came up and she..." She thought frantically of what could possibly distract Celine. "Maybe she caught the trail of a moose or an elk and decided to track it."

Irys didn't look entirely convinced, but she nodded. "I think trying to find her trail would be a good idea. Will your parents let you go?"

That did put a wrench in things. If Rowan's parents thought Celine had gone missing, there was no question of Rowan and Irys going to find her. And search parties from the village certainly wouldn't trespass in the Oak King's forest, not even to find one of their own.

"I'll think of something to tell them," she promised. "When can you be ready to leave?"

"As soon as you like," Irys said at once. "I didn't even bother to unpack my knapsack."

"I'll need to pack, but... I need to make sure my parents let me go. Don't worry," she said when Irys looked alarmed. "I won't tell them anything, but I can't just leave without a reason. If my mother won't let me visit Celine's camp in the *las graniczny*, I'll get my grandmother to cover for me."

Irys looked a little displeased with the idea of waiting, but she agreed nonetheless, telling Rowan to meet her by the crooked elm in the *las graniczny*.

Rowan went back to chopping wood, though her mind raced with ideas of what she could tell her parents. She needed an excuse to go looking for Celine—if there was something she could claim Celine had left behind or something she'd need...

She looked up and the sky. Clouds were moving in, and they looked heavy with snow.

You just need to be able to get away with no one questioning you. If you stay out longer than you said, there are any number of excuses.

She loaded up an armful of wood and went inside, stamping snow off her boots in the doorway. She dumped the wood in the crate by the fire, then went to the kitchen where her mother sat on a stool, reading a book as she stirred the stew on the stove.

"Mama?" she said, keeping her voice free of the worry she felt. "Would it be all right if I go visit Celine's camp tomorrow?"

"You, go to Celine's camp? Why?" Elzbieta asked, reluctantly tearing her eyes away from the page.

"I thought I could bring her some more food, and maybe a fresh change of clothes, since she's already been gone so long. And... well, I miss her. She doesn't seem like she likes spending time with me very much anymore, so I thought..." She was surprised at how honest her words were, even though she was using them as an excuse.

Her mother set down the book with an annoyed huff. "Don't be ridiculous, Rowan. I need you here. Besides, the woods are dangerous."

"But Celine's out there, I'd be just as safe as she is," Rowan burst out before she could stop herself.

Elzbieta shook her head. "No woman should have to do what

Celine does—it isn't right. Be grateful she's taken that work upon herself so you can stay here and learn."

"Learn how to be a wife, you mean?" Rowan snapped, no longer caring about convincing her mother of anything. "And does it matter what I want?"

Elzbieta stared at her. "You want what's best for yourself, don't you?" she said, anger prickling at the edges of her voice. "Your father and I have worked hard to make a good life for you. And you will not be happy if you stray outside of that life." She turned back to the stove and began stirring again. "Go hem your quilt."

Rowan didn't move, glaring at her mother's back. She wanted to yell at her, to make her listen to why she was wrong.

"I said go upstairs and hem your wedding quilt!" Elzbieta didn't even bother turning around.

Furious, Rowan stalked out of the kitchen and stomped her feet on the stairs as she went up. She knew her mother hated the noise, but that Elzbieta wouldn't let it rile her. Her mother would let her anger pass and then act as if nothing had happened once dinner was on the table.

See how you feel the day you come to wake me and my bed is empty, Rowan thought viciously as she slammed the door to her room.

The first sign of trouble came with the smoke. The cooking fire smoldered one morning, the scent of burning cinnamon wood spicing the air. I sat stoking it for a long time, trying to bring it back to flame. But all at once, the smoke twisted up into a column, and when I looked up, a pair of eyes stared back at me from behind the veil of gray. The eyes blinked. Then they vanished.

I told my mother what I had seen. She pressed her lips together, grim, and said nothing, but she was watchful after that day.

Not even a week later, my mother and I were hauling in fishing nets, glinting with the silvery skin of the spiky little fish we fried and ate whole. She hissed, and I thought one of them had pricked her. Then I saw she was staring at a dark boat that looked nothing like the fishing boats that passed our island.

She flung the net aside and pulled me with her, calling to the other children to go inside. She tried to order everyone into their huts, but the other adults refused.

"You will not face him alone again," spat my aunt. The fishbone bracelets on her arms clacking as she bristled, burning for a fight.

Several of our people had magic of a kind, though not nearly as much power as my mother had. But she shook her head at them darkly.

"His magic is different from ours. It ebbs and flows with the seasons of *his land. That's why he has waited until this time of year to come here—he is at the height of his power."*

But they stood fast, flanking her as the man leaped from the boat and strode up the beach to our village. I stood with the others, my aunt's hand fiercely gripping my own.

The man slowed as he neared the crowd of villagers. His eyes flicked from my mother to me, then back again. I had never seen hair like his before—gold curls, cropped short so it barely brushed the color of his shirt.

He halted just a few feet away.

"It's been a long time, Jasmine."

I was surprised at how gentle his voice sounded, how he smiled sadly at my mother as though he had missed her.

Her face remained stony. "You should not have come back."

"I had to."

His eyes found me again. Their greenness disconcerted me—bright as the skins of the snakes that slithered through the rocks on the beach. And flecked with copper like mine.

"You left thirteen years ago. There is no reason for you to be here now." My mother's voice rang clear and firm over the crash of the waves.

"Jasmine, a few years' absence means nothing to beings like us. We have centuries to make up for it." His voice was warm and sweet as syrup.

I couldn't understand it—he had left, before I had even taken my first breath in this world, yet here he was, speaking as though he cared about my mother and me.

"I do not know you, Oak, and you do not know me. I do not choose you, and thirteen years ago, you made it clear you did not choose me. Leave."

He made no move to obey.

"At least let me meet my daughter," he said, his voice pained.

I stiffened at the word.

"You have no daughter, Oak," my mother told him.

His brow furrowed, his eyes fixing on me. "What do you mean?"

"This is my son, Nash."

"But I thought—"

"He is a boy, and there is nothing more to say on the subject."

His eyes narrowed ever so slightly. "Very well."

He stepped forward, his attention solely on me.

"Nash," he addressed me.

My mother flinched, as though tempted to step in front of me. Oak caught the movement, and the corners of his lips twitched in amusement.

"I have come a long way to meet you," he said. "And here you are, already half grown."

I said nothing. There was a war within me—of dislike for this man who ignored my mother's wishes and of an intense feeling of warmth at his words. He had magic, my mother had told me, of a sort our people had never seen before, and he ruled a strange and distant land. His attention made me feel special, and I did not want it to.

"Your mother has raised you to use her magic, has she not? The magic of water?" he asked me.

"Oak—" my mother began.

"Please," he said without taking his eyes off me. "Let Nash answer."

I glanced at my mother, at my aunt behind her, both of them tense, as though waiting for a storm to break.

"Yes," I said at last. "She has taught me her magic."

He nodded, as though he had already known the answer.

"And has she told you about the other magic you possess?"

My eyes widened, and I looked at my mother. Her lips pressed together in a thin line, and I could see fear in her wide eyes.

"Other magic?" I echoed.

"My magic," he said softly, a look of satisfaction coming over his face.

"N-no." My stomach roiled. My mother had never told me I possessed another kind of magic. But it made sense—I had inherited hers. It was only natural that I had also inherited Oak's.

"You do not need his magic, Nash," my mother said, a note of panic in her voice. "It is tied to his land, not to ours."

"Why don't you let Nash decide that?" Oak's gaze landed on my mother, his tone admonishing. "Especially since you failed to even mention that she—"

"He," my mother corrected fiercely.

"Yes, yes, of course. Nash has more than one kind of magic. You of all people should know how dangerous it is, not to train a child to use their powers."

My breath caught in my throat. Was this true? Had my mother kept *this from me simply because she did not like that I had Oak's powers? Was I a danger to myself, to my people, because of it?*

"He is not a danger to anyone. We do not need your magic, Oak."

"But Nash has it, nevertheless. And I can show her—Nash, I mean—how to use it. I would teach you, Nash," Oak said to me. "If you would come with me and stay in my forest a while. It is your choice."

"It is not his choice!" My mother burst out, stepping between us. "He is a child—my child!"

"A child you refuse to teach properly," Oak fired back. "And Nash is of an age where she... he can decide for himself."

Then, in a low urgent voice, he told me, "My magic is different from your mother's. It comes from ancient, wild elements. Without training, it will build throughout your life until you can no longer contain it. And then it will break out of you like a hurricane."

I stepped back from him, horrified.

"Is this true?" I demanded of my mother.

"I—" She looked at me helplessly, at a loss for words. "I do not know. My magic is not like that, but I know so little of his magic, Nash."

The only person who did know was Oak.

I turned my back on all of them—on Oak, on my mother, on my village—and I went to the hut. I threw some of my belongings into a bag and stuck my dagger in my belt.

The curtain across the door rustled and my mother came inside.

"Nash, I am sorry I didn't tell you about your other power." She came to me and took my face in her hands. "I was worried you would seek him out if you knew of it, that you would leave and try to find him so he could teach you to use it."

"So you hid it from me?" I exploded. "Even though not learning how to use the power could destroy the village?"

She shook her head slowly. "Nash, we do not know for certain if he is telling the truth."

Tears pricked at the corners of my eyes. "But, mother," I said, my voice cracking. "Now I am not sure if you are telling the truth either."

I pushed past her and went outside. To Oak, I said, "I will go with you and learn how to use this power. But after that, you have no claim on me."

He opened his mouth to reply, but I was already striding toward his boat.

I would not risk the village's safety, even if my mother didn't think Oak was telling the truth. But more than that, it stung to know my mother had hidden the truth of my powers from me, had not trusted me to make the right decision for myself.

I climbed aboard the boat, and Oak leaped up soon after. He said nothing as he prepared the boat for sailing.

As we lurched off the shore, I looked back at the island where I had lived my entire life.

My mother stood on the dock, her gaze unwavering. Even from here, I could see silvery tears streaming down her cheeks, but she made no move to come to me. She was letting me go.

The boat sped across the water at an unnatural speed—Oak must have enchanted it, though I did not know how. The island behind us grew smaller and smaller until it disappeared in the dark of evening.

There were no blankets or bedrolls, so I wrapped my arms around myself and lay down, trying to let the rocking of the water lull me to sleep.

CHAPTER 8

Rowan

Some hours later, after much apologizing and cajoling, Rowan managed to get permission to take a basket of food to Grandmother Elie's house.

I'm just visiting my grandmother, she told herself, trying to walk normally. *I'm not doing anything wrong.*

But her heart still raced, and she kept looking over her shoulder, as if expecting to see her mother following her.

She doesn't know what I'm doing or why I'm going. She never has to know.

It wasn't unusual for Rowan to go stay with her grandmother for a day or two when she needed help around the house. But she was still nervous, partly about her mother discovering the real reason she had gone, and partly from worrying that her grandmother would tell her she was crazy.

She reached her grandmother's door and peeked into the flower beds on either side of the steps.

Elie's flowers always came up before any others, and Rowan was glad to see the first little shoots of snowdrops poking through the scum-colored dregs of the last snow.

Rowan rested her basket on her hip and knocked with her free hand. Bustling footsteps approached, and the door swung open.

Elie had been baking—her clothes, face, and hair were dusted with flour, but her eyes lit up when she saw it was Rowan at the door.

"Little Russet, come in!" She waved Rowan into her house. "Look at you, all bundled up like it was the dead of Winter—don't you know that Spring is only a handful of days away?"

She peered up at the sky before closing the door.

"Though Spring seems to come earlier each year—the Oak King gets more and more impatient every season," she remarked as she led Rowan to her sitting room.

Rowan nodded absently, trying to think how she could best bring up what she wanted to tell her grandmother.

"I brought you some things," she said, too nervous to start with her news. She pulled back the cloth and showed her grandmother the rolls and the bottle of spiced wine within.

Her grandmother cooed over the embroidered napkins tucked under them. "You get better at your needlework by the day, my dear. This is very fine work—they'd pay good coin for it in the city."

Elie always said Rowan could easily make a living in the city. She'd even offered to move there with Rowan and help her keep a house, but Rowan couldn't fathom making her grandmother make such a move in her old age. Besides, her grandmother always said she liked the ambling pace of the village better than the hectic dash of Javsbor, even if the people here were backward.

"Rowan?" Her grandmother tilted her head to one side, reaching out to brush back some stray hairs that had escaped from Rowan's braids, which she'd hastily wound around her head.

"I'm sorry, grandmother, did you ask me something?" Rowan looked down at the basket and fiddled with the cloth.

"Your mind is miles away from here, Little Apple. What's troubling you?"

Rowan tried to smile. Her grandmother could read her so well.

"Celine hasn't come home. And she was supposed to meet up with Irys yesterday—there was no sign of her."

A crease appeared in Elie's brow.

"Well, that's not good," she said finally. "But she may just be a day behind. Perhaps she had to camp further down the Border—a late snow can gum up the path like anything."

Rowan shook her head. "She wasn't in the *las graniczny*, grandmother."

Elie went pale. She slowly sat down in her armchair.

"She's been hunting in the Oak King's forest?" she asked, her voice suddenly hoarse.

Rowan nodded, her throat tightening.

Her grandmother exhaled sharply, bringing a hand to her temple.

"How long has this gone on?"

"I don't know," Rowan said, shaking her head helplessly. "I only found out this Winter."

"Why didn't you—" Elie cut herself off, forcing herself to take a breath before starting again. "You didn't tell her to stop?"

Rowan looked down at her feet. "I couldn't."

"Whyever not? Trespassing in the Oak King's forest is punishable by death, torture, slavery—anything he thinks necessary! How could she be so foolish?"

Rowan opened her mouth to defend her sister, but all the reasons she could think of sounded hollow in her mind.

Elie took another deep breath, releasing it slowly as she looked about her room as though it was foreign to her.

"So, she hasn't come back. And Irys was to meet her this morning?"

"At dawn," Rowan replied.

Her grandmother's eyes met hers.

"What do you think has happened, child?"

Rowan's nails bit into her palms as she clenched her hands.

"I don't know. But I'm going to go look for her."

"Don't be foolish, Rowan!" her grandmother hissed, looking close to tears. "If something has happened to your sister, think how heart-breaking it would be if you went headlong into the same danger!"

"I'm not leaving her alone out there," Rowan insisted, tears burning in her eyes. "She already hates our family because no one understands her—I can't pretend nothing's wrong and not at least *try* to find her. She needs help—I'm sure of it."

Elie opened her mouth, then closed it again. She rose and went to her window, staring through the curtains at the wall of trees that made up the *las graniczny.*

"Your parents will never allow you to go into the Oak King's forest," she said finally, her voice uncharacteristically stony. It was how she sounded when she was trying not to cry.

"I wasn't planning on asking them. Mother already told me I can't go after her. But they don't know she went beyond the Border."

Elie said nothing.

"I can tell them I'm staying with you for a few days. *Please*, grandmother. I think Celine's in trouble, and Irys and I are the only ones who have a chance at finding her."

Rowan's grandmother turned around, her face unhappy.

"Irys will go with you, then? I care about Celine as much as you do, but I'm not sending one of my own grandchildren into the forbidden wood on her own, with nothing to protect you. Remember, Rowan, Celine has been going on these excursions for years—you have not. It won't be an easy thing, searching for her."

Rowan nodded. "But I have to try. And Irys can help—she's gone hunting and woodcutting with Celine, and she knows where Celine might have gone. At least, to a certain point."

Elie didn't look pleased, but she bowed her head.

"Alright. Run home and tell your mother I need your help for a few days. I can't promise more than two, and if you aren't back in the village at that point, I'm telling anyone and everyone where you've gone, and we will send out a search party to scour the Border for you. That's not a threat, Rowan," she insisted, holding up a hand when Rowan started to protest. "If you're in the Oak King's forest for longer than two days, that means something has happened to you, and that something would likely be worse than any reprimand from your parents."

Rowan swallowed her objection. She needed her grandmother's help, and if this was the only way to get it, so be it.

"I've told you the story of the girl who went through the wood to her grandmother's house, haven't I?" Elie asked, growing wistful.

Rowan nodded, "Little Redcap."

"Her family warns her to keep to the path, not to stray from the known world into the unknown. I don't feel good about permitting you to do just that."

"Well," Rowan offered, "I would do it even without your permission."

Elie smiled ruefully. "Then perhaps I shouldn't feel too guilty."

Their uneasy laughter died quickly, and the two of them stood in silence for a beat.

"Run along home, Rowan. Say goodbye to everyone and come back. We'll pretend that you really are just coming for a visit for tonight. Tomorrow will be tomorrow."

Rowan walked home. The sun warmed through her many layers of clothing. At this point in the season, it was hard to justify bundling up, but this was how Rowan felt most comfortable—with scarf and hat and mittens, a coat beneath her sweater, and her thickest socks inside her boots. Soon enough Spring would come, and she would have to pack away her cozy woolen things. Until then, she was determined to dress as warmly and comfortably as she could.

In any case, she would need to dress warmly for her venture into the forest.

She got her mother's permission; in fact, her mother seemed glad to have her out of the house, despite the extra work it meant for her. That night, Rowan lay awake in her grandmother's spare room. She was too anxious to sleep, even though she knew she ought to try and get a few hours' rest if she could. In truth, she was also scared of falling asleep and not waking in time to meet Irys at first light. But truly there was no chance of it. She still stewed over her mother's words, over her parents' double standards. They said no woman should have to work to feed her family, that it wasn't her place, but they depended on Celine for food and money alike. She could be the exception, no matter what she or anyone else wanted.

Had they ever asked Rowan how she would prefer to help her family? Or Ademun, for that matter, always hanging around the kitchens hoping to be permitted to help.

Her parents operated under the assumption that, as soon as Ademun turned fifteen, he would take responsibility for hunting and woodcutting, while Celine would take up whatever womanly duties her parents assigned.

And just how did they think that would go? Rowan thought, furious. *No wonder she wanted to leave.*

Now she wondered if Ademun had ever dreamed of running away, of escaping the dread of the new, unwanted duties, so unsuited to his character, that loomed over him. She wondered if Danica and Kestrel dreaded the day they would be forced to give up their play for cooking, sewing, and preening themselves in the hopes of catching some boy's eye.

She sat up, unable to relax. After lighting a candle, she went to her pack and yanked out the quilt her mother had ordered her to embroider. She hadn't touched it then, but she brought it with her in case she needed something to do. By the flickering light of the candle, she pulled out her needles and threads and bent to work. Ignoring the hem, she started embroidering the center of the quilt.

There were times she hated herself for loving embroidery, for loving to cook and bake. Everyone praised her for investing in the skills that would make her a good wife, but that wasn't why she liked them. She loved making beautiful and delicious things, and she was good at it. It made her proud, seeing something come out the way she wanted it, or even better, but she was careful not to share those feelings, lest she be chastised for vanity. Though her likes and dislikes had nothing to do with the nameless, faceless husband promised by her future.

And this quilt, painstakingly stitched together since she was twelve years old, was meant to stay unembellished until she was at least engaged to someone, so she knew what details to add—her intended's family crest, flowers his mother liked, or some stupid things like that. She was supposed to add another inch to the outer border every year, building an intricate, unique pattern to showcase future embroidery. The week before her wedding day, she would add the binding, sealing off the patterns just as her own fate was sealed.

Why should I put all that work into it for someone else? She thought as she stitched brown thread into the trunk of a tree. *It isn't right that I will have made this whole damned thing without a shred of myself visible in it.*

She sewed quickly, and the mountain ash tree she was named for took shape against the silvery-blue cloth. The leaves and bright red berries were painfully small, but she had done fine detail work like this many times. And she couldn't set the quilt down again until *something* about it represented her.

After a few hours of work, the tree was recognizable. Rowan thought it looked rather nice—a little spindly, but then again, mountain ash trees usually were. She wished she'd made it a bit larger, so she could add one of the little waxwing birds that loved the berries so much, but then she would have had to sew around the little sprays of green leaves, and that would have been unbearably tedious.

She raised her head and looked out the window. It was nearly dawn.

She went to her grandmother's kitchen and packed herself food. Elie had told her to take whatever she needed, and so she took what Celine normally did—a few loaves of hearty wheat bread, dried fruit and meat, and several apples. Unlike Celine, Rowan couldn't simply hunt for more food if she ended up getting stuck in the forest somewhere, but she could only hope that that wouldn't happen.

She wrapped up in one of her father's old coats, her favorite red scarf, and whatever other warm things she'd managed to pinch from home. Then, without a pause, she kissed her grandmother goodbye and trudged into the snow, toward the meeting place she and Irys had agreed upon.

As she left, she noticed that her grandmother watched her from the window, her blue work shawl wrapped tightly around her shoulders.

CHAPTER 9

Celine

Adull ache pounded in Celine's head. Her eyes were reluctant to open; she forced them to anyway. She was lying on a cot in a cell. Shakily, she pushed herself up onto one elbow. The movement made the ache in her head sharpen, and she screwed her eyes shut until it passed. Holding her hand to the sore area, she sat up the rest of the way and looked around her. Peering at the bars of the cell, she realized they were made of wood.

That's odd, she thought, *that doesn't make for a good holding place.* Then she saw her axe, her big one, leaning against the foot of the cot. Relief flooded through her and she grasped its handle, hugging it to her like an old friend. Her smaller one must have been left behind.

But at least I can cut my way out of here... Except... Why would her captor allow an axe in a cell made of wood? As she sized up the bars again, Celine began to get a sick feeling in the pit of her stomach. It was too convenient. Perhaps if she tried to cut her way out, someone was waiting to snatch her up again as soon as she was free.

Keeping ahold of her axe, she stood and walked to the bars. The room beyond the cell was, to her surprise, a bedchamber—with a large, canopied bed, a great glass window, and a table set with dishes and food. Celine's stomach wrenched painfully and she turned away. Why the cell sat on the edge of a fine bedchamber, she had no idea, but she wasn't about to torture herself by staring at food she couldn't reach.

She focused instead on the bars. In truth, now that she was closer, they looked more like the trunks of young trees—imperfect, curved, and covered in rough bark.

Maybe that's decorative, Celine thought hopefully, *could be metal underneath all that bark.*

She scraped one of the bars with the blade of her axe, peeling away a layer of bark. All it revealed was green wood underneath, but only for a second. In the blink of an eye, the bark grew back over the area Celine had cleared, leaving no trace of disturbance.

Frowning, she sawed a deeper cut into the wood, but that too sealed itself up again within seconds, and she had to pry her axe head out with some effort. She backed away from the bars.

Now she knew why the axe had been left with her—if she tried to cut down the bars, they would regrow instantly, giving her no time to escape.

The sound of footsteps caught her attention. Vaguely she wondered if she ought to go back to the cot and pretend to be asleep, but the thought of quick movement made her head ache. She settled instead for sinking back into the chair and leaning her head into her hand.

"Awake already?"

That pleasant voice made her stomach writhe. The Oak King smiled brightly as he strolled across the room.

The doorway through which he entered looked to be the only way in and out of the room. He gestured to the bedchamber outside of the cell.

"What do you think of your quarters?"

Celine said nothing. She stared at him blankly. The less cunning he expected of her, the better. Besides, he seemed perfectly happy to do all the talking—she was hardly necessary, just an opportunity for him to listen to himself talk.

He grinned sheepishly, though every expression of his seemed planned, calculated, and unnatural.

"Oh, I know—you can't really get to any of it from there." He went to the table and sat down, kicking his feet up on another chair. "But I don't really trust village folk to behave themselves, especially in my own home. I'm sure you understand."

His eyes flickered to Celine, as though hoping for a reaction. She kept her face empty and dull, as though she didn't quite understand what he said.

"Don't worry, now. I don't mean to do anything too extreme—I'm just going to give you a little time, maybe a day or so, to adjust to the way things are. I need to trust that you won't run away if I let you out. This is a wonderful opportunity for you, you know. I could have punished you for stealing from my kingdom, but instead, since I came across you at such a lucky time, you get this chance to redeem yourself. That's so much more noble, don't you agree?"

He wants me to talk to him, she thought. And he wasn't going to wait all day for a response. This was a dangerous game, and she had to tread carefully. Already she'd seen his temper abruptly change for the worse, and she'd suffered the result of that. She didn't want it to happen again, not while she was entirely at his mercy. His whim was cruel.

"What is the opportunity?" she asked. She was relieved to see the flicker of annoyance fade from his face the second she gave in and spoke.

"Oh, I think you already know," he said, rising from the chair and ambling over to the cell, his hands clasped behind his back. "After all, you must have suspected for some time now that you have some kind of magic. How else could you have so successfully avoided notice for so many years? Other people have tried and failed to steal from me for centuries; I have *always* given them their due when they have been caught." He looked delighted by whatever memories he spoke of.

What a cruel person, she thought, disgust tempting her lips to curl. But she was good at hiding how she felt, of course.

"But I digress, my apologies. Let's you and I get to know each other a little better. Come here," he said suddenly, his eyes glittering. He stood right at the bars of the cell.

She didn't move.

"I said come here." His voice had turned ice-cold, though his face was frozen in the exact same smile.

Celine stood. Still clutching her head, she moved as close to the bars as she dared.

Irys, what have I gotten myself into?

He reached out and touched her hair, rubbing the strands of blond between his fingers.

"Lovely," he murmured.

She thought she might be sick.

"Simply lovely."

She kept her eyes downcast, determined not to meet his eye.

"Tell me about your magic," he said, twirling a piece of her hair around one finger.

"I don't have any magic," she muttered.

His hand tightened on her hair, and he yanked, hard. Her head smacked the sapling bars, making her already aching skull hurt even worse. She would have fallen, but he hauled her up by her hair.

"Now, that's not going to work," he chided, as though reprimanding a small child. "You really will make things very hard for yourself if you aren't forthright with me."

"I don't have magic," Celine hissed through gritted teeth, trying to pry his hand from her hair. "I've never had magic—I don't *know* anything about it."

After a moment, he released his hold on her. She sagged against the bars, head swimming from the knock he'd given her.

"Interesting. Then I suppose we'll just have to learn about it together," he said, his tone disconcertingly bright.

He turned and strode toward the door. Then, almost as an afterthought, he stopped and went to the table.

"Almost forgot, silly me. Here," he said, plucking up an apple.

He tossed the fruit into the cell. It smacked against the wall, spraying Celine with juice, and rolled under the cot.

"Enjoy!" He strolled out of the room, whistling tunelessly.

Celine waited until the sound of his footsteps died away before kneeling to retrieve the apple. It was badly bruised from where it had hit the wall, bleeding juice, but she was too hungry to let it go to waste. He obviously didn't mean to feed her properly.

Turns out the Oak King is real, and he's a madman, she thought, biting into the apple. She ate every piece of it, only discarding the seeds and stem. It was next to nothing, but she had no choice. Then, though the only thing she wanted was to crawl back into the cot and sleep, she made herself stand to check her balance. She stood on one leg, then the other, moving her arms up and out to the sides to see if she could keep herself upright.

I think I'm alright. Certainly not concussed. She didn't feel good, by any means, but at least the injury to her head didn't seem to have caused any concerning damage. With that confirmed, she took stock of the cell. She relieved herself in a bucket she found under the cot. The bucket, a pitcher of water in the corner, the chair, the cot, and her axe were the only things in the cell besides herself.

Besides a row of impenetrable saplings, she reminded herself as she crawled back under the thin blanket, pulling it over her head to block out the sunlit room on the other side of the bars.

The Oak King's threats still drifted through her mind like vile somethings swimming in the deep. Why did he insist she had magic? And why did it matter to him so much? She shuddered, wrapping her arms around herself as if that would somehow protect her. Her scalp smarted from where he had yanked on her hair. She had never felt so unsafe, so powerless, in her whole life.

She sat up, grabbed her axe, and lay back down, making sure the blade lay pointed away from her body.

If he tries to touch me again, she thought, comforted by holding her weapon, *I'll cut him into kindling.*

CHAPTER 10

Rowan

SIX DAYS BEFORE THE SPRING EQUINOX

Rowan found Irys huddled by a small fire near the elder tree in the *las graniczny*. She stood immediately, brushing dirt from her trousers. She kicked at the fire until it went out.

"This is where we usually cross the Border," she said, pointing to a narrow path illuminated by the remnants of moonlight filtering through the bare trees. Snow still coated much of the ground, but there were many open patches where the dirt peeked through, and the days were getting warmer and warmer—it wouldn't last much longer.

Rowan looked down at the path.

"Are these her footprints?" she asked Irys.

"These ones, here." Irys pointed down at some footprints that very nearly matched the ones Rowan was leaving behind. "But these..." She indicated another line of prints that also followed the path into the Oak King's forest. "These are fresher, and they aren't mine or Celine's."

"How can you tell? That they're fresher tracks?" Rowan asked.

"Well, I know when Celine went into the woods, to the day and time. Hers are more rounded and melted, since they've sat in the sun for a few days. But these, see how all the snow that was kicked up is still all spiky and unmelted? This happened last night, I'm sure of it." Irys looked ahead at the Oak King's forest, concern written all over her face. "Someone else is in there."

The two of them stood there silently, each thinking about what this meant.

Could someone have followed Celine into the forest? Rowan wondered as the two of them, without a word, set off across the Border. Immediately the hunter who had warned her on the Solstice came into her head. She wished she had something more than a dagger to protect herself with, though she didn't even truly know how to use that. The most useful combat training she had was when Celine had taught her how to punch. That had come in very useful when the baker's son got cocky and tried to corner her in an alley—she'd broken his nose. It was the proudest Celine had ever looked, when she told her about it. Rowan always tried to focus on that part, and not the part when the boy had tried to jam his hand down her bodice. She still had to see him on market days, but he avoided their stall. His nose never did seem to heal properly.

The Oak King's forest was oddly quiet, but then, Rowan had never been here this early. Her excursions into the *prawdziwy las* had always taken place in broad daylight, and she had never stayed more than an hour or two. The faintest flicker of morning light was just starting to bleed from the east. As the two of them passed through the dark trees, Rowan heard the birds begin to chirp.

As their feet crunched in the mud-splattered remnants of Winter, Rowan realized that the two other girls had certainly gone much farther into the forest than she had ever dared. As a child, she'd somehow gotten it into her head that as long as she didn't stay very long, no one would notice she had been there. That wasn't really an option now. She could only hope that they didn't come across anything or anyone that didn't want them there. Especially the hunter.

After maybe an hour's walk, Irys suddenly stopped and held up a hand. Rowan looked about for what had made her stop, and she realized with a jolt that the snow was gone. She glanced back the way they had come. There was a clear line where the snow ended sharply and the damp dark earth began. It was growing lighter, and the strengthening blue light of morning helped illuminate a great snowless ring that stretched maybe twenty feet.

Every inch of the space before them was green and completely free of snow, a stark contrast with the forest they had just passed through. Little leaves sprouted from the branches above their heads and the bushes clustered around them, where outside of the ring there were only buds and bare branches.

"Look," Irys breathed, pointing toward the center of the clearing.

A collapsed tent—Celine's tent, Rowan realized—lay puddled there, and the earth in front of it was torn up, like some great creature had been digging there.

Before Rowan could say a word, Irys tore over to the tent and ripped it open.

"Celine!" she cried, feeling for her in the pile of ruined fabric.

No answer, and after Irys made certain no one was inside the tent, she rose again. A glint of metal behind Irys caught Rowan's attention. Celine's axe stuck out of the ground, as though someone had half buried it in the dirt. The strap Celine used to bind it to her leg lay beside it.

Rowan went over to it and pulled. It came out of the ground with difficulty. She looked at the handle and was startled to see fine little threads dangling from it like roots. It was covered in tiny twigs and dried up flowers. She brushed at them and was perturbed when they didn't come off. Irys walked over and snapped a twig off; Rowan could see the place where it had grown out from the axe handle. *Grown* as if from a living plant.

"What..." Irys began, but she trailed off, both of them staring at the axe.

Rowan snapped off the rest of the twigs and pulled off every flower. She scraped the root-like bits off the base of the handle and strapped the axe to her own leg. It was still Celine's—she would want it back.

"I don't see the other one," she said, feeling the urge to keep moving, keep talking, if only to ward off the horrible sense that something very bad had happened in this clearing.

"She must have it with her," Irys said instantly, looking back at the fallen tent. "She'd never go off without at least one of her axes."

But what happened to this one? The unspoken question hung in the air as the two of them looked around for something else, some other clue as to where Celine went.

"There are footprints, here," Irys said suddenly, starting forward. Just a few paces from where the axe had been, there was a cluster of large boot prints.

"Whose?" Rowan asked, crouching next to them.

"I don't know." Irys looked troubled. She followed the footprints over to where the earth had been broken up. "These... These are claw marks," she said slowly. "These were made by an animal."

Rowan stared. The marks were at least the length of her body and they sank at least a foot or two into the ground.

"Those footprints," Irys said, drawing a line with her finger from where Rowan stood to the giant claw marks, "end here."

"But...what made them?" Rowan asked.

Irys shook her head.

Some giant creature... and Celine...

A flash of movement caught Rowan's eye. She yelled to Irys, who spun. Hundreds of tiny things flooded out of the trees from the west and poured through the clearing. They were so small and moved so quickly that Rowan could barely make out what they were. Then something ran into her leg and she looked down. It looked like a very small person with olive-green skin, standing no higher than the middle of Rowan's calf, wearing a suit of brown fur and a brilliant scarlet hat.

"Red Caps!" she yelped, flinching away.

Red Caps set upon people lost in the forests. They would swarm the unlucky traveler and tear into their skin, dipping their little hats into their blood until they were soaked through.

But the creature only blinked its enormous eyes at her and scrambled around her, fleeing with its companions. The last of the huge herd of little Red Caps trickled into the trees where Irys and Rowan had just come from.

"What in the world?" Irys gasped, looking incredulous.

Red Caps never came out into the open like that, and certainly not in those numbers. They usually crept about in the trees and underground, watching for travelers to play tricks on. They hadn't looked twice at Irys and Rowan.

Then a roar echoed through the trees, startling flocks of birds from their roosts. Rowan felt the ground rumble beneath her feet. Her eyes fell on the deep claw marks in the ground.

"We need to get out of here."

Irys nodded, but when they moved, it was in opposite directions—Irys east toward the village, Rowan west toward the heart of the forest.

"What are you doing? We need to leave—it's not safe!" Irys hissed.

"Celine is still in here; what if whatever *that* was is after her?" Rowan gripped the handle of her sister's axe and considered just how ill-prepared she was to fight anything, especially something as big as whatever was crashing around somewhere in the forest.

"Celine would *not* want you to get yourself killed!" Irys said, looking very much like she was about to grab Rowan and drag her out of the forest. "You don't know the kinds of things that are in here. Celine is the only person I know who actually stands a chance against them!"

"Something's happened to her and you know it!" Rowan retorted. "I'm not leaving!"

"We can't help her if we get ourselves eaten!" Irys sounded desperate now, and she was edging backward. More roaring came from between the trees--it was getting closer.

"There will be no one left to help if *she* gets eaten!" Rowan inched closer to the trees—she could hear a vast and rhythmic movement overhead, and it sounded awfully like wingbeats. *Enormous* wingbeats.

Her eyes met Irys's for a split second across the clearing. Then a curtain of fire blasted through the clearing, obscuring her vision. Heat seared across her face, and the force of it threw her backward. She landed on her back amongst the trees.

Scrambling up, she looked for the source of the fire and immediately wished she hadn't. It looked like a flying tree at first, but after a second she made out roots curled into claws, bark twisting like muscle and sinew, trunk haunches, and wings made out of millions and millions of tiny leaves. And worst of all was the face—a horrible contortion of wood and bark with jaws the size of her home's front door, yawning wide to spout another stream of flame down at the clearing. Rowan looked for Irys among the trees but couldn't spot her. There wasn't time. She turned tail and ran, not knowing which direction she was headed, only that she was moving as fast as she could away from the fearsome creature intent on burning the place where she had been standing only a minute ago.

All the care she normally took when passing through the Oak King's forest flew from her mind as she crashed through the underbrush, no idea of where she was headed or what she might run into in her haste to get somewhere safe. Her pack bounced painfully on her back, and her boots slid in patches of slick mud, black as tar. She didn't know if the creature she'd just seen was following her or had stayed and gobbled up Irys. She had never been so scared in her life—never had she ever seen anything so huge before, or anything so obviously created by magic.

She ran until she met with the river, where she was forced to stop. Swollen with Spring flooding, there was nowhere safe to cross. She turned and scanned the sky behind her. No sign of the tree dragon. Perhaps it had gone after Irys. Guilt swam up in her stomach. She hoped her sister's sweetheart had managed to get away.

And what on earth am I meant to do now? she wondered as she started to follow the river. *Should I try to get back to the village?* But she was here, now, deeper in the Oak King's forest than she had ever been. Surely she was closer to wherever Celine was. She decided she would see where the river took her. If it grew shallow enough for her to cross, she would. Otherwise, no plans came to her. She was alone. She had no one to help guide her through the forbidden kingdom of trees.

And she had to keep moving, otherwise her mind started to dwell on what might have happened to Irys, and she couldn't bear that.

The ground grew rocky along the riverbank and she was forced to leave the riverside to get around particularly shifty pile of rocks. As she crossed back into the line of trees, her footsteps suddenly became quiet. She looked down and saw nothing but green, loamy moss beneath her boots. It covered nearly every inch of the space before her, coating each tree trunk, rock and bit of ground. She had never seen moss grow like this, in the *las graniczny* or the bits of this forest she had explored. Its abrupt shift from the woods around it reminded her eerily of the snow-less ring where Celine's camp had been. Similarly, there was no snow here, though the area surrounding it still had the odd patch of snow.

She hesitated, unsure if she should continue through the strange gathering of moss or if she ought to try and go around it, just in case.

"Does the human walk, or does she not walk? Could it be she has not made up her mind?" A soggy voice sprang up suddenly, almost at her elbow.

Rowan reared away, slipping and falling over in the marshy greenness. Sitting up on her elbows, she gaped as a clump of moss rose from the forest floor and grew into the shape of a person. It had no real human features; where eyes would have been two little blossom-like fungi sprouted, pointing directly at her. She reached down and tried to yank the axe from the strap on her leg.

"No need to chop, for Sphagnum cannot be cut," the creature said through mossy lips, though Rowan noted that it shrank back a little.

"She knows better than to walk across the moss without pause. Some humans have wisdom, others luck. Which has she, Sphagnum wonders?"

Rowan cleared her throat, recognizing a question in the creature's strange speech. "Er, neither, I'm afraid."

"But afraid, yes, this is a good thing to be," the creature—Sphagnum—nodded vigorously, snails and bits of pine needles showering down from its head. "No need to fear the mossmen, but the forest, truly, yes." It quirked its head to one side, regarding Rowan. "Though she seems to know the forest better than some. To look before she steps..."

Sphagnum righted its head abruptly, its eyes extending like a snail's stalk-eyes. "Are you of Oak? Or Holly?"

"S-sorry, I don't know what you mean," Rowan stammered politely as she could. The entire exchange bewildered her, though she was able to remember the importance of good manners in the face of obvious enchantments. Her grandmother's stories made it clear to her that all magical things demanded respect. That likely included moving, talking moss.

"Whom do you serve? The Oak King, or the Holly King?" Sphagnum asked again.

Rowan could see a black beetle marching steadily up the side of its head. A riddle or question answered incorrectly meant death or ruin in nearly every fairy tale Rowan had ever heard, but she had no idea what the question even meant.

"I don't know," she said finally. "Neither?"

"But she must choose," the mossman insisted, twisting this way and that.

Rowan looked down and saw that where legs would have been on a person, the mossman simply grew into the ground.

"Every creature in this land must choose."

"Choose between the Oak King and the Holly King?" Rowan had never heard of such a thing. The Kings were worshipped equally, though of course some preferred one over the other—farmers gave more tribute to the Oak King in the hopes of gaining extra warmth for their harvest, while the hunters and trappers preferred to praise the Holly King in exchange for an abundant hunting season.

But the mossman nodded, sending the beetle flying off its head.

"Why?" Rowan asked.

"She would be wise to choose the Oak King," the mossman said, ignoring her question. "His rewards are great, and his wrath greater still."

"Is that who you've chosen?" she asked curtly, annoyed that it hadn't answered her.

The creature inclined its shaggy head.

"And what of the Holly King, then?"

Sphagnum drew itself up imperiously. "He is weak. The time came, and the Oak King called for his allies. So we came."

The little blossoms on its face waved in the wind as it looked at Rowan more closely.

"She carries the axe, but she is not the woodcutter. Yet she shares her features."

Rowan's jaw went slack.

"You mean my sister? You've seen my sister? Where?"

Sphagnum held up a loamy hand.

"She has been stealing from the Oak King's forest for many seasons. This was not wise."

"But do you know what happened to her? Where she is?" Rowan asked, impatient and eager for news of her sister.

Sphagnum paused.

"If I tell her how to find her sister, will she swear her fealty to the Oak King?"

A sly note had crept into the creature's voice, making Rowan's hair stand on end. What could this strange plant-person hope to gain from Rowan making some kind of pledge to the Oak King?

A sudden movement behind the mossman caught her eye; a huge black raven took off from a tree, one of the few trees already full of leaves. A holly tree, its berries long picked over by birds.

You see things for a reason, especially in a magical place. Tread carefully, Rowan thought, remembering how in her grandmother's stories, everything worth noticing had a purpose. The holly tree had called her attention, she was certain.

"I'm afraid that would be an empty promise, as I don't know what it would require of me," she said cautiously, trying to sound like she was only confused, which was easy. "But after I've been reunited with my sister, I swear I will use what you've told me to help me make my choice. I must find her, before I make any promises or pledges."

The mossman bristled. At first Rowan thought it would refuse, unsatisfied with her answer. But then it lifted a hand and pointed south.

"She will find her in that direction, across the bridge," it said as it slowly began to sink back into the moss carpeting the forest floor. "And should she change her mind before then, she may call to the moss; when Spring is here, we shall cover the forest again." And Sphagnum had melted back into the greenery coating the ground.

Rowan's plea for it to wait died on her lips. It obviously meant to offer no more help than a simple direction.

It's better than nothing, she thought dismally, heading south, eager to put some distance between herself and the mossy clearing. South turned out to follow the river much in the same direction she had already been going. As she picked her way along the riverbank, she thought on what the odd creature had said—should she change her mind, once Spring had come, she could call to the moss to speak to him again? It was nearly a week until the first day of Spring. She truly hoped she wouldn't still be searching the forest by then.

CHAPTER 11

Rowan

Rowan startled some deer making a meal of tree bark and young shoots; their spindly legs kicked up mud and rocks as they fled. Once from around a tree she saw a flash of red and black—a head poked out and watched her. At first she thought it was a speckled hen, but after it popped out from behind another much closer tree, she realized it was another Red Cap.

She bit her lip and kept going, pretending she hadn't noticed it. Ignoring them was supposed to make them lose interest, but she kept seeing its little head popping up between branches or out of holes in the ground. Just as she was starting to wonder if it was just the one Red Cap moving very quickly from place to place or an entire herd taking turns, she saw the bridge.

"Oh," she breathed.

She'd imagined a humble stone contraption, like the bridges in and around her village. This could only be described as ornate. Great green leaves carved from wood stretched across the water, with no railing or safeguard to keep folk from falling over the edge. It arched beautifully in the middle. The construction made Rowan shudder—who would want to cross such a delicate, precarious thing?

She stared at the bridge, and at the raging water rushing under it. Surely it was the only way to get across for miles, with the river as high as it was. But still she hung back, looking downriver to see what it looked like further on.

She breathed out, screwing her eyes shut. *I'm not doing anyone any good standing around like this. It's only a bridge.* Eyes open, she strode forward, intent on getting across the bridge as quickly as possible before she could change her mind.

But somehow, over the roar of the water, she heard a stretching sound, and her mind was filled with the image of a bowstring pulling taut somewhere behind her. She whipped around, tearing the axe from her leg and swinging it aloft.

A man—no, a boy, near the same age as Rowan—stood, bow at the ready and arrow nocked. But he didn't loose it. Something about him was familiar, though Rowan couldn't quite place it. He wore the leather jerkin and trousers of a trapper, but his dark hair and tan skin meant he couldn't possibly come from the villages that had produced Rowan's pale skin and auburn hair.

He was very tall and extremely broad-shouldered. Rowan gulped.

"Most folk who come this deep into the Oak King's forest know to stay away from this bridge," he said, not moving a muscle. "Are you an idiot or merely lost?"

"If those are my only choices, then lost. But I was told to come this way," Rowan answered, mind racing. He could fire at any second and end her before she could reach him with the axe, but if she feinted to one side, she might just make the bushes.

"Told by whom?" he asked, stepping forward a few paces.

His boots came into view—Rowan wondered if these had made the prints they'd found near Celine's at the entrance to the forest.

"By some talking moss," she said, watching his face for a reaction. To her surprise, there wasn't one.

"A village girl should know better than to listen to talking foliage," he said, frowning at her.

"How—" Rowan began, but then she realized she had seen his eyes before. The hunter on the Solstice, over a month ago, with only his eyes visible above his scarf. Those dark eyes with flecks of gold and brown in them—there was no mistake. She tightened her grip on her sister's axe.

"Where is my sister?" she asked through gritted teeth.

"I'm afraid I haven't met your sister, though I know we share the same hunting grounds," he answered curtly, though he lowered his bow.

Rowan reluctantly let the axe drop as well. "We found your tracks coming into the forest, nearly alongside hers." Accusation was written into her voice, though the feeling crept into her stomach that he truly didn't have anything to do with it.

"I promise you, your sister and I did not walk into this forest together. We just happen to use the same path now and then." He slid the arrow into the quiver on his back and looped his arm through the bow. "Now, what are *you* doing here? Not taking up hunting in the heart of the Oak King's forest, I hope, though I understand it runs in the family."

"She's gone." Rowan was pleased to see surprise cross his face. "She disappeared three days ago, somewhere in here, and I'm trying to find her."

He opened his mouth, then closed it again, his eyes no longer fixed on Rowan but off in the distance, his mind working.

"Where? Do you know where she was?" he asked finally.

"She made camp some miles back that way. We had just found her tent and this," Rowan lifted the axe. "But we were attacked by a... a dragon."

His eyes widened.

"The dragon came after you? And you ran *deeper* into the forest? How badly turned around did you get?"

Rowan huffed and began strapping the axe back onto her leg. "I told you, I came here to find her. I'm not leaving her here to get eaten by flying tree-beasts and mossmen."

He snorted. "The mossmen don't eat anybody. The worst they'll do is bury you alive for a few years and send you out again to try and find your way home."

She threw him a scathing look.

"And how would *you* know?"

He shrugged. "I've lived here a long time."

She nearly fell over.

"Here? *In the forest?*"

He shifted uncomfortably and didn't say anything.

"How on earth haven't you been caught?" She looked him over again. He looked strong, but certainly he was far too young to have lived in such a treacherous place by himself. And something about his features told her that he had come from somewhere far away, where the sun stayed warm and bright year-round. He resembled one of the Islanders from the south, who traveled the land and rarely settled.

"I suppose I'm just lucky," he muttered, though the bitter edge to his voice said otherwise.

"Why shouldn't I cross the bridge?" she asked, gesturing to the fragile-looking construction behind her.

"Because you'll land right in the middle of the Oak King's most closely guarded territory," he answered at once.

"I thought the whole forest was his," Rowan said, peering over the water to see what was so special about the other side.

"It is, but he's dreadfully lazy and doesn't send his patrols out very far. The mossmen watch the edges closest to the Border." The boy jerked his head back the way she had come. "Your village is that way—I can escort you back to where you came in, just in case the dragon—"

"I know which way the village is," she snapped. "And I've already told you—I came here for my sister, and I'm not leaving without her. Something happened—there were claw marks at her campsite, and her axe was sunk in the ground with *things* growing out of it. I can't just—"

"What?" His eyes widened again and he stared at the axe on Rowan's leg. "Growing? Are you certain?"

"Yes, I'm certain. Look at it." She pulled the axe out again and held it up so he could see the handle. "See all these bits where it's scuffed up? I broke handfuls of twigs off it—they were *growing* out of it, like it was part of a tree again. Flowers, too, though they had dried up. And—"

"Roots," he finished, running his fingers over the bottom of the axe handle, where a few stray tendrils still hung. "Oak made it start growing again."

He dropped his hand and looked over the bridge. Then he pressed his forehead into his hands.

"He's done it again. Gods *damn* him, he's done it again!" He looked furious.

"Who's done what?" Rowan asked, sounding awfully meek. She

didn't want to bear the brunt of this stranger's anger, if it happened to turn on her.

The boy stood at the edge of the bridge and looked very much like he was thinking of crossing and taking care of whatever he thought had happened right there and then. But with difficulty he turned away from it and focused on Rowan.

"I believe the Oak King has taken your sister. He used to go out and search for people to use for his *experiments*, but he was bound to the forest five years ago and hasn't been able to leave since. So he's been waiting for people with certain characteristics to fall into his clutches. I would assume your sister has those characteristics."

Rowan knew she was gaping but she couldn't help herself. "Why on earth would the Oak King want to kidnap a village girl? What does he mean to do with her?"

The boy shook his head helplessly. "I—I don't know. I'm sorry. I only know that he kidnaps people with magic sometimes, takes them to his palace and..." He gestured weakly, indicating his lack of knowledge. He did look truly sorry.

"Something horrible, though, I can assume?" Rowan pressed, stepping closer. He must know more; he *had* to. She forced herself not to wonder about the "magic" he spoke of—whatever it was, it didn't matter as much as finding Celine.

"Something not good, certainly," he answered, not meeting her eyes.

"Then I can't afford to waste any more time," she snapped, and she brushed past him, determined to cross the bridge.

But he grabbed her arm and yanked her back. "I swear, the second you set foot upon the other side, you'll be swarmed with his minions and that will be the last I ever hear of you," he hissed, all but dragging her from the bridge. "There's every chance you could have whatever magic your sister has, and then he would have the two of you to do with as he pleases. If you want to save your sister, *wait*."

"Celine doesn't have magic!" Rowan insisted, straining against his grip but unable to break it. Finally, she let her arm go limp.

"Wait for what?" She glared up at him.

"There's another option, a *safer* one, if we work together," he said, surprisingly calm for someone who had just dragged her from her path.

"And why would you help? What's in it for you?" she asked snidely. He was hiding something, keeping something back, and she didn't like it.

"Revenge." he said simply.

"On the Oak King?"

"And a sort of justice. Yes, that would be more than enough for me." The grim set to his mouth was surprisingly convincing.

Rowan believed he had true reason to hate the Oak King, though whatever that reason could be, she had no idea. "How?" she asked finally, too aware of time ticking away, time in which Celine could be tortured or murdered or abused in some way.

"We need to get to the base of the mountains," he said at once, "and meet the Bear Maiden when she descends. A wish from her will free your sister and see you both safely home, without the risk of you falling into Oak's clutches as well."

"She... she's real?" Rowan's voice was barely above a whisper. While the Holly King and the Oak King were easy to believe in, the Bear Maiden, so elusive and mysterious in all her stories, was so much harder to think of as real.

"She is," the boy said with a small, sad smile. "I've seen her myself. But she'll be making her way down from the mountains in six days to watch Spring unfold. She'll be much harder to find in the forest—we have a better chance of finding her right when she leaves the mountains. And we'll be safe from Oak, too; he usually doesn't send the dragon into Holly's territory until high Summer."

"Cross into..." Rowan felt even more confused. "Why should the Oak King want to cross into the Holly King's territory?"

"They..." The hunter searched for the right words. "They are at war with each other," he said finally, digging up dirt with the toe of his boot. "Oak wants Holly's power and his territory. Look," he said with exasperation as Rowan opened her mouth to ask more questions. "I could stand here all day recounting lore from the past few hundred years, but the Bear Maiden descends on the first day of Spring—if we're to have any hope of meeting her, we need to leave now. I'll explain what I can when I can."

Rowan looked him over again. The Kings she worshipped were at war with each other? Who on earth was this person and how would he know such a thing? He clearly had deep knowledge of the forest, and he seemed to speak truly when he said he had lived here a long time. What that said about the kind of person he was, Rowan didn't know. But looking at him, at his warm eyes, the dark beard that softened his jawline, the brown-black hair that flopped to his collar, the rumpled hunter's clothes, it was hard to ignore the sense in her stomach that she ought to trust him. Still, even with that certainty building in her, she wasn't an idiot.

"Who are you?" she asked at last.

"My name is Keziah." he said, though she was sure he knew her question required more of an answer than that.

She blew out a stream of air, trying to cool her own frustration.

"Fine. Take me to the Bear Maiden, please."

If he was relieved, he didn't take the time to show it. Jerking his head to indicate Rowan should follow him, he set off north, back along the way Rowan had just come.

"But I *just* came this way," she moaned under her breath, glaring at the twice-walked ground beneath her feet.

"Don't worry, we'll cross up ahead and leave the river in about thirty minutes time." Keziah looked over his shoulder at her. "You're not given to complaining much, are you?"

"Depends on the company," she replied sweetly.

"Hmm," was all he said to that. "What *is* your name? Your sister's was all over town, but then she's something of a spectacle there, isn't she?"

"My name's Rowan. And the only spectacle is that people make more of a fuss over a girl doing so-called *man's work* than they do over her doing it better than anyone else," Rowan snapped. *Spectacle indeed. Says the man living in a magical forest.*

"You said 'we' earlier. Is there another villager out running about in the forest?"

"I—I don't know," Rowan answered honestly. "My sister's... friend came to help me find her, but when the dragon attacked, we got separated."

"So her friend either got eaten alive, burned to a crisp, or fled safely back to the village?" Keziah shook his head in exasperation.

Rowan glared at his back but said nothing. He came to the village to trade—she couldn't risk giving away Irys and Celine's secret. She changed the subject.

"Are you... are you of Holly, then, if you're against Oak?"

She couldn't see his face but his shoulders tightened.

"Forest folk think their choices mean something. You could say that I'd choose Holly, I suppose, if I had to choose between them like that. But the choice is between a friend and a tyrant, so it's really not a choice."

Rowan fell silent. The way he talked, it was as if he knew both Kings personally. But of course, that was absurd.

He led her across the river on a path of stones. Rowan felt far more confident with her feet on solid rock than she would have if she had ever set foot on the leaf bridge to the south.

"Later in the year, after Spring flooding, the river gets much easier to cross," Keziah told her, leading her up a faint game trail that wound through the trees. "It'll start getting lower as Summer approaches."

Rowan certainly didn't think she'd need to know about the state of the river in Summer, but it was interesting hearing about the workings of the forest and its features from someone who knew them well.

All the same, she stopped short when she caught sight of a stone cottage wreathed in ivy nestled at the base of the next hill.

"What's that?" she asked when Keziah looked back to see what was the matter.

"My house. Or one of them, really. I need some things for the journey. Unless you happened to bring along enough supplies to last us more than two days?"

Rowan narrowed her eyes at him as they approached the cottage

"No, I didn't. Is it really going to take us *two days* to get there?"

Keziah reached for the door handle.

"Unless you move much more quickly than you have for the last hour or so, yes." He met Rowan's eyes. She must have looked miserable, for his shoulders sagged a little.

"Look, if I could spirit us both there in a second, I would. That isn't how this works. The forest is against us, especially as it's almost Oak's season. In fact, I'm surprised no one caught you after you made it this far into the forest." He eyed Rowan thoughtfully.

"Why are you surprised? You said you've lived here a long time without getting caught," Rowan pointed out, wishing he would just open the damn door so they could be on their way.

"Yes, well," he said, irritated, "I'm different, unfortunately." He seemed as though he had more he wanted to say, but then he shook his head and swung the door open.

After much rummaging around, he came out and had Rowan put her belongings in a new, much larger pack. He then added food and several bundles that he didn't bother explaining the contents of. It was far heavier when she finally loaded it onto her back.

"Too much?" he asked as she wriggled her shoulders this way and that under the intense pressure.

"I wouldn't know—I'm not given to much complaining," she said with a pointed look.

He laughed—a good-natured laugh, much freer and easier than she would have expected.

"I wasn't sure if you had a sense of humor. You'll be much more pleasant to travel with if you do."

Her mouth twisted, but given the jab, she didn't feel like giving him a smile back. Instead she looked around the side of the house, where a large garden was penned in by a stone gate.

"Will your garden be all right? If you'll be gone for more than a day..."

He waved a hand dismissively.

"My garden does just fine without me. Not much is happening right now anyway—the peas are only just putting out their true leaves, the beets need time, and everything else either has yet to sprout or yet to be planted."

Rowan thought his statement that not much was happening couldn't have been farther from the truth—blossoms on the apple tree and the huddled little strawberry plants were just starting to unfurl, shoots and canes of what looked like raspberries and blackberries poked up against the wall of the house, and a row of blooming crocuses at the back of the house wafted a tantalizing floral scent over her as they left the charming little house. Rowan watched it over her shoulder until it was out of sight. She felt just the tiniest bit sad that she hadn't gotten to see inside the quaint little dwelling.

He led them further north, through forest Rowan had never seen before. By the time they stopped to make camp near a small stream that likely fed into the river, Rowan's feet and legs were numb. She slid off the pack and sank to the ground with a moan.

"Best not to get comfortable just yet; we still need to build a fire and eat," Keziah remarked as he pulled a sleeping roll from his pack.

"I'm too tired to eat," Rowan mumbled as she draped herself over her pack, certain she could fall asleep even in that awkward position.

"I'm sure you are," Keziah said skeptically. "But if you wake up at midnight with your stomach rumbling, you might regret going to sleep without eating. At least get a little into your stomach first."

Rowan was used to stirring herself even at the point of exhaustion, so she peeled herself off the ground and helped Keziah gather wood for a cooking fire. He cooked sausages and potatoes in a cast-iron pan, tossing in a handful of torn spring leeks he'd gathered from a patch nearby. Rowan drowsily ate the hot mess from the bowl he handed her, her head drooping where she sat.

"Here," he said, grabbing her half-empty bowl as it threatened to tip out of her hands. "I don't even think you're swallowing anymore. I'll clear this up—why don't you try and get some sleep?"

"But don't you need to sleep, too?" Rowan asked, stifling a yawn as she pulled off her boots.

"I don't think I'm half as exhausted as you are—I do this sort of trekking all the time, so I'm more used to it," he said with a grin, watching her crawl into her bedroll.

"Well, wake me after a few hours so I can keep watch and you can sleep," Rowan insisted blearily, tugging her blanket up over her head to shut out the light from the sunset.

She heard him snort. "We'll see. I really don't need much sleep anyway."

What an odd person, she thought as she drifted off to the sound of birds chirping in the twilight.

CHAPTER 12

Nash

His land was cold and green. Once we left the ocean behind, water seemed to be scarce, aside from a pitiful river that wound through the fields.

"You'll get used to it, I'm sure," he told me as we walked the road from the port.

I didn't argue. It wasn't as though I planned on staying in his land—as soon as I learned what I could from him, I would return to my people. I hoped that by that time, the sting I felt at my mother's secrecy would have lessened.

I did not know how to talk to Oak, the man who should have been my father. And he didn't seem to think of himself as such. He asked me little about myself, other than my magical abilities, and he seemed content enough to talk about his own powers at length.

"We came to this land centuries ago, Holly and I," he said as he strode beside me. "Not seeking anything in particular. We were both from small villages full of small-minded people, both tired of dull, little lives. We'd heard rumors of a land where nature ran wild, of a forest and a range of mountains where magic seeped from the earth itself. We decided to see it for ourselves, and we met the Bear Maiden not long after entering the forest."

"The Bear Maiden? Who is she?" I asked.

"A difficult question to answer, even for me." He grinned at me, and I found it hard not to grin back. *"She is ancient, brimming with powers that put mine to shame. She was working to bind the gods' wild magic so this land would have order, so her beasts would live a little easier, but wild magic needs someone to command it, and she had found no one willing to harness it for her. Then we stumbled into her path."*

A faint bitterness hung around the corners of his mouth. I wondered where it stemmed from; surely he was glad to have his powers.

"She convinced us each to take the wild magic into ourselves, promising that we would both rule this land as a kingdom like no other. I admit," he said wryly, *"that what she promised and what the reality of ruling this land has turned out to be are two rather different things. She kept certain things from us, you see. Things about this land she didn't think we needed to know. But despite that, we have ruled, Holly and I, the year divided between us. Spring and Summer are mine, while Autumn and Winter are his."*

I frowned. "What are Spring and Summer and... the other things you said?"

He halted.

"Do you not know the seasons?" He sounded incredulous.

"I know the harvest season, the breeding season, the globe melon season," I listed off, counting on my fingers. We had twenty seasons on the island, but none of them shared a name that Oak had mentioned.

He stared hard at me for a moment.

"She really told you nothing of my land, did she?" He said at last.

My face burned. More information my mother had kept from me.

"In this land, the year is divided into four seasons. Spring, which will begin in just a few days; Summer, when the sun shines hot and most of the food in this region grows; Autumn, when many of the plants die or go dormant; and Winter, when the ground is covered with snow and nearly everything freezes."

I blinked. "And what happens after Winter? The cold must kill everything."

"Spring comes again. Many plants are simply sleeping through the cold months, and they wake again in the warmth. Whatever seeds fell the

previous year begin to grow as well. It is a cycle, repeating over and over again." He looped a finger through the air.

"Strange," I murmured. Things changed on the island, but never quite so drastically as the entire land freezing. I wanted to ask what snow was, but I already felt ashamed of how ignorant I was. I decided to ask another time.

"And where do you come into all of this?"

"Ah," he said, smiling once more. "In other lands, these things would happen on their own. Here, the elements have split from nature and grown wild. I must cast each season at exactly the right time. You'll see in just a week's time—Spring will begin, and you will help me start it."

I blanched. "But... but I have never used those powers before. I do not even know—"

"It will be all right, Nash," he said soothingly. "This magic is ingrained in your very being. Using it will be easy—you just require some instruction."

Whatever the reason, I needed to learn from him and he was willing to teach me. I would try not to question his reasons too much.

After two days of walking, I could see we were heading for a mass of trees that loomed to the horizon. There was a gray drizzle from the equally gray sky. There was no sand here, only an odd greenness everywhere covering the ground, in the branches of the trees that stood on either side of the soggy road. Green and brown, not a speck of blue in the sky or a shimmer of gold anywhere.

Oak didn't hesitate before plunging straight into the trees. I followed, more apprehensive here than I had ever been diving into the ocean itself.

The first twenty yards or so weren't terrible. But then something changed. I couldn't see it, but it was like stepping from a warm pool into a frigid one. I knew about magical Borders, make no mistake; the ocean around our island was full of them. But this one was unfamiliar, and all the more disturbing for it. The trees looked different here, more twisted and gnarled and ancient. And the sounds had changed, too. Where on the road I could hear the sounds of farms off in the distance or other travelers making their way along the path, here I could only hear the sounds of forest animals, the creak of trees, the drip of water. It was a world completely separate from the land around it.

I didn't like it. I didn't like not seeing the sky, the horizon laid flat against the line of water that had always surrounded me my entire life. But somehow I knew that a part of me felt akin to the trees standing around me. I couldn't help but remember what Oak had said—I had his power, too. That must have been it, the thing that was drawing me further and further into the forest. It didn't matter that I didn't like it; here I was.

We passed a pile of something white, stained with dirt and dead leaves.

"Snow," Oak remarked, pointing at it. "Frozen water that falls from the sky like rain."

I flushed. He had guessed that I did not know what it was. I brushed my fingertips over it, flinching back from its chill.

I dwelled more on what he'd said as we walked on through twilight, dappled green and yellow by the leaves waving overhead. I had his power. He planned to teach me how to use it. I couldn't help but wonder why.

Oak stopped. He stood silently, looking around him as though he were waiting for something.

Then he turned to me, a mischievous smile on his face. "You know, I don't see why I can't start Spring just a little early this year. What could it hurt?"

He raised a hand. A breeze rustled through the trees, rattling the budded branches. Something crackled in the air, though I couldn't tell where it came from.

Then, Oak pushed.

A swirling aura of green and gold emanated from his outstretched hand and broke over the trees. Leaves spilled forth, unfurling from their buds. Blossoms burst like tiny clouds down the lengths of branches, filling the air with a syrup-sweet fragrance.

I watched in awe and frustration. I didn't know these plants. I had no names for the things around me, yet I would have to learn how to command them in this way, if I was to control my powers properly.

"Try it," he urged me as green flowed from his palms.

"I—I don't know what I'm supposed to do," I said, rubbing my own fingers. They were tingling, and I couldn't tell if it was because of the magic around me or because of how nervous I was.

I swear he rolled his eyes as he turned away from me. "No matter. We can work on it later."

Oak began to walk, his hand still out before him, spreading the greenness throughout the forest. It was getting warmer, I realized, and creatures were beginning to stir. Birds far smaller than any who lived on my island flitted about; small, furred animals scampered across our path and into the brush; something I thought was an insect darted past my face to land on Oak's shoulder. I saw, upon closer inspection, that it was actually a tiny person, with gleaming gold wings.

"Welcome home, Lord Oak," the being whispered, bowing deeply. "Hail Spring."

"Hail Spring," Oak said with a sigh, and the creature flitted off. He did not seem to share their excitement for the season's change, but I did not know him well enough to ask him why.

We continued in silence for some time, Oak sending out his magic, me following and watching, trying to imagine myself doing the same. It was wholly unlike anything back home. We had no need of a person to cast a season—our seasons changed of their own accord. But in time with the cycles of the moon, my mother would stand waist-deep in the ocean on certain nights, using her power to command the tide. I had stood beside her countless times, using my own clumsy powers to try and help.

A terrible pang of homesickness clenched around my heart, and I had to force myself back into the present.

Oak's steps were slowing, and ahead of us, I could see some kind of building peeking through the trees.

As we neared, I realized just how large it was.

It was an immense structure, with spires even taller than the tallest trees around us.

Oak smirked when he saw me gazing up at it open-mouthed. He let his hands fall, the green glow dying.

"I'll tell you a secret," he said, nodding at the building. "My palace wasn't built by human hands; I merely bent the trees into a shape I liked."

I saw what he meant—the walls had branches and bark, and roots arched where the walls met the ground. It was a living palace, crafted from contorted trees.

Two figures came out of the front doors as we approached—one a slender being in a gossamer dress the color of sea foam, the other a sullen looking fellow with dull, dark hair and dull, dark clothes.

"Dew and Thaw," Oak addressed them.

They both bowed at once, their eyes darting from me to Oak.

"This is Nash. She has come to learn to use her powers."

"He," I corrected, irritated. I had told him more than once, and part of me wondered if he was saying the wrong thing on purpose.

Dew and Thaw exchanged a glance.

"Oh, yes, of course," Oak said without even looking at me. "See that rooms are arranged for him."

"The rooms were prepared before your departure, Lord Oak," Dew said immediately. She was a fidgety creature. She seemed poised to dart off into the trees at the slightest sign of trouble.

"Ah, excellent." Oak didn't seem surprised. It struck me that he must have been certain I would be accompanying him back here. Why else would his people have prepared my rooms before I even arrived?

"I wish to rest from my travels," he told Dew and Thaw. "The pair of you may continue casting Spring in my stead."

"Yes, Lord Oak," Thaw drawled, slouching down the steps and ambling off into the trees. He seemed to be mere minutes away from falling asleep.

Dew gave another quick bow, then sprang into the air.

Startled, I spun around to watch her fly off over the treetops.

"No one flies on your island, do they?" Oak asked with some amusement.

"Not that I know of," I replied, unable to hide the envy in my voice. To be able to fly, to be up above everything and go wherever you wished—truly a special power.

"You send them to cast the season for you?" I asked as I followed Oak inside. There was a roaring fireplace at the end of the hall, torches burning on the walls. I was grateful for it; I had been chilled ever since I first set foot in this land.

"They have sworn themselves into my service, so I am able to lend them some of my power. It allows me a little more freedom for other pursuits." He strolled down a hallway, dumping his travel sack on a chair.

I hurried after him, burning with more questions.

"*They also patrol on my behalf,*" *he continued, entering a room with shelves upon shelves full of books.* "*Especially this time of year. A good handful of villagers always sneak into the forest to try and find the Bear Maiden as she returns to the forest in Spring.*"

My eyes were drawn to the desk in the center of the room. A book sat there, the words Legends of the Underworlde *inscribed on its spine.*

"*Find the Bear Maiden? Why would they want to find her?*" *I asked, half distracted by the strange title.*

Oak paused, frowning. "*I'm sure I told you... Didn't I mention her power for wish-granting?*"

I froze, my mouth half open. The wish-granter. The one my mother had spoken of. She was here.

My mother had learned of her from Oak.

Oak caught sight of my expression and looked mildly concerned.

"*I suppose I didn't. Anyone who finds her, in the forest or in her mountain home during the Winter months, can make a single wish for their heart's desire. The villagers are forbidden from entering the forest, but of course the foolish ones pay no heed to that.*"

"*Why?*" *I managed at last, my voice cracking.* "*Why can they not come into the forest?*"

Oak gave a bark of laughter. "*Because it's my kingdom, of course! Who would want a herd of grimy, ignorant village folk traipsing about their home? And besides,*" *he added, sobering a little,* "*it isn't safe for them here. Magical beasts, fearsome ones, make their homes here as well. Drawn by the magic. Other things, too. You'll learn of them soon enough.*"

He steered me gently to the door.

"*Now, if you'll excuse me, I'd like to unwind a little after the long journey. Your rooms should be upstairs somewhere. Lessons will begin tomorrow morning.*"

With that, he deposited me outside the room and shut the door.

Alone in the hallway, I swallowed the rest of the questions burning in my throat. I would have to wait to have them all answered.

CHAPTER 13

Rowan

Rowan nearly had to pry her eyelids open when she woke to something nudging her in the leg. Her whole face felt cold, and she wanted nothing more than to roll over and bury her face in the blanket. Then the same nudge that had woken her came again—Keziah was prodding her with a booted foot.

"Why?" she asked, bleary with sleep.

He looked amused at the odd question. "Because of food, that's why. Coffee?"

She sat up at once. "Please." Her voice sounded awful, and her mouth tasted foul. She remembered the same sort of thing happening when she'd gone out woodcutting with Celine, though they'd had the luxury of a tent.

Keziah went to a steaming pot he'd sat on a stump. Using a spoon, he scooped coffee grounds off the top and dumped the spent grounds on the dirt. Once he'd cleared the grit from the coffee, he dumped hot water out of a mug waiting nearby and poured in coffee. He handed the hot drink to Rowan, who gratefully took a sip and immediately burned her tongue.

"I should have asked—milk?"

She blinked and looked around the campsite.

"Milk? Where—" But Keziah was already kneeling on the riverbank, fishing out a skin tethered to a nearby tree with a leather strap.

"I keep it in the river so it stays cold—it keeps longer that way. Would you like some?"

Rowan held out her mug and he poured some in. She didn't usually take milk with her coffee, but she was desperate to drink it soon; this would cool it off.

"How in the world did you get milk in the forest? Do you keep a dairy cow somewhere?" she asked, taking a more cautious sip.

He snorted. "Don't be silly. It's elk's milk."

She half spat out the mouthful she'd taken.

"What's wrong? Is it off? It was fresh yesterday," he asked with concern, sniffing the opening of the skin he still held.

"No, it's—well, I think it's fine," Rowan spluttered. "But how did you milk an elk? I didn't think that was possible."

Keziah shrugged. "They're used to me. Or maybe I just have a way with them."

Rowan nearly choked again. She had a clear image of Keziah herding elk through the forest, and it suited him very well.

"Well?" he asked, indicating the cup of coffee.

"It's good. Not much different, or not that I can tell—coffee's quite strong. Less fatty than cow's milk."

"Not surprising. Elk trek up and down the mountains throughout the year. No one's feeding them hay and corn or building them a nice warm barn to sleep in."

"What... *do* they eat?" Rowan asked tentatively. She really didn't know much about animals other than the ones they kept on the farm.

Keziah made a face. "Er, grass, I think? Mainly grass. And probably whatever else they can find when it gets cold," he said, rubbing the back of his neck. "I'm not an expert."

That made Rowan feel a little better. For all his knowledge of the forest, Keziah didn't know everything.

He cleared his throat. "On that note, breakfast?"

"Breakfast" turned out to be bacon and dark bread toasted over the fire. Keziah folded his bread around the bacon into a kind of sandwich.

Rowan ate hers separately, savoring every bit of it. She hoped she'd never feel so horribly hungry again.

The two of them packed up their bedrolls and shoveled dirt over the fire. Rowan quickly washed her face in the stream.

Keziah raised his eyebrows at her, watching her wipe her face dry with her sleeve.

"I don't like feeling dirty," she said. "I've never gone so long without a bath. It takes getting used to," she said, glaring at him when he rolled his eyes. "Something you've clearly had time to grow comfortable with."

He laughed and nodded. "I think a layer of grime suits me—brings out more of my rugged good looks. Maybe it'll bring out some of yours."

She gave him a withering look.

"Alright, alright," he said, holding up his hands as she opened her mouth to reply. "I apologize. Peace?" He held out his hand to her.

"Hmm." She reached out and shook it. His hand was warm and heavily callused. "Peace, I suppose, if you keep the witty retorts to a minimum."

"Oh, that'll be hard." He grimaced. "Better lower your expectations."

And they left the clearing, heading north through the trees. Rowan tried to take in more of Keziah as they walked. He really was different, leading this solitary existence within the Oak King's forest. She wondered how long he'd lived there like this.

She flexed the hand he'd shaken. It was odd, touching the skin of someone she'd just met and really didn't know. She tried to remember the last time she touched someone's hand, someone other than family. A few boys had asked her to go walking in the fields—none of them liked the *las graniczny*, where Rowan certainly would rather have gone walking—but the hand holding never lasted long. The boys always invited her out with the pretense of talking, getting to know each other better, but as soon as they were out of sight of the adults, then their real purpose became clear.

Rowan had given her fair share of slaps—and that broken nose—for the unwanted attention. And once in a while a boy she liked invited her out, and those experiences had been fairly pleasant. But she always found she didn't like the boy quite as much as she thought, afterward. Perhaps it was the awkwardness of seeing them around town afterward, or maybe the memories of them playing together as children, strange set against these new, more adult experiences.

Why am I thinking about this now? She forced herself out of her own head. *Look around. It's not every day you get a guided tour of the Oak King's forest.*

It was so different from the solitary blind stumbling of that first morning in the forest. Fortified by coffee, food, and the security of Keziah's presence, she felt less like an intruder and more like an adventurer. Now she could appreciate the white caps of the mountains peeking between the bare branches, or the birds, ever increasing in number, dipping into the river for a drink or flitting about the treetops. She supposed Celine had long been accustomed to this, trekking out here on her own.

The thought of her sister darkened her thoughts. It hurt, it truly did, that she had built this mysterious separate life for herself—both her relationship with Irys and her ventures into the forest. Rowan wondered about all the places her sister had gone, how far she had dared to go into the forbidden woods, keeping all of it hidden from her family. There was a time, long ago, when Rowan had considered Celine her best friend.

Clearly she never felt the same, she thought, her mouth tightening. *If she didn't even trust me enough to tell me...* But no, that wasn't fair. She couldn't fault Celine for pulling away like that, not when she couldn't be sure of how her family would react. Still, it stung, and there wasn't anything Rowan could do about it.

She tried to distract herself with the landscape as they passed through the trees, which turned out to be an easy task. The buds on the tree branches were all beginning to open into leaves, giving the air around them a dappled look. And there were mountain ash trees scattered here and there, dotted with the very last dried up bits of their bright red berries. In Winter, the berries drew huge numbers of waxwings, tawny birds with crests the color of sunrise and markings like swipes of black paint over their eyes.

The melting snow revealed earth thick with layers of pine needles and dead leaves, stamped with muddy footprints from the creatures of the forest coming awake and venturing out of their homes for the first time in months. Rowan made out the needle-thin tracks of birds, marshy, kicked-up rabbit prints, and the thick, wide pads of foxes. Narrow deer trails looped over the hills and the mud, littered with shreds of bark and twigs. There still wasn't much for them to eat, but it didn't surprise Rowan that the deer stayed inside the forest for the Winter; hunters could never find much in the *las graniczny* during the lean seasons.

That explains why Celine was always so successful; she went where the game was. Even though it had meant crossing into dangerous territory. She must never have come face-to-face with anything as fearsome as the dragon, or else she never would have come back as often as she had. *But then again, neither did I.* Though Rowan had never gone far—she had certainly never spent a night in the forest, until now.

After a few more hours they stopped to eat lunch. Rowan's legs and feet had felt numb while she walked, but as soon as she sat down and let her muscles relax, the ache returned.

"How are you holding up?" Keziah asked, passing her water.

Rowan grimaced. "My muscles feel ready to snap, but other than that, lovely."

"Take a moment and stretch, but don't hold your stretches very long—you might pull something if your muscles get too loose."

She looked at him blankly.

"Like this." He bent and reached for his toes, sweeping his fingers over the tops of his boots for just a second before straightening and reaching toward the sky. Then he repeated the motion.

"That way you give your legs and back a bit of a stretch without overdoing it. Save the real stretching for once we've stopped for the night."

She did a few sweeping motions, feeling rather silly, but her legs felt less tight afterward.

"Is this one of the tricks you've learned, moving around like you do?"

Keziah shrugged. "I've always moved around the forest, ever since —" He broke off, looking at the trees around them.

Rowan watched his eyes as they scanned the forest. At last she realized what their color reminded her of—it was the same color of sunlight spilling through a canopy of leaves in the Summer forest.

"Someone's found our trail already. *Damn.* I thought I'd been careful..." He trailed off, and that seemed to be the end of his sentence.

"Let's move on," Keziah said, cinching his knapsack shut. "They won't catch us, but I'd still rather they didn't get too close."

Keziah seemed more wary, stopping frequently to listen or peer through the trees, as though expecting someone to come out and greet them. Rowan grew weary and tried to distract herself by remembering some of her favorite stories brought by the peddler from the great city. There had been a particularly heartbreaking one last year—a princess was wrongfully imprisoned in a cave by her brother, with only a single maidservant for company, but they had broken out to freedom. She was straining her brain, trying to remember how they had gotten out, when she ran straight into the back of Keziah—he had stopped again and she hadn't noticed.

He caught her hand and stopped her falling, a finger across his lips. Then he pointed down the slope of the slight hill they had climbed. At first Rowan couldn't see anything.

But then a large boulder shifted, and a chill ran down her spine. At first it seemed like the boulder moved of its own accord, but when a reedy black claw snaked into view, it became clear that something else was rolling the boulder off itself. There was a hissing, spitting sound, and with one last great effort, the boulder rolled over completely. A sharp-faced black creature writhed and wriggled itself out of the hole in the ground, luminous purple eyes fixed on Rowan and Keziah.

Keziah raised his bow—Rowan hadn't even realized he'd loaded an arrow—and fired down at the creature. The arrow struck the creature in its paper-thin chest and promptly disappeared with a puff of smoke.

Keziah swore and notched another arrow, but a second creature was already scrambling out of the hole and up the slope toward them. Rowan slid Celine's axe from its strap and held it at the ready.

"Don't bother!" Keziah hissed at her. "If it's near enough for you to hit it, it's too late for you. Stay back!"

And he fired again, but this time the arrow hissed past the creature.

Keziah cursed again and drew something from his waistband. Rowan only caught a glimpse of gleaming metal before he took off down the hill, running to meet the wriggling creature head-on.

But that's not an issue for you? She kept the axe up anyway—she had nothing else to defend herself with. And she was glad of it. There was a crash behind her, and she turned to see another boulder rolling its way down from higher up the hill, tumbling along the path. She leaped up to avoid it and caught sight of another purple-eyed creature making its slithery way toward her, following the rolling boulder.

Oh, no.

And she had no time to call for Keziah; the creature's gleaming violet eyes fixed on her, and it arched its back, dragging its long claws through the dirt. Then it sprang into a run and leaped at her. *So be it.* Glaring at it, she swung the axe like a bat. She caught it across its middle with the screeching, grating sound of metal on metal.

She opened her eyes just in time to see the split halves of the creature shrivel into tapers and fall to the ground, twitching. She blinked. *I did it. I killed it.* Though that last part was more uncertain—she didn't like that the pieces of whatever that creature was were still moving, and she had an awful vision of it somehow coming back from those little shreds.

A crashing sound distracted her, and she cast about for Keziah. She caught sight of him, just as he plunged a shining shard of something right in the face of the creature he fought. It let out a metallic scream, its face withering into almost nothing, shortly followed by the rest of its body. It fell to the ground like a pile of dead leaves, and he quickly knelt and did something Rowan couldn't see.

Then he stood up and stepped back, turning and looking up the hill.

"Rowan! Where's the other one? Did you see it?"

She pointed with the blade of the axe. He dashed up the hill, impressive for someone laden with a full knapsack. When he reached the path, he looked down at the ground where the pieces of creature lay. Breathing heavily, he looked from them to Rowan, then to the axe she held.

"You... you did that?" he said, still trying to catch his breath.

"Yes, I think so. Is it dead?" The pieces were still moving, twitching closer together.

Keziah quickly bent down and separated them, then kicked dirt over them.

"As close as they'll ever get to death. We'll have to burn the pieces to keep them from growing back together. That's... How did you..."

He looked at the axe again, narrowing his eyes.

"May I see that?"

It was barely a question, and she got the impression that even if she said no, that wouldn't be the end of it. She handed it to him. He looked it over, checking its weight and the sharpness of the blade. Then he shook his head and handed it back to her.

"An ordinary axe shouldn't have given that imp a scratch. You shouldn't have been able to kill it with that." His mouth twisted as he looked her up and down.

"What kind of magic runs in your family?"

Rowan frowned. "I told you, there *isn't* any magic," she said, uncertain. "Why are you so sure that there is?"

"Hmmm," was all he said. Then, with a glance overhead to check the position of the sun, he jerked his head. "Come on, we need to get a fire started."

Soon bits of imp smoldered in the newly grown shoots of grass. Rowan wrinkled her nose; it smelled worse than a pigsty on a hot day.

"Are there a lot of those around here?" she asked.

Keziah, apparently satisfied that the imps weren't going to sneak themselves back together, began to kick dirt over the fire. "Not many, but when you run into a clump of them, there are likely to be a good amount writhing together in one of their pits. They're invasive, from somewhere to the east, so they don't do well everywhere in the forest. Once they find a nice dry, sandy place to burrow and wait for prey..." He gestured at the warm rocks under which the creatures had been burrowing.

"Don't let them get ahold of you—they burn." He showed her a blackened welt across his forearm.

"That looks bad," Rowan said, reaching out a hand. It was an evil-looking wound—his skin looked as though someone had lain a red-hot poker against it.

He drew his arm back before she could get a better look.

"It's fine. I heal quickly. We should keep moving."

"I'm sure you do," she snorted. "No sleep, no wound care—you seem quite impenetrable. Just watch; you'll get an infection and your arm will swell up and *then* you'll wish you'd at least cleaned it out."

He rolled his eyes. "Much as I appreciate your concern, I'd rather not waste the time. I have a—injuries just heal quickly for me. I don't really want to go into it."

"So mysterious. Tell me, which persona are you set on cultivating—the brave, stoic *man* who can't be bothered to take care of an injury in a responsible way? I've read the stories—those kinds of people don't last long in any of them," Rowan snapped. She was sick of him waving away her questions and professing that he didn't *need* basic necessities.

He looked impressed by the outburst.

"If you're going to be a bully about it, fine. Get me a rag from that pack."

She wet the rag using the water skin and helped clean his arm. Then she tied another rag around it for a bandage.

Nothing else accosted them as they made their way through groves of birch trees, growing dense as fine white eyelashes. Walking through them bothered Rowan's eyes—birch trees were pretty enough on their own, but moving through row after row of them with their black-and-white stripes made her dizzy. She was relieved when the last of the birch trees were behind them and they were back in the mix of oak, pine, elm, and ash. She was still more relieved when Keziah suggested they stop for the night under the boughs of a massive maple. He asked Rowan to help him string up a tarpaulin over their sleeping area.

"Not that I think it's going to rain," he said, shielding his eyes from the setting sun as he looked up. "Or snow, for that matter, but I'd rather take the precaution."

Rowan looked up as well, holding the rope taut. Pink and gold wisps of cloud streaked the sky, with only thin shreds of blue visible.

"If all those clouds stay put, we might be fine," she said, looking west, "but it looks like they're thinning, and there's not much wind. I'd bet my dry socks there's going to be a frost tonight."

Keziah looked amused. "Are your family farmers, then?" he asked as they hoisted the tarp higher and knotted the rope to keep it in place.

"Not for money, if that's what you mean. We grow most of our own vegetables, for table, so it helps to know if a frost is likely." She gave him a pointed look. "And what about your family? What do they do?"

He gave her a cheeky grin and bent to pick up a piece of wood.

"As it happens, I don't mind telling you that. My mother's family fishes and makes goods for trade. At least, I assume that's still what they do."

"And your father?" Rowan started picking up twigs and smaller pieces of wood for kindling.

"My father is nothing," Keziah said shortly, "and my mother deserved better than him. Thankfully, he's left her alone for the time being."

He glanced at Rowan, who realized she had frozen while reaching for the ground. She closed her hand on nothing and scrabbled, feeling for the branch she'd been so certain was right beneath her fingers.

"Your father is ill, you said?" Keziah smoothed his way out of his own story.

"Yes, and my mother runs the household for the most part."

"And your sister is the eldest?"

She nodded.

"And not married? Surely if she's older than you, your parents must be trying to find a man for her. Or have things actually gotten better for women in the villages?"

Rowan blanched and shook her head. "They—they decided, until my brother is old enough to take over the woodcutting and hunting, they can't spare her for marriage. But I don't think…"

For the life of her, she couldn't decide how much was safe to tell this man. On the one hand, he certainly didn't seem like the type to go to the village and blab some girl's secrets to her family and neighbors. But on the other hand, it wasn't her story to tell.

"I don't think she would marry anyone they chose for her," she said finally.

"And why's that?" he asked, stacking wood in an area he'd cleared of dead grass and leaves. "Does she have someone in mind already?"

"Y-yes," Rowan said cautiously.

"And that person would be deemed unsuitable by your parents?"

Rowan nodded, not trusting herself to speak. What would happen if he guessed it?

"Why? No money?" Keziah bent over the stack of kindling he'd made.

"Not money, no," Rowan said, feeling uneasy.

"Bad stock?"

"No, nothing like that."

"I'm stumped," he said, leaning back from the small blaze he had somehow created without Rowan noticing. "What possible problem could your parents have with a suitor if money and blood aren't an issue?" He looked up at Rowan and finally took in her expression.

"You don't want to tell me, do you?" He sounded surprised, and he rose and waved her over to the fire.

She moved closer slowly.

"I shouldn't have pried, I'm sorry," he said seriously. "I don't need to know your sister's business. I was just curious."

"It's fine," Rowan said, rubbing her arms, grateful for the warmth of the fire. "I just don't feel it's my place to tell anyone."

"Not even someone who doesn't know her, or your family? I admire your dedication." He grinned at her again, and she felt herself finally relax again.

He is *a good person,* she decided, watching him gently lay more branches on the fire, *and I'm lucky I happened across him.* It surprised her that she hadn't been sure up until this point, despite his generosity, but it had taken time for her to appreciate his willingness to listen and understand. Most village men, or folk in general, didn't value that.

"Food? Food." Very businesslike, he started pulling potatoes and apples from his knapsack.

"I hope you don't have issues eating around hot coals," he said as he nestled the potatoes in the fire. "Because that's the price of today's hot meal. These, too." He held up the two apples, glinting rosily in the firelight. "Though I'll wait to put them in until the potatoes are done; they won't take as long."

Rowan watched the fire curl and lick around the potatoes, blackening their skins and hissing with steam. She'd had potatoes like this a few times, when she'd gone with Celine to help with the cutting ages ago. She liked them best in Winter, when they dropped them in the snow as soon as they came out of the fire—this cleaned them and helped make the skin easier to peel off.

She looked at Keziah, who sat staring into the fire as well. He looked tired, something she hadn't thought possible from the insane pace he'd kept that day.

"I'm impressed," he said out of the blue, not taking his eyes off the fire. "If I'm honest, I thought you'd give up halfway through the day. I should have given you more credit."

The praise, though unexpected, felt good. Rowan allowed herself a small smile.

The potatoes were delicious, despite there being nothing to put on them. Their steamy insides had turned creamy, while their outsides were charred and crisp. Rowan ate every bit she could, spitting out some of the too-blackened pieces. The apples were even better—tart and bursting with juice.

"It's amazing that an apple and a potato could make for such a good meal," she remarked as she lay down in her bedroll.

"I'd like to take credit for it, but you're probably just starving." Keziah grinned at her over the fire. "I must say, I didn't think much of potatoes until I ate them after days of almost no food. Fish was always my main staple before that."

"That couldn't have worked very well for you," Rowan said, frowning. "What did you do when the river froze over?"

Keziah's mouth opened, then closed again, his lips pressed together. He poked at the fire with a long stick, unnecessarily adjusting the pieces of wood he'd lain over the top. He glanced up and saw Rowan still watching him, still waiting for his response.

"There are some places where the water doesn't freeze three months out of the year," he said finally.

Rowan sat up straight. "You mean... Is that where you're from, then? You said your mother's people fished..." She trailed off at his expression.

"I don't know if I'm *from* there anymore. It's been a long time." He sighed, dropped the stick, and rubbed his hands over his face. "Look, I'm tired, and I really don't feel like talking about it. Why don't you try and get some sleep?"

Rowan's face burned—she was glad of the growing dark because at least he wouldn't be able to tell—and she murmured something about that being a good idea. She'd really been hoping to ask him how he knew so much about the Oak King, but that certainly wasn't an option now. It seemed the topic of Keziah's old home was completely off-limits. And of course that only made her more curious about it.

She pulled the blanket over herself and turned onto her side so she faced away from Keziah. She kept having to remind herself that she really didn't know him all that well, and it wouldn't do to get too comfortable, especially since she kept accidentally bringing up subjects that turned out to be painful to him. He was only doing her a favor, after all.

I only need to reach the Bear Maiden and wish for... For what? Would the Bear Maiden tell her what she needed? If the fairy tales she had read were any indication, that didn't seem likely. She would have to think about it, determine exactly what she would need to wish for to be able to rescue Celine. And with her only source of information on the Oak King unwilling to speak of his experiences with him, she would have to figure it out for herself. Somehow.

And so she closed her eyes and tossed and turned her way into a fitful sleep.

CHAPTER 14

Rowan

FOUR DAYS BEFORE THE SPRING EQUINOX

The next morning there was no offer of elk's milk with breakfast, but Keziah seemed to have put the events of the previous night behind him. He only spoke of the path they were to take that day as he handed Rowan a bowl of porridge, sweetened with honey.

She eyed his knapsack. "Did you really bring honey with you?"

He pointed at her with his spoon. "Don't scoff. It's well worth the extra weight, and it never goes rotten."

She shrugged. It did make plain old porridge taste better, though she thought wistfully of her mother's spiced cream, which was her topping of choice at home. She watched Keziah scrape the last of his out of his bowl. He seemed to be in a rather good mood, considering. He hummed as he looked toward the hills, which had just begun to gleam gold-green in the early morning light.

"What are you so jolly for?" she asked finally. She felt awful, having slept badly and worried most of the night about her sister and whether or not Keziah was angry with her for asking about his home.

"Oh," he said, wiping out his bowl with a handful of dead leaves. "Just enjoying the weather. Everything's coming alive again—it's good to see all the color."

She looked around. True, grass had begun to poke up from the ground, and there was a sprinkling of little leaves popping from the tree branches overhead.

"Hmm," she said, noncommittally.

He raised his eyebrows.

"A young maiden not overcome by the wonders of Spring?"

She nearly choked on her porridge laughing.

"Don't be daft," she said, managing to swallow her mouthful of food. "I like Spring just fine, but I don't like that everything gets hotter and hotter from now on. I like the cold."

Keziah rolled his eyes.

"Do you also like everything withering away and dying, and all the animals leaving for better climates?"

"Yes, I do," she replied without hesitation. "The leaves are beautiful in Autumn, and everything smells heavenly. And plenty of animals stick around—don't you pretend they don't. All the best food, and you can dress up warmly and stay cozy inside, or go out and find chestnuts and hazelnuts at last."

"Anything else?" An annoying little smile played around his mouth as he watched her speak.

"Pears!" She ignored his infuriating expression and let herself get carried away imagining all her favorite things. "It's the only time of year we have pears. And apples are finally ripe, and plums and blackberries. The game is better, too, and mother doesn't mind heating up the house all day with the oven, turning out fresh bread and pastries."

Keziah grunted, obviously in disagreement, and began to tuck away his bowl and spoon.

"And you prefer this time of year, I take it?" she said, challenging him. "Why?"

"It's *infinitely* better, that's why," he fired back. "It's insane that for half the year, this land is basically uninhabitable for humans. So yes, I prefer the warmer periods. And not specifically Spring—it snows almost as much as it does in Winter. Summer, when all the best fruits and vegetables are in season, the animals are all in the middle of raising their young and living in the forest again—you can go about in hardly anything, no bundling up in scratchy wool or bulky clothing. Swimming, fishing without breaking through ice or nearly freezing to death —*that's* what I like."

Rowan wrinkled her nose. "Sweat and everything going rotten because of the heat, skunks and raccoons getting into everything. You keep it—I'd gladly give it up."

Keziah opened his mouth to say something, his eyes aglow with mischief, but abruptly he closed his mouth.

"No quips? No jibes? Or did I make that good of an argument?" Rowan asked as he turned away.

"Not nearly good enough," he said with a shadow of the happy energy he'd just had seconds ago. "Just not worth debating the subject—I'm clearly not going to convince you." He gave her a grin, trying to repair the moment.

She returned it a little uncertainly. *Why did he stop? I was enjoying that.* But the moment had passed, so they broke camp and started on their way.

A few minutes in, Keziah said over his shoulder, "Know any good stories?"

"Plenty. Any kind in particular?"

"Anything involving sea voyages and pirates, or ogres and treasure troves in the mountains. No Forests and Kings of the Seasons, if you please."

Rowan obliged and began with the tale of Calden on the Sunlit Sea, a story the peddler had brought her of a young adventurer who had to pass three tests set by the God of the Ocean. She followed that up with the story of three princes who climbed a mountain to rescue a princess guarded by a dragon, but the princess turned out to *be* the dragon.

Each time she finished a story, Keziah would glance over his shoulder and say, "Any more?"

It was hard avoiding stories about forests. Those were the ones she tended to like most and remember best, but luckily she had received so many books from the peddler and devoured them over and over again, so she was well-versed in stories. After a while, she began to make up a story about a girl with the ability to change her shape into that of any animal in the world. And when she got bored of telling stories, she turned her attention back to the forest around her.

They made their way through the stretch of hills, then came down into an area thick with trees. Rowan felt oddly comforted, surrounded again by gnarled trunks and rivers of roots. The snow was truly gone now—it had seeped into the ground the past day or two, soaking it a deep dark color, and green began to show up everywhere; fine moss flushing up a tree trunk, early leaves poking their tips from buds. Where the late Winter wood had been brown and gray, now there was more contrast, more richness.

Rowan caught sight of a bush with brilliant yellow flowers, or maybe they were leaves, coiling itself against a tree.

"Forsythia," Keziah said, nodding his head at the plant. "The first flower to bloom, if it can get the sun."

The striking plant sat in a patch of sunlight. Rowan could see dust floating in the warm golden glow, giving the air a shimmering look. Then she realized a pair of wide eyes were staring through the bush's yellow foliage. The deer poked its head around the forsythia, craning its neck to watch them as they passed by. Velvety green antlers coiled like corkscrews from its head. It delicately peeled a forsythia blossom from a branch and chewed, its eyes fixed on them until they rounded an elm and lost sight of it.

They passed a colossal tree, so old, Keziah said, that it had turned to stone. Its trunk had split into five pieces, making it look like a giant hand reaching for the sky.

Rowan was still looking over her shoulder at the stone tree, so focused on trying to catch one last glimpse of it that she didn't hear Keziah's first warning.

"Rowan!" he shouted, grabbing for her.

Startled, she instinctively shrank back from him. Then she saw that she stood in a ring of white mushrooms, and the stout little things began to swell and blacken.

A mushroom ring—oh, gods...

Keziah had gone around the ring and stood at its edge, reaching for Rowan, who, when she tried to follow, found she couldn't move her feet. They were sunk deep into the earth, and she was being pulled deeper with every second. She realized in horror that the earth would close over her head and the mushrooms would grow over the top of her, living off her body after she suffocated.

She strained to reach Keziah's hand, but he was too far away, and he didn't dare let his feet cross the line of growing mushrooms, lest he, too, became stuck.

I can't get around them, she thought desperately as the mushrooms swelled into one another, forcing Keziah to back up. *The only way out is up.*

She looked at the tree branch above her and reached up, though she knew it was too high, far too high.

"Please," she murmured, hoping, *hoping* she could somehow stretch just a little further.

And then the branch dipped, just low enough for her to grab on and pull with all her might. The earth that had climbed up to her knees crumbled back to the ground, and she hoisted herself up onto the branch, swinging a leg over it and scooting herself back, until she was no longer over the growing clump of mushrooms, which had reached the size of several woolly sheep clustered together.

Clinging to the branch, Rowan tried to catch her breath—and process the fact that the tree had *bent down* so that she could reach it. A difficult feat, because the mushrooms were still getting larger. At the rate they were growing, Rowan worried that they would soon consume the tree she was in; they were already eating away at its roots.

"We need to get out of here," Keziah said urgently, bracing himself against the side of the tree. More mushrooms began to pop out of the ground around him.

"Go around," Rowan said. "I'll drop down on the other side."

She climbed through the branches, over to the other mushroom-free side of the tree. Keziah helped her down, and the two of them ran as the tree creaked and groaned under the mushrooms' attack. Rowan looked over her shoulder, watching as the tree that had saved her—an elder—shook, then swayed, then fell, its branches snapping as it crashed to the ground.

She didn't know how far the mushrooms could spread from their ring, but Keziah pulled her by the hand until they reached a rivulet that Rowan supposed eventually fed into the river.

He let go of her hand, knelt, and began washing his hands, his arms, his face. Then he pulled Rowan closer to the water.

"You need to wash everything—these clothes, yourself. And I need to clean off our packs." He turned his back on Rowan. "I'll keep a look-out, don't worry. You and I are covered with mushrooms spores right now, and we need to get them off of us, or else those things will start popping up anywhere we go, possibly even inside of us."

Shakily, Rowan pulled off her clothing, trying very hard not to think about the fast that she was now naked in the middle of an enchanted, very dangerous forest. She stepped into the rivulet. The water was, unsurprisingly, ice-cold, and Keziah nearly turned around when she gasped.

"Don't!" she hissed at him, and he snapped his head back the opposite direction. "It's just cold!"

"Get your hair, too. A good amount of the spores probably settled there."

Teeth chattering, Rowan bent over and dunked her head in the freezing water. She nearly wept at the chill. Then, hoping she had rinsed the spores off, she grabbed her clothing and submerged them, shaking them out under water. She watched grimly as a cloud of something murky billowed from her coat—she hadn't even realized she'd been covered with the stuff.

"Are you ready for dry clothes?" Keziah asked. "I'll need to wash off, too, when you're done."

"Th-this was not the bath I was d-dreaming of," Rowan stammered, her skin stinging with cold.

Under Rowan's directions, Keziah awkwardly passed her a dry shirt and breeches over his shoulder. Then they traded places, Rowan continuing to wipe down the outside of the packs while Keziah stripped behind her and doused himself in snowmelt.

She was a little satisfied to hear the little noises of shock he made when the water splashed over him.

"Good gods, this is freezing!" he exclaimed. "And you hardly made any fuss about it!"

Rowan almost turned around to give him a snide smile.

"If you peek at me, I'll splash you. And I won't give you a second change of clothes, either," he warned.

Rowan hastily faced away again, red flushing up the back of her neck. She'd forgotten he wasn't wearing anything.

"I am sorry I haven't managed to find you a warm bath yet," he said, "but I can promise both of us a good hot fire in a moment. We need to get warm again, if we don't want to catch cold."

"It may be too late for that," Rowan sniffled. She thought she'd been cold last night; clearly, she'd been mistaken.

"Well, consider that your lesson for not listening to me. Clothes?"

She opened his pack and found a dry shirt and a pair of trousers.

"Trousers first, please." She obliged, holding them out behind her. She felt his hand fumbled at her back before he managed to get them from her. She held the shirt out behind her until she felt him take that as well.

"Can I turn around now?" she asked after a moment.

"There." He came into her line of vision, buttoning up the last few buttons on his shirt. "Now you may look at me again."

She rolled her eyes. "You mean now I *have* to look at you again," she corrected, but that blush still burned through her cheeks.

"I think we should move on a little ways in case any spores fell here. That way." He pointed across the rivulet, toward a cluster of young birch trees encircling a boulder.

They lay their wet clothes over the rocks, hoping the bit of warmth promised by the coming Spring would dry them off.

Keziah looked down at the wet clothes skeptically. "We really ought to burn them. Rinsing them might not have been enough."

"How common are those mushroom-things? If we go burning our clothes every time we have a run-in with them, we won't have anything left to wear," Rowan said, looking about for another ominous white ring of fungus.

"They're common enough, but easy to spot, especially when someone *warns* you about them. Doesn't work, though, if you ignore the warning and stomp your way into them," he said, smiling cheekily at her as they walked to the cluster of birch trees.

"I didn't *ignore* you," Rowan retorted, sliding her pack off and leaning it against the boulder. "I just didn't hear you."

"You weren't listening to me at all," he corrected, snapping a dead branch off one of the birches. "Your face had gone all dreamy, and you were staring off into the trees."

"And what of it? Neither of us died, did we?" Rowan began gathering twigs for kindling.

Keziah watched her, twisting the dead branch between his fingers. "No, I suppose we didn't," he said finally. "Though no one dying is a low bar for me." Then he snapped the branch into pieces.

"Are you any good at cutting firewood, or do you only use that axe to kill imps?" he asked after he had constructed a pile of kindling.

"I know how to cut firewood," she replied.

"Good. There's a dead tree over there—go hack it up."

"A 'please' costs you nothing," she said, not budging an inch.

He looked up at her, amusement dancing in his golden eyes. "Fair enough. Fair—no, *Fairest* Rowan—"

She snorted.

"Would you *please* do me the great favor of slicing up yon tree into manageable pieces?" He clasped his hands over his heart. "Or shall I sing a sonnet about your auburn hair, or the mud and leaves stuck to your boots?"

Her mouth threatened to break into a smile. "That will do," she managed, her throat aching from the effort it took to keep from laughing. She turned and quickly walked away, grabbing Celine's axe as she headed in the direction he had indicated.

"I really do know a sonnet like that," he called after her. "Don't think you can escape my singing it."

He really is something else, she thought as she swung the axe and buried it in the side of the tree, which lay propped up slightly over another, far more decayed fallen tree.

She hadn't gotten much practice splitting up an entire tree over the last few years, but slowly she remembered the technique Celine had taught her. She cut the tree into pieces, then worked at splitting them into fire-sized chunks. Then she hauled them by the armload over to the little fire Keziah had built.

She half hoped he would be impressed by how quickly she had worked, but if he was, he kept it to himself. He did, however, jump up and fetch his own armful of wood, helping Rowan stack it next to the boulder, on top of a crosshatch of sticks to help it stay dry.

Then all of a sudden, he grabbed Rowan's arm and pulled her to the ground.

"*Don't move*," he whispered, dropping flat on his stomach, his eyes fixed on something across the water.

Rowan pressed herself as close to the ground as she could, head raised only slightly to try and see what had given him such a fright.

Then a flicker of silver caught her eye.

A slight figure wound their way through the trees, delicately slipping over root tangles and under branches. They reached a hillock and perched at its peak for a moment, like a deer stopping to listen, poised to flee at the slightest noise. Now Rowan got a good look—it was a young woman, wide-eyed and slender, dressed in gossamer-thin silk that hung from her like drips of candle wax.

Keziah's hand tightened around Rowan's arm.

"*Dew*." He spoke barely above a whisper, yet Rowan could hear the contempt in his voice. He closed his eyes and began murmuring something under his breath.

Rowan felt a tingling sensation in the air around her, heard a kind of whispering through the trees. A chill ran down her spine.

Dew turned her head slowly, like an owl, her large eyes taking in every inch of the forest before her. Then, she descended from the hillock and airily picked her way through the trees and out of sight.

Neither of them moved for several minutes. Then Keziah slowly sat up, and Rowan followed suit.

"Was she following us?" Rowan asked, keeping her voice low.

"I think she was trying to," Keziah said, though he sounded uncertain. "If she truly had our trail, she certainly would have found us—we were right in front of her. I think she was out on patrol, more likely, and just happened to cross our path. She's one of Oak's most ancient Sentinels, and one of the most perceptive, so we'd be wise not to let her get so close to us again."

Trying to put the close call behind them, they ate lunch. Keziah talked about the forest, trying to dispel the unease that had settled over the bright afternoon.

"This time of year, when everything starts waking up—it's disconcerting sometimes, after the months of quiet. The color, too—it's startling, in a good way; a reminder that things can grow and live. It's easy to forget that here, sometimes. That's why I like to do my trading during Winter—have a break from the monotony." He waved a hand vaguely at the trees around him, which, to Rowan, looked anything but monotonous now that the snow had all melted and the buds had started to sprout into leaves.

"But why not come live in the village, then?" Rowan asked. "Why do you have to stay in the forest?"

Keziah poked at the fire with a long stick, thinking over his reply before he gave it.

"I can't leave the forest for very long," he answered finally. "And there are reasons I don't live among people like your villagers. Things about me I know they wouldn't like. Here, I have the freedom to be myself, provided I don't let the Oak King know I'm here."

Rowan's brow wrinkled. "Why can't you leave the forest for very long? Is it because of your debt to the Bear Maiden?"

Keziah looked uncomfortable. "Not exactly, though it *is* somewhat related... Look, it's a long story that will only confuse you further, alright?"

Rowan fell silent, feeling guilty for once again pressing him with too many questions, but his unwillingness to answer even simple things still irked her. It was as though something was at stake, and if he answered her, something bad would happen.

"Tell me about your grandmother," Keziah said suddenly, changing the subject. "She sounds like a marvelous woman."

Rowan grinned. "She is. Sometimes I don't know how my mother managed to be so different from her. She always gives the best presents, tells the best stories, and she listens to what we have to say. She wants us to do the things we like, and she's always told me that marriage isn't the only option for someone like me, if I don't want it to be."

"What a woman." Keziah grinned. "Is it just because she came from the city? Or does her openness stem from something else?"

"I don't know," Rowan said, hugging her arms around her knees. "I don't know what her life was like in the city. It got bad enough that she and my grandfather decided to leave, but I know she loved working in the bookshop; she talks about it all the time."

"And what did your grandfather do? Run the shop?"

"Oh, no—they didn't work in the same shop. He worked for a toy shop, carving. He would come to the bookshop looking for ideas in fairy-tale books, and that's how they met. Once they married and my grandmother was pregnant with my mother, they decided they didn't want to raise a child in the city, so they bought land near the *las graniczny* and moved all the way out there."

Rowan waved a hand in the direction of her village.

Keziah frowned.

"How do you know that's where your village is?" he asked sharply.

Rowan stared at him. His mood had shifted so abruptly.

"I..." She was going to say that she hadn't really known—that she had just waved in a random direction—but that wasn't true, now that she thought about it. She *knew* that, if she were to walk straight in the direction she'd just indicated, that she would come to her village. "I just knew. I have a good sense of direction."

"Most folk don't, in here. If you don't know the forest or have some of its power, it works at turning you around, disorienting you so you lose your way, as a way of teaching a lesson to trespassers."

Rowan shrugged. "I'd always heard about that in the stories, but I've never gotten lost here. Neither has my sister. I assumed it was just a story."

Keziah looked thoughtfully off in the direction Rowan had indicated.

"But you pointed exactly in the right direction. As the crow flies, your village falls right there," he pointed west.

"You're so surprised that *I* know that—how are *you* so sure?" Rowan asked, brow furrowed.

Keziah shrugged, but she got the impression he was only trying to appear casual. "I've lived here a long time—I know my way around."

So often she got the feeling that he was keeping back over half the truth from her. Tired of trying to wheedle information from him, she only shrugged, then pulled out her embroidery from her knapsack.

"Needlework, here?" he asked, but he scooted closer so he could see what she was working on. "A good likeness of your namesake," he said, running a finger along the trunk of one of the mountain ash trees. He squinted at the red cap poking its head around another of the trees.

"What's that?"

"I thought they were Red Caps," Rowan answered, expertly threading her needle with green thread, "A crowd of them followed me for about a mile my first day in the forest, just before I met you. I was scared witless they would all jump on me and shred me to ribbons, but they got bored and left me alone after a while."

Keziah was quiet for a moment.

"A herd of Red Caps followed you, and *nothing* happened?" he asked, incredulous.

"I thought they seemed awfully sweet—not one of them touched me," Rowan said, starting a leaf pattern curling around the outside of the mountain ash grove. "They just seemed like they were waiting for something." She glanced up and met Keziah's eyes.

He looked extremely skeptical.

"Why, what do they normally do when you come across them?"

In answer, he pulled the collar of his shirt aside and showed her a nasty patch of scars on his shoulder. Her eyes widened.

"Ever since my first run-in with them, I haven't made a point of sticking around long enough to strike up a conversation," he said dryly, pulling his collar straight again. "I scurry away as fast as my legs will carry me, and I burn yarrow all night long to keep them away from my house; they hate the stuff."

"But why didn't they attack me?" Rowan asked, unable to concentrate on her leaf. "They didn't seem vicious at all, just curious."

"Maybe they took a liking to you." Keziah's eyes traveled over Rowan, as if looking for what had appealed to the Red Caps. "You do seem to have a connection with the forest—perhaps they could see it."

"But you have a connection, too, don't you?" Rowan couldn't stop herself from asking. "After all, didn't you say the Oak King would know you were here if the trees didn't like you so much?"

His lips tightened. "You're right. I shouldn't have told you that, but you're right."

"Why is there so much you 'shouldn't' tell me? What would happen if you did tell me everything, every 'long story' that you think will just confuse me?" Rowan didn't honestly expect him to answer and was shocked when he did.

"There are a number of reasons I don't want to tell you certain things. One." He held up a finger. "Some of it is extremely unpleasant. No, I mean it," he said when Rowan sniffed in disbelief. "There are things I wish I didn't know. Sad things. Awful things. Second." He held up another finger.

She noticed the nails on his fingers were very round and white against his tan skin. Extremely clean, too, for someone who'd been trekking through the woods for years.

"Knowledge can get you into trouble. There are some in this forest who think knowing makes you a part of what goes on here, even if it was set in motion long before you were even born."

"Is that what happened to you?" Rowan broke in, watching his face. She caught the little flicker of reaction that he couldn't manage to hide —a sorrow darkening around his eyes.

"In part, yes. And third." He held up a final finger. "You seem very much like the sort of person who would want to help if you found out there was a problem or something that needed fixing. I'd rather you didn't get involved—enough pain has gone on here. Everything hangs in a delicate balance, and people's lives depend on it staying that way."

At first Rowan thought he meant Celine, but it seemed to be more than that. His face looked distant, haunted, and he looked like he had forgotten she was there for a moment. But it was only a moment, and then it passed.

"Enough reasons?" he asked, resuming his stirring of the fire.

"I suppose so," she said reluctantly, watching the fire between them dance across his face.

The conversation was over, so she bent her head and resumed her quiet stitching. She kept her body angled slightly, so that Keziah couldn't see what she was working on. When she got tired of the swirling leaf pattern around the trees, she rethreaded her needle with gold and started working on capturing the outline of the dagger Keziah wore on his belt.

It helped to have the subject of her work right before her face, though she had some difficulty making out the smaller details. It would have helped if she could have moved closer, but then he would see what she was doing, and she didn't want to make him uncomfortable.

All of a sudden, something white flashed through the air and rammed into Keziah, knocking him to the ground. It was gone in a second, but Keziah was back on his feet instantly, blood trickling from his lip.

"Snowbelly," he hissed at Rowan, as though that explained anything. "Get down!"

But Rowan looked up and saw the white thing flying down toward her. She just had time to make out black eyes, a bloody mouth, and dark, outstretched claws before it hit her in the chest and brought her to the ground. Not knowing what else to do, she rolled, pushing hard against the creature to keep its claws from her throat. Heat seared her ankles; her feet had gone through the fire, scattering coals in the dirt around her. Sharp pain shot from Rowan's collarbone to her shoulder, and she realized in a panic that the creature had sunk its teeth into her.

Something exploded, and suddenly Rowan felt the creature fly off her. It crashed into the bushes and struggled back up. It was the size of a cow, but long and skinny except for its white, sagging stomach that hung from it, oddly distended. Its snout was longer than a wolf's, and it bared black fangs stained with blood. Its mangy white tail curled up and lashed out as it flicked its dark eyes from Rowan to Keziah, who stood with his hands raised and directed at Snowbelly as though he was about to throw something at it.

The foul beast gave a loud sniff, then whipped its tail across the ground, throwing dirt into Keziah's face before he could react. When the dust cloud cleared, Snowbelly was gone.

Rowan sank to her knees, hands clutching at the bite across her shoulder. Her skin itched and stung, and blood was slowly soaking her shirt.

Then Keziah was there, ripping open the torn shoulder of her shirt and pressing a cloth to the wound.

"He won't be back. He thought he would catch us off guard, but now he knows that's not enough."

For all his certainty, Rowan couldn't fathom why Keziah sounded so panicked.

I must be bleeding too much, she thought vaguely as she slumped against him.

"Close your eyes for a moment. This may sting."

Rowan closed her eyes. She felt his palm against her collarbone, warm and solid. Then heat blistered over her skin like someone had pressed an iron to her. She yelped and sat straight up, clutching at her shoulder. She felt for the bite marks she had seen, but all she felt was her unbroken skin, smooth and unmarred.

"What did you do?" she asked, incredulous.

Keziah sat back on his heels. "Nothing. I just fixed it," he said, not meeting Rowan's eyes as he wiped blood—*her* blood—off his hands with the cloth.

She reached out and grabbed his arm. "*How* did you fix it?" All that remained was the ghost of the pain that had brought her to her knees moments ago.

Keziah met her gaze, uncowed.

"Does it matter? You're alive. I think that's all that counts." He pulled his arm out of her grasp and stood. "Do you feel strong enough to move on in the morning?"

Rowan glared at him. "I suppose so. You're sure that thing won't come back?"

Keziah nodded. "And if he does, I'll be listening for him. He's a quiet one, but now that I know he's in the area, it would be much harder for him to sneak up on us if I'm on the lookout."

"So I'll need to rely on your keen hearing to keep from getting mauled again. Lovely." Rowan brushed dirt off the front of her shirt, then realized it was still damp with blood.

"I need to change," she told Keziah, "unless we want every carnivorous creature for a mile to come looking for the walking blood-soaked rag I've become."

Keziah snorted and pulled a clean shirt from his pack. Then he turned his back so she could change.

Rowan found her fingers trembling so much that the buttons kept slipping sideways as she tried to fasten them.

"Nearly finished?" Keziah asked after a few moments.

"I—almost," Rowan muttered, which was a lie. She'd only managed one button, and the shaking only seemed to get worse.

Finally, she sighed and gave up. "Can you help?"

Keziah turned around, concerned. Rowan gestured to the buttons. "I'm shaking too much—my hands are useless."

She'd taken care to close the shirt as much as she could, but she still saw Keziah hesitate. Then he walked over and started buttoning the shirt for her.

"I'm sorry," he said as he started on the second from the top. "I forget not everyone has had a run-in with an animal that wants to kill them."

"Is that what that was? An animal?"

"At the end of the day, yes, I'd call Snowbelly an animal," Keziah answered, his fingers sliding to the next button. "But he's very old, and he has a long memory. Holds long grudges, that one."

"Grudges?" Rowan looked up at him and instantly wished she hadn't. She could make out a hint of stubble across his jaw, see beads of sweat at his temples, could suddenly smell cedar and smoke and something else, something bright and peppery, like ginger...

"He hates me, and I'd wager that's the only reason he attacked us the way he did. Though I'm having a hard time figuring out why he attacked *you* instead of focusing his energy on me."

"But why would an animal hold grudges?" Rowan asked.

She could have sworn Keziah smirked. "Snowbelly is a mountain creature who in recent decades started coming to the forest to hunt. Maybe he was tracking Dew—he hates anything and anyone of Oak, so anytime he senses Oak's power, he attacks."

Rowan thought about that for a moment. "But then why would he attack you?" she asked slowly.

Keziah's copper-colored eyes met hers for a moment.

"Must not like me, for some reason. Can you imagine?" he said with a wry grin, though his eyes looked sad. But that was all he'd say on the subject.

Keziah promised there was no chance of Snowbelly returning, so they kept to their plan of staying the night there. They built the fire back up and stomped out the coals that had been scattered by Snowbelly's attack. Keziah had caught a fish in the rivulet, and Rowan helped him stuff it with dried herbs and roast it over the fire. They made a mess of themselves eating it with their bare hands.

"Time for another wash in that snowmelt," Keziah joked, tossing the fishbones into the rocks.

"Oh, don't even *say* that," Rowan groaned, aching at the memory of the painfully cold water.

She poured some water from her skin on a rag and wiped her face and hands. Keziah did the same. Even though the fire had long warmed the dampness from their clothes, they sat there until dark, striking up conversations when one of them felt like talking. Then, when it was too dark to excuse staying up any later, Rowan volunteered to take first watch and keep the fire going. Keziah lay down in his bedroll and turned his back to the fire.

Rowan sat and looked into the dancing flames over the top of her embroidery. She felt guilty, guilty for sitting and talking and eating and resting while her sister was out there, most likely without any of those comforts. *We should have moved on,* Rowan thought, her anxiety growing. *We should have kept traveling as soon as we got dry. We didn't have to sit around talking.*

And she was angry at herself, because she enjoyed sitting with Keziah, getting a handful of new facts about him, adding them to the faint idea of his character she was building in her mind. She liked him. That was why she hadn't pushed for them to move on. She liked him very much, even though she only knew a little about him.

And you are letting it distract you, she chastised herself. *You're supposed to find your sister, not lust after some forest boy.*

But she had always been like this, growing infatuated with someone over a short period of time, then slowly realizing they weren't as wonderful as she'd thought they were. Her feelings always fizzled out as quickly as they had risen up in the first place.

But Keziah was no village boy. Here was a person who lived in a forest entangled with legends, a man with knowledge of the creatures and magic Rowan had dreamed of since she was young. He had built a life for himself here, alone, without any of the oppression or small-mindedness of Rowan's home. She wondered, again, what the home he had run away from had been like.

Then she sighed and accidentally jabbed herself with her needle. No matter how worthy he was of her infatuation, it wouldn't do her any good to keep thinking of him like this. It would only make her awkward around him, make her care too much what he thought of her. She didn't need that, and it would only annoy him if he noticed. She'd rather keep things how they were, their quips at one another, their playful bickering—she hadn't been permitted to form many close friendships back at home, since her mother needed so much help.

And who decided that men and women can't be good friends? Rowan argued with herself. *If he's so wonderful, who's to say I like him as anything more than that? It doesn't have to be romantic.*

She sighed again. *Or maybe this is just what happens when you spend every waking minute with someone as charming as he is.*

If she'd been trying to prove something to herself, she was growing too tired to properly consider it. She made herself get up and add more wood to the fire.

Celine

Celine jerked awake. The Oak King's black boots were the first thing she saw, at her own eye level. It took her a moment to realize, with relief, that he was still on the other side of the bars. She'd slept horribly the past few days—or was it weeks now?—fearing he'd come into the cell while she was asleep. But now, as she raised her head, she could see he was dressed for travel—a cloak as rich and brown as moleskin over his shoulders, clasped with an intricate gold leaf at his throat, and his boots looked a good sight sturdier than the decorative shoes he'd worn when he'd visited her before.

"I came to tell you I'll be leaving you for a time," he said, smiling as though he were popping by to visit a neighbor instead of the young woman he'd kidnapped. "But when I return, then it's time for me to extract your magic. I'd like to begin on the Spring Equinox, since my powers will return in full force. It's unfortunate you've disrupted my schedule so much—I have a standing appointment on that day every year, a meeting with an old friend that simply *must* be kept, and now I've had to move our meeting earlier. But no matter."

She kept her face dull and stupid, pretending sleep still befuddled her.

He frowned. "I suppose you'll need to eat. I'll have someone bring food. Really, your magic had better be worth all this effort. I *hate* to waste my own time."

He was hardly talking to her, more just to hear the sound of his own voice . He turned and left her, continuing to prattle as he made his way down the corridor. Her empty stomach roiled and threatened to turn itself inside out. Her head pounded, and she thought she might be going mad. She sat all day in a cell, with nothing to do, with the threat of his horrible intentions hanging over her.

She didn't know how he meant to do it. He'd spent the last few days asking Celine all sorts of strange questions—things about her parents, how animals acted around her, even the precise time, day and year she'd been born. However odd his questions had been, her answers must have satisfied him enough to "extract" her magic, though she shuddered to think what that might involve.

Worse—he came one morning with a strange flat dish and said he needed some of her blood. "To test it," he'd said. He had instructed her to present her arm. She hadn't moved. Then the saplings that made up the bars of her cell had sprouted branches and wrenched her from her cot and dragged her over to the Oak King. He had tutted and smiled at her as he cut her arm, allowing her blood to drip into the dish. Then he'd pressed a finger to the wound. A searing heat burned through Celine's skin, and when he'd lifted his finger, the cut was gone.

"See? Not bad at all," he'd said soothingly. The saplings released her and she shrank back from him. He didn't seem to notice, already striding away with a dish of her blood.

At least he was gone now, however briefly.

She glanced at the little table that sat beside her cot and saw that bread, cheese, and apples had appeared on it. She ate as quickly as she dared. At least she finally had a meal large enough to fill her stomach.

As the food settled, she tucked the rest away—she didn't know when she could expect more—and she began to think. The Oak King was gone. He was going to be gone for at least a few days. That gave her time to plan a way to escape. Though she was sick of sleep, she forced herself to lay back down, determined to think of something the next day.

The next morning, she rose, washed her face with water from the pitcher, and looked around the claustrophobic little cell.

She gripped the handle of her axe, as she did often now for comfort. It was so tempting to strike at the saplings that enclosed her cell. They looked so weak, so ready to give to the slightest blow, but she knew, she *knew* they would grow back immediately.

She began to pace around the cell. She wanted to move, to get her blood flowing, her heart rate increased. This lifeless sitting around did not suit her. She had not been made to sit and wait for the worst—she was made to act.

Pacing turned into jogging in a small circle, jumping up and down, using the tiny space she had to do whatever she could to break up the monotony her life had been for the past week.

He would not *extract* anything from her. She was going to find a way out.

Breathing heavily, she went to the bars and leaned her head against them. Surprisingly, the rough bark felt good against her face. She wondered what kind of trees these saplings would become, if they were permitted to grow outside where they belonged instead of inside a palace.

"Get me out of here," she whispered, to no one and nothing in particular. "*Please.*"

No one answered, of course. There was no one who could help her here.

Celine let go of the bar and raised her hand to push her hair out of her eyes, but she stopped before she'd moved even an inch. Her hand had brushed against something soft.

She looked at the bar. It was covered in rows of tiny leaves. Her eyes widened. Those had certainly not been there before.

She leaned in, looking closely at them.

"Willow," she murmured, noting how long and skinny the leaves were, as well as their bright, yellow-green hue.

As if in response, the leaves grew longer, thinner, and small branches began to shoot from the sapling's sides.

She watched in amazement as the saplings swelled and twisted, beginning to wrap around each other. The growing slowed, and she got the sense that the trees were waiting for something.

"If you can break through the ceiling," she said slowly, reaching for the bag of food she had just tucked away. "You can get to the sunlight."

At once the trees sprang into motion, coiling around each other into one massive trunk. Their leafy tops shot up, breaking off when they hit against the ceiling. They kept growing, however, and Celine heard cracking as they continued to press up. Moving quickly as she could, she started climbing. Great chunks of wood fell around her as the ceiling broke and gave way. She pushed on, following the trunk of the tree up, up, up.

And all of a sudden she felt warmth, the heat of the sun on her skin, and she smelled fresh air, free of the sickening, stagnant sweetness of her cell. She risked a look.

She was high on a building, high above a sea of trees that stretched as far as her eyes could see. As she became accustomed to the brightness, she made out dark shadows on the horizon. *The mountains,* she realized with a horrible lurch in her stomach. *They're so far away.* That meant home was far away, too.

She had no time for this. She needed to get as far away from this place as possible, and hope that none of Oak's allies paid her any notice this time.

She pressed a hand to the willow's trunk, looking up at the conjoined trees that had kept her a prisoner.

"You just wanted to grow, didn't you? I didn't realize you were a prisoner, too." The tree's long tendrils of branches swayed in the wind.

Celine found her footing on the roof and steadily made her way between the many decorative spires. As she hoped, the roof lowered the closer she got to the edge. She peered over the side. It was still a dizzying drop, one she couldn't possibly make without the risk of injury.

She sat on the edge with her feet hanging over, wondering if it would help for her to hang off and drop that way.

This is not *going to work,* she thought, frustration making her screw up her face.

She turned to see if there was anything on the roof she could use to make a rope. Then her eye fell on an olive-colored vine, which lay just a foot from her hand, its end dangling off the side of the palace.

That was very much not there a moment ago, she thought, casting about on the rooftop for the person casting spells and making plants do things without her noticing.

But there was no one. She tugged on the vine. Whatever it connected to, it held fast, even when she tested it with her own weight, leaning back as far as she dared. It would hold her.

Keeping the rope taut, she stepped back carefully, her feet leaving the roof for the side of the palace. She hoped the vine would be long enough to reach the ground—somehow, she predicted it would be—and she rappelled down.

She dropped to the ground and crouched, holding her breath. She waited there, in the dead leaves and unfurling shoots of ferns, for shouts of alarm at her escape.

None came.

Shakily, she stood and looked at the forest surrounding the Oak King's palace.

It finally hit her. She was free of him, free of that horrible cell. And right now, she most wanted to get somewhere where she would never set eyes on this foul palace and its ruler ever again.

Armed with only the axe on her back and her small bag of supplies, she headed east into the trees, toward home.

CHAPTER 16

Nash

"*Try it again.*"

My face stayed buried in my hands, my stomach roiling with frustration.

"*You must try again. It is the only way to improve your skills.*"

"*I've been trying, and they aren't improving.*"

"*Then you need to try harder.*"

Oak stood with his back to me, looking out the window. I was seated in his study, slumped forward onto the table so I would have to look at the pot of earth before me. There was a seed inside. Oak had not told me what it was, and I was supposed to make it grow.

Several half-rotted sprouts lay on the table, evidence of my failed attempts.

"*I'm working as hard as I can,*" *I told Oak.*

There was a pause, just long enough to let me know that he didn't believe me.

"*Try again, Nash.*" *His voice came out softly, but I could tell he was displeased.*

I lifted my head and stared hard at the pot of dirt.

"*Just tell me what the seed is and I'll be able to grow it,*" *I said, for what must have been the tenth time since our lesson for the day had begun.*

"*If I tell you what it is,*" *Oak said, irritation bleeding into his tone, "then you'll never learn to recognize seeds by their nature. You must decipher it yourself. I really don't understand why it's causing you such trouble —you ought to be able to just sense it." A phrase he had repeated through a tight smile several times already today. It never got easier to hear.*

It obviously also hadn't occurred to him that I had never encountered these plants before coming to his forest—I was almost certain that this was why I had such trouble identifying them. Reading about plants in books was one thing. Interacting with them for years was another.

I gazed longingly out the window. After a few months of the chilly season Oak called Spring, the weather had turned pleasantly hot. It wasn't the humid heat of the island, but it was close enough to feel like home— almost. And the forest was full of berries, of fascinating foliage, of animals I had never seen before and loved to observe.

And here I was, stuck inside until I could successfully identify the seed in this damn pot.

I closed my eyes and focused on the seed buried in the earth before me. I could sense it, almost even see it, suspended in darkness—minuscule, round and long and skinny, with a point at one end. I thought it was an apple seed at first, but it wasn't. Something in it, though, had the same feel as an apple seed—something cool and crisp and tart...

"It germinates in Autumn," I said suddenly, sitting bolt upright in my chair.

Oak blinked, then smiled at me. "Indeed, it does, Nash. But that isn't what I asked."

"I know," I said quickly, my energy renewed by this discovery. "But I learned how to sense when a seed will germinate! Isn't that a good thing, that I'm learning something?"

Oak sighed. "Of course it's good that you're learning. But the point of these lessons isn't for you simply to learn things—the point is for you to master them."

Just as I opened my mouth to ask what the difference was, a knock resounded throughout the palace.

Oak's mouth twisted with bitterness.

"Ohh," he groaned, spinning to look at the clock in the corner of his study. "I thought we had more time than this!"

"More time?" I asked as he stormed around the room, grabbing

various books and pieces of paper and shoving them into a bag, which I recognized as his travel sack.

"Autumn approaches," he said irritably, struggling to jam a particularly sturdy text into the travel sack. "And I make it a point never to be here during those godsforsaken months. Cold, clammy, everything dead," he muttered, cinching the bag shut.

Indeed, the reminder of the coming change of the seasons had wrought some kind of change in him that I had noticed in the past few weeks. He had been irritable, quick to anger, and displeased with almost everything. I had chalked it up to my poor performance as a student, but now I could see it was tied to the dwindling of his season—and his magic.

"Where are you going, then, if you don't stay here?" For he sounded eager to get as far away from this kingdom as possible.

"Somewhere warm," he muttered distractedly. "Always somewhere warm."

My eyes lit up. "Am I coming with you?" Somewhere warm, maybe near the ocean...

He frowned. "No. I think it would do you good to spend the Autumn and Winter months here, in the forest. Keep practicing what I've taught you, and don't let Holly's lot distract you. I'm sure they'll all think that I've finally— Oh, never mind. Just keep practicing."

And he hurried out the door.

I gave the still-empty pot before me half a glance. Then I followed Oak.

He'd already made it to the front doors and was throwing them open when I caught up.

Two women stood upon the doorstep, one pale with a sumptuous figure, and the other with faintly shimmering skin several shades darker than my own. Her eyes immediately found me over Oak's shoulder, and I was struck by their deep blue color. It reminded me of the ocean on a windy day.

"Ladies," Oak said cordially, "is it that time of year already?"

The shimmery being said nothing but looked on Oak with an almost cold expression. The pale one smiled graciously.

"Near enough, Lord Oak. The Holly King begins his journey soon." The figures both had long hair and large, luminous eyes, though I was *certain neither were entirely human. Their bodies seemed to be made of something other than skin and bone—it was as though clouds had sunk from the sky and assumed the shape of humans.*

"Preceded by you and the lovely Fog, as always, Mist; I'm aware. And Frost not far behind you, I presume?" Oak asked, his eyes darting over their shoulders to the forest beyond them.

Mist shook her head, silvery tresses rippling over her shoulders. "Frost felt the urge to spread some early chill over the farmlands. They will join Fog and myself soon, I expect."

Oak's expression soured. He strained to keep smiling.

"Seems earlier and earlier every year. Can we not keep to the Equinox, as agreed? I find myself increasingly encroached upon."

Fog's brows drew together, her eyes narrowing.

"I seem to remember a number of early Springs, my Lord Oak, including this year," Mist said smoothly, not missing a beat. "And I believe it was agreed that the Equinoxes and Solstices were to be thought of as guidelines, rather than strict dates. If you'd prefer to postpone your journey until Lord Holly arrives, I'm sure he would be more than glad to discuss—"

"No, no, I cannot sit idly waiting for Holly to get here," Oak interrupted, passing Mist and Fog and hurrying down the steps. "Give my regards, and so on."

He disappeared into the trees without another word to me.

Mist and Fog shared a look, one that indicated a long history of similar interactions with Oak. Then, as one, they turned to me.

"Good day," Mist greeted me, as though she'd expected to see a thirteen-year-old boy upon the Oak King's doorstep.

"Hello," I returned, feeling incredibly awkward. Was I supposed to welcome them? Was I their host, now that Oak had gone away? I wished he had warned me before he rushed off on his travels.

"What is your name, child?" Fog rasped. Her voice sounded hoarse, barely above a whisper.

"Nash," I replied, "I'm... Oak is my..." I found I couldn't say the word "father." For my people, a father was one who stood by his family, worked alongside them, supported his partner and his children the same way a mother did. Oak had done none of these things; he had only sired me.

"I see the resemblance," Mist said softly, saving me from having to finish the sentence. I did wonder what she meant—the faint curl in my hair, perhaps?

"What was all that about?" I asked, nodding to the place where Oak had vanished from view.

The two women exchanged another look.

"Your—the Oak King prefers that the rules be followed when his own season draws to an end," Mist said carefully, "but when Lord Holly's months dwindle, Lord Oak becomes more... lenient with them."

"He doesn't like his own season cut short, but he happily ends Winter early when it pleases him," Fog muttered.

"And have you come for a long visit, Nash?" Mist asked, pretending Fog had not spoken.

"I've come to learn to use my powers," I explained. "Then I'll go back home."

The pair had a great deal of questions for me about my home, and I found them surprisingly easy to talk to—easier than Oak by far. They were sisters; that was about all they would tell me of themselves and their history.

"Our story is not nearly as interesting as yours," Mist told me when I pushed to learn more about them.

Fog merely pressed her lips in a thin line and remained silent.

The next morning a noise woke me. It was still dark, but the faintest pinpricks of dawn had begun to poke over the treetops. The mornings had grown chilly, and so I wrapped my blanket around my shoulders as I sat up in bed to look out of the window.

Mist and Fog walked from the palace into the trees. As they walked, Mist lifted her arms and swept them dreamily from one side to the other. Faint clouds drew from nothing and poured into the trees like steam, softening the darkness.

Something about their magic drew me in. I scrambled out of bed and pulled on clothes. I bound my hair back as tightly as I could and ran down the stairs and out one of the side doors. I spotted the swirl of Fog's skirts disappearing into the trees and took off after the sisters. I didn't know why I felt the need to see what they did. Maybe it was because they seemed like *such a natural part of this world, while I was still struggling to feel like I belonged here.*

They walked slowly through the trees, neither of them seeming to care that I was trailing them. Mist kept up her smooth, slow dance, while Fog walked in peaceful quiet next to her.

Then they reached the bridge.

A great arching structure made of carved wooden leaves stretched over the rushing river. I had never been across it—Oak hadn't thought it necessary for me to explore that portion of the forest yet, as it was too close to some of the villages. But the two sisters walked to the very center of the bridge, halfway across. Mist dropped her arms and let her wisps dissipate.

Then Fog screamed.

She sank down, arms thrown back behind her, and roared into the canyon below. Great gray clouds billowed from her mouth and poured over the water. She didn't stop for breath. I grew dizzy watching her scream and scream and scream until the canyon was obscured. I clutched at the tree next to me, grateful to have something solid nearby. I could no longer see the sisters, but after a moment, the screaming stopped, and then their soft footsteps came back toward me.

A cool hand found mine and gently pulled me from the tree.

"Come, child, we shall lead you back," came Mist's soothing voice.

I let her lead me back to Oak's palace, which looked even more otherworldly than normal, wreathed in the gentle mists.

I followed them every morning. I began to wish I had followed Dew and Thaw while they resided in the palace, but the two of them had vanished.

"Dew and Thaw will return in Spring. I am surprised Lord Oak did not introduce you to more of his court, but perhaps it was for the best," Mist told me. "Smoke and Blaze can be... a bit much." She was the only one who spoke to me, much of the time.

Fog seemed to like silence. Perhaps she needed to reserve her voice for her screaming.

CHAPTER 17

Rowan

THREE DAYS BEFORE THE SPRING EQUINOX

Chirps and the beating of many tiny wings woke Rowan at dawn. She groaned and started to pull her blanket over her head to block out the light, but the noise persisted. It kept her from drifting back to sleep, though she couldn't say how it was different from the other mornings in the forest.

For some reason, it sparked her curiosity.

Rowan couldn't shake that sense she had—that something just over the hill was causing the unusual sound, and she ought to go see what it was. After all, this was likely the only time she'd ever venture this far into the enchanted forest, and if something magical and marvelous was within earshot, it would be well worth looking at.

Leaving Keziah slumbering in his bedroll, she climbed what was left of the hill and crept through the trees. At the bottom of the slope lay a marsh that opened onto a pond. They were still close enough to the river that its flooding could have created this marsh, and over time, made it permanent.

Blackbirds with red wings flitted among the reeds, while frogs croaked and insects buzzed. The water was still, except for where the reeds thinned and the pond began. There, ripples billowed out into the water from a figure hovering above its surface, swaying back and forth.

Rowan's fingers went cold, though from awe or fear she couldn't say. The figure looked like a woman with long dark hair, dressed in a rough brown shift. She held a branch in her hand and drew intricate patterns in the air with it, letting it dance over the reeds growing in front of her.

What on earth is she doing? Rowan had to get a closer look. She inched down the hillside, taking care to stay behind the trees and only peeking out every so often. The floating woman maintained her odd, airy dance, swirling the tip of the branch over the bobbing reeds. As Rowan came closer, she began to hear a chorus of chirping coming from the reeds. She saw that a group of the blackbirds had come into the reeds and begun flying about in them, keeping time with the woman's dance.

Rowan stood transfixed, only a few feet from the start of the marsh. It was an oddly beautiful sight, birds and plants swirling all in the same direction, turning back over themselves.

What could it all be for? She wondered. She found she was swaying in almost the same pattern, turning a gentle figure eight without realizing it. She blinked and tried to stay still. It was harder than it should have been. A sweet haze had descended over her, a strangely comforting numbness that left her only with the vague desire to keep moving, to stay a part of the dance conducted by the woman with the branch.

No... That wasn't right. Her movements thick, Rowan forced herself to take a step back up the hill. The feeling faded a little, returning some clarity to her. She made herself look at the woman, trying to make out her face under the curtain of dark hair. She could see pale skin and warm brown eyes, but as sunlight passed over her face, it shifted to dark, bark-like skin and white pits where her eyes had just been. Then it was a normal face again.

I shouldn't be here. Rowan took another step back. A branch snapped beneath her foot.

Without missing a beat of her soundless music, the floating woman turned and looked at Rowan. Once again, her eyes flashed from warm brown to empty white. For a moment, Rowan thought perhaps the woman didn't care she was there, for she didn't stop moving.

Then, suddenly, she made a swiping motion with her branch, as though gathering an armful of nothing toward herself. The birds stopped cold in the air and fell into the water. The reeds withered and disintegrated into nothing. The patch of life on the riverbank turned dead and brown, and the remaining blackbirds flitted off screaming.

The woman drifted over the water toward Rowan, the skirt of her shift gently parting the reeds. The branch she held aloft until she hovered right in front of Rowan. She lowered the branch and let it dance above Rowan's head, as though testing her.

Rowan desperately wanted to turn and run, but she couldn't pry her feet from where they met the ground. She could only watch as the woman slowly began to swirl the same pattern with her branch that had killed the blackbirds, could only whimper as she felt herself once again begin to sway along with it. Something was rising in her throat, something vital that should not be taken out of her this way...

No, she thought, and she reached out and *pushed* the sensation away.

The floating woman drew back and hissed. Whatever had risen in Rowan's throat sank back down instantly. Withdrawing the branch, the woman slithered back across the water, winding her way out of the reeds, until she was across the pond from Rowan. She drifted under the hanging branches of a willow and sank into the water, her hair billowing out as she disappeared.

Rowan stood there for five minutes, thirty, maybe even an hour, trembling. That woman had been about to snuff her out exactly like the sweet little birds now floating in the water before her. *But what made her stop?*

She heard Keziah calling for her, but when she tried to answer, she found her throat bone-dry, unable to make a sound.

He saw her from the top of the hill and came sliding down.

"Why on earth did you wander off like that?" he asked, grabbing her by the shoulder. He looked more frightened than angry, but his expression softened when he saw the look on her face.

"What happened?" he asked in a low voice, looking her over for injury.

"There—" Rowan's voice broke. She swallowed and tried again. "There was a woman on the water."

Keziah's brow furrowed. "On?"

She nodded. "She was... dancing, with a branch, and the birds were dancing, too."

He stared at her for a moment.

"Where did she go?"

Rowan pointed to the willow across the pond. The water was smooth as glass, and the willow fronds swayed ever so slightly in the wind. No sign of the floating woman.

Keziah's lips pressed together grimly.

"That was a willow witch. Likely a young one, if she was only after birds. But even a young one can transfix a human and drain them, if they get the opportunity." He turned back to Rowan. "Be grateful she didn't see you, or otherwise—"

"But she did, she did!" Rowan exclaimed, knees wobbling, "She tried to—she had her, her branch-thing over my head and..." Rowan made a figure-eight motion in the air.

"She did?" Keziah looked thunderstruck. "Then how are you still alive?"

"She s-stopped." Rowan felt tears prickling in her eyes. "I think I tried to push her away, and she stopped. She hissed at me like a cat and sank down in the water over there."

She swiped at her eyes with the back of her hand. She didn't know why she was so upset—she hadn't been hurt, and the willow witch was gone. But Keziah implying that she ought to be dead from her encounter made her want to curl up in her bedroll and never come out again.

When she looked up again, Keziah was staring at her with that expression she was beginning to grow used to—appraisal.

"What?" she snapped, suddenly disgusted with herself for crying.

"A willow witch only lets a potential meal go if it outpowers them," he said, his tone unreadable. "For example, a willow witch would never dare to work their magic on Oak. They know they'd never stand a chance."

Rowan stared at him.

"And do they ever try it on you?" she asked after a moment.

He returned her gaze steadily. But before she could ask the question again, he turned and walked up the hill.

"Come have some breakfast," he called over his shoulder.

Cursing him under her breath, Rowan marched up after him.

They had barely finished eating breakfast when a great *CRACK* rang through the air and white light flashed overhead. Stunned, Rowan blinked her eyes, partially blinded by the momentary brightness. When she regained her vision, she found herself standing alone with both bedrolls; Keziah was hauling himself up the nearest tree. Bits of new leaf fell to the ground as he climbed.

Rowan looked around for a moment, wondering if she ought to climb the tree as well—if he was trying to get away from something, she'd probably do best to follow suit.

But when she reached the base of the tree Keziah had climbed, she found she had a good enough view of what he was staring at—he was looking at the mountains, one hand crooked around a branch for support.

"Oh, no," he breathed.

Rowan followed his gaze. Orange flames licked up the side of the great mountain in the center, and smoke billowed into the hills.

"Damn. Damn, damn, *damn!*" Keziah cursed, grinding his fist into the bark, "He's gone and done it. I only hope—"

There was another loud *CRACK,* and a piece of the mountaintop broke and smashed into the side of the mountain next to it.

"No! Damn that evil—" He dropped back down, swinging himself roughly to the ground again. Rowan couldn't believe how well Keziah moved through the trees, especially for such a large person.

"What is it? What's happened? A fire in the mountains?" she asked breathlessly, watching Keziah roll up his bedroll and fasten it to his pack.

"Yes, a fire in the mountains indeed. But a very unnatural one. Oak called up some lightning, and it looks as though he's trying to force him back from the mountains. The blasted shite-demon!"

"Force who out? And what are you doing?" she asked, panic rising in her as he set his pack aside and pulled out a hunting knife.

"I'm going to try and distract the prick so my friend can escape."

She had never seen him look so angry. His face flushed and he looked like he wanted nothing more than to hit something. His face faltered a little when he finally looked at Rowan.

"I..." What he was about to do seemed to dawn on him. "Stay here. Don't leave this clearing. I'll be back, hopefully soon. If anyone comes by that isn't me, get the hell away from them. I'll find my way back to you somehow."

Despite the fear and uncertainty she felt, Rowan couldn't help but notice a sudden flare within her at the words *I'll find my way back to you.* She wanted to say something, anything, but she couldn't think of a thing, and so she watched Keziah turn away from her and disappear into the trees. Smoke already filtered down the mountain and coated the air with the scent of fire. His frame was slowly swallowed up by foggy white.

Is it the Bear Maiden? That was the only person Keziah would know in the mountains, surely. But from what Keziah had said, Oak had no quarrel with the Bear Maiden, so it didn't make sense that he would attack her or drive her from the mountains. *And Keziah said she comes down to the Forest on the Spring Equinox.*

Whoever Keziah was rushing off to rescue, Rowan had no way of finding anything out, so she threw more wood on the fire and sat leaning against her pack, trying to stay warm. But the smoke grew thicker and thicker. Some rabbits raced through the clearing, followed shortly by a deer and fawn, who struggled to keep up with their mother.

The animals were clearly fleeing the fire. That made Rowan worry that the fire had spread from the mountains to the *prawdziwy las,* possibly in her direction. *I'm sure Keziah knows to keep out of the way of a fire,* she told herself, but she couldn't stop herself imagining him trapped under a burning tree, or choked by smoke, left gasping for air on the forest floor.

Stop it, stop it, stop it. But there was nothing to distract her from her thoughts. Unless... Her eye fell on Keziah's pack. She should leave it where it was—she had no business snooping. But, if the fire *did* get close, she would have to move their packs in order to save their supplies, and she needed to know what was in his pack, just to make sure it wasn't too heavy for her to carry alone.

That's what she told herself as she pulled open the drawstring of his pack. But when she only saw clothing and parcels of food, the disappointment she felt pointed out her ulterior motive. She rooted through it all anyway, taking in how much food was left.

Her hand brushed something hard and rough-edged. Startled, she closed her hand over it. It bit into her palm. She yelped, but she kept hold of it and drew it out of the knapsack.

The thing was round, thin like a disk but curved like a shallow bowl. It was a little smaller than Rowan's palm, and the inside of it was smooth and shiny pink, like the nose of a newborn lamb. She flipped it over. The outside was rough and gray. If she'd seen it lying this side up on the ground, she'd have taken it for a rock, but the inside was lovely as a jewel. Some of her blood had smudged on the thing; she did her best to clean it off with a handkerchief and some water from her waterskin, taking care to avoid the sharp edge. She couldn't tell if Keziah had sharpened it or if it just happened to be deadly keen-edged.

What a strange thing to keep around, she thought as she turned the object from one side to the other, marveling at the contrast between its inside and outside.

When guilt finally prompted her to stop looking at Keziah's possession, she tucked it back where she'd found it, underneath his clothes. Then she pulled the drawstring tight and closed his knapsack. She wondered where he had found such a thing—it certainly didn't seem like anything she'd ever found in the forest.

After a moment, she realized she could hear something. She listened hard. Whatever it was, it was far off, and it almost sounded like the rush of the river, except that it was growing louder. And there was a rhythm to it, a rise and a fall...

Rowan leaped to her feet, her breath coming rapidly. Wingbeats. She could hear the wingbeats of something immense.

The dragon.

She scrabbled at the straps of her knapsack, clumsily pulling them over her shoulders. She started forward, then skidded, remembering Keziah's pack. She stacked it awkwardly on top of her own smaller knapsack, then took off for the nearest tree. For some reason, it made her feel safer to skirt the edges of the trees, as though by staying beneath their branches, she was somehow safer from the giant thing coming closer through the sky.

She had no idea how far away it was, only that the sound of its wings beating grew louder with each second.

I need to find cover, she thought desperately. But then she tripped over a tree root she could have sworn was not there a second earlier. She tumbled, the straps of the packs pulling painfully at her shoulders, and fell much further than she expected into darkness.

When she came to a stop, she lay, stunned, waiting for the sound of the wingbeats. But when they came, they were fainter than she thought they'd be, as though something were dampening the sound.

Pushing herself up onto her elbows, she looked around. The light was dim where she had fallen, but she had a flashback to the day she and Celine had jumped into a ditch and dug a tunnel into the side of it, a pretend house for one of their games. As her eyes got used to the light, she could see she was indeed in a tunnel. The opening was some few feet behind her, spilling morning light over the network of roots that held up the earth.

What could have made this? It had the smooth look of a water-worn cave, but the river wasn't even close to this spot. *An animal, then?* But what animal could dig so smoothly, leaving no trace of claws or paws? And it would have to be an animal of some size to create a tunnel so large.

She stood, brushing dirt from her knees. With the dragon about, she didn't like the idea of returning to the forest above her, so she started off down the tunnel, promising herself she'd turn around if it got too dark to continue.

If the tunnel had been created by an animal, she'd have expected it to slope downward, or at least open up into a den, but it stayed fairly level. She could make out light up ahead of her and never lost her ability to see. *There must be another opening.* She hurried, wondering where it was leading her.

She didn't have long to wonder. The tunnel came to an end, with tiers of tree roots stacked like stairs leading up to a hole that opened to the sky. Rowan poked her head out. There was no sound other than the chirping of birds and the chattering of squirrels. The dragon must have moved on.

She had only just managed to pull herself out of the hole when the ground rumbled and shifted beneath her. She scrambled backward, watching as the tree roots she had just climbed slid back and forth, crumbling earth into the tunnel. The opening closed up, and the dirt settled again, leaving no trace of the tunnel she had just traveled through.

Rowan stood clutching the handle of Celine's axe, staring down at the ground.

The roots.

She looked up sharply at the trees surrounding her. She was certain of it; the trees had created that tunnel and destroyed it as soon as she had exited. But now they stood and pleasantly bobbed their branches in the slight breeze, their new young leaves flickering in the sunlight like tiny candle flames.

Flames, she thought, remembering the forest fire, but the smoke was gone. *The fire must be out, but surely that wouldn't mean the smoke would already be gone, would it?*

What she needed was a view of the mountains. She reached for a branch, thinking to climb the nearest tree, but all of a sudden her feet were swept out from beneath her, and she felt herself being lifted up by something hard and rough. She looked down and found a tree branch wrapping around her middle as it drew her up into the air. It cleared the canopy and stopped, dangling her above the treetops.

She waited for it to drop her, or to draw up another branch and hit her into the sky like a child's ball, but nothing happened. *It's showing me the mountains,* she realized, as she took in the view before her. *It's showing me what I wanted to see.*

And the fire was indeed out. Wisps of smoke still curled up the mountainside, but the orange glow was gone. *How did it get put out? Did it rain?* She didn't think so; the sky was as clear as it had been when she and Keziah had woken up. *Did Keziah somehow...* But how could he possibly put out a forest fire by himself? How could he have even *reached* the mountain that quickly? It didn't make any sense.

She had seen enough, but now, how to get down?

"Er, thank you," she addressed the tree branch holding her. "But I'm finished now. Could you please put me back on the ground?" She wondered if she needed to be specific and say, "Don't drop me," but the tree seemed to know what it was doing. With creaks and groans, the branch drew back into the forest, uncoiling from around Rowan's waist as it set her relatively gently on the ground.

"Much obliged." She awkwardly bobbed a curtsey to the tree—a solid sycamore—and felt a little foolish when there was no discernible response. But either way, the tree had helped her. And other trees, too, if that tunnel was their doing.

I wonder why they're helping me, Rowan thought as she picked her way over mossy tangles of roots, making her way in the direction of the mountains. *I thought they were only loyal to the Oak King.*

"She ought to tread carefully, the young ashling," a croaking voice broke through the peaceful sounds of nature. "The Oak King does not take kindly to usurpers."

Despite the warning, Rowan slipped on a patch of wet moss and fell painfully, jarring her tailbone.

"Sphagnum!" The mossman sat cross-legged on an arching tree root, and at Rowan's naming of him, he stood and bowed in his slithery way.

"A most admirable instruction of the trees, but she would be wise to limit herself. The Oak King believes he is the only one with the right to command the forest. Whenever it seems to favor someone, he is liable to fly into a rage."

"But I didn't instruct them at all." Rowan hauled herself back to her feet, rubbing her lower back where it had collided with a rock. "I only thought I needed to climb up so I could see the fire."

The mossman hissed. "*Fire.*" He shook as he spat the word. "The Oak King had agreed to restrict its use to the end of Summer, to keep the health of the forest. But he has not kept his word." He shook his mossy head mournfully. "There are birds that roost on the cliffside, who build their nests with mud and moss in Spring. Sphagnum does not know if they survived."

Rowan felt sorry for the moss creature. "I didn't know you had friends in the mountains. I'm sorry. I hope they are all right." She didn't know how to properly convey sympathy to a mossman, but he seemed comforted by her words.

"Still she has not found her sister? I gave her directions, and she ought to have followed them."

At this, Rowan bristled. "Why? So your king could capture me, too? Thanks very much for that. Luckily I found someone who can guide me to the Bear Maiden, without any risk of being snapped up by the Oak King."

Or at least, I had *found someone, but now he's disappeared,* she thought ruefully.

Sphagnum perked up.

"She seeks the Bear Maiden, does she? Intends to wish for her sister's freedom, does she?"

Rowan suddenly had the very strong sense that she ought not to have told the mossman anything. But then something strange happened. The mossman leaned forward and spoke in a soggy whisper:

"*The blackened deep, you first must seek*
And circumvent it without fear
But do not wake the sleeping beast
Or you will find your end is near."

He sat back, looking immensely smug for a pile of moss.

Rowan, utterly befuddled, blinked several times. "Is... that supposed to mean something to me?"

In the stories her grandmother told her, sometimes people were given clues or riddles they had to solve, but she had no idea what Sphagnum's words might mean. And besides, he served the Oak King—he couldn't possibly be trying to help her. He'd already tried to lead her astray once.

"She must *think* about what it might mean," Sphagnum pressed, nodding vigorously.

"I think," Rowan said slowly, "that it sounds like more nonsense, and that you're probably just distracting me from finding my sister."

Sphagnum's smugness faded abruptly into irritation. "If the girl thinks it is mere nonsense, then Sphagnum does not have high hopes for her," he snapped. "And she ought not to linger—should the Oak King find her here, he will not be pleased."

Rowan frowned. "He burns the mountain, endangers your fellow mossmen, and you are still loyal to him? Why?"

The mossman bristled, sliding from his root seat up the side of a tree.

"One does not change allegiance overnight. Sphagnum serves the Oak King as he has for centuries; he will do right by the mossmen again. The mossmen must trust."

Somehow Rowan picked out the note of anxiety in his soggy voice.

"Or else?" she prompted.

"Hmph," the creature grunted, shrinking himself into a bright green puddle of fuzz on the tree's trunk. "Not all creatures serve themselves as humans do. The Oak King can command vast fires. If a forest creature were to displease him, he could bring on a most terrible and unseasonable fire, one that kills the seeds in the ground instead of fertilizing the earth. He has done it, too. Better to keep him in good humor. There is very little he wants from mossmen, for his attention is elsewhere."

"And where is that?" Rowan asked, but Sphagnum had clearly tired of their conversation.

His warning given, his puddle of moss morphed back into the green stuff coating the forest floor, and he was gone.

Rowan slept curled between the roots of a tree that night, not wanting to risk a fire or going much further away, in case Keziah found his way back in the night. Several times, loud thundering *BOOMS* rang out across the valley. Rowan woke with a start each time, fearing another bout of lightning and fire, but even after she coaxed one of the trees to lift her up so she could see the mountains, she could not determine where the sounds came from. She knew they must be coming from the mountains, but whatever caused them was invisible to her. She managed a few uninterrupted hours of sleep until the first slight fingers of dawn crept around the edges of the trees.

CHAPTER 18

Nash

Mist found me stuffing clothing into a knapsack in my room.

"Child, what are you doing?" she asked quietly.

"I'm bored out of my mind. I think I need a change of scenery."

It was nearing the end of September, almost a week since Oak had left, and without lessons, I felt aimless and idle. Back home, we harvested magnalia fruits this time of year, and I was itching to do something. I even wondered if I could justify going home for a visit, though the thought of returning when I had not yet mastered my powers quickly drove the idea from my mind.

Mist looked troubled. "I do not think it wise for you to leave this part of the forest."

I gave her what I hoped was a reassuring smile. "I'll be fine."

"Nash... You are still very young, and..."

There was something she wanted to tell me, but she seemed to have trouble finding the right words.

"I know you are not a girl. But to many humans, a person's body can mean only one thing. If you get too close to the villages, if someone were to see you and guess that—"

I understood what she was trying to say. She thought somebody might *hurt me, if they were to realize that my body did not match my identity as a boy.*

"Is that how things are in the villages?" I asked, continuing to stuff my belongings in the sack.

She nodded. "They do terrible things sometimes."

"Why doesn't Oak do something about it? Doesn't he rule them?"

Mist looked uncomfortable. "He... doesn't seem to care. Or perhaps he doesn't notice it."

Both were equally likely.

"Don't worry about me," I told Mist grimly. "I won't go near the villages. I just want to explore a little."

And see if I could find my way to the Bear Maiden. My wish had been burning in my heart all these years, and this could be my chance to finally see it come true.

Mist still looked doubtful.

"The Holly King has not yet arrived, and I do not think the Oak King would like to hear of you exploring the forest unaccompanied."

I gave her as bright a smile as I could muster.

"Well. It's a good thing he isn't here, isn't it?"

She said nothing as I left the room.

Fog also said nothing as I passed her on my way out the door, though she raised a hand in farewell. Even though Mist was the one who usually spoke to me, I tended to prefer Fog. Mist was too concerned with keeping Oak happy, even though he wasn't even there.

I noticed an odd amount of mist still hanging around the forest as I moved through the trees. Perhaps it was Mist's way of trying to deter me from going. I found myself irritated. Was I not a "real" enough boy for her, that she worried about me running across some small-minded villagers?

I crossed the arching leaf bridge over the river gorge. My pack bounced on my back as I strode through the now familiar trees, aiming myself toward the mountains in the distance.

After a few hours, I began to feel uneasy. It wasn't the forest—the trees sang faintly in the back of my mind, glad of my presence and my powers. I checked over my shoulder several times, the back of my neck starting to prickle.

It was the strangest thing. I almost had the feeling that I was being watched.

A patch of strangely dense mist swirled through the branches of nearby rowan. It moved so differently that I stepped closer for a better look.

Then it leaped at me.

It wasn't mist at all—it was a creature as long as I was tall, white, muscular, all claws and teeth. It knocked me to the ground, scrabbling at my face and chest with its claws. I could feel my skin tearing, could feel it crush the breath from my lungs.

I *cannot* die this way, not in this body, *I thought as I struggled to breathe.*

"Snowbelly, cease," a low voice barked.

The creature sprang back from me, sniveling and cowering as it slunk away, its belly dragging along the ground. Its red rat eyes stayed fixed on me, but it kept moving, slinking off into the trees and out of sight.

I lay where I was, dazed and stinging from where the creature had clawed me. A pair of boots came into view. Their owner dropped to his knees, and a bearded face swam into my vision.

"I apologize," he said gently, turning me onto my back. "He thinks he does me a service, clearing out unwanted visitors, but I'd prefer he let me deal with..."

He trailed off, his brow furrowing. I could see him taking in my features, could see his confusion deepen.

He seemed to come back to himself. "Here, for the pain—"

He pressed a hand to my forehead, and a warmth flooded over my face, trickling through the rest of me. The many wounds on my chest and face flared briefly, then numbed. I reached up to touch my cheek and found the claw marks had vanished, leaving only a little half-dried blood behind.

I sat up, feeling my ribs. They were sore from the creature's weight, but nothing had broken.

The man eyed me, and I eyed him right back.

"Who—" we both began at the same time.

He broke off, smiling. I found myself tempted to smile back.

"My name is Nash. I am here to study with Oak," I told him.

He raised his eyebrows. "Really? That is most... unexpected. He never mentioned that he had finally selected an heir."

It was my turn to furrow my brow. "An heir? Is that what I am?"

The man looked as puzzled as I felt. "That's what I assumed. Has he not mentioned it?"

I shook my head.

"I suppose I should not make any further assumptions. Why has he invited you to study with him, then?" the man asked politely.

"I'm his... He was..." Not for the first time, I struggled to name exactly what Oak was to me.

"Did he sire you?" the man asked softly.

I nodded, relieved not to have to say it.

"And you have his power?"

"His and my mother's."

The man paused, considering.

"He... did not tell me any of this. Strange. Is he still at the palace?"

I shook my head. "He left nearly a week ago."

The man sighed.

"That's a shame. We haven't spoken in some time."

He glanced at me.

"Well. In any case, I am pleased to meet you, Nash. You can call me Holly."

I blinked. Then it all clicked. Of course this was the Holly King. I had been so dazed by the creature's attack that I hadn't realized it yet.

"That... that thing that attacked me—you know it?" I asked, glancing uneasily at the trees around us. I hoped it would not come back.

"Snowbelly is one of my creatures. He comes down from the mountains occasionally to patrol the forest, though I've tried to tell him it isn't necessary. He doesn't care much for Oak—my guess is he sensed your power and thought you were him."

"Why doesn't he like Oak?" I asked, wondering if the bizarre animal had also attacked Oak at some point.

Holly scratched his beard.

"It's a long story. Why don't I tell you while we walk back to the palace?"

My face fell, just as Holly's gaze fell on the pack on my back.

"Ah. Unless you had other plans?"

I hesitated. This was what I had been dreaming of since the first time my mother had told me the story of the wish-granter.

"What if you joined me for dinner?" Holly suggested, his face lighting up. "I've been longing for a decent conversation for months—the dragons are all in foul moods because of the weather, and the gnomes have all burrowed into their caves to get ready for Winter."

A grin spread across my face. I could have used a good conversation myself. And besides, he looked so hopeful, I couldn't turn him down.

"I can always go another time," I said at last, unable to pass up the opportunity to hear Holly's stories. And it was true—I would have plenty of time to go seek out the Bear Maiden. Besides, the Holly King resided in the mountains for half the year—perhaps he knew where I could find her.

He grinned at me. "Excellent. I suppose I'd better start at the beginning. Oak and I met when I had just begun traveling—I called it 'adventuring' back then, because I was eighteen years old and an idiot. I passed through his village and he decided to join me..."

I listened as we walked back the way I had come, enjoying the story. Holly left no details vague, answered my questions, and seemed to genuinely enjoy talking with me. It was a pleasant change from Oak's indifference.

Celine pressed her back into a maple tree, too afraid to breathe.

The pad of paws drew closer to her hiding place.

"The Oak King attacked early again this year," came a voice as gentle as a mother singing to her babe.

"I fear it has become a habit," returned a deeper, gruffer voice.

"I do not like the fires. Not so early."

"I do not like how he has changed Narra."

The first speaker hissed faintly. "You feel for the dragon?"

"Her people and mine are not so different. How long until the Oak King decides he can control us all better if we are bound with wood?"

A pause.

"He would not do that," the first speaker said, though they didn't sound so sure.

"I do not think we can say what he would or would not do," the second speaker countered. "Not given the events of the past five years. This war with the Holly King—it is vengeance he seeks, nothing more. I do not like to imagine what he will do, to ensure that he gets it."

The voices were so close now. Celine squeezed her eyes shut, her back pressed so hard into the tree that the bark cut into her skin.

Please don't see me please don't see me please don't see me...

The steps came to a halt.

"I should warn you, Carzen, your words are most peculiar today," the first speaker said slowly. "If I did not know you better, I might even say they sound treasonous."

Celine risked opening her eyes a fraction. A colossal cat—a panther, black as night and at least a head taller than Charly—faced a creature with the head of an eagle and the body of a lion.

A griffon, Celine realized, eyes widening.

The griffon bristled, his feathers ruffling along his back.

"Then it is a good thing you know me so well, Sezara," he replied. "For I could never speak ill of the Oak King."

"Indeed," Sezara agreed. "At the rate the Oak King discovers traitors among us, we must all take care. Now, let us finish this patrol."

The two creatures passed Celine by and vanished into the trees.

She waited. A minute. Two minutes. Ten, maybe twenty.

Then she sagged, her back scraping against the tree as she slid to the ground.

She had only just got herself free, and she had been a mere breath away from getting caught again.

I need to be more careful, she told herself. She'd had only moments to hide herself—some kind of tremor, or *something,* had alerted her to the creatures' approach. Still, she hadn't found a very good hiding place, but they hadn't seen her. That seemed odd, especially if the panther and the griffon really were patrolling the forest for the Oak King.

She put it from her mind. It didn't matter as much as getting back to Irys.

A glance at the sky told her it was almost evening. She would need shelter for the night, perhaps more; she needed to build up her strength if she was going to make it all the way across the forest in the next few days.

And then I'll never come back, she promised herself fiercely. *I will never set foot here again, never shoot another animal, never cut down another tree.*

It had almost cost her everything.

She hurried onward, trying to go the opposite direction of the patrol. She could just barely hear the sound of rushing water, and she realized she was parched with thirst. She sped up. Water could also mean fish, game, edible plants—she needed to reach it.

She rounded a bend and—there it was. A curtain of water cascading from a tumble of mossy rocks into a pool nearly twice the size of the millpond back home. She sank to her knees at the water's edge and scooped up handful after handful, splashing down her front as she drank.

Shivering, she stood, suddenly worried that she might have been spotted in her haste to get to the water. Desperation had overcome her and she hadn't been careful.

I need rest, she thought wearily, wiping her mouth on the back of her hand, *and shelter.*

Her eye fell on the waterfall—a beautiful thing, though she was almost too tired to appreciate it. As she watched the water spill over the rocks and swirl into the pool, her eye was drawn to something *behind* the falls. A darkness.

A cave. Her eyes widened, and at once she went over to the tumble of rocks. Peering behind the sheet of cascading water, she strained to see into that darkness. It looked like enough space for her.

She pressed her back to the stones and edged along, trying to keep out of the spray of water. She would have a difficult time drying off, especially if she wasn't able to build a fire tonight.

The narrow ledge opened into the cave, and Celine waited for her eyes to adjust to the darkness.

It was a decent amount of space, larger than she'd initially thought. Much of the ground was rock, with jutting boulders and smooth stones. Very little soil, though great roots stretched from ceiling to floor to what small patches of dirt there were.

Celine set down her bag. All she wanted to do was curl up on the ground and sleep. But she knew she needed to take care of a few things first.

She forced herself to inch back outside, staying hidden behind the curtain of water until she was sure there was no one about. Then she hurried through the trees, collecting an armload of wood and sticks. She paused long enough to set up a quick snare in a narrow little trail littered with rabbit prints. Then she returned to the cave.

She built a small fire. Soon she was roasting an apple on a stick, struggling to keep her eyes open as she turned it. She needed to eat something before she went to sleep. She had traveled all day on half-wasted muscles, and there was no way she would be able to travel again soon if she did not regain her strength.

She ate the apple, some cheese, and the last of the bread. Then she curled up as close to the fire as she dared, resting her head against a rock.

It was nothing close to comfortable, but she would sleep on rocky ground for the rest of her life if it meant never setting foot in the Oak King's palace ever again.

Irys, she thought miserably as she closed her eyes, *I'm coming home to you. I swear it.*

CHAPTER 20

Keziah

Keziah soared over the treetops, his eagle, Isbel, keeping low enough to just barely brush the highest reaching leaves. The dragon was busy setting fire to the clusters of brush and small trees leading up into the mountains, but if it were to look up at any given moment, he wanted to give it only the slightest chance of catching sight of him.

It helped that night was falling.

He nudged the eagle, directing him around the other side of the mountain. Isbel was almost the size of an elk, which made her just about the perfect size for Keziah to ride. They needed to break the dragon's focus, distract her somehow.

But as they rounded the side of the mountain and the next slope came into view, Keziah saw a dark shape move across a scree and dart into a cave.

"No, Holly, don't move now," Keziah moaned, "just *wait.*"

But the dragon had already taken off. She was turning her head, directing her flaming mouth to the rocky slope above her. She landed almost sideways on the slope, her claws scrabbling for purchase among the rocks. She reared her head back, drawing in breath to blast fire into the cave.

Keziah squeezed the eagle's shoulders. She let out a shriek, high and piercing.

The dragon's head snapped in their direction. Keziah kept his body flat to the eagle's, praying he wasn't visible against the tawny gold of her back. She darted as a lick of flame spat toward them, circling up above the dragon, who let out a roar and sprang into the air after them.

She could smell him, he was almost certain of it, but he hadn't let her get close enough to get a good look at him. Provided he could get away, she wouldn't be able to give Oak a description. He hoped.

But as the eagle swooped to reenter the trees, the dragon veered off instead of following them. Keziah's heart sank as he wheeled the eagle around, just in time to see the dragon descend to allow a man upon her back. Once he had mounted, the two of them flew back toward the mountains.

"Damn!" Keziah curled his hands into fists. "So he wants to do his own dirty work now, does he? Damn him!"

Keziah squeezed the sides of the eagle with his thighs. "Come on. We've got some more fires to put out. That should get his attention."

But as he looked up at the mountain, a white flash of light nearly blinded him, and he almost fell from the eagle's back. A great *CRACK* rent through the air, and something dark hurtled out of the cave, sailing over the treetops and out of sight, leaving the dragon and her rider behind.

Keziah stared in the direction the figure had flown. Then, while the dragon and her rider appeared to start conferring about what to do next, he urged the eagle forward again, toward the nearest fire.

Now that Holly was no longer safe in the mountains, all Keziah could do was keep Oak off his trail for as long as he could.

CHAPTER 21

Nash

Frost arrived bitter and blue, their spiky garments jingling faintly like coins in a pocket. It was only a few days after Holly had arrived. I answered the door.

"Please direct me to the Holly King—I must make my report at once," they said, bustling in past me.

My skin stung where they brushed against me. Frost hurried anxiously at my side, eager to see their king.

"Lord Holly," they burst out when we entered Holly's study. "I have news I must share with you."

"Welcome, Frost," Holly said, a smile twitching at the corners of his mouth. He seemed unsurprised by Frost's demeanor. "I hope your journey has been pleasant."

"Yes, yes, quite," Frost waved a hand, which sent a shower of icy spray all over the wall behind them. "The Oak King has left the country again, headed for lands unknown. None of his sentinels know where he has gone this time, just like last year!"

Holly cleared his throat and glanced at me. "Frost, I now know the reason Oak left this past Winter."

Frost stared at me, then looked back at Holly. "Surely not," they said slowly, realization dawning on them.

"This is Nash. He has inherited Oak's powers, as well as those belonging to his mother," Holly told them.

"Then... Then he has selected an heir at last?"

Holly's eyes met mine for a moment.

"I... do not believe he has. True, he is teaching Nash to use his powers, but he has not explained the Bear Maiden's proclamation to him. In fact, he failed to mention it at all."

Frost looked thunderstruck. "But then, why teach the boy at all, if he does not mean to pass his crown to him?"

Holly sighed and leaned his chin on one hand. "I am not sure. Perhaps he simply wishes to make sure Nash is capable of taking up his seasons before he makes the offer."

We had discussed this at length. I had told Holly that Oak wanted to teach me to master my powers for safety's sake, but Holly didn't think Oak was telling the complete truth.

Frost looked extremely skeptical. "I don't believe one bit of it," they said stoutly. "He rages and blusters over the Bear Maiden's commands for centuries, then suddenly decides to play along? Forgive me, my Lord, but that does not sound like the Oak King I know."

"I agree, Frost, but let us give him the benefit of the doubt for now. Nash is here and wishing to learn as much as he can. Let us all swear to see to his education this season so that he may return home as soon as possible."

"Actually," I interrupted, unable to keep the question inside me any longer. "There was something I wanted to ask you about."

Holly waited, but I glanced at Frost, feeling uncomfortable at the thought of bringing it up in front of them.

Holly seemed to understand.

"Frost, could you give us a moment of privacy?" he asked.

Frost bowed, their face still troubled, and exited the study.

"The Bear Maiden," I said as soon as the door closed behind Frost. "I'd like to try and find her before I go."

Holly looked stunned.

"You... have a wish you'd like to make?"

I nodded fiercely. For some reason, my heart was racing. I needed to know if he could help me find her.

Holly took a deep breath, his brow creasing.

"*This wish—is it something that could be attained in another manner? I ask because the road to the Bear Maiden is incredibly treacherous, even for beings with powers like us. And there is no guarantee that you would find her.*"

"*I-I can't get what I want any other way,*" I said, my voice cracking. The answer couldn't be no, not after leaving my home and coming all this way. "*It... my body. I need her to change my body.*"

Holly looked puzzled. "*An injury you need healed? Some kind of...*" He trailed off when he saw my face.

"*I want my body to match who I am,*" I said, clenching my hands.

Realization dawned on his face. "*Ah,*" he said softly. "*Yes, it makes sense that you would need the Bear Maiden's magic. You are certain?*"

I nodded.

He rubbed a hand through his beard, lost in thought.

"*Well, I cannot promise we will find her. But I will do my best to guide you there. Not this year,*" he warned, seeing my face light up. "*Your powers are not yet strong enough—I would not risk you against the mountain's creatures as you are now. But let us see how things stand in a year or so.*"

"*A whole year?*" I burst out, disappointed.

"*Nash, it will be worth it,*" he assured me. "*Believe me—the mountains hold a darkness that the forest does not. I will not bring you there unprepared.*"

I argued furiously, but he would not be swayed.

CHAPTER 22

Rowan

TWO DAYS BEFORE THE SPRING EQUINOX

Unable to sleep any longer, Rowan rose and rooted in the packs for food. As she munched on walnut bread, she tried to make up her mind. Time was running short. She needed to find the Bear Maiden before she made her way into the forest. But other than a sense of how to find the mountains, she had no idea of how to actually find her.

I should have made Keziah draw me a map or something. Keziah. She wondered what he was doing, where he was, if he was headed back toward her or still fighting a fire somewhere. If he had even reached the mountains yet. She frowned.

Keziah had said it would take them the better part of a week to reach the mountains. But from the way he had spoken as he left, he thought he would reach the fire in time to distract Oak and make him stop what he was doing. It just didn't make any sense; he would never have made the two day journey fast enough. Would he?

Rowan rubbed at her temples. She knew there were things Keziah had not told her about himself. That was fair; they were practically strangers, and he seemed to have good reasons for secrecy. But now she was left alone without direction or the comfort of information, and she had no idea what she ought to do.

I'd better not go much further. I'll stay in this area until something makes me move.

First, she decided she was overdue for a bath. As politely as she could, she asked an elm if it knew the direction of the river. It shifted, its trunk groaning as it twisted and bent northeast. She bowed her head in thanks and, armed with a bar of soap and a fresh change of Keziah's clothes, she headed in that direction.

The river was perhaps marginally warmer than it had been the day she washed at Keziah's cottage.

I am so tired of being cold. And of being outside, she thought miserably, trying to comb tangles out of her wet hair. *Oh, crumbs.* She gave up and began twisting her hair into two braids. *At least it's clean.*

She peered at her reflection in the cool water. Bedraggled was the only word that came to mind, and she thought longingly of her warm robe and cozy slippers back at home. Wistfully, she made her way back to the packs by the elm tree. She sniffed at the bag of coffee, wishing she could spare a moment to brew herself a cup, but she made herself pack everything up and head for the campsite of the previous night. She didn't want Keziah to go off in another direction to look for her if he came back.

She had only gone a few paces before a branch sank down in front of her, stopping her in her tracks. She looked up at the tree. The oak stood motionless, its branch blocking her next step.

"Erm, excuse me," she said, and she went to step over the branch.

Another branch lunged out, this time from a nearby yew, and it stacked on top of the oak branch, giving her no room to step over it.

"Oh, I..." She looked between the two trees. "Should I not go back this way?"

Neither tree moved. Slowly she turned and took a tentative step to the side. The two branches shifted with her, keeping her from passing by their trees in the direction of the campsite. She tried going directly to the oak tree and skirting around its base, but a quaking aspen bent down and whipped its thin branches out in a fan in front of her.

"But why?" she exploded finally. "Why won't you let me pass?"

Nothing, of course. The trees only kept their branches blocking her way, and at last she turned and strode away in the opposite direction.

"Fine. Clearly you'll let me know if I'm going the wrong way, so I won't bother thinking about it myself."

The faintest voice in her head reminded her she ought to be polite to the trees, but they hadn't been so very polite to her themselves. Whatever the case, she found herself directed north again, and any time she tried to shift direction, even slightly, a tree would lean down and block her path.

This was what I hoped for, wasn't it? Direction? She thought wryly as the river came into view. But the trees ended at the riverbank. She looked at a willow, whose long tendrils of branches had only the barest coating of their trademark millions of leaves, straining toward the water.

"Shall I cross?" she asked it, a little irritably.

Nothing moved. *Maybe willows don't act up as much as other trees,* she mused. She looked at the water. She didn't like the idea of crossing it by herself. The river ran high, fed by snowmelt from the mountains and the forest.

Her reluctance at last prompted her to slide the packs from her back, find a comfortable spot to sit, and pull out her quilt. She needed to do something that wasn't trekking through the forest or finding another way to get sopping wet, and this was the only home-like thing she had with her, so she set to embroidering with a vengeance.

The first spool of thread she pulled out gave her pause. Its pink pearly color reminded her of the inside of the object in Keziah's pack. She rubbed the thread between her fingers for a moment, then passed the end through the eye of her needle. She began to stitch.

Of course I'm not doing this because I think he'll be my husband some-day, she reminded herself. *I barely know him. I just like whatever that thing is—it's pretty.* And what did it matter what went on her quilt, after all? She wanted to sew things that mattered to her, or beautiful things that had struck her somehow. The strange smooth sharp thing in Keziah's pack was unlike anything else she had ever seen—it felt right to depict it somewhere, and this as her only available medium.

Besides, I don't even know if I like him all that much. Most of the time.

But of course, she did like him. It was impossible not to like him. Besides his mildness and his sarcasm and his deep knowledge of the forest, he was a fine looking young man. She poked her finger through the quilt and yelped, more out of anger at herself than out of pain.

Do not *be silly,* she ordered herself. *You don't know him. He doesn't know you. Don't go making things awkward for yourself by getting ideas into your head.* Her father's cruel words trickled through her head—*not pretty enough to attract that kind of attention.* She shook her head. His voice was the last one she wanted echoing in her mind.

And so she stitched, switching the pink thread for a dark gray-brown for the outside. *I wish I knew what it was called,* she thought as she added one of the bumpy ridges she remembered it having. It all felt odd to her; sitting by the river in the middle of a forest where her elders had forbidden her to go, waiting for a boy she barely knew to return to help her find the sister she knew so little about, as it turned out. And she was sewing, to boot.

An odd activity for an odd situation, she thought grimly.

Her stomach rumbled, so she finally rolled up her embroidery, tucked it into her pack, and rummaged around for some lunch. She'd hoped she'd somehow missed a roll of sausage or something more savory, but all she found was more walnut bread and fruit. She was getting so tired of the bread that she considered not eating at all, but her groaning stomach convinced her it was wiser to eat than to starve.

She had just pulled the parcel of bread out of the pack when something large and dark fell from the sky above her and crashed into a thornbush.

She ducked behind the pack, scared breathless by the sudden violence. When nothing came and tore the pack from in front of her, she slowly raised her head and looked over the top of it.

Something black flapped from inside the thornbush; a large raven was snarled up between rows of prickly branches, making pitiful squawking sounds as it tried to free itself.

"Oh, dear." Rowan hurried forward, pulling out her knife.

The raven, seeing her approach, thrashed even more fiercely, streaking the dirt below it with blood.

"No, no, hush," she spoke with as calm and soft of a voice as she could, gripping one of the thorny branches at its base. "I'm trying to get you free. Please try not to move—you're getting all cut up."

The raven paused, and for a moment she wondered if it had understood her, but it must have only stopped to catch its breath, for when she knelt down, it threw itself this way and that again, straining to get free.

She worked as quickly as she could, her own fingers pricked and bleeding all over as she sawed through the branches that had trapped the poor bird. Some of the thorns were so long they had stuck entirely *through* the bird's wings. When she cut the last branch loose, the raven hurled itself past Rowan, trying to fly off, but either it was too wounded or the branches still stuck to its wings weighed it down too much. It flopped miserably on the ground, still struggling to get up again.

"Here." Rowan knelt and gently pulled at one of the thorn branches, hoping she wasn't hurting the bird too much. "Just try and keep still."

The raven let out a great shuddering breath, and as she watched, the raven's feathered form morphed, the lines of its body shifting and swirling into something else entirely. The lines settled again, and the body of a man, clothed in black, lay on the ground before Rowan.

She dropped her knife.

"Oh," she whispered, wide-eyed. Of the magics she'd seen thus far in the forest, this was one of the more surprising. Of course, she'd heard stories of people cursed into animal form, or others who could change their shape at will, but never had she dreamed she would come across it herself.

The man was unconscious, but she saw his chest rise and fall—he was alive, at least for the time being. She knelt down and gently shook his arm.

"Are you all right?" she asked gently.

He didn't wake.

Oh, dear. She looked up at the sky. The clouds were gray—it could just as easily rain as not, and whatever was wrong with the person lying before her, it certainly wouldn't be improved with a cold. His cheeks were gaunt and there were dark shadows under his eyes—he looked as though a meal and a full night's sleep were distant dreams. His beard was long and tangled, hair blacker than Keziah's. But she noted that, despite his unkempt appearance, his tattered clothes had once been fine

—she could feel the excellent quality of the black fabric. Looking closer, she saw that there was a network of embroidery over his shirt, though it was in black thread, which made it difficult to read the design from a distance.

Her hand felt wet and she pulled it back, damp with blood. Horrified, she yanked his sleeve up. Thorns stuck out of his arms and torso—when he'd crashed through the thorn bush as a raven, he must have been impaled many times. Rowan would have thought that changing back into a human would have rid the man of the thorns, but clearly whatever magic was at work here didn't agree.

She got her knapsack, pulled out the bag of healing supplies, and tore a shirt into strips for bandages. Then she cut away the man's black shirt.

As she pulled away the collar, she gasped, her fingers faltering. A pale, vicious scar ran across the base of the man's neck. Two others exactly like it ran at the seams where his arms met his shoulders. She could even see another, just above the line of his trousers.

"What happened to you?" she whispered as she made herself focus on the task at hand. She pulled out every thorn she could find, moving slowly so she didn't break off the tips and leave the poor man with an infection. Then she spread yarrow salve over the wounds and wrapped the worst ones in bandages. It was odd, to tend to a stranger, particularly one who didn't even realize she was there.

She was just pulling out another of Keziah's shirts over the man's head when he gasped and struggled to sit up.

"He's coming!" He choked for breath, hands scrabbling at his chest in panic.

"It's alright, there's no one—"

"He's coming! He's coming! I have to—"

Their words were cut off by a great roar.

CHAPTER 23

Nash

I had assumed, with Oak gone, that my lessons would pause until his return in Spring. To my surprise, a week after Holly's arrival, he knocked on my door early in the morning.

"I thought we might take a walk," he said.

I saw that he was already dressed in a warm blue cloak and thick-soled boots.

"Perhaps I could help you practice with the trees."

"The trees?" I was already halfway reaching for my cloak, but his words made me pause. "What do you mean?"

Holly's brow creased. "Commanding the trees. Surely Oak has worked with you on that?"

"He told me he's the only one who's supposed to command the trees."

Holly threw back his head and laughed. "What a ridiculous thing to say! I suppose he also didn't mention that I have the exact same power over them that he does?"

He smile faded as I shook my head.

"Well, by the gods. How does he expect you to master all of your powers if you don't practice? I know he doesn't like to share control, but this is important."

I fiddled with the hem of my cloak and didn't respond. It struck me as odd, too, but I didn't know Oak as well as Holly did.

Holly cleared his throat. "In any case, it would do you good to work with your powers. Will you join me?"

I was bored out of my mind after being cooped up in the palace, so I agreed at once.

The Autumn forest was a thing of beauty and despair. The foliage turned copper, scarlet, orange, and yellow as the leaves died, spilling from the treetops like handfuls of coins. The underbrush wilted and withered. Once, through the trees, I caught a glimpse of a grand woman dressed in a trailing brown gown. She ran a hand along a patch of vibrant green ferns. They shriveled at her touch, slumping to the ground. Her work done, she vanished into the shadows of the trees.

"Who is that?" I whispered to Holly as we crossed over the bridge. The river was full of dead leaves that glittered like fish scales in the weak Autumn sunlight.

"That is Wither," Holly replied. "One of my allies. She and Oak dislike each other rather strongly, and she refuses to come live in the palace. I'm afraid her companion, Decay, shares the same sentiment. We will likely only see them out here in the forest."

I wondered that Oak had done to make Holly's allies refuse to live in his palace, even when he wasn't there.

We came to an opening in the trees and Holly stopped.

"This should do nicely," he said, scanning the trees around us. "A good mix of different tree types. Good."

He turned back to me. "Now..." He paused, frowning.

"What's the matter?" I asked nervously, remembering how unpleasant my lessons with Oak had been.

"I'm trying to remember how I started when I first received my powers. I'm afraid it was such a long time ago that the memory is rather foggy. I seem to recall..." He lifted a hand toward the beech tree beside us. "I was sleeping among a tree's roots when I realized I could feel the tree, hear it the same way I heard animals moving through the forest. And it suddenly struck me that I could influence it. I told the tree to grow a new branch, and it did."

He bit his lip. "But I'm not certain if what worked for me will be helpful to you. After all, you've had your powers since birth—quite a different situation entirely from mine and Oak's. What do you think, Nash?"

I considered what he'd said. Oak's lessons had mainly taken place in the palace, with strict instructions from him on what I was to do and how I was to accomplish it. Oak had never once asked me what I thought about his teaching methods.

"I think..." I went over to the beech tree and settled at its base, placing my hands on the roots that arched up from the earth. I closed my eyes. Instantly, I felt that hum of life, that presence I had felt in every seed I had sprouted. It felt like someone returning my gaze, waiting.

"H-hello," I said, feeling extremely self-conscious.

The presence did nothing.

I was being a fool. Of course trees didn't care about human pleas-antries.

Grow, *I told it.*

It resisted. It could feel the chill of Autumn, the lingering death of its own leaves. But I urged it again, GROW.

And I felt it comply. I looked up and watched its branches stretch, felt sap pouring to the tips of every twig. Buds popped and unfurled new lime-colored leaves—a wash of green amid all the yellow and brown of the decaying forest.

"Good," said Holly from beside me. "Excellent work, especially for your first time."

I flushed with pride. I couldn't remember Oak ever complimenting me.

"Now, how about trying something else?"

My hands slipped off the beech roots.

"Something else? What else can trees do besides grow and die?"

Holly grinned. He spread his fingers and reached for the beech tree. It groaned and bent its crown low to the ground, splaying its branches at Holly's feet. He stepped lightly onto the thickest one, and then the tree rose up again, carrying him into the canopy.

"Try it!" he called down to me.

Excitement rushed through my veins. I hadn't thought anything like this was possible. I ran over to a nearby willow and pressed a hand to its bark, willing the tree to bend and lift me the way the beech had for Holly.

Instead, its thin tendrils whipped around my waist and hoisted me up. Holly laughed as the willow branches deposited me on a branch of his beech tree, and I found I couldn't keep from laughing either.

"The trees certainly take some liberties with us when it isn't our season." He held out a hand and helped me to my feet. "I think you'll find them far more responsive to your instructions come Spring."

"I mean, technically it did what I asked," I chuckled, brushing dead leaves from my sleeves. "Even if it chose to go about it its own way."

"In any case, don't feel too bad about it. The only person the trees obey without question is the Bear Maiden—not even Oak gets the forest to do what he wants all the time, no matter how he blusters at it."

This made me feel a great deal better, both about my powers and about Oak. He presented himself as a true master of his realm, but in reality, he struggled, too. I desperately wished that Holly could be the one to teach me to use my magic. But I quickly realized that would never work.

Holly did not have the same powers as I did. Where Oak and I both had the powers of fire, warmth, and storms, Holly had the power of snow and rain, and he could speak to beasts. Aside from our powers over the forest, the only other power we shared was control over water. And since that was the only power I had practiced since my birth, I didn't need his help learning to control it. A pity—Holly was a good teacher, and an even better friend.

I went walking with Holly many times that Winter, shivering enough to come apart from the cold. He would find creatures that had stayed out too long or gone too long without food—squirrels who hadn't burrowed into their nests in time, birds who hadn't flown and now were too weak to travel south, green pixies that had failed to slip behind the veil before the first frost. He would cup them in his hands or lay his fingers against their fur. Sometimes he talked to them until they struggled to their feet and found their way to warmth. Other times, he talked them to their deaths, easing their pains along the way. He was always kind.

I watched Holly leave at the start of Spring, returning to his mountains. He never seemed truly at home in the palace, his eyes always cast toward the imposing darkness lining the treetops to the north. But the forest was a kind, peaceful place while he ruled, for all that the weather was harsh. It taught me something—that death and the ruin brought on by the cold wasn't cruel and didn't have to be.

Oak returned a few days later.

CHAPTER 24

Rowan

The wood dragon. Rowan cast about wildly, trying to guess which direction it was coming from. Her patient seemed not to care—he scrambled to his feet and staggered, falling against a tree.

"You're hurt, you can't possibly run like that," Rowan hissed at him, going and helping steady him.

But he seemed beyond reasoning. His dark eyes darted this way and that, not focusing on anything.

"I must get out, I must get out," he mumbled, falling to his knees.

The roar came again, louder this time, and Rowan caught another whiff of smoke.

She couldn't let the dragon find them.

She joined the man on his knees and put her hands against the ground. She tried to think of what she had done when the mushrooms had threatened to envelop her and the tree had moved to save her—it *must* have, there was no other reason why she could have suddenly reached it.

"Please," she whispered desperately. "Please!"

And the ground rumbled and broke around them. Roots shot up and started twining together over their heads. Layer upon layer twisted, blocking out all daylight. The ground beneath Rowan shuddered and she felt them drop. Then all was still.

A weight suddenly sagged against her and she nearly fell over. Her companion seemed to have lost consciousness again. She tried to push him back up but there was no room in the tiny enclosure of roots. She had to lean back against its wall, his head laying on her shoulder.

What did I get us into? She wondered as she absentmindedly stroked his hair, as she'd done when the younglings were little and needed someone to hold them while they slept.

Another roar resounded, though it was more muffled than the others. Rowan thought that they must be underground.

Then everything lurched. Something snuffed and huffed overhead. Rowan held her breath. The dragon must have landed. Rowan found a crack in the roots that hadn't been covered up. She could see the great wooden haunch of the wood dragon.

"There's nothing here," a voice snapped.

Rowan heard something slide and hit the ground, then footsteps. The dragon had a rider?

"Are you sure there isn't something wrong with your nose? You lost his trail after just a few hours."

A creaking growl rumbled, making the root enclosure tremble. Rowan shifted closer to the opening for a better look.

A man, handsome and golden, came into view, staring intently at the forest. His eyes passed over the area sheltering Rowan and her sleeping companion without a flicker.

The dragon snuffed at the sandy riverbank, as though trying to catch the scent of something.

"I don't see anything," the man said curtly, turning back to the dragon. The dragon growled and sank its claws into the riverbank. It stuck its head up in the air and breathed in through its monstrous nostrils, shifting its head back and forth like a dog who has caught wind of a squirrel.

"Stop it." The man kicked wet sand at the dragon. "You useless thing. What good are all of these enchantments if you still can't find him? You lost his trail, again."

The dragon shrank from the man, even though the spray of sand from his boot couldn't possibly have hurt it. It slunk its body close to the ground, strangely cat-like for such a large creature. The man looked once more at the forest surrounding them. His nose wrinkled with displeasure.

"Let me make this clear, just in case the real dragon in you starts to poke through again. I designed you purely to hunt Holly. Any allegiance you owed him when he was your master is now obsolete—you are *my* creature."

A crack rang out, and the dragon crumpled to the ground, out of Rowan's vision. Dirt trickled down over her face—she didn't dare move to brush it away.

"If you continue to fail me, I will have no choice but to resume my experiments. I'd rather *not* take such a tremendous step backward. Would you?"

Silence. Then the dragon let out a low, resonant growl.

"I thought as much. You will find his trail again before the week is out, or I will be *extremely* displeased."

The dragon groaned and reared to its feet once more. The man stalked toward it.

"You should count yourself fortunate. I found a guaranteed source of magic not five days ago; if I don't catch Holly this year, I'll at least extract the village girl's power."

Celine, Rowan thought, her eyes widening. She knew who this man was.

"After I finish with her, we'll catch his trail again. We always do. And *this* time, we won't let him get back to his precious mountain before Winter, will we?"

He addressed this last question coldly to the dragon, who rolled its head on its long neck anxiously. Rowan felt a pang of sympathy for the creature—it was clearly terrified of its master. The man strode up to the dragon, grabbing its jaw with one hand.

"He *owes me,* Narra. He *stole* from me. You dragons are always so concerned with justice. *Where is* my *justice?*"

The dragon shook its head out of his hand. The man's lip curled in disgust.

"Fewer and fewer of you take his side, you know. It won't be long before all of Holly's allies count among *my* faithful. Unless you'd like the dragons to be eradicated from the mountains, I'd encourage you to accept your fate with a little more grace."

The dragon bowed its head, and the Oak King climbed onto its back once more.

"Come. Back to the palace. Let us see what this village girl's magic has to offer."

The dragon spread its wings and leaped into the air, out of sight. Rowan didn't move until the sound of its great wingbeats had faded into the distance.

Then she looked down at the face of the man leaning against her breast.

Holly? Surely not...

Rowan coaxed the roots open—they split like an eggshell, revealing that they had sunk Rowan and her unconscious companion a few feet into the ground. Rowan struggled to lift the man—the Holly King?— out and almost dropped him. He wasn't particularly heavy—the poor soul was practically emaciated—but limp and unhelpful as he was, she couldn't get him out.

"Could I, er, *please* have some help?" she finally entreated of the roots, gasping for her breath against the side of the pit.

With a creak, the roots pressed up, bringing Rowan and the man level with the rest of the ground.

Rowan thanked them as courteously as she could—they were tree roots, after all—and looked around for her pack. Once she found it, she returned to the side of the sleeping man.

She stared down at him for a moment. If this *was* the Holly King, if the Oak King truly was searching for him, then it would only be a matter of time before he was found. He was certainly in no state to make a run for it.

I can't just leave him here.

But Keziah was somewhere out there, possibly even looking for her, if he'd managed to stop the fire, and she was miles away from the place where they had parted. And it was almost the first day of Spring—the Bear Maiden would soon begin her journey down from the mountains. If there was any hope of catching her, Rowan needed to reach the mouth of the mountains as quickly as possible. She shivered—that *vile* man she'd just witnessed was the Oak King, whom she had paid tribute to her whole life. That man had her sister locked up somewhere and meant her nothing but evil. But even as she thought it, her eye fell on the Holly King. Blood still trickled slowly from cuts across his face.

Rowan threw down the pack in frustration and slumped against the nearest tree. Her head swam with the events of the past day—the past week, too, for that matter. It was supposed to be straightforward—entering the forest to save Celine from some kind of injury or animal attack, or even a fallen tree that might have broken her leg and pinned her, keeping her from dragging herself home. Certainly not being kidnapped by a wicked magical king, certainly not something that required her to *quest* to save her sister's life. Her sister's welfare depended on her succeeding, and she couldn't seem to get more than a few miles at a time on her own without something awful happening. And now she had lost her guide. Hands clenched together, Rowan thought a quiet prayer for Keziah, cut short when she remembered that the Holly King, to whom she prayed for the protection of those she cared about, was lying just a few feet away from her. *He* couldn't hear her.

But surely this couldn't really be the Holly King. His power was equal to that of the man she had just seen commanding a dragon—a dragon he seemed to have *created*, or changed in some way to make it hunt the Holly King. Someone with that kind of power shouldn't be this weak, should they?

Rowan got to her feet. If Keziah were here, he would insist they care for the wounded man, despite it costing them time. She was certain of it. Perhaps fate was at work even here—in the stories, people were thrown off their course only to find themselves on the path they were always meant to take.

She circled the area where the man lay. If she was going to keep watch over him until he healed, he couldn't stay out in the open like this.

"I, er..." She felt so silly addressing the silent trees—each time made her flush, even though no one was around to hear her. "I have an idea, if you'd be willing to help."

She explained the overall design, then talked each tree through what it needed to do. One by one, they extended their branches and thrust up their roots from underground. The circle of trees grew into one another, their trunks sinking into the sides of the trees next to them. Overhead, their branches twisted around each other, forming a crude roof that would at least block the rain, if it came, as well as the view of anyone flying over.

Rowan was proud when it was finished. It did indeed look like something out of a tale, though she wished a flowering tree had been a part of the process. She thanked the trees sincerely and went inside. She'd asked them to create a sort of platform underneath the unconscious man. She supposed the arch of roots resembled a bed closely enough, but she thought it must be dreadfully uncomfortable.

She could only hope, if he *did* wake up again, he'd be grateful to be alive, even if his back hurt.

She covered him with a blanket and went outside to cook—helpful though the trees had been, she didn't feel right setting a fire inside the dwelling they had created for her.

Soon, tender ramps sizzled in the pot—a patch of them poked through the thatch of dead pine needles and leaves, and she had to keep herself from harvesting the lot of them. She threw in some dried mushrooms from the knapsack, chunks of potato she carved with her knife, and pieces of dried fish. Then she filled the pot with water, wistfully remembering the pot of rich stock always simmering on the stove at home, and let it come to a rolling boil. She moved it slightly off the heat of the fire and let it simmer and reduce.

The final product, once she added some salt and a handful of cow's parsley, was savory and flavorful, for all that the broth was mostly water. The mushrooms added richness and a meaty flavor, and the ramps and cow's parsley made it aromatic. And, of course, the potatoes made it filling.

Rowan ladled a bowl and ate quickly, shoveling down the hot soup as fast as she could. She hadn't realized just how hungry she was. Then she filled a bowl with mostly broth and carried it carefully into the shelter. The man had shifted a little in his sleep but hadn't woken.

She gently shook his shoulder. "I have food, if you're able to wake up."

His eyes opened the slightest crack, bleary. He tried to sit up but slumped back down at once.

"If you please, some assistance?" Rowan addressed the root platform on which the man lay.

The roots complied, pushing until the man sat almost upright. He blinked but still seemed unable to keep his eyes open. Rowan spooned small amounts of broth into his mouth. He swallowed with difficulty but ate almost half the bowl. Then he lost consciousness again, his head slumping to one side as broth trickled from the corner of his mouth. Rowan wiped his face and asked the roots to lay him down again.

I suppose he needs sleep more than anything else, she thought as she went to collect more wood for the fire. She spent the next few hours collecting wood, harvesting wild herbs and plants she found—small brown mushrooms, blue cabbage blossoms, golden woodthyme, and young garlic shoots that would all help make for hearty meals to help her patient recover.

She hung the herbs from small root tendrils inside the shelter and stored the mushrooms and cabbage blossoms in a little hollow. She heard a gasp from behind her and whirled around. The man was sitting up on his elbows, staring wildly around him.

"Where...?" His eyes fell upon her and widened. "*Niedźwiedzia Dziewica*, where did you come from? Where is Oak?"

"Oh," Rowan said, startled by his strange address. "I'm... Sorry, I'm not the Bear Maiden. Please, don't try to get up!" She hurried forward as he tried to climb off the platform. "Don't —you were hurt quite badly, and the trees helped me hide you from him. You need to rest."

He tried to stand and she pushed him back down, as gently as she could. It didn't take much. He fell back exhausted from the effort.

He blinked several times, his eyes just beginning to focus. "You...you are not the Bear Maiden," he said at last, with some effort.

"N-no," Rowan said slowly. She was so terribly confused. "I assure you I am not."

"Forgive me... It was the hair," he murmured, and he closed his eyes again.

Rowan stared down at him. Then she ran a hand through her hair. It had come loose from her braid, she realized, and it hung wild around her face. What on earth about her hair would make him think she was the legendary *Niedźwiedzia Dziewica*?

He must be out of his head. She lay a hand on his forehead to check for fever; he was a little warm, but not feverish.

Troubled, she left him to sleep undisturbed and went to boil water for drinking. He did not wake for the rest of the day. As evening cast bruised shadows over the trees and the water, Rowan bade the roots close up the entryway to the shelter. She spread her bedroll on the ground beside the sleeping man, propping herself up a little against the root wall—she didn't intend to sleep deeply, just in case he woke in the night and needed her help. He slept fitfully, tossing and turning this way and that, muttering at unseen enemies. Rowan had trouble ignoring him. Every now and then she caught a glimpse of the scar at the base of his neck, whenever the collar of Keziah's shirt pulled to one side.

Rowan finally managed to doze off, only to be awakened some hours later by shouts.

The man had fallen or rolled off the platform and begun thrashing about, fighting for his life against nothing. He yelled wordlessly, screamed with anguish as he clawed at the blanket wrapped around his legs and throat.

Rowan scrambled out of her bedroll and over to him on her knees.

"Shh, shh," she whispered to him, hoping she sounded comforting. "It's all right. You're safe."

His writhing eased a little, and she was able to unwind the blanket from around his neck. Then all of a sudden, he had her by the arms and wrenched her close. Panting, sweat glistening on his brow, he glared up at her.

"Who *are* you?" His voice sounded stronger than it had earlier.

"My name is Rowan." She sounded a good deal calmer than she felt. "I'm from a village on the Border."

He stared for another long, disconcerting while. Then his grip slackened and he leaned back against the root platform.

"A villager."

He sounded dejected, though Rowan had no idea why that information should disappoint him.

"And... are you the Holly King?" she asked tentatively.

He choked out a laugh, bitter and thin.

"Barely. I don't know if I deserve the title anymore." He took in a shuddering breath and let it out again, slowly. "You'd have done better by me if you'd left me to bleed out in the thorn bush."

"You should get some more sleep," Rowan said quietly. Lord of Winter or not, he was not in his right mind.

He snorted at what she said, but he grudgingly grabbed the blanket and yanked it over himself.

"Excuse me if I don't climb back up on that," he jerked his head at the platform behind him. "I don't particularly like sleeping on a sacrificial altar."

Rowan said nothing, and soon the man's breathing slowed and deepened. He slept.

After a time, she, too, fell into a troubled sleep.

CHAPTER 25

Nash

I excelled that Summer. Oak was pleased with my progress, though I think he gave himself most of the credit for my success. I didn't say so, but I thought I had started to do better once he had left the forest. The weight of his expectations had been holding me back; once I learned to work without them, I did better.

I learned to name the seed that had given me such trouble before—mountain ash. I could name any seed Oak set before me.

Then one day I made the mistake of mentioning the journey I had planned with Holly.

"Holly promised to take me to the mountains if my powers have strengthened enough," I was saying as I swept up the dirt from our last lesson.

Oak dropped the pot he was carrying, and it shattered, spattering both of us with dirt.

"What? Why on earth would he take you to the mountains?" he thundered. "What possible reason—"

He caught himself.

"I think it would be most unwise to travel anywhere at the moment, Nash," he said in a more composed tone, brushing down the front of his tunic and trousers. "Especially to the mountains. They are very dangerous for someone of your skill level."

"But you said just the other day—"

"I cannot allow it," he said, as though I hadn't spoken. "It is best if you remain here until your training is complete. Swear it to me, Nash—swear that you will not leave this land until your powers have reached their full strength."

His eyes bored into mine, and I felt like I couldn't look away.

"Alright," I said at last. "I swear it."

His shoulders relaxed, and his careless smile returned to his face.

"Good. Now, clean up the rest of this mess. I have work to do."

After he left the room, I stood there staring at the pile of dirt on the floor. Something was very, very wrong. Oak had essentially forbidden me from traveling, and try as I might, I could not convince myself that it was out of concern for my safety. There had to be another reason.

It wasn't until he left again and Holly arrived that the pieces fell into place.

I was on my way to Holly's study, ready to talk to him about my misgivings about Oak, when I heard Frost's voice from within.

"It is terrible—terrible! I've just been to the border of Zetambique, and he was there! He was there!"

"Frost, I don't understand you—slow down, take a breath," I heard Holly say calmly.

"He's been planning this! He'll never give up his powers—never!"

"Frost."

Frost took a shuddering breath. I slipped inside the study. Holly caught my eye and shook his head before I could speak. Then he turned his eyes back to Frost.

"Tell me everything. From the beginning."

Frost inhaled sharply and began.

"I followed him. I know you said to leave it alone, but I couldn't. There was such a sense of wrongness to him and I couldn't let it lie. He crossed the border into Zetambique, and of course, I couldn't follow him, but I had a feeling... So I waited. Just a few days. And then—"

Frost broke off and gulped. Tears sprang in the corners of their eyes.

"He came back, pulling a boy with him. He couldn't have been more than..." They glanced at me. "There were people chasing them— the boy's family, maybe, or his village. But they were too late. Oak *stopped just before the Border, and he started singing the willow witch's song."*

Holly's shoulders stiffened.

"And he drained the boy. He must have had some kind of magic—I could see it spill directly from him into Oak." Frost wept, tears spilling down their cheeks. "Then he leaped across the Border and ran off."

"The boy," Holly asked quickly, "was he..."

Frost shook their head miserably and buried their face in their hands.

Holly looked stricken. I felt sick.

"Where is he now, Frost?" Holly asked, his voice strangely tight.

"He went south," they choked out, wiping their eyes. "I believe he was heading toward the pass leading to Asla, but I couldn't bear to follow him again."

Holly said nothing. A haunted look had come over his face.

"He... killed that boy?" I asked, my voice coming out very small and very young.

"Killed him and took his magic," Frost said bitterly. "And I believe that is the purpose of his travels—seeking out people with magic and tearing their powers out of them."

"But... but then why hasn't he done that to me?" I asked, my hand sliding into my pocket to grip the shell knife my mother gave me on my tenth birthday. It helped me feel a little less scared.

"I think," Holly said slowly, "that he may have a similar plan for you, Nash."

"It must be your powers," Frost gasped, their eyes widening in horror. "You have his magic and your mother's. If he waits until you are fully grown, you will be incredibly powerful—then he'll take it from you."

Shaking, I took a step back. "But won't his powers leave him once the thousand years are up? I thought the Bear Maiden said he'll lose them whether he chooses an heir or not."

Frost and Holly exchanged a glance.

"Willow witches are very dark creatures," Holly said softly. "And their draining spell extracts magic from their victims. It seems Oak has found a way to use the spell himself. I would assume that any magic he... collects in such a way would fall outside of the Bear Maiden's jurisdiction."

"But that's horrible!" I burst out. I couldn't believe it. The man who

had promised to teach me to control my magic, the person I had willingly accompanied to this strange land, was a murderer and a thief of magic. And I might be his next victim.

"It is." Holly turned and looked out the window, his fingers curling into fists at his sides. "I cannot believe I didn't realize what he was doing until now. The secrecy, the avoidance—how long has this been going on?"

"We have to stop him," I demanded, looking to Frost.

They opened their mouth, glanced at Holly, then closed it again.

"I agree," Holly said, turning back to face me, "but I have no idea of how. If he has been amassing magic for years, then he is far more powerful than I realized. We cannot do this alone."

"Then what do you suggest, Lord Holly?" Frost asked, a note of terror in their voice.

Holly looked at me.

"Nash, we'll be taking that trip into the mountains a little earlier than expected. It seems I also need to pay a visit to the Bear Maiden. We leave within the hour."

CHAPTER 26

Rowan

TWO DAYS BEFORE THE SPRING EQUINOX

Rowan woke to the splashing and honking of geese in the river. The Holly King lay curled on his side, like a creature in a burrow, still sleeping deeply. She got out of her bedroll as quietly as she could and took the food bag outside. She brewed coffee and cooked several slices of bacon. While she waited for the bacon, she ate a piece of the dark walnut bread Keziah had packed, trying to enjoy it even though she was very, very tired of eating it. She couldn't quite pick out all of the spices—cinnamon and nutmeg, to be sure, and probably clove, but there was something else adding gentle heat that she couldn't name.

Then a scream came from inside the shelter. She nearly dropped everything as she scrambled through the root opening.

The Holly King's eyes were open, but he didn't seem to see Rowan. Wide-eyed with fear, he thrashed and threw himself this way and that, screaming like a fox caught in a trap. He swung and swiped at nothing.

Rowan stood in the doorway, frozen by indecision. She knew she shouldn't try and wake him—it would only make things worse—but she couldn't leave him in such a state of terror.

"It's all right," she called to him, keeping her voice as calm as she could. "It's all right—there's no one here. You're safe."

His thrashing became more subdued. Finally, he cowered on the ground, hands covering his head. Sobs shook him, and he crumpled.

Rowan slowly, uncertainly, moved closer, crouching down beside him. She was careful not to touch him.

"You are safe. No one is coming. No one knows you are here," she murmured.

His sobs eased. Tentatively, Rowan reached out and brushed his hair out of his face. He flinched. She drew her hand back.

He drew a shaky breath and let it out slowly. Then he pushed himself up until he sat with his back against the platform. His eyes were shut.

"Where am I?" he asked. His voice was hoarse from screaming.

"In a tree by the river. I wish I could offer you a more specific location, but I'm a little lost myself."

His face twitched, as though he wanted to smile but didn't have the energy. He opened his eyes a sliver, then closed them.

"My mysterious savior," he murmured. His lips were dry and cracked. "What on earth possessed you to stay with me?"

"You were hurt," Rowan answered immediately. "Leaving you was a death sentence."

"For me alone. Don't you know not to cast your lot in with a hunted creature?" He opened his eyes and stared at the sunlight streaming through the opening in the roots.

"I'm afraid I don't know much about hunting," Rowan replied, standing and brushing dirt from her trousers. "I deal more with human beings."

He stared at her, then with effort he managed a faint smile.

"Surely you know that's not what I am?"

"You look plenty human to me." Rowan was growing tired of this. "You bleed when you're hurt, you fear when you are attacked. What does it matter if I wanted to help you?"

He looked down at his hands, which were clasped around his knees. "I must say, I haven't been talked to like this in a long time."

"Well. Maybe it's a good thing I came along, then, Lord Holly." Rowan extended her hand. "There's food, if you want it. Coffee, too."

He looked at her hand. Then his dark eyes flicked up to hers.

"Lord Holly." He spoke dully, as though the name meant nothing to him. "Something else I haven't heard in a long time."

He reached up and took her hand, wincing as she pulled him to his feet. He swayed, then sat down on the root platform, breathing hard.

"I'm afraid I can't walk at the moment," he said once he caught his breath.

"That's all right." Rowan went out and brought in the pot of coffee and the pan of bacon. She cut a piece of walnut bread for him and ate the rest of her breakfast sitting on the ground beside the platform.

He took small bites and chewed slowly, stopping often, as though even eating was almost too much exertion. He glanced at Rowan between mouthfuls.

"You must know, I can't reward you for any of this. My power is greatly diminished from... from what it once was."

She frowned at him. "Of course, the only reason one person helps another is for the hope of *reward*." She took a drink of coffee. "Set your mind at ease—I don't want anything from you."

His mouth twisted wryly.

"Tell me, what is a village girl doing so far from her village? The forest is more dangerous now than it ever has been."

The food turned to ash in Rowan's mouth. She looked down at her second piece of walnut bread with distaste.

"I suppose it is. I'm looking for my sister—she went missing almost a week ago, and I tracked her into the forest, and..." She looked outside at the river glistening in the Spring sunlight. "The Oak King has her. I don't know—"

She heard a sharp intake of breath and looked quickly at the Holly King. His bread had fallen from his fingers, and he stared back at her, that wide-eyed, fearful look returning.

"How do you know?" he asked swiftly, hands shaking. "What did you see? Tell me!"

Taken aback, Rowan set down her food.

"I met a boy, here in the forest," she began, wondering how much she should tell him about Keziah. After all, the Holly King ruled these woods as well. Weakened though he seemed, he might not take kindly to someone living there in secret.

He froze.

"A boy? What kind of boy?" His voice had become very quiet.

"He... He's a hunter and trapper. He knows the forest, and he knows... what the Oak King does." Rowan's spine prickled. The Holly King seemed to be hanging on her every word.

"What is his name?" he asked sharply.

"K-Keziah," she answered. She didn't feel like she could lie to him, not with him watching her so intensely.

"Keziah." Relief spread across his face, and his shoulders relaxed. "So he's still alive." Rowan could see the start of tears glimmering in his eyes, but he blinked them away. "It was worth it, then," he said to himself, "worth *something*, at least."

"You know him?" Rowan asked slowly, her mind working. That would explain how Keziah knew so much about the Oak King, if he was friends with his rival.

"I knew him years ago, by another name. We... share a common enemy, you could say."

"The Oak King?" Rowan asked, and she immediately regretted it.

He flinched again, as if just the name alone could hurt him.

"I'm sorry."

He shook his head. "It's not your fault. Like I said, no one has spoken to me much these past few years. The one good thing about it is not having to hear about... about him." Before Rowan could ask why mentioning the Oak King brought him such pain, he cleared his throat and looked around.

"Where is he, then? Keziah?" He sounded out the name, as though trying to get used to it.

Rowan looked at the abandoned travel pack. "I don't know. When the fire started in the mountains, he said he had to go stop it. He said—" She broke off as the pieces finally clicked in her mind, only confirmed by the horror that spread across the Holly King's face. "It was you, wasn't it?" she said, though it wasn't a question. "Keziah went to help you—he said... he said Oak does this every year, but this time he came early, to drive someone out of hiding. He went after you, didn't he?"

Holly swallowed and nodded, his eyes beginning to dart in their frantic way.

"But Keziah didn't come back?" he asked.

Rowan shook her head, worry creasing her brow. "Not yet. I don't know what happened. He told me to stay put, but then..."

"The dragon."

She nodded.

The Holly King picked up a piece of bread and absently crumbled it between his fingers.

"Almost more than anything else, I hate seeing what he's done to her. Narra was one of my closest friends. But once he got his hands on her, he made her into such a... machine. Designed for one purpose, really." His trembling hand clenched around the piece of bread. "To hunt me."

Rowan let him talk. She didn't want to distract him, now that he finally seemed able to speak about what had happened.

"She was one of my creatures, you see—an ice serpent from the mountains. So she always knew how to seek me out. He used his magic on her, forced her to combine with some tree of his and his fire power, and now... now..."

He ran a hand over his face, smearing tears over his cheeks.

"She was a fascinating beast. Incredibly intelligent, a wonderful companion. Now he's reduced her to a brute, set upon destroying everything in her path. I didn't *think* about what would happen, if—" He broke off and sank his head into his hands.

Rowan burned to ask him what on *earth* he was talking about, but clearly he didn't want to go on. She held out the mug of coffee.

"Here."

He looked at the cup as though he didn't know what to do with it.

"You can have tea, if you'd rather have something less—"

He took the cup without a word. He took a sip, staring down into the liquid, both hands clasped around the cup. "Your sister, you said?"

Rowan nodded. The Holly King's mouth twisted and his eyes narrowed.

"He's doing it again. After all we've done to stop him, it hasn't been enough," he muttered.

"Doing what?" Rowan couldn't help herself from asking. Keziah hadn't explained it to her, but maybe the Holly King would.

"He wants magic," he said bluntly, setting the cup beside him on the platform. "More than what the Bear Maiden granted him, all those centuries ago. The powers she gave us—we were never supposed to keep them forever, but he can't imagine life without them now. And he wants more. He used to travel the world, find people with magic, and take it from them. For the last five years, however, he has been bound to the forest. Trapped, unable to go looking for magic himself. Once he even—"

He broke off, his hand going to his mouth.

"What? What did he do?" Rowan pressed, both horrified and, despite herself, fascinated.

"He had a child, with a woman who had powers of her own in a land far from here. He brought the child back to the forest, saying he intended to teach them to use their powers, but..."

"He wanted their magic?" Rowan guessed.

He nodded, though he was watching her with an odd expression.

"He did. He meant to take it from them—'extract' it, as he called it —once they were fully grown and their powers as strong as possible. I couldn't let that happen."

Rowan recalled the Oak King telling Narra that Holly had stolen something from them. That must be what he'd meant—his child and the powers he sought to steal from them.

"What happened?" she asked tentatively.

He hesitated, his hand clenching and unclenching. Then he reached up and pulled his collar to the side, revealing the scar she'd noticed before.

"Oh." She covered her mouth with a hand.

"He did his best to... well, you can guess. And after that didn't go the way he had planned, well..." He let go of his collar and gripped the edge of the platform so hard his knuckles turned white. "We bound him to the forest, the Bear Maiden and I, tried to make sure he couldn't leave. All we needed was for everyone else to stay *out*." He released his grip on the platform and ran his fingers through his hair. "Of course it wasn't enough. The villagers have always been so curious about this forest. It wasn't as though we could warn anyone—he was still far too powerful for that."

"But I don't understand. You said the Oak King—"

"Please, he's not the King of anything. Don't treat him with any respect—he doesn't deserve it, any more than I do. You can call us 'Oak' and 'Holly.' Neither of us truly rule this land anymore—he is a tyrant who only serves himself, and I... I am broken."

"Fine. You said the Oak—that Oak was bound to the forest. What does that mean?"

Holly smiled sadly.

"It means I gave up a portion of my power to keep him from leaving. Three months of power, to be precise. I am..." He took a shuddering breath. "Half of what I used to be. And it was all for nothing. All Oak had to do was wait for someone to cross the Border, and he could snatch them up and start again."

"Do you—do you mean—" Rowan's mind refused to accept the idea. "My sister," she said desperately. "What exactly does he mean to do, by *extracting* something from her?"

Holly looked back at her helplessly.

"I'm sorry," he said at last. "I wish I knew what he intended. I wish there was something I could do. He has been hunting me for years—I haven't had a chance for my powers to grow. He keeps me on the run. If I could stop him..."

He trailed off, and the two of them sat in silence, the heat of the day creeping in through the cracks in the branches twined overhead. Rowan closed her eyes and inhaled deeply. The scent of the season's first blossoms filled her nose. Spring was Celine's favorite time of year, and the only dress Rowan had ever seen her wear willingly was the exact color of the lilacs that grew outside their bedroom window—pale purple.

"I have to find her." She stood and began gathering up the breakfast things. "I'm sticking with our plan."

"And just what is that plan, exactly?" Holly asked, trying to push himself to his feet and failing.

"I'm looking for the Bear Maiden. Keziah said I can wish for her safety, and it should fix everything."

His hand shot out and gripped Rowan's arm.

"You cannot just wish everything well. That isn't how it works," he hissed. "Keziah should know that better than anyone else—there is more that needs fixing than a single kidnapping."

Rowan tried to shake off his hand, suddenly very aware that, despite their conversation, he was still a stranger who, though he said his power had diminished by half, still had a great deal of magical powers. But he clung all the tighter.

"What should I do, then? Please, if you have any suggestions as to how I can save my sister from a tyrannical forest god, do let me hear them," she snapped. "I'm afraid my concerns are solely for my sister."

He stared up at her for a long moment. "And yet you stopped long enough to help me. Why?"

Underneath the long, tangled beard, she could see that he had been —was still—rather handsome. Fear and hunger had taken their toll on him, hollowing his cheeks and darkening the areas under his eyes, but his dark features and soulful eyes still made Rowan's breath catch a little in her throat as she looked at him.

Oh, no, she chided herself. *First rule of any fairy tale is not to trust the handsome ones.* The Oak King had certainly been handsome—painfully so, and in such a cruel way that he didn't seem real. Holly was every bit as real as she was. Perhaps it was only his loss of power that made him that way, but even so, Rowan could not reconcile him with the Lord of Winter she had worshipped her whole life.

"Just look at any of the old stories," she finally answered him. "Choosing not to help someone in need is unforgiveable. The princess who helps the bird whose breast was pierced by an arrow discovers him to be the prince she was looking for all along. The woman begging for scraps of food just so happens to know the secret of the enchanted castle. I know better than to leave someone lying in the dirt when they might have the answers I'm looking for. Or they might come back to curse me some day," she added, giving Holly a dubious look. He didn't seem the cursing type.

Holly smiled bitterly. "Fairy tales? Surely you're not following rules from stories meant to produce good behavior in children and teach young women how to find husbands?"

"If you think that's all fairy tales are, then clearly you haven't heard any of the good ones." Rowan gently pulled her arm away and turned her back on him, packing the rest of the food in the bag.

"Who are you?" he asked, though it didn't really sound like a question.

"I told you, my name's Rowan," she said without bothering to turn around.

"That's not what I meant. How have you come so far in the forest without being found? And why hasn't Oak picked up my trail yet? I haven't slept a whole night in years."

Rowan looked at him over her shoulder.

"In *years?* How are you still alive?"

He winced and leaned back against the platform.

"Here, push up for him again," she told the roots, going over to help him swing his legs up.

He froze. "Who are you talking to?" He leaped when the platform shifted beneath him.

"Just the trees. How do you think I built this place?" She waved a hand at the shelter around them.

"Built..." Holly looked around the enclosure as though seeing it for the first time. "You commanded the trees?"

"Certainly not," Rowan said firmly. "I just asked them if they could help. They've been quite nice to me the whole time I've been here. I understand," she said quickly as Holly opened his mouth, a skeptical look on his face. "That isn't entirely normal."

"It's not just abnormal—it's unheard of." He was looking her over, the way Keziah had after she killed the imp. "Normal people can't ask the trees to do anything for them."

"Keziah can," Rowan pointed out.

"Exactly my point," Holly replied, sitting back against the raised bit of platform. "Surely you don't think Keziah is just some village boy."

Rowan opened her mouth, then closed it again, thinking.

"Who is he, then?"

Holly fiddled with one of the buttons on his shirt. "That isn't my story to tell," he said softly, "And you haven't answered my question."

Rowan rolled her eyes. "Which one? Not that I have answers for any of them."

"Why hasn't he found me yet? It usually only takes him an hour or two to pick up my trail if he loses it."

"I don't know. There isn't anything special about me. Keziah said Oak should have known I was in the forest to begin with—that his sentries should have reported me, but they didn't, and he didn't know why that would be. He did say it might be because the trees like me." Rowan absently patted one of the branches near her. "But I don't know how that would affect you."

"Yes, I'd say the trees do like you," Holly murmured, his eyes scanning the length of the branches stretching above him. He looked as though he was having trouble keeping his eyes open.

"Why don't you try to get some more sleep?" Rowan asked, holding out the blanket he'd discarded on the ground.

"Are you going to be here when I wake up?" he asked, not moving a muscle to take it from her.

"Do you really think I would leave without another word? I'll at least stay a few more hours—I need to get to the mountains as soon as possible, or I'll miss my chance to find the Bear Maiden."

Holly blanched.

"I only meant—if Oak should happen to come back, he'd surely find me."

"Won't that happen anyway? You seem to expect him to show up at any second."

Holly looked pointedly at her. "For whatever reason, *you* made him lose my trail."

"But the trees—"

"The trees don't care if I live or die in Springtime. They know I'm not their ruler this time of year, and they know the thousand years are nearly over. *You* made them help me, so they've been keeping me hidden the same way they've kept *you* hidden from him." He spoke calmly, yet his words made Rowan's pulse quicken. He made it sound as though she had some kind of power, which was preposterous. "If you go away, I think your protection will go with you. Do your stories have anything to say about abandoning people to die?"

"I thought you scoffed at stories," Rowan grumbled, setting the bag back down. She wondered what he meant by *the thousand years are nearly over.*

"Consider me convinced by your argument," he said, amusement dancing around his mouth. "Will you stay? At least until I'm a little stronger?"

Rowan looked out the entryway at the mountains—they seemed so close, and yet they were still miles and miles away. And without Keziah's guidance, she had no idea of where to go once she reached them.

As though he had read her thoughts, the Holly King spoke.

"I can guide you to the mountains, if Keziah still hasn't come back. I know them better than any creature alive, with the exception of the Bear Maiden herself. Please. I've been alone for such a long time. I won't last another night by myself in these godsforsaken woods where everything wants me dead."

Rowan looked at the man lying on the platform. Keziah's words about the Holly King came flooding back into her mind, as well as her own reasonings informed by fairy tales. *I met him for a reason.* She was sure of it. Maybe helping him would lead her to her sister. In any case, she really couldn't proceed to the mountains without a guide.

"I'll stay," she said finally. "But only if you try to get some more sleep. I promise I'll be here when you wake up."

"Thank you." He took the blanket from her.

She helped him drape it over himself, then left him to sleep.

There was no true path through the forest. But Holly seemed to know exactly which way to go, even when I became so turned around that I could not have pointed the way back to Oak's palace.

He frowned when I told him this.

"If you have Oak's powers, then you should be able to find your way in the forest quite easily. Did he never show you how?"

I shook my head. The set of Holly's mouth turned grim.

"I suppose I shouldn't be surprised anymore."

He stopped walking and placed a hand on my shoulder. "But there is no reason why you shouldn't learn now. You have mastered your command of the trees, yes?"

"Yes, some. He didn't like to let me try it too often."

Holly snorted. "I'm sure he didn't. Reach for the trees, as though you are about to give them a command."

I obeyed, stretching with that same part of myself I had used to sprout seeds and grow plants. The life I sensed around me bristled, still full of life even as the sunlight grew sparser and the leaves changed into their dying colors.

"Now." Holly's voice came from far away. "Look with the forest."

Before I could ask what he meant, I found I was already doing it. I *felt as though I was rushing through the trees at great speed, hurtling past every stone we had just passed, every stream we had stepped over. Oak's palace loomed before me, and I raced past it, sailing over terrain I had not walked since I first came to the forest. The dying green of Summer, streaked through the gold and orange of Autumn, streamed together into a death-tinged blur. I reached the very end of the forest, where I had first entered it with Oak—but I could not see beyond it, not matter how I strained to look past this cold land and see the crystal-blue waters of my home.*

"Nash?" Holly's voice sounded all the more distant. "Nash!"

His hand closed around my arm, dragging me back into myself. My knees threatened to give way, and I slumped against a yew, panting.

"That was a little too far for your first time, I think," Holly said gently. "I should have warned you."

"I want to try again," I said at once, pushing myself upright.

Holly shook his head. "Now is not the time. We will have plenty of time for you to practice once we make camp, but we ought to get as far into the mountains as possible before nightfall."

I didn't like it, but I obeyed.

Leaving the trees behind after so many months spent within their ranks felt bizarre. We moved into sparse pines and cedars as the ground sloped steadily upward. The vegetation gave way, too, from lush ferns and shrubs to scraggly bushes and grayish-green lichen.

I paused and stared up at the mountain before us. It looked impenetrable, inaccessible to the two of us, small as we were in its shadow. I had never climbed a mountain before, had never even stood this close to one. My island had great rocky cliffs overlooking the sea on one side, but there was no true peak, and the climb took my thirteen-year-old self all of ten minutes.

"Are you all right, Nash?" Holly asked.

"How do you climb something like this?" I asked, waving at the heap of stone and earth before us. "Where do you even start?"

Holly grinned. "Just a little at a time."

He strode forward, toward what looked like nothing more than a pile of rocks. But as he picked his way through, I saw that there was a faint path through the spill of stone, much like the hint of a trail deer and elk left in the forest.

Of course. Animals moved from the mountains to the forest, too. And so did Holly and the Bear Maiden, for that matter. It only made sense that they would wear their footsteps into the ground here as well as in the trees.

I squared my shoulders and followed him.

The climb was excruciating. I had always thought of myself as rather strong, but the sheer endurance it took to climb and keep climbing was more than I had in me—or, rather, more than I had thought. Each time I considered stopping for rest, I remembered that Oak could decide to return at any moment, could hear a report from one of his allies that we had fled. He could come after us and catch us easily, exposed as we were on the slope of the mountain. Or, if he took the time to consider his options, he might decide I wasn't worth the trouble. He might cut his losses, might seek out my island again and take my mother's magic instead of mine. I could not afford to waste any time.

The path led us up and around the base of the first mountain before delving between the two behind it. We stopped and made camp in a patch of tall stones plastered with lichen and ivy.

Holly built a fire, and the two of us sat staring into it in silence.

"We ought to eat something," Holly said at last, reaching for his pack.

"I don't feel hungry," I said.

He started pulling out food regardless. "You may not need food to live, Nash, but you will feel better if you eat. It's good to remind yourself now and again that part of you is human."

I didn't say anything, but I took the cheese and dried meat he handed me without protest.

As I chewed, I tried casting my mind out again, feeling for the forest and trying once more to see beyond it. It was even more difficult this time, and I let out a growl of frustration.

"What's the matter?" Holly asked, alarmed.

"Why can't I see my home?" I asked miserably, blinking back sudden tears.

"Your home? You mean you were trying to reach your island, miles away?" Holly asked.

"I have my mother's powers, as well as Oak's. Why shouldn't I be able to see the island, too?"

Holly considered that. "I don't know, Nash. Perhaps you are too far away from it. Or it could be that you need practice. This is the first time you've tried this sort of seeing—you may need to build up your strength in order to see farther."

Another thing that had to wait. I set my half-eaten food on the ground beside me and wrapped my arms around my knees.

"It doesn't help that you are tired," Holly continued gently. "No one can expect great things from themselves when they are exhausted. Why don't you try to get some sleep? Then you can try again in the morning."

Part of me wanted to stay up, practicing this new way of seeing until I caught a glimpse of my home, but I found I could not keep my eyes open. So I did as Holly suggested and laid out my bedroll. I fell asleep almost at once.

CHAPTER 28

Rowan

Rowan scraped at a piece of wood with Keziah's hunting knife. She was trying to sharpen it into... well, she wasn't quite sure what it would be when it was finished. A fishing spear? Not an arrow—she didn't have the slightest idea how to make one of those. Something stabby to use on fish, whatever that was called. She didn't like using the little bat on them—she wasn't quite strong enough to put them out of their misery with brute force. So she needed something sharp, and she wasn't about to dull Keziah's knife by using that.

She'd caught a fish the day before and was planning on going back to the same collection of stones in the river to try her luck again. The Holly King—Holly—had slept through dinner and woken briefly for breakfast, and she wanted to have a meal waiting for him when he finally woke up again.

Poor man seems like he needed the sleep. She looked over her shoulder through the entryway. He lay on his side, turned away from her.

Gods, what am I doing here? After the hustle and bustle of the past few days—or had it been a week now?—Rowan wasn't sure what to do with herself. She went back and forth, cursing herself for staying put while the Bear Maiden made her way out of the mountains and into the forest, where Rowan would surely never find her. Then she chastised herself for wanting to leave—Holly needed help. The man had been hunted, and badly hurt at some point.

Admit it, you're just curious about what happened to him. She swiped viciously at a knot in the wood. It split the piece in half, ruining it. That wasn't entirely true—she did feel sorry for him. She wanted to help him, but the thought of her sister, the things that might be happening to her...

She shook her head. In this forest, all she had to trust was her instincts, now that Keziah wasn't with her. And those instincts told her not to leave Holly to whatever fate Oak intended for him. Chills went down her spine at the memory of his voice.

She had spotted the dragon from a distance a few times today, but it didn't spot them. It seemed to be sweeping over large stretches of forest, scanning everything below. While it didn't seem to have picked up Holly's trail, it came unnervingly close to their camp.

We probably ought to move camp to somewhere safer, Rowan worried.

She watched it now as it swept back up to the mountains, fearful that at any moment it would turn and head straight for them. She had no idea of how to protect Holly if it did.

"She's still beautiful, isn't she?"

She nearly leaped out of her skin.

Holly stood in the entryway, watching the dragon as she rippled over the treetops. "I like to think that, after everything he's done to her, he still hasn't managed to break her character."

"You should be resting," Rowan said, getting to her feet. "Are you hungry?"

He waved her concerns away.

"I'm feeling better. I do need to move around a little, if I don't want to forget how to use my legs." He pressed a hand to his hip, as though it pained him.

The scars Rowan had seen there that first day flashed through her mind, but she didn't think it right to ask about them. Still, she wondered if they still hurt.

He moved slowly from the entryway to the boulder next to Rowan and eased himself down on top of it.

"Actually." He cleared his throat. "I'm feeling better than I have in years. Maybe from sleeping through the night without the threat of... well, the threat of being found."

He glanced at the trees behind them.

"Though I really can't seem to guess why none of his sentries have found me yet."

"Has he really been hunting you nonstop for so long?"

Holly looked down at his feet.

"Not exactly. He gets bored, especially when his powers are weak in Autumn and Winter. I usually manage to get back into the mountains on the first day of Autumn, but he sends Narra after me throughout year, keeping me from recovering properly. And it never fails that as soon as Spring arrives, he finds some way to drive me out again."

He smiled bitterly at Rowan.

"I don't look like much of a king at the moment, do I? I still have to find a way to bring Winter to the forest every year, whether I get time to rest and recover or not. The Bear Maiden intended for both of us to spend six months of the year storing up power for our next six months of ruling. But he doesn't give me that. He hasn't for nearly five years. I don't know if I will ever regain my strength properly."

He looked up as the dragon roared and sped off over the hills, out of sight.

"It wouldn't be quite so hard if it wasn't so lonely. All my friends have abandoned me, or else it's too dangerous for them to come close."

Keziah flickered into Rowan's head. Though he hadn't been able to communicate with Holly all these years, he had clearly been doing what he could to help. And though Oak had taken the dragon and turned her into something else, she still seemed to hate him, still seemed to miss her old companion.

An idea struck Rowan. She opened her pack and pulled out her embroidery again.

"Tell me what she looked like, before... before he took her," she said to Holly, her fingers hovering over her thread. "Which color is closest?"

He looked at her for a moment. Then his eyes dropped to the thread.

"This one."

He reached into Rowan's lap and rubbed a silvery-green bunch of thread between his fingers.

"Her scales were this color, at their outermost edge, but they darkened the closer they got to her skin. Her underbelly was more like this." He picked up the black-brown. "And she was shaped more like—well, here." He bent and used a stick to draw a rough outline in the dirt. "She was shaped more like a cat, before. He made her bulky and brawny, but she was never that way when I knew her. She had whiskers, here, and her tail was full of blue feathers."

It was the happiest she'd seen him. He sketched, adding details to the image of his old friend.

"That's as much as I can do," he said finally, sitting back up.

Rowan saw that he was holding his side again, but his face was free of pain. She looked down at the drawing in the dirt. A reptile with feline features sat on its haunches, her face as expressive as the barn cat Rowan's family fed from time to time. The whiskers Holly had mentioned spiraled in tendrils from her cheeks, and her tail curled on the ground beside her. Almost unrecognizable from the fearsome beast setting fire to the forest.

Rowan threaded her needle and got to work. It was hard not to try and rush while she was being watched, but Holly was a good observer. He kept quiet, following the line of thread with his eyes. Rowan finished the outline for the face.

"Eyes?" she asked, pulling out the silvery-green thread.

"Gray," he murmured without taking his eyes off the picture developing before him.

She guessed at the shape and showed him. His brow creased.

"A little less round, more of a slit than that."

She pulled out the threads and began again. He nodded at her second attempt.

"That's it."

The whiskers, he told her, had been gray as well. And so the two of them went on like that, Rowan stopping to ask about color and shape and placement, Holly offering what answers he could.

Until finally he said, "That's her."

Rowan could hardly believe she had managed to turn out such a beautiful work of art. The dragon seemed to ripple on the quilt under the sun. At the last minute, Rowan made the tail coil around the base of one of the holly trees. The dragon looked so peaceful, too, like a deer in a glade.

The silvery-green creature was beautiful, every inch the kind of magical being Rowan had longed to see since she first set foot in the forest. And she wanted to get it down before she forgot some of the most striking details—the rows of horns that ran along the ridge of its head and down its back, the tendrils that swept from its face like a cat's whiskers, the elegant, swanlike arch of its impossibly long neck.

She had to be strategic with her silver thread, for she didn't have much of it left, but she had enough to outline the dragon and give a good impression of the way Holly said she had glittered in the sun.

She handed the quilt to Holly and set about making food. She would have to try for a fish later. They ate in silence, Holly absently running his fingers over the lines of the trees and the dragon. Rowan kept looking up to find him watching her, though he quickly looked away each time. When they were done, he rose, wordless, and made his way back into the enclosure, leaving the quilt on the rock he'd sat on.

Rowan let him go. He seemed to want some time to himself, anyway. She packed up her embroidery and took the fishing trap and spear to the water. Several damp hours later, she had at least one fish to show for it. She decided to cook a stew with some bacon, a potato, and another handful of greens harvested from the riverbank.

Holly got up again for dinner and promptly went to lie down again when he was done.

She sat outside, keeping guard over the sleeping Holly King, adding wood to the fire when it burned low, until at last she could not keep her eyes open. She nodded off, leaning against her pack, and dozed until dawn.

CHAPTER 29

Keziah

Keziah was so tired he could barely see straight. Oak's dragon, exhausted and overworked, had been sent away. Now Oak himself was following Keziah's trail through the forest on foot, and he had called upon a griffon to accompany him.

So this is what it's been like for Holly, Keziah thought bleakly. *Except he's been doing the opposite—trying not to leave any trace of himself.*

But Holly was so easy to sense in the forest when it wasn't Winter. The forest rebelled against him, crying out against the potential of unseasonal frost, even though the poor man meant no harm. Keziah could tell that Holly had been in the forest, though it was more difficult than normal to sense his presence.

In contrast, Keziah knew how well the forest liked him, how it relished his presence at this moment, just as it relished Oak's. The trees accepted him completely and would not give him away to his enemy. That's why he had to purposely leave tracks, bits of snapped twig, handfuls of ash from a pouch—giving Oak something to follow. He didn't know how long he could keep it up. Sooner or later Oak would get bored, as he always did, and decide it was more important to return to his search for Holly, or perhaps return to his palace to commence the vile torture he called "experiments."

Keziah shivered as he let a fistful of ash crumble onto the riverbank.

He didn't envy the girl her position. But there was no way he would attempt to free her from the palace himself. Rowan would have to find a way to free her sister on her own.

And that's fair. I will help her as much as I can. I don't need to do any more than that, he told himself. She was surprisingly resilient and had learned quickly from her time in the forest, despite being raised without the skills Keziah had had years to learn.

He hoped she was all right. She'd almost certainly have needed to move from where he left her—she knew to hide from the dragon. He just hoped she'd found somewhere safe to hide until he could find her again. He found he was hoping he *would* see her again—he liked her, and he didn't feel good about how little he had told her about the truth of the forest.

This was exactly what I didn't *want to have happen,* he thought, swatting at a bush with a branch, breaking up some of its foliage. *I didn't want to send her off in the forest on her own. It's not safe for someone with no powers.*

But then, she wasn't completely powerless, was she? The same thought that had been nagging at him since he met the girl prodded his mind once again. Rowan had a connection to the forest. It had shielded her the same way it shielded him—he hadn't known she was coming until their paths had crossed. And the trees were so ready to aid her. It just wasn't normal.

He stopped walking and rubbed his eyes with his ash-free hand. He had lived here so long, he had almost forgotten what the lands beyond the forest and the villages were like. He strained to summon up the memory of blue waters, rich golden sand, hot, singeing sunlight. One day, he had promised himself, he would no longer need the knowledge he had accumulated about this damned place. He would be free to leave and forget he ever knew it. He could live out his last days in his true home, if it still existed.

One debt, and once it's paid, I'm free.

He took a step forward but froze, mid-stride. A pair of putrid yellow eyes burned through the leaves above him, and the griffon stepped out from behind the tree. Keziah turned and saw Oak, flanked by another griffon, holding a piece of wool he had left snagged on a bramble.

Two griffons. Idiot.

Keziah let his face go slack with fear, and he let his hands tremble—anything to make his face not betray the hatred that burned within him.

"You know, I usually punish trespassers quite fearsomely," Oak drawled, his face free of his usual snide smile. "But you can count yourself lucky today, boy. You've been traveling with a girl, have you not?"

He doesn't know me.

Keziah tried to hide his confusion. He was relieved Oak hadn't recognized him, but he thought he would at least know him to be the poacher living within his forest for the past few years.

He didn't dare refuse to answer, but he also didn't dare speak, lest his voice spark Oak's memory. He ducked his head respectfully.

"Good. I seem to have lost a valued houseguest and must make do with a replacement. Luckily, the sister seems to share the same magical knack for avoiding detection. And *this* time, I need assurance that she won't run off. Seems I can't rely on my trees for anything anymore."

He shook the handful of wool at Keziah. "*You* were sloppy, to my good fortune. My trees used to be such good sentinels, warning me of anyone who dared cross over the Border. But now..." He kicked a root next to his foot. It splintered, and he ground the broken wood into the dirt with the heel of his boot. "Useless. I have to do everything myself."

Oak turned with a flourish of his cloak. "Bring him along," he ordered the griffon nearest Keziah over his shoulder.

Keziah barely had time to brace himself before the creature grabbed him with its clawed foot and slung him onto its back.

Another time, he could have fought it off with ease, but he couldn't risk using his powers in front of Oak. Oak would be all too happy to realize just who he had found in the forest.

Keziah tried to keep himself calm. *He didn't recognize you. He just wants you for a prisoner. He can't sense your magic.*

And once they got wherever Oak was taking him—Keziah hoped it wasn't the palace—he could then work on trying to escape when Oak lost interest in him. The thinking brought him little comfort, but it was all he had.

CHAPTER 30

Rowan

ONE DAY BEFORE THE SPRING
EQUINOX

The first thing she was aware of was a reddish light. She opened her eyes. Her head had lolled back on top of the pack. She was staring up into the early morning sky through a crack in the roof of branches, cast into a peachy glow by the rising sun. She lifted her head and let out a groan. Her neck ached horribly, possibly from the cold or from sleeping at such an odd angle.

Holly had risen before her, to her surprise. He crouched by the fire, stirring it with a stick. She noticed he had added wood to it too—maybe he was feeling better.

"What's the matter?" he asked, watching Rowan rub her neck.

"I can't get used to being outside all the time, that's all," she said through gritted teeth, stretching her neck gently from one side to the other. She got to her feet, every inch of her complaining, and she tried to warm up her sore muscles by moving around a little. "I feel like an old woman," she complained when she found every limb to be stiff and unwilling to wake up.

She looked over just in time to catch a small smile on the Holly King's face.

"Don't Kings of the Seasons get aches and pains as they age? Or are you excused from that experience?" she asked, giving him a look.

He suppressed a laugh. "I've had plenty of those, but I think you're a little young to start complaining about aging."

She pulled out bacon and the last potato. Once breakfast sizzled in the pan, she brewed coffee and sat with her back against her pack. It was the most comfortable thing she could find to lean on that wasn't a rock.

"We should probably break camp today, since tomorrow is the first day of Spring," Holly said grimly.

Rowan yelped. "The Spring Equinox is *tomorrow?* Oh, I lost track of the days!" She scrambled up, sloshing half her coffee from her cup as she did so.

"Peace, Rowan." Holly nodded his head at the mountains. "We're much closer than you think. As long as we reach the base of the mountains tomorrow, we will find the Bear Maiden. There's no need to rush."

Rowan shielded her eyes with her hand as she looked toward the mountains.

"Are you sure? You're still quite weak—I wouldn't want to make you worse by hurrying."

He held up his cup. "Provided I have another cup of coffee in the morning, I'll be perfectly fine. Don't worry about me, Rowan—your help has done me a world of good. I'm feeling better than I have in years."

Pleased, Rowan tried not to smile too broadly.

"I'm going to try and catch a fish," she told Holly, "and hopefully we can have something other than walnut bread for luncheon."

Holly grimaced. "It's very nice bread, but it does get tiresome after a day or two. Not to offend you," he said quickly.

"Oh, I didn't make it, and I'm quite sick of it, to be honest," she laughed, heading toward the water.

She had good luck; two perch darting around, snapping bugs off the stream's surface, speared easily with the stick she'd sharpened. She stabbed them each through the head and cut their gills with her dagger. After she gutted them and rinsed them in the stream, she went back to show Holly her good fortune.

But the King of Winter seemed lost in thought and barely smiled at the promise of fresh fish.

"I've been thinking," he said, watching Rowan slide the fish onto spits made from peeled, sharpened branches. "Since Oak does seem to have trouble finding me while I'm with you, it might be a good opportunity to replenish some of my strength."

"Isn't that what you're doing now, by resting?" Rowan asked as she filled the cavity of the fish's stomachs with ramps and cow's parsley.

"My physical, human strength, yes. I'm talking about my magic. If I can find a grove of holly trees, there's a kind of... ritual I can perform—it would help me recover some of what I've lost. I used to go every year, sometimes more than once, but he's kept me on the run for a long time." His voice turned shaky, as it always did when he talked about Oak.

Rowan thought about his suggestion for a while as she set the fish above the fire to roast. "You just need a grove of holly trees?" she asked.

"And the ability to make a small fire. A torch from our campfire would do," he said, his face anxious. "There should be a grove somewhere near here, if I remember correctly. My memory..." His face drew in on itself a little. "I can't remember things quite properly, since..."

Since Oak hurt him. Rowan nodded. "If you like, I can scout around this area and see if I can spot the grove."

Holly looked relieved. She realized he must have seriously expected her to refuse.

"That would be most helpful, thank you. It's been such a long time since I've had the use of the forest—it's kept me very weak."

"But doing this will help you regain some of your power?" Rowan wondered exactly what he was going to do, if it involved trees and fire.

"Yes," he said heavily. "It's a little difficult for me, but it will be worth it."

They dined on roasted perch and a handful each of dried fruit. Rowan's stomach still ached for more food—she couldn't remember the last time she felt full—but the fish was still extremely satisfying and a welcome change from meager soup, dried fruit, and that infernal walnut bread.

Wistfully thinking about dessert, Rowan cleaned up and set her pack up. According to Holly, the grove shouldn't have been more than a half-hour's walk from their shelter.

CHAPTER 31

Nash

I woke to the bitterest chill. Holly still sat before the fire, and I was certain he had not slept a wink.

The fire itself drew my attention for the first time. In my weariness the night before, I had not paid much mind to it, grateful for its light and warmth. Now, as I watched it flickering in the morning light, I realized we had brought no firewood with us, and it certainly wasn't possible for Holly to have gathered enough from our surroundings to keep it going all night.

"How—" I started to ask.

Holly smiled and raised a hand. Beside him, a sapling sprang from the ground and grew swiftly into a stout juniper, its reddish bark splintering as its trunk thickened. In the space of a breath, it grew until it reached just above Holly's head, its feathery fronds brushing his shoulder.

When its growth slowed, Holly passed his hand over its bark. The fronds blushed orange and withered, and the little tree split into pieces, showering the ground with pale blue berries.

I saw that the ground around Holly was littered with even more juniper berries.

"You've been doing this all night?" I asked, huddling closer to the fire.

"It seems wasteful, I know," Holly said, adding another chunk of wood to the fire. "But there are creatures in the mountains that might not take kindly to the Oak King's son paying a visit. Fire is the best deterrent."

"But you rule the mountains," I said, confused. "Can't you just command them to leave us alone?"

Holly rubbed at his beard.

"I do not 'rule' the mountains the same way Oak and I rule the forest. Otherwise, I could never leave it for six months every year. It's simply where I make my home during Spring and Summer, when the forest is cared for by Oak."

"Why are there two of you ruling it? I've tried asking Oak, but his answers are always vague."

Holly sighed. "I know he would have preferred to rule it by himself, especially in recent years. The Bear Maiden wished to divide the powers of the forest. She thought that all of them would be too much for one human, and I agree with her. She also thought it wise to divide the powers between us in accordance with the seasons so that neither of us housed powers that conflict with each other. My powers of ice, for example, and Oak's powers of fire."

"But you both grow things and make them die," I pointed out. "Isn't that a conflict?"

"You would think so, but no. With plants and animals, they are constantly in the process of growing and dying. So it is no more a conflict in us than it is in them."

I recalled the times Oak had called on me to use my powers of rot and decay. I shivered. The way the life had completely gone out of the juniper tree just now reminded me horribly of Frost's report of Oak taking that other boy's powers.

"Couldn't she have split your powers up more?" I asked, trying to keep my mind off Oak's horrible doings. "So that neither of you were so powerful?"

"I suppose she could have," Holly mused. "But I think, at the time, we proved ourselves capable of providing leadership—of ruling the forest and the beings who help bring on the seasons—and that's what she was looking for."

The beings?

"You mean, Frost and Dew and the others—they were already there?"

Holly's mouth twisted, but he nodded.

"There was a battle, long ago," he began, "the old gods fought for this territory, for the great pools of wild magic throughout the forest and mountains. It was utter chaos, until the Bear Maiden drew together a force of other beings to bind the gods to the Underworlde. But with the gods gone, there was no one to direct the wild magic, no one to guide the seasons in this land. The unbound forces of nature—with frost, with mist, with fire—and ran rampant through the forest and the village, and each of them bound themselves to a human, stealing them from their homes to cause further chaos."

I listened closely. I did not know the stories and gods of this land well, and I had never realized that Frost and the others had once been human.

"We arrived not too long after that final battle and found the Bear Maiden trying to instill order. We helped her. In exchange, she told us of two pools of magic—one in the forest, one in the mountains—that we could each call our own, provided we stayed and helped her rule over the seasons. We each absorbed one of the pools and bound that magic to ourselves."

"So... you took the place of the gods," I said slowly.

Holly made a face. "I wouldn't call it that. Gods demand worship. There's a certain ego needed to be a god, a certain disregard for human welfare, and I don't think I have it. Oak, on the other hand..." He trailed off and sighed. "He seems to have taken to that role with more vigor than I initially thought. But no, the Bear Maiden never intended for us to be gods. That's why she set the limit of a thousand years. The power is supposed to pass to someone else."

I considered this for a moment. "I think you'd make a good god, Holly," I said at last. "Especially because you don't want to be one."

He chuckled and shook his head. "Eat some breakfast, Nash. We need to get moving."

CHAPTER 32

Rowan

After lunch, Rowan set out, leaving Holly curled up by the fire, wrapped in a blanket.

Being by herself again was odd. First she'd had Keziah with her, with his sarcastic quips and charming grins, and then she'd cared for Holly. *Two very different companions,* she thought as she made her way northeast, through a cluster of cedar and pine. Keziah had welcomed her company, while Holly... well, he needed her.

She hiked up the hill Holly had described, remembering he had said she should be able to make out the grove from its peak, but once she reached the summit, she stopped. The holly grove should have stood on the next hill over, but all she faced was a blackened mound. The hill had been burned, and the holly grove with it.

Her heart sank. She couldn't bear to bring the news back to Holly— it would crush him.

She wondered if she ought to go back and tell Holly right away, but then a patch of green on the hill caught her eye. *I already came all this way. I'd do better to make certain there's nothing there that can help him, just in case.*

She hiked her way up the burned hill. The fire had happened recently—perhaps in the last few months, but enough time had passed that a few faint patches of grass had begun to grow. Soon brush and maybe even some saplings would again start poking their way through the blackened earth. Rowan couldn't help wondering what kinds of mushrooms would pop up here in a year's time.

She reached the top of the burned hill and looked down the other side. There, on the slope, was a badly burnt holly tree. Despite its injury, the tree looked to be alive—it had managed to grow some leaves.

Maybe it will still work, Rowan thought, turning her body sideways to keep from sliding as she made her way down to the tree.

Poor thing, she thought, running a hand up a blackened branch, *and I don't have to wonder who did this to you.*

This was the only area of the forest that had burned. The base of the hill was free of the signs of fire—something had stopped it from spreading, for it certainly should have spread. There was dry brush growing all around, and there were plenty of other trees that would have ignited just as easily. Rowan wondered if Oak had gone through the forest and torched any places like this, where his counterpart may have come to regain his strength.

Well, Oak was sloppy, Rowan thought, leaving the lone tree behind her and walking back up the hill. *And hopefully it will be to Holly's benefit.*

Lost in thought about the burned grove, Rowan made her way back through the trees without looking around her much. She was over halfway back to the cave when she got the prickling sensation she was being watched. She stopped and turned around.

"Hello?"

A patch of moss on the tree nearest to her shifted and morphed into the shape of a human's torso, jutting out from the tree like an odd limb. A marshy voice called out:

"Next a tree that turned to stone
   And hardened to a mask of fear
   But watch your step as you proceed
   For beasts are born of ivy here."

"Are you following me, Sphagnum?" she asked, a little irritated. She didn't know how long he'd been watching her.

"Why does a human girl take interest in the remnants of a fire?" the creature asked, their voice soggy in her ears. "I fear she did not take Sphagnum's advice about the Oak King."

"I fear your directions did not help me find my sister," she retorted, her irritation growing. "In fact, I think you sent me straight in the direction of danger, knowing what the Oak King would do if he came across me. Now answer me—have you been following me?"

"Sphagnum cannot follow the girl through the forest," Sphagnum said, sliding his patch of moss to the ground before Rowan. "As soon as she leaves his sight, it is as if she is no longer in the forest. Strange, it is, and most unusual. Quite a puzzle to Sphagnum."

"And why should you want to follow me in the first place? I told you before, I only want to find my sister and go home."

The mossman shook his head. "And send her toward her sister, Sphagnum did. She was with the Oak King."

Rowan opened her mouth to tell the creature off again, then froze. "Was?"

The mossman inclined its head. "She has managed to escape his prison, in a most curious and unusual way, and no one knows where she has hidden herself—only that she has not yet left the forest. She, too, is hard to find."

Celine had escaped the Oak King. Rowan felt a burst of hope in her chest. But quickly, anger returned.

"So you knew where she was, when I first met you, and you said nothing to me. You sent me to join her in captivity."

"Yes," the mossman said simply. "Sphagnum's Lord, the Oak King has commanded that all trespassers into his forest be caught and punished. To disobey him by helping the girl openly would mean Sphagnum's death."

"And you think that's fine? You don't question what he does, or what he orders?" Rowan asked disbelievingly.

The mossman gestured back the way she had come. "The girl saw the holly grove. That is what the Oak King does to those who make an enemy of him—destroys. Sphagnum leads the mosses of this land. He cannot condemn them to burn to save his conscience."

The creature tilted his head.

"Does the girl know the whereabouts of the Holly King?" he asked, his voice gone sly.

"No." Rowan lied, glaring straight into Sphagnum's feature-less face. "Do you?"

"Usually, he is most easy to find. He is of the mountains this time of year, more so than of the forest. But he has vanished, much in the same way the girl vanishes unless she walks across Sphagnum's path, as she did today."

He leaned forward.

"Much in the way of the Bear Maiden, who walks the woods without the Oak King's knowledge."

Then he chanted at her again, more insistently this time:

"Next, a tree that turned to stone
And hardened to a giant's hand
But watch your step as you proceed
Or soon your bones will feed the land."

Rowan gritted her teeth, fiercely chastised herself for not noticing the moss. She would need to look around herself more carefully.

"Why do you keep doing that?" she asked, willing her voice to stay polite. "What do your rhymes mean?"

"If Sphagnum could tell the girl that, he would not concern himself with riddles in the first place," the mossman replied haughtily.

"I haven't seen the Holly King, or the Bear Maiden, for that matter," she said stoutly, "and you've already caused enough trouble for me. I'll thank you to leave me alone. I'm not in need of any mossman poems, and I want nothing to do with the Oak King—I will not ally myself with a man who kidnaps people for gods know what purpose. He sounds like a terrible ruler."

The mossman stared intently at Rowan. "Maybe so, but a ruler nonetheless, and the only one with the full power of his seasons. The Holly King cannot stand against him for much longer. And five years from now, when the thousand years are over, the Holly King will lose his powers, but the Oak King has other powers to keep him strong. He will still reign while the Holly King returns to mortality. The girl would be wise to see that she is no longer in the forest when he finally falls."

"If you had been honest with me to begin with, my sister and I could have been home by now," she shot back. "And what do you mean, 'returned to mortality?' What will happen to him?"

"Perhaps if the girl listened a little better, she might have everything she wanted, and more," the creature retorted. "But Sphagnum's duty is to his king, not to the girl. He has helped where he could. The advice he has given the girl was out of his own kindness. By rights, Sphagnum should have told the Oak King of the girl the moment she first appeared, but he did not. No matter. Sphagnum will leave her now."

And the mossman shrank back into a puddle of moss on the forest floor.

"I hardly call sending me into a trap advice!" Rowan glared at the patch of moss for a moment, then turned and slowly made her way back through the trees. Every minute or so, she would turn back, convinced the mossman had followed her, but she saw no bright green anywhere she looked.

Still, she took a more winding route back to the shelter, hoping that, if the creature was indeed following her, it would grow weary and give up. She hoped it was enough.

Next, a tree that turned to stone
And hardened to a giant's hand

Rowan stopped with a blink. Lost in thought, she had been walking in time to Sphagnum's silly little poem. Gods, couldn't he leave her alone? But something about this second poem nagged at her. Hadn't she and Keziah passed that tree shaped like a hand? Keziah had explained how it had become stone over time, but she hadn't had much time to think about it before she'd walked into that mushroom ring.

"Maybe he's been following me this entire time and thinks he's being funny, mocking the mistakes I've made," she muttered darkly. She firmly resolved to put the infuriating mossman and his poetic nonsense from her mind.

She entered the root shelter, her heart sinking as Holly sat up, his face bright with expectation. It fell away when he took in Rowan's expression.

"What has happened? Did you find the..." He trailed off.

"I found where it was," she said as gently as she could. "But it looks as though there was a fire. There was only one tree left standing."

That awful, tortured look had returned to Holly's face. Rowan thought it would break her heart.

"He's burned it all," Holly said, his voice going raspy. "He's burned every single grove in the forest."

His hands were shaking again, and his breath came fast and panicked.

"Every safe place is gone. I can never escape from him."

He was losing control, his breath coming in great sobs, and his eyes cast wildly about the enclosure, as though expecting Oak to appear from the shadows at any second.

Rowan knelt and took Holly's shaking hands, holding them tightly. "He's not here. He doesn't know where you are, I promise. He won't get you again." For now she was certain Oak *had* caught up with Holly at one point, and whatever horrible thing he had done to him had broken the poor man completely, leaving him terrified every waking second of his life.

"Holly," she said softly, trying to break through his panic and calm him in some way. "There is a tree left at the grove. Is that enough to help you, even in a small way?"

He took gulps of air, struggling to slow his own breathing.

"It could," he gasped out finally. "It could help. Not as much as..." He shook his head, still pained by the knowledge that his grove was gone. "It would help, to have a little of that tree's strength," he managed to finish.

"Then you'll have it," Rowan said firmly. "When do you want to go?"

"I...I..." He was still anxious, his breath uneven. "I don't know. If he's been there before, he might come back at any second. I don't know when it's safe to...to..."

"You'll be with me," Rowan reminded him. "He won't find us if I'm with you."

She hoped she wasn't promising too much, that she wasn't wrong about Oak's inability to sense her presence in the forest. But Holly needed to grow stronger, needed to connect with the tree on the blackened hill—she was certain it would be good for him, remembering how fondly he had talked of it the day before. She needed to get him there.

"I... just need a few minutes. Please." Holly turned away from her and pulled his hands from her grasp, wiping his eyes.

"Of course." Rowan rose and brushed dirt from her knees. She set the water skin next to him without a word, then went to sit by the river. She'd never met a man with so much pain, so much terror in his mind as the Holly King. She wished she knew what to do to help him.

After a while, she heard him walk up behind her. She put on her pack and the two of them started out together.

Holly didn't speak much. He seemed to have more energy than the previous day, but he still labored to keep up with Rowan. She tried to move as slowly as she could, but he seemed impatient to go as quickly as possible.

She desperately wanted to ask him about what Sphagnum had said —would he really lose his powers in just a few years? And why?

When they reached the hill where Rowan had first seen the burnt-away grove, Holly only stopped and stared across. His face looked so weary, deadened of emotion.

Then, without speaking, he started down the hill. Rowan followed, letting him set the pace. He reached the empty peak and looked down the other side. His shoulders relaxed a little, and he went to the blackened tree.

He gripped the branch, pressing his forehead into the bark. Rowan held back, staying near the peak of the hill. She hoped she wasn't intruding by watching, but Holly seemed to have forgotten she was there.

He lit the torch they'd brought and singed some of the twigs, smoke spiraling through the branches. Then he dropped the torch and breathed in the smoke. Rowan stepped back when the branches creaked and grew several inches longer before her eyes.

The noises of the forest died away, overcome by the sound of a breeze that appeared to come from Holly and his tree. An icy blue swirled around him, blurring his dark edges until his form threatened to melt into the tree. Rowan could feel the earth beneath her tremble slightly.

Then, with all the peace of a deep breath, Holly's shape solidified again. His face, when he turned back to Rowan, still looked weary, but he had lost his look of hopelessness.

"I feel better than I expected to," he said, a small smile touching the corners of his mouth. "Stronger than I thought one tree would—"

But his eyes grew wide, staring at something behind Rowan, and he moved back to the tree, clutching at the branches with both hands.

Rowan turned around.

The Oak King stood there her on the crest of the hill, smiling down at Holly.

She backed away, down the hill, but he didn't seem to care that she moved. He didn't even seem to realize she was there.

"Hello, old friend. Feeling better now?"

Rowan glanced at Holly. He looked like an animal backed into a corner. His hands were white where he gripped the branches of his burnt tree. She wanted to get in front of him, wanted to block out the image of his enemy staring down at him. But what could she do? This was the King of Summer.

"You look a sight better than the last time we met," Oak said pleasantly, taking a step down the hill.

Holly tensed, as though he would run, but Rowan didn't know that it would help anything if he did.

"Though, you did seem so much braver then, so much more prepared to face me." He tapped his chin with a finger. "I wonder why you don't seem so ready now?"

Rowan could see Holly was shaking. She knew the same panic she'd watch come over him in the cave was likely coursing through him now, but he was afraid to move. And Oak was taunting him with reminders of whatever he had done to make him so afraid. She felt sick. She had to do something, something to keep him from getting to Holly.

She almost asked the trees for help, but Oak twitched and blinked in her direction, as though a fly had buzzed past him. But he ignored whatever it was he felt.

Idiot, Rowan cursed herself, *the trees are his—he won't let them help you.*

But then, a chill ran over her back. She looked down the hill and her jaw dropped.

Trees creaked, and two tawny beasts stepped out from the forest. They were even taller than Celine's horse, Charly, and their faces had beaks and feathers like birds, though their bodies were most definitely feline.

Rowan's mouth fell open.

Griffons. Creatures straight out of the fairy tales her grandmother told her.

Then she noticed one of them had something slung over its back. The griffon twitched and let its burden drop to the ground, where it lay for a moment before struggling up.

Keziah. Oak had caught him after all.

"Don't you have anything to say to me, Holly? Not after all this time?" Oak took another step and lifted his hand suddenly.

Holly flinched. Oak laughed.

Rowan took another look at Keziah. Keziah stood at the base of the hill, flanked by the two griffons. One of his eyes was blackened, and he swayed where he stood, but his eyes were fixed on Oak. Rowan had never seen such seething hatred in all her life.

Keziah's lips moved, as though he were speaking. Whatever he was saying, he did it quietly enough that the two hulking beasts on either side of him took no notice. Rowan wondered what on earth he was doing, until the chill ran over her again, and she caught glimpse of movement over the line of trees. Something—something huge—glittered and swelled there.

"Has the King of Winter truly been made so low? Or are you finally starting to regret what you took from me? Of all people, I would have thought *you* would understand my situation. But I was never as *good* as you were, was I? Never quite as suited to this damned kingdom."

Oak waited for a response but none came. He rolled his eyes.

"Still nothing to say? I thought performing your little ritual might give you a little more feist. I left this one..." He gestured to the holly tree.

"... in the hopes that you'd stop by. Don't you like what I've done with the rest of the place?"

Rowan looked back at Keziah, and at whatever approached them through the trees behind him. His hands lifted slightly at his sides, and Rowan's knees nearly gave way as a colossal wave drew up through the forest.

The river, she realized, her mind blank of anything else. *He's bringing in the river.*

"This is getting tiresome—I have much more important things to be doing right now," Oak said, looking irritated, "But first, some answers. How have you been hiding from me, these past few days? You always stick out like a butchered cow in a field during my months, and yet I couldn't tell where you were this year. Who helped you?"

Keziah closed his eyes, his words intensifying, though Rowan still couldn't hear them. The wave grew higher and higher. Realizing what he must mean to do, Rowan began to edge slowly down the hill, trying to keep her eyes on Holly.

"No one. Only the girl." Holly's voice was quiet, painfully quiet. Rowan froze.

"What was that?" Oak asked, his face spreading in a smile. Rowan was sure he had heard Holly, for his eyes flicked to her, but he seemed determined to make a show of how badly he had damaged his counterpart.

But Holly only stared at Rowan, pale-faced and desperate. He didn't seem to have seen the wave, blind to everything but the evil man taunting him. She wished she could say something, give him some kind of sign that they would save him, but with Oak looking at her, she couldn't do a thing.

"Ah. The girl. Sphagnum tells me you're looking for your sister."

She hated his handsome face.

"That makes two of us. The little bitch escaped somehow, and after I find her again, I'm going to find whoever helped her and see they never do so again." He gave Rowan a meaningful look. "And you will accompany *me* to search for her, if you care anything for your former traveling companion."

She lowered her eyes from Oak, in what she hoped was a compliant sort of way. A faint crashing sound pricked at her ears. She worried Oak would hear it, but he had turned his attention back to Holly.

"I wonder that you managed to convince this girl to help you at all," he said, jerking his head at Rowan. "Not very much of you to offer these days, is there? What did you promise her, to help you?"

"Nothing," Holly choked out.

"Nothing," Oak repeated, his eyes burning with rage. "Just another person you've corrupted to your cause. Does she know what you did to my own flesh and blood? Did you tell her what you did to Nash?"

The wave above them wavered; Rowan's eyes darted to Keziah—he looked as though someone had slapped him.

Holly's lips tightened. "Don't."

Oak struck out with his hand. A flash of fiery light rolled from his fingertips and struck Holly in the chest before he could move. He cried out and wrapped his arms around the tree, keeping it between Oak and himself.

"Don't what? Don't talk about my son? Is a father not permitted to grieve?" Oak looked anything but grieving, his eyes alight with the pain he was causing Holly. "He took him from me, you know," he said to Rowan, his eyes flashing gold and red. "Took my son from me. My only child."

"That isn't the whole story, and you know it," Holly spat through gritted teeth.

Keziah had turned pale, his hands clenched into fists.

"Oho!" Oak cried, sending off another flash of fiery light that blew branches off the holly tree and sent them crashing into Holly. "The King of Winter has some spine left! Strange, I could have sworn I left that spine dangling from a tree. No matter." He raised both his hands and framed them around Holly. "I'll do a better job this time."

Rowan felt water dripping over her shoulders, felt the sun give way to shadow. And now, before Oak could bring the light to his fingertips yet again, she saw Keziah bring his own hands down forcefully. The waiting river crashed down upon the Oak King's head. Rowan only caught a glimpse of it before the river washed her feet out from beneath her.

Holly stood, frozen, watching the river sweep Oak down the side of the hill. Keziah staggered, obviously struggling to keep the water from rushing everywhere. Rowan was certain he would lose control soon, and Oak would recover—she was sure he would.

"Holly, go!" Keziah yelled over the crashing water.

Holly looked down at him, then at Rowan, frightened as a deer. Then his shape blinked and shrank before her eyes, feathers sprouting through his skin. The huge black raven took off toward the mountain, a sprig of burnt holly grasped in its claws.

Keziah's shoulders sagged, and finally he released his hold on the water.

Rowan watched as the water seeped into the ground before her and the river reverted from its altered course back to the riverbed.

The ground rumbled beneath her, and she fell, tumbling down the hill as the earth tipped her. She landed in a heap at the bottom.

"What was *that?*" She looked up.

Oak was striding toward her, his face furious, his fine clothes soaked in muddy water. He gripped her by the collar and dragged her up, spitting into her face as he spoke. "*How did you do that?*"

Rowan was too shaken to understand what he meant. "D-do what?" she stammered.

His eyes narrowed.

"Don't think I'm going to underestimate you," he said, his voice as low as a growl. "Your sister managed to trick me that way, and I won't let it happen again."

He released her, and she stumbled. *Oh, gods, he thinks* I *controlled the river?*

"I have something you probably want," he said, snapping his fingers. One of the griffons shoved Keziah forward with its beak. He fell to his knees, keeping his eyes on the ground.

"I found him making his merry way through the wood—led me on quite a chase this one. Somehow, I can't seem to sense him as easily as I do most mortals in the forest." Oak pointed an accusatory finger at Rowan. "Just as I struggled to sense you. And the only reason I knew your sister was here is that she happened to catch the attention of the mossmen. But as I understand it, she has been stealing from my forest for years until now."

Oak flipped his wet cape from over his shoulder. "What I would like to know," he said, furiously, "is who has been hiding you from me? Who has been undermining my rule of my own forest and making it impossible for me to find you?"

Confused, Rowan shook her head. "No one has been helping me."

Oak smiled condescendingly. It was alarming how abruptly his expression could change from furious to pleasant and simpering.

"Do you really expect me to believe that *you,* on your own, are capable of commanding the trees to shield you? Of commanding the river? Even I can't do that."

Rowan didn't answer. She had done a great deal more with the trees than that and nothing at all with the river, but clearly he didn't know or expect that of her.

He sighed and waved a hand to the griffons.

"Bring the boy."

One of the griffons seized Keziah's collar in its beak and dragged him through the dirt to Oak's side.

Keziah looked terrible. He looked like he hadn't eaten in days, and his face was bruised and battered. Guilt swam over Rowan. She had been safe, comfortable, and well-fed in the past few days since he had left. She'd assumed he was safe, too.

"Tell me who has been helping you," Oak said sweetly, "or I will kill the boy. And if you still won't tell me, we'll find your sister and see if you care any more about her."

"That's an awfully long time to wait for an answer," Rowan said, trying to sound reasonable as her mind raced, trying to think of how to save Keziah. "Surely there's a better way—"

Oak waved a hand dismissively. "I don't bargain—I rule. Bargaining is only an option when *I* decide it is."

Rowan's thoughts bounced frantically around her head. *What do they do in the stories? What do they do when they're cornered by magic?* Then she remembered.

"Then I demand a trial," Rowan said stoutly, looking him dead in the eye.

His face tightened, making his smile seem skeletal.

"You... *what*?" he whispered, his voice harsh like glass grating.

Rowan hoped this gamble would pay off.

"I demand a trial. By all the laws of the forest, the mountains, and their magic, you must set me a trial. And if I pass," she said quickly, before Oak could speak, "you will release my friend and myself." She indicated Keziah. "And let us go on our way through your forest."

Behind her back, she crossed her fingers for luck. She had no idea if the Oak King was actually bound to set trials if challenged, but the stories said he was, and she had to trust in something.

An incredulous smile broke over Oak's face. "A village bumpkin reads a few fairy tales and thinks she can get the better of an immortal *king*? Fine! Have your trial and see if it doesn't lead you to your ruin!"

He waved a hand at Keziah, who vanished. Then, in a flash of light, a row of boys appeared. As Rowan looked at them, she felt the color drain from her face. They were all Keziah. Rowan felt her insides twist.

They were identical, all dressed exactly the way he'd been dressed. But, more disturbingly, they each had different expressions. One was smiling kindly at Rowan. Another watched her, fearful and trembling. Still another glared at Oak, his eyes full of hate. And another looked straight ahead, dead-eyed and listless.

"Tell me which of these men is your companion. If you name him truly, I will let you both go, as you have demanded," Oak said with a hateful smile, gesturing to the line of Keziahs.

Rowan walked down the line of boys, looking at each one. It made her horribly uncomfortable, for as she reached the next Keziah, his expression would shift, happy to sorrowful, angry to afraid. Her throat tightened. The real Keziah might not even be in this line—Oak could have hidden him away. But then how would she guess? She couldn't tell, couldn't tell at all.

"Truth be told, I was a little surprised to find an islander skulking around my forest," Oak mused as Rowan peered anxiously into every face. "Though I suppose I only have myself to thank, now that their people have started spreading to the continent. I've known one or two with such *interesting* magic."

Rowan ground her teeth, trying to ignore Oak's voice. She looked at the Keziah at the very end of the line—he looked back at her with an awful hopelessness. She wanted to cry—she *couldn't* fail him, not now.

Then, as she turned to make her way back up the row of Keziahs, something caught her eye. There was something different about the second one from the end. She moved closer slightly, and she saw that a snowflake had fallen and got tangled in his long black eyelashes. This Keziah stared back at her, his eyes desperate as his face was twisted against his will into a winning smile.

Out of the corner of her eye, she saw something dark take off from the top of a tree. She didn't dare turn to look at it properly, but she could see what it was.

The raven, unnoticed by Oak, had come back to help her.

Holly.

She waited until she could no longer see the raven before pointing at the Keziah before her.

"This one," she said firmly, taking his hand in hers. "This is him."

She looked at Oak. His eyes burned as he strode toward her, waving a hand. The line of Keziah's disappeared in a puff of smoke, leaving behind the boy in front of Rowan.

"Impossible!" he snarled, pushing up his sleeves. "Impossible! No mortal woman could ever hope to tell the difference!"

And he raised his hands, his promise of letting them go clearly forgotten in his rage, but then he blinked and stopped. Snow was falling, large, fluffy flakes cascading from the sky.

"Holly!" Oak roared, and he spun where he stood and swirled himself up into a fiery burst of light.

The griffons shied away from the flames and tore off into the trees without a second glance at their king.

The funnel of fire that was the Oak King took off, directed at the mountains, speeding like a burning arrow up the slope. But then it stopped, plumes of smoke rolling off, and the fire dissipated, leaving only a darkened form screaming up at the mountain.

"He can't cross into the mountains."

Keziah's voice startled Rowan, and she turned to him.

"He spent too much of his power." His glassy eyes reflected the mountains. He looked at Rowan. "Holly hasn't been strong enough to keep him out like this in years. What did you do to him?"

Startled, Rowan dropped his hand. "I helped him get to the last holly tree here," she said, indicating the broken hill behind them. "He was able to do his ceremony, to recover."

Keziah shook his head. "That shouldn't have been enough. It would have helped a little, but he needed more trees than that to regain enough strength." He looked at Rowan for a long moment. Then his knees gave way and he fell forward, knocking into her.

At first she thought he had fainted, but then he gripped her arms very hard as she tried to keep him from falling to the ground. Then she realized he was shaking badly.

"Are you all right?" she asked as she helped ease him to the ground.

His face was screwed up, as if he were about to cry. "He didn't recognize me," he gasped out finally, "he didn't recognize me at all."

"How did you do that, with the river?" Rowan asked, unable to keep her questions to herself, "And who are you to him, that he should have recognized you?"

Keziah looked at her, his face stricken. "I—"

But before he could answer, a golden light burst across Keziah's chest, and he lifted up, out of her arms, and into the sky. Rowan jumped up, reaching after him, but he was out of her grasp in seconds.

Then Oak hurtled down, cloak flapping in the wind, his face screwed up and ugly with anger.

"He's safe and snug inside his fortress, it appears," he snarled as he landed, his boots slamming into the dirt. "And you're to blame for this; don't think I don't know it."

He paced back and forth, his eyes fixed on Rowan. She tried not to stare up at Keziah, dangling in midair. Falling from that height would not be good.

"He shouldn't have that kind of power—not after living on the run, and not after a simple commune with a single holly tree." He reached out a fist and clenched it; with a *CRUNCH*, the sole remaining holly tree crumbled into dust. "He has been drawing on another source of power, and you must have it. What is it?" he demanded.

Rowan shook her head. "I don't have anything. And I passed your trial—you have to let us go."

He stared at her. Then that awful, chilling smile slid back into place.

"Actually," he said, his voice sounding horribly pleasant once more, "I don't."

He waved his hand, and Keziah shot away, far over the trees and out of sight.

"I've decided my trial hasn't quite finished yet. Go find your village boy. If you succeed at that, well..." His smile deepened cruelly. "I'll be quite surprised. I'll even give you a trail to follow—though even with that generosity, I still don't think you'll manage. See that you don't stray; the moment you veer away from the path I've set, it will vanish."

He waved his hand, and a glittering wisp of gold appeared, hanging in the air and winding through the trees in the direction Keziah had just been flung. Then, with a swirl of his cloak, which would have been more impressive if it hadn't been stained with mud, Oak spiraled back up into the air and soared off to the south.

CHAPTER 33

Nash

The air turned chillier the higher we climbed. Holly led me over rocky screes, past crashing waterfalls, beyond a herd of elk nestled near a hot spring. As we passed through a maze of rocks, I heard growling and looked up. That same snow-white creature, with his long snout and horrible distended stomach—the one that had attacked me a year ago—glared at me from his perch atop a boulder.

"Peace, Snowbelly," Holly said, putting a hand on my shoulder. "He is with me."

Snowbelly snorted and turned his back on me. Holly jerked his head at the path, and we continued.

I kept looking over my shoulder, hoping that Snowbelly wasn't following us.

"Don't worry about him, Nash. Snowbelly is closely tied to the magic of these mountains—he will listen to me." Holly sighed. "Though I will admit, I've had problems with him following the Bear Maiden down into the forest in Spring and attacking Oak's people, as you experienced last year." His expression turned sour. "I wonder if he somehow found out what Oak was doing and was trying to stop him, in his own way. A pity he cannot speak."

As the day wound toward night, I kept waiting for Holly to stop to make camp, but he pressed on, until the sun barely clung to the horizon.

"Are we going to keep going all night?" I asked, desperately hoping he would say no.

Holly laughed. "I wouldn't do that to you, Nash. My fortress is nearby —I thought we could rest there for tonight. It will certainly be more comfortable than camping on rocks."

It was so dark by the time we reached the fortress that I would have completely missed it if I had been alone. Thankfully, Holly stopped and pointed out the doorway, barely visible in the growing dark.

We went inside. I was so tired that I hardly took in any of it. I had a vague impression of a roaring fireplace and rich, cozy rugs as Holly led me down the dim hallway. He pointed me to a room with a bed in it. I dropped my pack and fell onto the bed, asleep before my head hit the pillow.

CHAPTER 34

Rowan

Rowan stood alone beside the burnt hill. She could see the broken branches of the final holly tree sticking up from the muddy ruin of the former grove. Her pack had ripped from her back during Oak's onslaught of the hill—it lay on a mostly dry patch of earth. She went and picked it up.

She had no idea of what to do now. Keziah was gods know where, Holly had escaped back to his mountain, and she was still no closer to finding Celine.

She knelt by her pack and checked it for damage. Both straps had broken, but the rest of it looked largely unharmed. She pulled out her needle and thread and, hating that she had to waste fine dyed embroidery thread on mending, she set to fixing the straps. She cursed herself for not thinking to bring plain old linen thread, but then again, she had hoped to be home by now.

How long have I even been in this forest? she thought dismally, tears welling in her eyes. *And Celine, how long has she been out here by herself?*

At least she knew Celine was no longer the Oak King's prisoner—that was a comfort. But that knowledge still didn't give her an idea of where her sister might be, or if she was still alive.

I still need the Bear Maiden, she thought, *and I still need someone to lead me to her.*

She pressed a fist to her head, trying to sort through her thoughts. This had all gone so terribly wrong from the first moment she'd set foot in the forest.

Keziah. She had to find Keziah.

She checked the straps, yanking on them to make sure their stitching held fast. Satisfied, she pulled on her pack.

She had to keep going. Though all she wanted to do was crawl back to the shelter she'd shared with Holly, she couldn't afford to let herself sink into her tiredness. People were depending on her.

She stared off uncertainly in the direction Oak had sent Keziah flying. The trail Oak had left glimmered faintly in the afternoon sun. She needed to get going. Oak might have sent him into a den of Red Caps, or sunk him in a swamp.

Of course, her insides squirmed. Every instinct told her there was danger lurking somewhere along this winding golden trail of Oak's. But if it truly led to Keziah, then it was her only hope of finding him.

So she set off, oddly comforted by having a path to follow at last, even if it was likely treacherous. The woods were strangely quiet, empty of the Spring bustle from earlier that day. Rowan didn't know if it was because of the altercation with the river or if Oak's presence sent the forest's inhabitants into hiding.

I'd hide from him, too, if I thought he was nearby, she thought, *hateful man.* There was something so wrong about him, the evil joy he took in causing pain.

And he had a child, apparently, she thought, her brow wrinkling. He'd said Holly had taken him away, and Holly, rather than denying it, had only said it wasn't the whole story. *Does that mean he killed the Oak King's son?*

He hadn't told her the whole story. Rowan wondered if that was why the Oak King had attacked him, but surely Holly would have told her the reason. Wouldn't he? And besides, she couldn't imagine gentle Holly hurting anyone.

After a while, she noticed that the sound of her footsteps had grown muffled. She looked down and realized the ground beneath and before her was carpeted in the bright green moss of the swamp. A flash of fury ran through her, and she stomped her foot.

"Sphagnum!" she spat, pulling out her flint and striking it on a stone. The sparks flew into the moss and sent up a hiss of smoke.

"Come out now, or I'll burn you up," she snarled at the mossy forest floor.

There was a loud squelching sound, and his human-like figure detached from the side of a dead tree.

"Really, so rude! No need!" he spluttered, sliding across his mossy brethren toward her.

"That's far enough," she growled, raising her flint menacingly.

The creature waved dismissively.

"Such an act would not be justified." His mossy lips brushed together as he spoke.

"How wouldn't it be justified? You told Oak where I was! You led him straight to Holly!" She wanted someone to pay for what had happened—for the look of pure terror she'd seen on Holly's face, for the hurt that had been done to him, for the Oak King's smug look of triumph on the mountain.

"Sphagnum told the Oak King where he believed the Holly King to be," Sphagnum corrected. "And since he is Sphagnum's enemy and the girl is his ally, then it appears Sphagnum was right to tell the Oak King of her position, also." The creature spoke with such simplicity, as though he were commenting on the weather.

"I told you when I came here, I'm not on either side. I have no allies," Rowan said through gritted teeth. She was growing tired of the mossman's insistence that she choose a side.

"Yet she tends to the Holly King and sleeps by his side in a dwelling made from the Oak King's trees? If that does not make her his ally, Sphagnum must ask what does?"

"I only helped him when he was wounded—I would have done that for anybody."

The creature shook its head. "But she is female, and he is male. If a child were to come of such a union, they would inherit some measure of the Holly King's gifts. Where would the balance of power fall then?"

Rowan gaped at the creature.

"*That's* why you told Oak where we were? Because you thought we *slept* together?"

The creature shrugged, and a snail fell from his shoulder.

"Sphagnum prepared for the worst. He is a ruler himself—he must think of his people."

Rowan glared at him. "Absolutely *nothing* like that happened. You were wrong. And you nearly cost three people their lives today."

He inclined his mossy head.

"Sphagnum chose Summer long ago. He must remain loyal, despite his personal preferences."

Rowan rolled her eyes. "Don't you think you would do better to stay on good terms with Winter? You act as though he wants a land full of snow and ice year-round. He doesn't. And for that matter, don't you think ought to be on good terms with more than just one season? Surely *that* would give you the best chances."

Sphagnum quirked his head. "As long as the year is divided in two, the Oak King will not rest until he has the power of both halves. There is no one else to keep him in check—once he broke the Holly King, even he could not stand against him. What could a simple mossman hope to do in the face of one with so much power?"

While his words sounded hopeless, his tone had an odd energy to it, and Rowan could almost swear his empty eye divots flashed at her.

"What are you trying to say, Sphagnum?" she asked, exasperated.

Sphagnum tilted his head the other way, his floral features sly.

"Last, before the day is done,
The snowdrop garden must be found.
Follow lights of blue, not red
And leave before the sun goes down."

The creature sang at her.

Rowan frowned. The mossman insisted on telling her these little rhymes. Surely they must mean *something,* even if he was on Oak's side. "You've mentioned a pool, a... hand? And now a garden," she said slowly. "Is this some kind of warning? That something will happen to me if I see these things? Or is it another trick, like when you gave me directions straight to Oak's palace? Because I swear, Sphagnum, I'm sick to death of your meddling, and—"

"If the girl thinks Sphagnum meddles only to her detriment, then he truly cannot help her." The mossman sniffed. "She will never find the Bear Maiden at this rate."

Rowan threw up her hands. "What does that have to do with you? I *will* find her, and she'll help me find my sister."

She brushed past the mossman, walking along the path outlined by the golden wisps.

"She would be wise to ask for something else," Sphagnum called after her. "Many seek the Bear Maiden for favors, things that could be easily achieved even without her aid. Few ask her for real power."

Rowan ignored him. Or at least she tried to, but she was so distracted that she didn't see the person in the path ahead of her until their outstretched hand slammed into her chest, forcing her to halt.

The gossamer-clad Dew was far stronger than she looked. Up close, Rowan could see every inch of her skin was beaded with moisture, glistening as though she was coated in minuscule jewels.

Without taking her eyes off Rowan, she called in a high, clear voice, "Aiding the Oak King's enemies, mossman? It's a bit early in the year to start working against your king. Don't you agree?"

Rowan heard Sphagnum shifting uncomfortably behind her, mumbling something about, "Nothing of the sort," and "Sphagnum would never."

"I promise you, he hasn't been helping me," Rowan said, holding her empty hands up to show Dew. "I only came here to bring my sister home, and he has been nothing but a hindrance."

"'Nothing but a hindrance?'" Dew high-pitched laugh rang in Rowan's ears, making her head ache. "I heard what he told you—*The snowdrop garden must be found.* And that's the third piece, which means he's told you the other two already. Have you found them, then? The Hand and the Pool?"

"The... what?" Rowan took a step back. Sphagnum had chanted poems about both of those things earlier, but he had only been trying to distract her so Oak's allies could capture her. Hadn't he?

Dew's eyes narrowed. "Don't tell me you don't even know... Good gods, *humans* are so *dense* these days!"

She stepped around Rowan and picked her way over to the hump of moss that was Sphagnum.

"Be gone, mossman. No more trailing this girl through the forest. I've got my eye on you, and I'll know if you disobey."

Grumbling, Sphagnum slumped flat to the ground and slithered off over the tree roots and out of sight.

Rowan took a tentative step backward. Dew whirled around instantly.

"He's already told you what you need to know," she said in a low, urgent voice. "It's up to *you* to make that brain of yours put it all together."

Rowan's foot slipped on a wet root and she stumbled to the ground, still gaping up at Dew.

"W-what do you mean? What did he tell me?"

"Gods damn you, I can't say anything more!" Dew whispered fiercely, her eyes darting through the trees. "I crept up on you and the mossman and heard every word he said; someone else could easily do the same now."

A twig snapped in the distance, a faint sound, but Dew's head snapped up. "Someone's coming! Smoke, perhaps, or Thaw. You've got to get out of here," she hissed.

"I don't understand! Why are you helping me? I thought you served Oak!" Rowan whispered.

Dew turned her large, luminescent eyes on Rowan. There was a hardness in them that belied her delicate exterior.

"He's gone too far. He went too far the day he began stealing powers, and he went too far the day he decided to try it on his own child. I cannot stand against him outright, but I can at least do *something*. Now go!"

As Rowan climbed back to her feet, Dew thrust out a hand. Her palm filled with an orb of water the size of a melon, and she flung it at a nearby tree. It burst, spattering Rowan as she stumbled along the Oak King's path.

She looked over her shoulder and saw Dew flit off through the trees, pelting the underbrush with fistfuls of water.

"She came this way!" Rowan heard Dew call. "Quickly now, before she vanishes again!"

Her lungs burning, Rowan ran as fast as she could, following the swirling trail that wound through the trees. Part of her was convinced Dew had tricked her and would soon have the others on her trail. Or that they would hear her crashing through the forest and come after her despite what Dew told them.

But she couldn't run forever. Soon, her aching legs seized up, and she had to slow down. She made herself keep walking, for she thought she might vomit if she stopped moving entirely.

But she made herself breathe deeply, trying to put her fear from her mind. Instead, Dew's words came back to her.

He went too far the day he decided to try it on his own child. The Oak King had tried to take his own child's powers for himself, a choice that would have killed them if he'd had the chance to do it. Rowan shuddered. She wondered where that child was now, if they were still alive, if they were still near the forest, or if they'd gotten as far away from the place as they could.

But speculation would get her nowhere. For now, all she cared about was getting to Keziah before the glittering gold trail vanished.

We left early the next morning, after breakfasting in a cavernous room that overlooked the forest.

"So this is your view all Summer?" I asked Holly as I chewed on my fruit-studded bread. The kitchens had produced a full, hot breakfast, though I had yet to see any of the kitchen staff, if any such people existed.

Holly leaned his head against the rocky wall, his troubled gaze fixed on the forest. "Yes, though I usually break up the Spring and Summer months by traveling through the mountains. As I said before, I don't exactly rule up here, but there are just as many creatures up here who need help now and again. The dragons, for one—they're quite the political bunch, and they fight over territory constantly. I'll intercede now and again if their battles start to affect other creatures."

He drained the last of his coffee. "In fact, we'll be passing by a dragon's den on our journey today—I'd like to warn them that Oak may pursue us if he catches wind of our venture. I find it very hard to believe that none of his allies have noticed our absence back in the forest."

The thought of Oak coming after us made my stomach turn, and I abandoned the remainder of my breakfast.

Soon after we departed the fortress, Holly paused before a large heap of frost-kissed stones. He held out a hand, and a snowburst spun from his *palm into the rocky pile. The ground rumbled, the stones shifting and spilling, and an ice-blue snout poked out from among the rocks.*

"Holly?" the dragon hissed, blinking sleep from her silvery eyes. "What in the gods' names are you doing up here? Is it not Autumn?"

"Sorry to disturb your rest, Narra. I'm afraid I had to return to the mountains on urgent business." Holly indicated me.

The dragon's eyes flicked to me, and I took half a step back. Never before had anyone's gaze chilled me to my very bones.

"The Oak King's son," Narra said slowly.

"Oak means to sacrifice him and take his power," Holly said in a low, urgent tone. "And I mean to get to the Bear Maiden and ask her to help me stop him, once and for all."

Narra shifted and grumbled. "Well, good luck to you. We shall guard the pass if the Oak King approaches."

"Thank you," Holly said, but Narra had already slid her snout back into the rock pile. He smiled at me and shrugged. "Dragons," he whispered.

"I heard that," rumbled Narra from deep within the scree.

Hours later, after Holly and I had hiked for an age along a treacherous cliff, I was beginning to regret ever asking to make this journey.

"Is this really the only way to reach the Bear Maiden?" I asked through chattering teeth. It was far colder up here than down in the forest, and the wind cut straight through me.

"This time of year, yes." Holly didn't seem bothered by the cold in the slightest.

His cloak whipped loosely around him, and he didn't even bother with mittens. I, on the other hand, had my cloak wrapped around me as tightly as possible, and I had wrapped a scarf around my face for good measure, too.

"If it were Springtime," Holly continued, "we could have simply waited for her to come down into the forest. She can be a little difficult to track down, but if we sat at the base of the mountains, we'd most surely find her as she made her way down."

And couldn't we have done that? *I didn't voice it, but I dearly wished we could have stayed in the forest and let the Bear Maiden come to us.*

Holly seemed to guess my thoughts. "It is an uncomfortable journey, I know, but Oak might have decided at any moment that your powers were strong enough for him to take. As long as you are out of his reach, you are safe."

He was right. Of course he was right. That still didn't change how much I wished to be sitting by a fire with a warm cup of cider in my hands. Nonetheless, I resolved to keep my complaints to myself.

The cold and the wind made the next two days of travel blur into a haze. We passed through, what Holly called the "nevető sziklák," or "laughing rocks," in total silence at Holly's request, anxiously watching the sleeping faces carved into the cliffsides as we crept along. Once my foot slipped and dislodged a few stones, which rattled off down the mountainside and made a great deal more noise than I had expected. The eyes of one of the stone faces flew open, and they let out a sharp, barking laugh.

Holly motioned for me to freeze, and the pair of us stood there like startled deer, staring wide-eyed at the cliff face. They looked us over eagerly, as though hoping we would entertain them, but when we didn't move or make a sound, they seemed to grow bored. They yawned widely and their eyes fluttered shut again.

We moved on, and I took greater care to step wisely.

The labyrinth came next. We entered the cobweb-laced network of passages the next day. The second the sky was out of sight, my chest seized up. I struggled to take in air, even after unwinding my scarf and undoing the top buttons of my shirt collar. The tunnel walls pressed into me, and I had the horrible image of them squeezing together until I was crushed.

"Breathe, Nash," Holly told me, taking hold of my shoulder. "You can still breathe. It's just the tunnel. We'll come out into the open again soon, I promise."

It took a few minutes, but I was able to draw a deep breath and calm myself.

Somehow Holly seemed to know where we were going—I, for my part, had absolutely no idea. If he had asked me to find my way back to the entrance, I would have gotten us horribly lost.

The hours felt like days. Perhaps they were—I completely lost track of time, without the sun or the stars visible. The stagnant air of the tunnels sat heavy in my lungs, and my feet crunched on what I sincerely hoped were sticks and twigs.

Even worse, there were things *living in the labyrinth. The most harmless were translucent little bats the size of moths that liked to swarm our faces without warning, scrabbling at our mouths and eyes with their clawed wings. I crushed a good handful against my face trying to swipe them away, and the resulting mess made me wrap my scarf around my face once more, despite the oppressive darkness.*

Holly wouldn't let us stop for the night; to fall asleep in the labyrinth was an invitation he did not like to extend, he said. I tried not to think too hard about what that meant.

Even more disturbing were the spiny things creeping after us in the shadows. Holly had asked me to summon a ball of fire to light our way. Every time I turned to look over my shoulder, something—or somethings—scuttled back around the bends in the passages before I could get a good look at what they were.

"The Bear Maiden lives here?" *I asked Holly more than once.*

"Not in these passages, no, but somewhere nearby. The journey to reach her is difficult for a reason."

I couldn't help but wonder if that reason was good enough.

The very worst was yet to come.

I had just turned around abruptly, trying to spot the scuttling creatures behind us, when I ran into the back of Holly. He had stopped and was now surveying the passageway ahead of us with a frown.

Cobwebs thick as ropes stretched from ceiling to floor and wall to wall. There was such a dense layer of them that I couldn't see through to the other side.

"Is this the only way through?" I asked, though I could already guess the answer.

"I'm afraid so," Holly said grimly. He stepped aside so I could use my fire.

No sooner had flame touched the first bit of web, something dark and massive crashed through them, knocking me to the ground. I heard Holly yelling something as I struggled under the weight of the beast, trying to keep myself from realizing what it was.

But there was no denying it, as its pincers scrabbled at my face, shredding my scarf to rags.

"Yield, Pająk!" Holly's voice was closer now.

Whatever he meant to do, I hoped he did it soon—the spider was crushing the air from my lungs.

"You bear the revenge of Winter if you do not yield!"

The spider hissed and paused for a moment, which gave me enough time to wriggle out from under it. It must have decided to stick with its initial course, however, for it snagged my cloak and yanked me backward, clasping me to its horrible, furry body as its chelicerae closed on the back of my head.

The look of rage on Holly's face chilled me even more than the vile spider. He threw out a hand and a burst of orange light shot from his palm. It struck the spider's bulbous abdomen, eliciting a piercing shriek from the beast. It released me and, I flung myself away from it. From behind Holly, I watched as its body shriveled in upon itself, its legs curl under and snap under its weight. It twitched violently, then lay still.

"What... what was that?" I asked, my voice nearly as shaky as my hands.

"Pająk is a—" Holly broke off when he saw that I was staring, not at the spider, but at his raised hands. He let them drop by his side. "Ah. That was the power of Withering. I only hold a portion of it—the rest is held by the lady we saw in the forest."

"I thought Withering would only be used on plants," I said slowly.

Holly grimaced. "Yes, I can see why you'd make that assumption. But our powers have no restrictions in that way. It takes a little more power and practice to use Withering like this, but it's certainly manageable."

I filed that fact away, just in case it ever came up for my powers.

"In any case, the webs have been cleared, and we should be getting close now. Let's keep moving."

True to his word, around the next bend, I could see a faint glow of light up ahead of us. I stepped out into the weak Autumn sunlight and thought I had never been so glad to see the sky, gray and cloudy as it was.

We had come out into an odd circular area, lined with a half circle of different tunnel openings. The area sat upon a ledge that overlooked a deep canyon. If I squinted, I could just make out the river far, far below, nothing more than a glint in the ground.

And in the center of this strange ledge stood a tree, its leaves yellowed with Autumn's chill.

"What is this place?" I asked Holly as I peered into one of the other tunnel entrances.

"This is it," he replied, studying the tree. "This is where the Bear Maiden appears to anyone who successfully makes the journey we just made."

"Where is she, then? Do we have to do something, to make her come out?" My foot crunched on something. I looked down and found I had stepped on a splintered ribcage, ancient and bleached stark white by the sun.

"Oh, I'm already here, young one," a deep voice rasped from behind me.

I leaped back from the tunnel. There now stood a woman—or someone like a woman—with long, tangled auburn hair and a golden cloak of warm fur. Her face was covered by the same fur, and black claws curled around the edges of the cloak.

Her dark eyes were fixed on me, and she smiled, displaying a mouthful of sharp black teeth.

"Lord Holly," she said without turning to look at him. "What on earth has possessed you to leave the forest at the height of Autumn?"

"Oak," Holly said grimly. He strode over to stand beside me, his hand on my shoulder. "This is his son, Nash."

"Ah," the Bear Maiden studied me with a faint smile. "So, he has chosen an heir after all?"

"That's what we all thought."

The Bear Maiden glanced at Holly, noting the bitterness in his voice.

"But no. In his travels, Oak has been stealing magic from children, killing them in the process. Likely others, too, but we have no way to confirm it. We believe he is helping Nash's power come into its full force so that he may do the same to him."

The Bear Maiden's lip curled. "I knew the day I met you that he would bring trouble. He was a selfish boy, more concerned with getting himself power than with doing anything good with it. You deserved better than him, Holly."

To my surprise, Holly blushed.

"That was a long time ago. He was a different person when we first came here—I believe he could have done great things, if only—"

"He had the same choices you did, the same opportunities to grow," she snapped. "Now he has taken the gifts I gave him and turned them to a dark purpose—he holds the same ambitions that the gods did, and he deserves to be banished."

"Then you can do it?" Holly asked. "You can banish him, just as you did with the gods."

The Bear Maiden sighed, shaking her head. Dead leaves tumbled from her auburn tresses.

"If, as you say, he has amassed powers from other lands that we do not even know of, then I am afraid I cannot simply banish him. Nor can I strip him of any of these new powers. Not of my own free will, in any case—you know how the magic works."

"A wish, then? What if I—"

"You have already wished, Holly," the Bear Maiden said regretfully. "I cannot change the magic, even for you."

Dread seeped into my stomach. I knew Holly would turn to me and ask me to use my wish to break Oak's powers, to give up the chance I'd been waiting for to help save the world from the man who had fathered me. I braced myself for it, for how could I refuse?

But to my surprise, Holly squared his shoulders and said, "What if I returned some of my powers to you? Would you be able to use them against Oak in some way?"

My head reeled. Holly would rather give up his powers than take my wish from me? I was already struggling to wrap my brain around the Bear Maiden's implication that Holly and Oak had been... involved in some way long ago.

The Bear Maiden scratched her chin, thoughtful.

"Hmm. I could use them to intensify the Border, trap Oak inside so he cannot do any more mischief in other lands. Then we could work to break his power, little by little."

My face fell. "Little by little? Is there nothing else we can do to stop him properly?"

"He is too strong, little one," the Bear Maiden told me. "And I would not have you and Holly risk your lives against him. Besides, the magic of the forest must be governed. If we did manage to defeat Oak somehow, his powers would break free and ravage the countryside. He

has done an extremely dangerous thing, trapping all that power within himself."

"But it is possible," Holly insisted. "Even if it cannot happen all at once, we can keep him trapped in the forest and take his powers away, one by one."

"Yes," agreed the Bear Maiden, "and we must take care to keep this power from falling into his hands again." She nodded at me. "I am glad to see you have little of your father in you, boy. Let's see that it stays that way."

I flushed.

"Actually," Holly said, stepping back. "Nash has something he would like to ask you. He and I had planned on making this journey long before we discovered Oak's treachery, but even so, I would still like to see that he gets his wish."

He walked back to the cherry tree, leaving me alone with the Bear Maiden.

"So, you have a wish, young Nash?" She sounded pleased. "I cannot recall the last wish I granted. Not many villagers make the climb through the mountains these days."

"Yes, I—" I stopped, hands balling up into fists at my sides. It didn't feel right, to make this wish for myself when so much in the world needed fixing.

"If you aren't certain, perhaps it would be best to save your wish," the Bear Maiden said kindly. "After all, you only get one."

"No, I am sure! At least, I was, but... All the terrible things Oak has done—all the terrible things he's still out there doing. I feel like my wish should be something that stops him. Something that makes a difference to someone other than me."

"Ah," sighed the Bear Maiden. "You're afraid you're being selfish, aren't you?"

I nodded, tears pricking in the corners of my eyes.

"Nash, a wish is a selfish thing by its very nature. Something for yourself that you cannot get any other way. What you want for yourself does not need to change the world—you have already promised to do that work, and as Holly said, it can be done. There is no need to sacrifice your wish to serve the world."

Her clawed hand squeezed my arm. I wiped my eyes on my sleeve and nodded, swallowing the rest of my tears.

I opened my mouth, ready to make my wish, ready to commit to the promise I had made to myself—when a great BOOM of thunder echoed across the mountains, causing the ground to shake beneath my feet.

A rush of wings came from overhead. Holly's head snapped up, as did mine. Narra, all silver and blue scales flashing in the light, came rippling down from the sky and landed in a crouch by the cherry tree. There was barely enough room for her on the ledge.

"The Oak King approaches!" she barked at Holly. "The dragons have gone down to meet him, but they cannot stand against him alone."

"They will not have to," Holly promised. He turned to the Bear Maiden, dropping to his knees. "We don't have much time. Please, take the power you need from me."

The Bear Maiden hesitated. "Without you to guide the power, the season—"

"My people will guide the season. They can manage without me until Oak has been stripped of his powers. Please. We must bind him before he can reach Nash."

The Bear Maiden looked as though she had a great deal more to say, but she set her mouth in a grim line and placed a paw on Holly's head.

"I will take the season of Autumn from you," she said, her eyes turning to glittery black, "and leave you with the powers of Winter intact."

Gold light burst from her paw and swirled around him. Holly's chest heaved, and tendrils of orange and brown magic began to spill from his eyes, his hands, his mouth. The magic poured into the Bear Maiden, who shuddered as the magic took root within her.

Holly collapsed forward onto his hands and knees, gasping for breath. The Bear Maiden turned her face upward and raised her paws to the sky. The power of Autumn glowed in her palms for a beat, then burst into the air, spreading wide like a net. The Bear Maiden waved her hands back in the direction of the forest, and the net sped away, falling out of sight.

"It is done." Breathing heavily, she looked down at Holly, still curled over himself on the ground.

"G-good," he choked out, a hand clasped to his chest.

Another peal of thunder rang out, and the very mountains shook with the force of it. I nearly fell over, clutching the cherry tree to keep myself upright.

The Bear Maiden frowned. "It is done, but it may not be enough. If he is strong enough, he may be able to break the Border."

Holly's eyes met mine. I do not know what he saw in my expression, but I am certain it made him do what he did next.

"Then we must make certain he is not strong enough to break it." He struggled up from the ground, nearly staggering over.

"Holly, you ought to rest," the Bear Maiden told him, watching as he stumbled over to Narra. "It is no small thing to have power taken from you—you will be weak for some time."

"And we will all be weaker still if Oak should break the Border and find us here," Holly replied, climbing onto Narra's back. "Nash, make your wish," he told me. "I will make sure Oak does not find his way to you."

The Bear Maiden and I watched as he urged Narra into the sky.

"But... does he mean to face Oak? He doesn't have his full powers anymore!" I cried, dread pooling in my stomach.

"Child, I think he knows that." The Bear Maiden's voice was heavy with sorrow. "It appears he has made his choice. Let us hope it makes a difference."

She turned to me, her voice growing urgent. "We may not have much time. If you still are certain of your wish, I encourage you to make it now."

I swallowed hard, my thoughts still half with Holly as he flew back down the mountain. Oak would be waiting for him—I was sure of it.

"I wish... I wish for my body to become physically male, as if I had been born that way. Please."

A wide grin spread across the Bear Maiden's face. "It would be my pleasure to make it so."

She waved her hand, and a beam of gold light arced from it, striking me in the chest. The warm light filled my vision, and then all went dark.

CHAPTER 36

Rowan

Rowan pressed on, struggling where the trail took her through thick brush.

The path led her on through the quiet forest for another hour or so without incident. She was just starting to think the Oak King had set her a trail to nowhere in particular, to get her out from under his feet.

Last, before the day is done,
The snowdrop garden must be found.

Sphagnum's silly rhymes kept dancing through her head. Rowan sped up her pace, as though she could outrun his ridiculous poems. What did he mean by spouting those little phrases at her? And why had Dew been so angry that Sphagnum had told them to her? Rowan had no idea why—Sphagnum had always seemed a bit addled to her, and his little ditties had certainly done nothing to help her through the forest.

Abruptly, the trees gave way, opening onto a wide black lake.

Rowan stared across the glassy surface of the lake. The water was dark—she couldn't see the bottom, only the waving tops of weeds just under the surface, and in one spot the tip of a tree trunk stuck above the water, bleached white. It looked like the bone of a colossal animal.

She swallowed. The glowing trail extended directly across the lake—

not around. She knew that if she went the wrong way, she would lose the trail to Keziah. Or so Oak had said.

Well, what am I supposed to do? Swim? she thought angrily, but her gaze fell on a thin wooden object in the water. A narrow boat, not tied to anything, but gently bobbing in the water near the shore nonetheless.

That's just a little too *convenient,* Rowan thought uneasily, reaching out with a toe to prod the watercraft. It seemed watertight, with no visible leaks, and there was a worn dark wooden oar resting against one side.

Rowan rubbed her temples. This seemed to be the only way forward; she just couldn't convince herself that the trail would stay if she changed course. She slung her pack into the boat and stepped in, easing herself down on the bench. She paused, though why she did she wasn't sure. Maybe she expected the owner of the boat to burst out of the bushes to chase her off. But nothing happened.

Come on, now, she thought, gritting her teeth and seizing the oar. The smooth water did not invite disturbance, and she realized that there were hardly any sounds of life at all; there were faint bird noises back in the trees, but they were distant. Nothing seemed to live around the lake, or in it—there were no ripples of fish or swimming fowl to be seen, just the monotonous sway of the weeds, turned gray-green by the water.

It should have felt peaceful. It didn't.

Or maybe life in an enchanted forest doesn't lend itself well to relaxing, Rowan tried to convince herself, bucking up what little courage she could muster. *A calm ride across a lake should be good for me.*

And so she dipped the paddle into the water and pushed off from the shore. The dark water rippled against the oar like a silky blanket.

She watched the ripples pass over the tops of the weeds like a gentle breeze as the boat passed by. Forcing herself to look ahead, she dug in with the oar and made steady progress across the lake. There was bright green in the water ahead, along a bank that wove into the center of the lake like a peninsula. She couldn't help but crane her neck to look— giant lily pads, larger than her head, perfectly tessellated together, forming a great green pathway on the water. Dotted here and there were bulbous yellow lilies, with striped black-and-white centers. She would have expected to see insects, or maybe even frogs, but there was nothing but plants; the lilies and their pads, the weeds under water, the thin green reeds stood stock-still in the shallows.

Eerie. The word finally came to her halfway across the lake. This place should be beautiful, *was* beautiful, but something about it made it impossible to enjoy.

She felt an odd tugging on her oar and looked down. The water should have been swirling its way behind the boat in the wake of her rowing, but instead, it went backward, spilling back over her oar as she tried to row the opposite way. Something was pushing the water.

She looked over her shoulder and nearly dropped the oar.

Water spilling from its limbs, a colossal bone-white creature lifted itself from the depths she had just crossed, from the place she'd thought she'd seen the submerged tree. As it creaked its way to its full height, she realized two things; that it seemed to be made of bone instead of wood, and that the lake was far deeper than she'd thought.

Then the thing turned its black, pitted eyes toward her. Its mouth stretched and gaped at her, revealing jagged shards of bone around a hideously dark maw.

It shrieked, so loud that she thought her ears might burst.

Rowan wasn't breathing. Her hands shook as she tried to move the oar, and this time she succeeded in dropping it into the boat with a loud clatter. The creature twisted its osseous head at an awful angle and shrieked again. Then it lurched forward, swimming toward her.

With a cry of terror, Rowan snatched up the oar and tried to row for a moment. The boat hardly moved, the vile creature rushing toward her in a curtain of black water.

Do something!

Rowan stretched her hands forward, silently begging the trees on the opposite shore for help.

She couldn't catch her breath, couldn't form a plea for help—she almost sobbed with fear. But she saw roots explode from the ground on the far bank, reaching out over the water for her. She choked on grateful gulps of air, standing up in the boat to reach out her hands.

Then a bone-white limb the size of an oak tree crashed down on her, breaking through the boat and dragging her underwater.

Freezing water filled her mouth and nose, along with the flavor of rotting fish. She vaguely wondered what must have died in the water, to give it that horrible taste, before she snapped out of her shock and struggled against the limb pinning her to the broken boat, pulling her downwards.

She could barely see anything in the murk. Lungs burning she felt out again for the roots that had reached for her, hoping they could still sense her under water. Her own senses were so deadened by the vile water that she felt nothing—no presence of trees or plants at all, just the rage of the bone-beast swimming her down to her death.

Its crooked limb swung her through the water, bringing her before the black holes it used for eyes. It stretched open its horrible jaws again, but instead of noise, all it released was a gush of foul water, full of half-decayed animal bits and plant-muck. The refuse hit her full in the face, and she knew, with little guesswork, that the creature meant to turn her into the same half-digested stuff it spat at her.

She squirmed against its limb, but the jagged bone caught on her clothing and dug into her skin. The creature tightened its grip cruelly, squeezing the last bit of air from her lungs as it drew her toward its mouth. She couldn't close her eyes, couldn't block out the nightmare of its sharp, pointed fangs, its black, vile mouth. All she could think of was Celine—she would never see her sister again, never know if she was safe.

And then, the creature's face exploded. Roots burst through its empty sockets, twining around Rowan and pulling her back up through the water. They wrenched her above the surface, holding her high above the churning water as they carried her toward the opposite shore.

She heard a horrible screech and saw the bone-beast burst from the water, its head in fragments. It flailed its limbs but couldn't reach far enough out of the water to pull her back in. The loss of its eye sockets and most of its head seemed not to affect it much. Furiously, it swam beneath Rowan and her tangle of roots, standing up to swat at her, but the roots simply swerved her out of the way and kept sailing through the air.

The root tangle deposited her on a sturdy elder branch overlooking the lake. She clutched at them as they released her.

"No, don't go—it's coming for me!"

But instead of returning underground where they belonged, the roots turned back to the water, shooting straight at the pursuing bone-beast. They punched through its center, wrapping around it and tightening. An awful grinding noise echoed off the water as the roots crushed the creature into bits. A few sickening *crunches* later, all that was left were clumps of splintery white, floating on the dark water.

Shaking off bits of bone, the roots slithered apart and back into the broken earth on the shore. Other than the floating remnants of the bone-beast drifting in the water, the lake was as undisturbed and glassy as it had been when Rowan first saw it.

Rowan's hands clattered against the bark as she tried to climb down from the branch. Her muscles, weakened by fear and cold, gave up on her and she fell in a pile to the ground. She allowed herself to stay like that a while, palms and kneecaps smarting from the impact. But she knew she needed to move on, to dry off, to continue on the trail.

The trail!

She scrambled up, casting around her, ducking her head this way and that to try and catch the ghostly golden shimmer that had led her to this point. But it was gone.

It had vanished. She had left the trail, and it had disappeared, leaving her with nothing but the dimming light of evening.

She sank back down to the ground. There was no energy left for tears, no emotional effort left in her. The journey across the lake, the horrifying brush with death—to survive it only to lose her one guide to Keziah. It left her hollow and without the will to move.

Her shoulders sagged forward, giving in to gravity, and she crumpled. There was nothing she could do.

CHAPTER 37

Rowan

She was vaguely aware that her eyes were pressed against the damp sleeve of her shirt. She must have dozed off, for the next thing she was aware of was a rustling sound and the faint glow of the sunset above her.

She opened her eyes a crack.

The bruised color of the forest nearly matched the color of her own closed eyelids.

She squeezed her eyes shut again.

I've ruined everything.

The bitter cruelness of the words going through her own head made tears burn in her eyes. But it was true. The first day of Spring had come. The Bear Maiden had already descended from the mountains, and Rowan had not been there to meet her. Her chance to help Celine was gone, and now so was her chance to help Keziah.

Why did I think I could do this? I'm a weak little village girl, who likes baking and embroidery.

Not for the first time, she wished *she* had been captured by Oak and Celine had been the one to come after her.

We'd probably be home already. She never would have lost her way.

But, unbidden, another thought flitted through her mind.

Celine would not have come for her.

Rowan blinked as tears spilled down her cheeks. The very idea made her heart ache, made her throat tightened and her lungs burn. But she couldn't deny it.

She loved her sister, loved her just as much as she had when they were little and each other's best friends. And perhaps Celine did care about her still, in her own bitter way. But she had been planning to leave and never come back. She wanted to live the rest of her days far away from her family. Rowan couldn't blame her for it—of course she couldn't. But that was the difference between them.

Celine was strong, brave, incredibly capable. But Rowan was the one who cared enough to come after her.

"And a lot of good it's done us both," she mumbled, wiping her tears ineffectively with her damp sleeve.

There was nothing left to do now. She had no way to help Celine, no way to find Keziah. She had no choice but to try to find her own way back home. Celine and Keziah would surely get themselves out of the trouble they were in—Celine had already escaped, after all. Maybe she'd already gone back home, and now Rowan was the fool who'd gotten lost in the forest. Either way, they were all better off without her help.

Hollow and aching from her bout with the bone-beast, Rowan clumsily got to her feet.

I probably need to eat something, she thought dully. But she made no move to take the pack from her back. Instead, she started walking, slowly, stumbling blindly over rocks and roots alike.

Her legs felt weak as jelly. She staggered and fell against a tree, but instead of stopping to rest, she pushed herself back up and kept going.

She continued blinking away her tears, but the more she walked, the angrier her tears became.

Why on earth did I think I could do this? What kind of idiot am I? I'm not cut out to be a hero. I'm not even strong enough to help Celine with woodcutting. What did I think was going to happen? Me, a soft, weak village girl, only good for marrying off and having babies. My own parents know I'm nothing special.

This last thought cut deeper than the rest, so deep that she stopped in her tracks, big, gulping sobs forcing their way up her throat.

She forced herself to catch her breath, scrubbing fiercely at her eyes.

"The least I can do," she told herself through gritted teeth, "is get myself home."

And she started forward again.

But as she went to take her next step, her foot froze midair. A ring of white mushrooms sat before her, nearly identical to the ones she'd run into with Keziah.

She blinked at them, then looked up.

There was that strange stone tree, the one she'd thought resembled a hand.

A hand.

Sphagnum's strange rhyme came back to her:
First seek a tree that turned to stone
And hardened to a giant's hand
But watch your step as you proceed
Or soon your bones will feed the land.

Slowly, she turned back in the direction she had come. Though she could not see it, she pictured the dark pool and the bone-beast rising from its depths.

The blackened deep you next must seek
And circumvent it without fear
But do not wake the sleeping beast
Or you will find your end is near.

The pool, the hand. Dew had said Sphagnum was helping Rowan, though she had not said how. But Sphagnum had known what—*who*—Rowan was seeking. Could he have been trying to help her find the Bear Maiden all along?

Her boots scrabbled for purchase in the mud as she sped back toward the black pool. When she reached it, she ignored the boat this time and went around, scanning the dark water warily. She was sure the roots had destroyed the bone creature completely, but part of her worried that here, in a clearly magical pool, the creature might piece itself back together again. Thus she kept her steps as quiet as she could.

Once she had reached the other side of the pool, she paused, looking back the way she had come. *The hand, the pool. The snowdrop garden.* Was there some sort of pattern in Sphagnum's rhymes? She wished now more than ever that a map of the *prawdziwy las* existed. She had no idea which direction she ought to go next.

Staring up at the sky, she noted that the stone hand lay in the west, while the black pool had been decidedly further east. She frowned.

If the hand comes first and the pool next, then perhaps the garden is further east still.

But what if that wasn't right? She rubbed a hand across her forehead, turning first one direction, then the other.

I can't just stand here. I have to do something.

Then a little flicker of blue light flitted past. Then a flutter of red light sped off in the opposite direction.

Rowan blinked. *Follow the lights... blue, not red.*

That was all she needed. She took off in the direction the blue light had gone—east, opposite the last burning dregs of the sunset.

Her feet sank deep in yellow loam as she made her way through a grove of larches, the earth around them soft and dense with centuries' worth of shed needles. A pair of rabbits in fine brown waistcoats scattered as she plunged through new-leaved shrubs. Little blue lights streaked past her, illuminating the trees with an eerie glow.

All the while, she tried only to think of east, of finding the snowdrop garden. And as she hurried onward, something started to grow within her, a pull from her very center, burning somewhere between her lungs and her heart.

She came into a clearing and stopped, eyes closed, hunched over and panting, to catch her breath. And when she opened her eyes, there, by her boot, was a single snowdrop. Its pendulous bell-shaped blossom bobbed gently in the fragrant breeze.

Rowan's eyes immediately found another just beyond it, and a cluster of three beyond that. She straightened and saw that snowdrops *blanketed* the forest floor ahead of her, so densely that she couldn't see the green of moss or brown of tree roots in between them.

"I found it," she whispered, not fully daring to believe it. "I found the garden."

"Yes, it appears you did," came a deep, rasping voice from behind her.

Rowan whirled around. A figure in a long cloak sat on the arch of a tree root before her, their feet nestled among the snowdrops. In the dying remnants of daylight, they nearly blended in with the trees behind them.

Rowan's eyes glided over black claws clasped together over the buttons of a long brown coat, over a tartan scarf knotted at the neck, to a furred, golden face. A face framed by long, auburn tangles of hair, almost identical to Rowan's and just as full of leaves and dirt. A fanged mouth spread into a smile.

Decidedly not human, despite the clothes.

"Welcome," the golden being said with a warm, pleasant growl, like a dog falling asleep.

Rowan realized she was gaping and promptly closed her mouth. She didn't know why, but she suddenly felt extremely conscious of how dirty and unkempt she was.

"A-are you of Oak or Holly?" she asked nervously.

The person shook their head. "Not a question I need to answer, as it happens. Consider me *your* friend, dear girl. You look as though you've had a terrible time in the forest."

"I'm looking for my sister," she said, trying to keep her mind straight. But she was so very tired.

"Really? I wondered if you might be looking for me," the person said, tilting their head to one side. "Very few people know my path through the woods, you see. This place is rather hard to find if you don't know the way."

Rowan blinked. *Of course.*

"You're... are you the Bear Maiden?"

She inclined her head. "Most folk who enter the forest come for a look at the Oak King's court these days. Not many seem to remember his reputation for punishing trespassers. Nor do they remember my reputation for rewarding them." She grinned, flashing rows of pointed pearly teeth.

"I need to find my sister—she's been missing for over a week now, and I've been—" Rowan began, but the Bear Maiden held up a claw.

"I'm sure you are very worried for your sister. However, I ask that you not make any requests of me just yet, not until I've had time to speak with you. You see, I know you, Rowan, and your sister, Celine, too."

Rowan stared at the Bear Maiden.

"I've never seen you before in my life," she said finally, feeling very stupid.

"But *I* have seen *you*, Rowan, slipping into the Oak King's forest in Spring and Summer, pretending you're in a fairy tale. Or wandering through the Autumn leaves falling, or the drifts of Winter snow, marveling at how different it is from your own side of the forest." The Bear Maiden grinned again.

"I've seen your sister, too, though she doesn't wander in quite the same way. She and her sweetheart make a pretty pair, don't you think?"

Rowan shrugged. Getting swept up into Holly and Oak's conflict had made thoughts of her family and her village seem very small and distant.

"Haven't you wondered why you haven't been caught? The Oak King's minions have snatched up every person to cross the Border for centuries, but you and Celine have escaped their notice for years now."

Rowan didn't like the way the Bear Maiden was watching her—like she knew more about her than Rowan knew about herself.

"We were just lucky, I suppose," she answered slowly, though she got the feeling she was wrong.

"It's a little more than luck," the Bear Maiden said, rising. "I knew it the moment I laid eyes on you. You are descended from one of my cubs."

Rowan was so tired that she was sure she misheard the Bear Maiden.

"I'm a what, sorry?"

"One of my descendants, child. You and your siblings."

Rowan gaped at her for a moment. The Bear Maiden stared back pleasantly.

"I'm sorry, but that's just not possible," Rowan managed to say at last. "I don't see how we could possibly be descended from you. I don't... We don't have..."

She gestured to her fangless mouth, feeling rather silly.

The Bear Maiden chuckled in amusement. "I see. Fangs and fur aside, do you know your family's lineage, all the way back to the beginning of time?"

Rowan opened her mouth, then closed it again.

"Exactly. You see, I am not entirely bear, and neither are my cubs. They usually roam too far for even their children to return to this forest, but one of my descendants returned some time ago. I remember her walking the Border, so close I could almost call to her. She never crossed, but I could hear the echo of her in the stories you and Celine told each other."

Rowan immediately thought of her grandmother, who had instilled such a love of stories in her. If anyone fit the Bear Maiden's description, it was her.

"I should think it would explain a great deal to you," the Bear Maiden rumbled. "Why else would you be so drawn to this forest, despite the wrath of the Oak King?"

"We weren't *drawn* here," Rowan protested quickly. "Celine came here to hunt and cut wood, and I..." But she couldn't explain it. Simply saying she *liked* it here didn't seem like enough, for some reason.

"My point is, you and your sister have each formed your own bonds with these trees. They like you. They accept you and keep you from Oak's notice, no matter the time of year. You never take more than you need, and you have always been respectful—just as Oak and Holly were when they first entered this land, centuries ago." Her face drew in gravely. "Oak changed. Holly did not. Perhaps if they had both changed, it would have been better. But that isn't Holly's way."

Her luminous golden eyes settled heavily on Rowan.

"You've met Keziah," she said evenly.

"Oak had him," Rowan said at once, trying to stand. "He sent him off and said I had to find him. There was a trail, but I lost it when that... that *thing* attacked."

The Bear Maiden held up another claw.

"He's safe for the moment. Oak is in one of his groves, replenishing his power. You made him use up quite a bit of it. He wants his power to be limitless, you see. Never wants to give it up, wants an even more powerful source he can draw from. That's what he tried to do with Keziah, and what he was trying to achieve with your sister."

"With Keziah?" Rowan's head swam. "What did he have to do with Keziah? What do you *mean?* Who is he?"

The Bear Maiden looked at Rowan for a very long time. "I thought the boy might have told you," she said softly, "though perhaps I shouldn't have assumed. It's a difficult thing to share, but it seemed the two of you grew close, even over a short period of time."

The Bear Maiden looked out at the still black pool before them, her eyes wide and dark.

"Oak is Keziah's father. Keziah is the heir to the powers of Spring and Summer."

Befuddled, Rowan rose, now at eye level with the seated Bear Maiden.

"But that's not possible. Oak saw Keziah, he *had* him as a prisoner, and he thought he was just a boy from my village traveling with me."

The Bear Maiden inclined her head. "It has been some time since Oak has seen Keziah, and the boy has changed a great deal. I am not surprised he didn't recognize him."

Rowan rubbed her hand across her brow. "Then... then Keziah is the one Sphagnum was talking about? The one Oak said Holly took away?"

"The very same," the Bear Maiden said. "He has been through a great deal, Rowan. And he has lived in the forest, in almost constant danger, for the past five years."

Rowan turned away from the Bear Maiden, rubbing her hands over her eyes. "Why didn't he tell me any of this? All this secrecy is keeping me from helping anyone properly!" she burst out in frustration.

"If you want to help, then listen." The Bear Maiden rose. She stood a good few feet taller than Rowan, and Rowan was all at once reminded that this person was very much still part bear.

"Long ago, when I first gave the power of the seasons to Oak and Holly, I set a limit: they would rule this land and its seasons for a thousand years, no longer. And after that time, they were to select heirs for their magic, train them to take up the kingdom. Then they would return to their mortal lives once more. Oak agreed to the terms at the beginning, but he has long since decided he will not give up his powers, whatever the cost. Now he has turned vicious in his lust to consume magic."

The Bear Maiden bared her teeth. "I want to see Oak removed from power. Removed from this very earth, as it will likely come to that. But the forest and the mountains are a great source of magic, and there must be people to serve as conduits for that power—people chosen by representatives of the forest. Do you understand?"

Startled, Rowan nodded, though she wasn't sure she did truly understand.

"Good." The Bear Maiden nodded in approval.

"Magic only serves humans; animals have no need for it. But magic comes from something in nature, so it is only fair that users of magic seek to benefit both humans and the environment from which the magic stems. Oak understood that once, but now he thinks of magic as his and his alone, to serve his own ends. And he wants more. He has grown frustrated at the borders controlling where he can perform his magic, frustrated with the boundaries of the seasons that weaken him and strengthen him by turn throughout the year. He is determined to grow his power the only way he can—by absorbing it from others who have it.

"Some twenty years ago, he left the forest and found an island with its own magic and folk who served as conduits for it. Their seasons barely changed, so their powers were more constant. He fathered a child there with a woman of great powers, and he returned some years later to claim that child, determined to use his offspring to steal himself an even greater power. He intended to absorb his own child's power once it reached its full potential, and he also planned to make a bid for Holly's power." Her lip curled in disgust.

"Keziah has both his father's powers and those of his mother's people, but he wants nothing to do with his heritage from Oak." The Bear Maiden gave Rowan a meaningful look. "As I'm sure you can understand. Oak manipulated him, you see. Convinced him it wasn't safe for him to live in his village without learning to use his magic properly. Keziah believed he was doing the right thing, while all the while Oak was planning to use him to make himself more powerful. If it hadn't been for Holly, I don't know what would have become of Keziah."

"Oak said Holly took his son away," Rowan said slowly, trying to piece things together.

"Holly *saved* Keziah, and in doing so, he destroyed the person Oak was hoping to use. The only loss that Oak grieves is that of power," the Bear Maiden said primly, crossing her claws over one another.

"But... But why don't *you* get rid of Oak, if you know what he is? Or help Keziah take his powers from him?" Rowan asked, turning back to the Bear Maiden.

"My power is limited. I, too, am bound by the seasons—unable to move from one place to another until the right season has come. I am bound also by the bargain I made with Oak. I must permit him to rule until the thousand years have ended. And I can only help folk through a wish they make. Keziah made his wish—two wishes, as a matter of fact: one for himself, and one for someone else, with a sacrifice. I cannot help him again in that way, even if he wanted to take up his father's role, which he does not. And Holly made his own wish long ago. So when he asked me to help keep Keziah safe and to keep Oak from leaving the forest, I could not do it freely. He had to sacrifice half his power to make it so. Believe me," she said earnestly, "if I could, I would. Magic passes through my fingertips—I cannot use it for myself, but I can direct it where it needs to go."

"Then what can be done? How can he be stopped, if you can't do anything against him?"

The Bear Maiden grinned savagely.

"I never said that. Why do you think fate crossed our paths, girl? Now, if I'm not mistaken, you have a wish to make."

Rowan leaned back against a tree. Her head ached, and all she wanted to do was close her eyes and rest.

"I don't know what to wish for," she said suddenly, her throat unpleasantly tight. "There are too many people who need my help, and I don't know how to help all of them."

"Your sister and the boy?" the Bear Maiden asked.

"And... and Holly, too. He's not safe with Oak out there." She turned and looked at the Bear Maiden. "I don't suppose I can wish for Oak to be destroyed?"

The Bear Maiden shook her head. "The power that would take is unimaginable. I simply do not have it."

Rowan thought for a long moment.

"What if," she began tentatively, "you gave me your advice on what to wish for?"

"Wish for the power Holly forfeited," the Bear Maiden said at once. Rowan got the impression she had been waiting all this time for Rowan to ask that very question. "Wish for the power to rule an entire season. For the last five years, that magic has done nothing more than confine Oak to this forest—useful, yes, but not with Holly so weak, unable to stand against him and neutralize the threat he brings."

"But—" Rowan struggled to think through it all. "But if Oak can leave, he'll start doing those awful things again."

"My dear child, he does them still, to any person of magic who happens to fall into his clutches. He would have found a way around it eventually—he was always going to. The power must be contained within a person—that was Holly's mistake in giving it to me. Once he did, it could not be used for anything else, and I could not give it back to him, not without some kind of payment. But this is the only wish that will give you what you seek. That sister of yours—with Holly's power, you'll be able to find her." The Bear Maiden pointed a single claw at Rowan. "And when you find her, see that she comes to make her own wish."

Rowan tried to think, but her head was swimming at the very notion.

"That... that doesn't sound like something I could do," she said finally. "*You'd* be better off finding Celine for me."

The Bear Maiden quirked her head to one side.

"And why is that?"

"Because I've made a mess of everything, from the moment I set foot inside this forest." Rowan's throat began to tighten. "I couldn't save my sister, I couldn't save Holly, and Keziah—"

"None of these people are currently in any kind of dire situation," the Bear Maiden interrupted, "and it isn't your responsibility to save any of them. I would say, however, that they are all better off than they would have been if you hadn't come along." She extended a single claw. "You braved the Oak King's forest to rescue your sister." She extended another claw. "You protected the Holly King and helped him recover strength he hasn't had in years." She held up a third claw. "And now you are on your way to save Keziah from whatever trap his vile father has placed him in, after besting Oak in the trial he set you. Perseverance is all well and good, but in the face of the almost impossible, I'd say you have also shown remarkable strength and courage."

"Perseverance hasn't helped me save anyone," Rowan muttered.

"*Yet*. That's the point of perseverance, isn't it? And with what I'm offering you, you *can* save the people you care about, in the short *and* long-term."

Rowan looked up quickly.

"Long-term?" she said shakily.

The Bear Maiden bowed her shaggy head.

"Child, did you think you were called here merely to play amongst the blossoms and harvest wild mushrooms?" she asked, amusement dancing in her gruff voice.

"I have to say, I didn't think I was *called* here for anything in partic-ular," Rowan snapped. "I wanted to save my sister."

"And just what is your plan, may I ask? Continue to fight your way through the forest by the skin of your teeth? You're incredibly fortunate to have made it this far with only the gifts of my bloodline to protect you. The trees," she said, in response to Rowan's blank look, "they shield you, they serve you when asked—as they do for me. But I am old. Oak knows I am powerless to stop him on my own, and he cannot find me. My powers shelter me, and I have many caves hidden throughout the forest that Oak knows nothing about and couldn't find if he did. All I can do is hide from him, as Holly does. I cannot act against him. I cannot use Holly's power for myself—I *need you*."

Protests rose up in Rowan's mind again, but a single thought broke through them. *Why not?* Why shouldn't she make the wish? Why shouldn't she accept such a bizarre, magical gift? After all, the only things waiting for her at home were a life of drudgery and the promise of yet more drudgery once she was forced to marry somebody. And didn't the heroes of the stories accept change when it was offered them? She couldn't remember a single one where the main character said, "No, thanks," and trotted off home to live out the rest of their days. Not any of the good ones, anyhow.

"What is it, exactly, that I would be getting if I wished for the portion of Holly's power that he gave up?" she asked, wording her question carefully. The Bear Maiden was not a trickster in any of the stories, but not all the stories were turning out to be true, lately.

"The powers of Autumn," answered the Bear Maiden with a sweep of her clawed hand. "The power to put nature to sleep, to ripen the last fruits, to bid the world prepare for death. The power that kills Summer, in the end."

Rowan shivered. She'd certainly never thought of Autumn as having anything to do with death.

The Bear Maiden noticed.

"I know the Holly King to be a good and gentle man," she said softly, her claws digging into the dead wood. "But never forget—he is the knife that slides into a fallen deer's heart, when they have no more to eat and the frost has come early. The cold that leaves a songbird frozen on the ground, if they have lingered too long past the first snow. A job that must be done. Death can be kind, but it is still death."

Try as she might, Rowan couldn't imagine the dark-eyed man she'd cared for hurting anything.

"And I can help him?" she asked, clasping and unclasping her hands. Nerves bubbled in her stomach.

"All of them," the Bear Maiden assured her.

Rowan blew out a deep breath. It didn't help.

"Alright." She bounced anxiously on the balls of her feet, wishing her heart wasn't racing the way it was.

"I wish for the power of Autumn," she said slowly.

Nothing happened.

She frowned and looked to the Bear Maiden.

"Is that enough?" she asked nervously.

"It should be," the Bear Maiden said with a toothy grin, and she reached out and sank her claws into Rowan's shoulder.

CHAPTER 38

Nash

I woke in the dark, my head pounding like I had drunk too much rice wine. I sat up and banged my head on the rocky ceiling of the cave.

Groaning, I crawled toward what little light I could see. As I crawled, I noticed my body felt different. I had more muscle in my arms and chest. My shoulders were broader. My legs felt longer, too.

I came out into daylight, shielding my eyes from the sun.

When my eyes had adjusted, I saw the Bear Maiden sitting some distance away, staring into a crackling fire.

"What—" I began, but my own voice made me jump. It was deeper than before, richer in tone. I touched my throat gingerly. Then I looked down at myself properly for the first time.

My chest was flat, and when I touched it, I felt the absence of the bindings I had worn before.

"It worked," I whispered, looking at the backs of my hands. "It really worked."

"Good, you're awake." The Bear Maiden rose from the fire and cast a hand over the flames. They went out immediately, leaving behind a smoldering pile of ash. "We must leave at once."

"What happened? Where is Holly?"

Her brown eyes met mine, and I thought I could see the remnants of tears. "He did not return. I heard sounds of a battle, and when they ended... nothing."

It was as if an icy hand had wrapped around my heart and squeezed it.

No. Not Holly. Not after all he'd done for me.

"He... he can't be gone, can he?"

The Bear Maiden's expression darkened into a scowl. "That is what you and I will find out. Come."

She held out a clawed hand to me. I took it.

Wind swirled around us. Dust stung in my eyes until I screwed them shut, and I felt my feet leave the ground, though my hand stayed firmly in the Bear Maiden's grasp.

I tried to open my eyes but found it almost impossible in the rush of wind. Squinting, I could barely make out rocks and stones rushing past us as we hurtled down the mountainside.

Then all of a sudden we lurched to a stop. The Bear Maiden released my hand and I stumbled against a tree.

We were back in the forest. The journey up into the mountains had taken days, yet the Bear Maiden had brought me back in the blink of an eye.

"Come," was all she said to me as she set off through the trees.

It was easy enough to find where it had happened. There, at the base of the mountains—a smoking, blackened area where the trees had been burned away.

Together we stared at the destruction. It stretched for at least a half mile. And there was no sign of Holly.

Just as my knees wobbled and threatened to give way beneath me, I heard someone weeping in the trees.

I ran toward the sound and found Frost, their back pressed against a tree, hand clamped over their own mouth to stifle their crying.

"What happened?" I asked.

Frost took a step back from me, their eyes widening in confusion.

"It's me, Nash—I've been to the Bear Maiden. Tell me what happened here, Frost, please!"

They closed their eyes, shaking their head as more tears spilled from their eyes.

"*Frost, what happened to Holly?*" *I demanded, wrenching their hand away from their mouth.*

"*He broke him!*" *Frost gasped, doubling over as if in pain.* "*He tore him apart like a rag doll! My king!*"

I took a step back. My hands felt numb, my stomach turned stony.

No. Holly couldn't be dead. He couldn't be.

"*Where is he?*" *My voice shook as I spoke.*

Frost's mouth trembled.

"*Where is he, Frost?*"

They raised a shaking finger and pointed behind me.

"*Th-th-there, I think. And there. It's... the strangest thing—there's no blood, no blood at all...*" *Their eyes welled up again and they buried their face in their hands.*

A sharp intake of breath came from the Bear Maiden as she surveyed the spot where Frost had pointed.

"*Nash, help me find the rest of him, quickly!*"

I wanted to ask her why, but my stomach threatened to turn itself out each time I tried to form the words. Instead, I did as she asked. I went and started picking up the pieces of my friend.

My mind seemed to blur out what I was doing, as if the horror of what had happened to Holly was too much for it.

Frost joined us at some point. Their face was deathly pale, but they worked quickly and quietly alongside me.

At last, we had found all of him. We laid him out, doing our best to fit him back together.

As we stood there, staring down at the wreck Oak had made of Holly, my vision blurred again with tears.

I should have waited. I should have saved my wish and used it for him. He had risked everything so that I could be safe, so that I could have the wish I'd been dreaming of my entire life, and now he was gone.

I covered my face with my hands. My eyes hurt from crying, and yet it seemed the crying would never end.

"*He's not dead.*" *The Bear Maiden's voice cut through the silence like a knife.*

I peeled my tear-streaked hands away from my face. Beside me, Frost swayed dangerously and grabbed my arm for balance.

"Not dead? How is that possible?" they asked.

"His magic." The Bear Maiden's voice came out in a raspy whisper. I couldn't tell if she was surprised or if she had expected this.

"What Oak did was not enough to tear his magic from him. But he is broken, and most certainly in a great deal of pain."

She knelt at his side and reached a trembling claw toward his face. But she stopped, her hand falling to her side.

"Can't you do anything for him?" Frost asked miserably.

"Without the prompt of a wish, I do not have enough power to fix him." The Bear Maiden's claws curled and she bared her teeth. "Never have I hated the boundaries of my own magic so deeply."

"Use mine," I said at once, "take my power, like you took Holly's."

"You what?" Frost asked, horrified.

"Please," I begged the Bear Maiden, "we have to help him."

"Nash," she said slowly, as though each word was painful. "You are our best hope of defeating Oak now—I could not possibly take any of your powers."

"You have to!" I screamed, my hands curled into fists. "We have to help him!"

"Perhaps I—" began Frost, but the Bear Maiden cut them off.

"You are not human enough to make a wish. As for your magic, you are so infused with the Godpower of Freezing that to take it would mean your death. And the power would do us no good here—my power is the only thing that can save him."

"And the only thing that could make your power work is a wish?" My mind began to race with possible solutions—we could travel to the nearest village, beg some farmer to come to the forest and wish for Holly to be restored. But I knew it would never work. Who would make such a wish willingly? Not to mention that Oak could be back any second to finish him off. I was sure his attack on Holly had weakened him greatly, and that he was now off recuperating in a grove somewhere, but he would most certainly be back, especially once he realized he could not escape the forest.

I was so lost in my thoughts that I didn't realize the Bear Maiden had not answered my last question. Not until Frost asked it again.

"Is a wish the only thing that will work?" they prompted.

The Bear Maiden rose and looked at me.

"There is... another way. Possibly. I do not have any guarantee that it will work, but it is worth a try. That is, Nash, if you agree."

"Of course I do," I said at once. "I'll do anything."

The Bear Maiden's eyes flashed. "Never say anything like that again, boy. That's a dangerous statement to make, and it cannot easily be undone," she said sharply.

My jaw jutted forward, and I refused to drop her gaze. "I meant what I said."

She growled deep in her throat. "Very well. If you, Nash, promise to use your powers to serve me for as long as I deem it necessary—for as long as Oak is bound to this forest—then that can serve as a trade for a wish. I wish to clarify," she said, holding up a claw to stop me from interrupting, "again, that this may not work... But it may be our only option."

I was already nodding. "Yes. I'll do it. Please hurry."

The Bear Maiden grasped my hand in hers, and for the second time, her golden magic swam around me, drowning out the rest of the world. She was saying something, but the roar of her magic in my ears kept me from hearing what it was.

Then, abruptly, the golden light swept away from the two of us, streaming down toward Holly's body. It enveloped him completely, glowing so brightly in the growing dim of evening I had to shield my eyes from it.

When the light faded, Holly was whole again. I wasn't certain we had succeeded until I saw the gentle rise and fall of his chest.

He was breathing. He was alive.

Frost dropped to their knees and clutched Holly's hand, pressing it to their forehead.

"He should wake soon." The Bear Maiden was breathing heavily, but I could hear the joy in her voice. "It worked, Nash." She smiled at me, but I looked away. If it hadn't been for me, none of this would have happened to Holly in the first place.

"What happens now?" I asked her, keeping my eyes trained on the mud on my boots.

"We wait for the opportunity to strike at Oak again," she said simply. "It may be tomorrow, or many years from now. But as long as he is trapped in this forest, he cannot steal more magic. And as long as no one *else with magic enters the forest, he will have no opportunity to grow his powers. One by one, we will strip him of his allies and the magics he stole, until he is mortal once more."*

She glanced at Frost. "You and I will help Holly get back into the mountains. Oak will most certainly come for him again."

"I'll help, too," I said.

But the Bear Maiden shook her head. "I need you here, Nash. You swore to serve me, and this is my first order. While Oak is bound to the forest, you must never leave it for long. Your power calls to the trees. It makes them question Oak, and that weakens him. In your absence, he will only grow stronger."

The full weight of what I had vowed to do sank in. After all that had happened, I was still stuck here, and far away from my home.

But it was only fair. Oak had nearly killed Holly because of me. If this was the only way to make it up to Holly, then I wouldn't complain.

The Bear Maiden knelt down and gently shook Holly's shoulder. Suddenly, I felt terrified at the idea of him waking, of having to face him after what he had suffered on my behalf.

"Nash, where are you going?" Frost said as I started off through the trees.

"Help him get back to his fortress," I called. "I'm going to make sure Oak never gets his hands on my power."

The Bear Maiden said nothing. I knew she'd find me when she needed my help again.

For now, if I was going to be staying in the forest, I needed to make sure Oak would never recognize me again. The wish had changed my physical appearance, true, but I would need a new name, a new identity, if I was going to hide from him right under his nose. I would trap some animals, harvest their furs, then go to the nearest village and buy myself a set of new clothes. I'd build myself a home, here in Oak's own forest, and make sure he never finds me and grows strong enough to break free of the Bear Maiden's border. I would command the trees he selfishly kept to himself, spread whispers through the forest about what a brute he was, sow discord among his allies. I would work against him here, in his own kingdom, until I could destroy him for good.

Part of me, the part that wasn't torn with grieving for the hurt I'd caused Holly, was thrilled at the idea. Here was a chance to start over, with my body newly changed and my entire life thrown into chaos once more. This time, instead of Oak, I would choose my own way forward. I would choose who I was.

Keziah. The fragrant cinnamon trees that grew on islands near my home. It was the name I had turned over and over again in my head on sleepless nights, when all I could do was dream of a day when my body suited me and felt like a real home. The name warmed me to my very core. A name I chose for myself, when my life had already been overturned at Oak's whim countless times. A new name and a new beginning. I hoped both would serve me well.

CHAPTER 39

Rowan

Rowan would have cried out, except the pain was far away from her. The darkening sky dropped away, leaving only trees and trees and more trees around her. She could feel them growing, could feel the bark swelling, the leaves pushing further out, the roots drinking up water deep underground. She could feel the gentle steps of deer in the distance, feel the arching of a bird's neck as it prepared to take off from a branch, could feel the scuttering feet of the Red Caps dancing around their dens.

And then, she felt a coolness, a calming energy like the constant flow of water from the stream, but it wasn't the stream. She pushed at the sensation, curious as to why it had caught her attention.

There was a waterfall. She was aware of the water thundering down upon stone, foaming up where it met the pool below it. And that coolness emanated from *behind* it.

She caught a flash of Celine's face, pale against dark rock. Her sister huddled inside a cave behind the waterfall, clutching her larger axe to her chest. She was alive. She was *safe*.

Then Rowan came rushing back to herself, falling to her knees beside the black pool. She looked up. The Bear Maiden was gone. There was no sign she had ever been there.

Rowan pushed her hair out of her face with a shaking hand. Just what, exactly, had the mysterious Maiden gifted her with? It was similar to reaching out to the trees for help, except now she really could see parts of the forest she had never been to. She had clearly seen where her sister was, and now that she thought about it, she could point out the direction she would need to take to find her.

But Keziah...

She closed her eyes, thinking of him, forming the question in her mind, but there was nothing. She got to her feet, frustrated.

I thought she said she gave me the ability to save all *the ones I care about,* she thought angrily. But then, something buzzed, roughing up her skin like a cat being pet the wrong way. She took a step forward and the buzzing faded. She stepped back and it started up again.

She took a step in a lightly different direction, and the buzzing intensified slightly. Trusting her instinct, she continued in that direction. The further she walked, the greater the buzzing sensation became. It had a sense of wrongness, of unhappiness. She realized it was the trees themselves, the closer she got to where the buzzing was stronger.

The trees were unhappy about something. Their branches quivered, their entire trunks vibrating with that wrongness. Rowan sped up, no longer concerned about heading in the wrong direction. It was all around her now, impossible to miss. Up ahead of her she heard yells and the crash of metal.

She broke into a clearing and caught sight Keziah, hands full of fire, sending bursts of flame into the face of a gnarled bear. The hackles on its back were like the ridges of bark on an old, bent tree, and its snarling mouth was filled with razor-sharp leaves that gnashed at Keziah, though it flinched from the fire and ducked to dodge it.

Without a moment's pause, Rowan reached for the trees nearest the bear. Their branches moved at her faintest of thoughts now. They reached out and wrapped around the bear, plucking it from the ground and swinging it up into the air. Together, they bent, then flung the bear into the sky, aimed south.

Keziah watched the creature sail away, then he turned to look at Rowan. His hands still burned. He realized this and shook them, extinguishing the fire like a guilty child caught reaching for a forbidden treat.

Rowan saw there were gold chains around his ankles, fastening him to the stump on which he stood. She hurried to his side, calling up a tangle of roots to break apart the chains. She could feel the roots sinking into the invisible little gaps in the chains, prying them into pieces. They fell away and Keziah stepped down, looking bewildered.

"How did you..." he began, then he shook his head. "I suppose I should stop being so surprised at what you can do."

"I suppose we both should," Rowan said, giving his ash-covered hands a meaningful look. "I met the Bear Maiden, as luck would have it, and I made my wish."

He didn't say anything for a long moment.

"Did she... Did she say anything about me?" he asked finally, without looking at Rowan.

"She did, though I think I feel more confused than I did before. Oak is your father?" she asked pointedly.

His lip curled. "Technically. Yes." His voice had gotten dangerously low.

"And when Oak confronted Holly back at the grove, *he* said that Holly took his child away," Rowan continued.

He smiled bitterly. "Was that how he put it? What an interesting perspective."

"And the Bear Maiden told me Holly *freed* you. Is that true?"

"Yes," Keziah said immediately, "Holly saved me from Oak. He did nothing wrong."

Rowan waited for him to say more, but he said nothing. She sighed.

"You don't have to tell me anything, but I'd like to help if I can. That's... that's all," she finished lamely.

Keziah kicked at a pile of dirt, looking very much like he'd like to leave.

Finally, he turned to Rowan. And he told her. He told her of the island where he had been born, how Oak had come and tricked him into thinking he had to leave. How he and Holly had uncovered Oak's plot to steal Keziah's powers—and his life.

"Holly promised he would never let Oak do it. He needed to ask for the Bear Maiden's help, so he took me to the mountains to find her. I... had a wish I wanted to make, as well." Keziah bit his lip suddenly, looking afraid to continue.

"What did you wish for?" Rowan asked softly.

Keziah took a deep breath. "In my village, they don't tell children they are boys or girls—they let them figure that out for themselves. They don't have to be either, if that isn't who they are. When I was born, my body was like my mother's. But I knew I was a boy. From the moment I was old enough to think, to remember, I *knew*. And my village accepted it, as easily as accepting that I had curly hair instead of straight."

His eyes met Rowan's, still full of that fear. Rowan, head swimming with all this new information, nodded for him to go on.

He took another deep, shuddering breath, then continued. He told of the journey he and Holly had made to find the Bear Maiden, of Oak's pursuit, of Holly's decision to go and face him while Keziah made his wish.

He looked down at his hands, clasped together.

"I didn't know it would weaken him so much. He had given the Bear Maiden half his power—the whole season of Autumn—to bind Oak so he couldn't go after my mother, or anybody else. So he was weak, too weak to fight against Oak properly. I found him, afterwards. I asked the Bear Maiden to heal him. She said she couldn't help me, that I'd used my wish and she had no more power to use for me unless I could pay for it. But I promised her my service, that I would be bound to her as long as Oak was bound to the forest. And so I became her servant, and she put Holly back together.

"He wasn't dead, you understand. His magic kept him alive, somehow. Even Oak couldn't kill him outright, not just like that. But he was in horrible pain, and, as I'm sure you've seen, he still hasn't truly recovered. Oak came back for him again and again, wanting his revenge. He thinks I ran for it. He thinks I left the forest to live out my days far from him, and I've let him believe it. But I can't leave, not while my debt to the Bear Maiden—and to Holly—still stands."

He looked at Rowan finally, his eyes dry and his voice hoarse.

"I swear it's true. I know how it must sound, but every word of it is true." He tapped his chest. "This is who I am. I haven't kept any of it back."

Rowan spoke carefully and slowly, not wanting to say the wrong thing. "I don't know if I understand completely, but I'd like to."

Keziah managed a small smile.

Rowan, feeling emboldened, went on. "This is the only way I've ever known you. I trust you to know who you are, better than I ever could. And I know, from the time I've spent with Holly—I could tell that Oak did something terrible to him, but I didn't realize... But I do believe you," Rowan said finally. "Thank you for telling me. You didn't have to."

"It's better for you to know, I think," Keziah said, shaking his head. He looked at her. His brow furrowed. "Something's different."

Rowan was confused until she remembered she had just been endowed with half the Holly King's power.

"What did you wish for, from the Bear Maiden?" Keziah asked, sounding troubled.

"I—I..." Rowan didn't know how to tell him. It had just struck her that Keziah might not like the idea of Oak once more free to roam the world, if he figured out the magic no longer bound him within the forest.

"It feels..." Keziah took a step closer, his face focused like he was trying to hear something. "It feels like Holly."

Before Rowan could open her mouth to respond, a roar echoed through the trees.

"Damn! That bear must have found its way back to us!" Keziah cursed.

Sure enough, the bizarre beast thundered into the clearing—and this time, it wasn't alone. A band of twisted tree-beasts followed it. Rowan made out a prowling wildcat with vines for limbs, a boar with jagged branches for tusks, and a wolf whose coat was made up entirely of leaves.

"More of Oak's 'experiments,'" Keziah muttered, taking up a defensive stance. Rowan followed suit, raising her arms and preparing to call for the trees' aid.

But just as the pack of tree-beasts prepared to spring in their direction, something pale hurtled out of the night and rammed into the side of the tree-bear. The figure whirled and struck at the beast with something that glinted in the moonlight. The other beasts fell back, the wildcat baring its teeth in alarm at... the *axe*.

Celine! Rowan realized with a start.

"Who is that?" Keziah's arms fell slack as he stared.

"Look out!" Rowan spotted the tree-wolf leaping out of the corner of her eye. Swiftly, she bade the ash tree beside her to whip the creature back. Its branches struck the tree-wolf hard across the snout and flung them sideways.

Then the neighboring beech bent and walloped the wildcat in much the same manner, striking it from the air just as it leaped out of the shadows straight for Rowan. It went crashing through the underbrush and out of sight.

Rowan froze. She had made the ash tree strike down the wolf, but she hadn't even seen the wildcat. She turned and saw Keziah, his hands raised in precisely the same manner hers were raised. He gave her a pointed look.

"Looks like there's more we need to talk about," he said, nodding at her outstretched hands.

"There's no time for that now—*that's* my sister!"

Rowan pushed past Keziah and made for the tree-bear, which was swatting at Celine with its treacherous paws. Celine swatted right back with her axe, but the bear had her backed against an elm, leaving her little room to maneuver.

Rowan called up the elm's roots from beneath the earth. They wrapped around the tree-bear and yanked it down with them back into the dirt. The creature's claws scrabbled wildly but to no avail. The earth closed back over it, cutting off its roar.

Celine started at the spot where the bear had disappeared. Then slowly, she raised her eyes to her sister.

"Rowan?" she whispered.

A loud snort interrupted the moment; they both turned to see the boar wheel around and take off into the trees, abandoning the fight now that it had no fellow tree-beasts to back it up.

Keziah watched it go, a grim but satisfied grin playing around his lips.

Rowan turned back to her sister.
"Is it really you?" Celine asked, her voice shaky.

CHAPTER 40

Rowan

Rowan couldn't speak. She only nodded, her eyes welling with stupid tears. Celine looked so thin, her face bruised and hollow-cheeked.

Celine dropped her axe and ran to her. Rowan threw her arms around her sister and squealed when Celine picked her up and swung her around.

"Don't!" she gasped, the and sorrow mingling with the dirt on her face. "You're going to snap yourself in half, you goose—you look like you haven't eaten in weeks!"

Celine set her down, looking winded. "How in the world are you here? And how did you find me? I thought you'd all assume I was dead!"

"I—" Rowan didn't know how to explain it in a way that sounded sane. So she didn't. "I saw you. I met the Bear Maiden, and she showed me where you were," she said, wiping her eyes.

Keziah hung back in the trees, giving them some space. Celine barely spared him a glance.

"The Bear Maiden? Does that mean you made a wish?" she asked Rowan excitedly.

Rowan tried to smile back, but her face resisted.

Celine own face fell.

"Oh." Realization dawned across her features. "Please don't tell me you wasted your wish on finding *me*."

Rowan huffed and gave her sister a little shove.

"That's *hardly* a waste, you dunce. What would I do without my big sister? Besides," she continued haltingly, not sure how much she should say, "that wasn't the whole wish." She looked over Celine's shoulder at Keziah, who crossed his arms, frowning.

"What *did* you wish for, then?" Celine pushed. "You've dreamed of meeting the Bear Maiden since we were children. What did she give you?"

"She... she gave me the power of Autumn." Rowan bit her lip at the expression on Celine's face. She could only imagine the look on Keziah's.

Celine blinked. She bent slowly to pick up her axe, absently wiping dirt from its blade before slipping it back into its place on her back.

"Why on earth," she began, her voice surprisingly level, "would you wish for that?"

Rowan opened her mouth, closed it, looked at Keziah, who looked just as shocked as she'd expected, then shook her head.

"It's a long story. And I don't think I should tell it here—those... *tree-things* might come back."

Celine's mouth twisted, but she pointed back behind her nonetheless.

"There's a cave back this way—we can stay there for the night."

Then she looked at Keziah and frowned, as if seeing him for the first time.

"*You're* the new hunter from down south. What in the world are you doing here?"

Rowan, irritated by the cold note that had come into her sister's voice, nudged her with her elbow.

Keziah's mouth twisted wryly as he shared a look with Rowan.

"I know the *prawdziwy las* quite well, and Rowan came to me for help."

"Help finding me?" Celine asked, a challenge in her voice.

He nodded.

Celine did not look pleased. "How did you know where to find me?" she said to Rowan. "Do mother and father know you're out here?"

Rowan shook her head. "Irys told me you didn't show up at your... your meeting place. We started out looking for you together, but she had to go back to the village. And you know mother and father would never let me go into the *prawdziwy las* if I told them. They're probably just as worried about me now."

Celine opened her mouth, and Rowan wondered if she was finally going to say something—about Irys, about her secret ventures into the forest—but then she closed it again, her brow furrowing. Instead, she turned away and started into the trees.

"Let's get to the cave. A panther and a griffon patrol this area for the Oak King, and they'll probably come by soon."

After Celine stopped to grab a pair of rabbits from a set of snares nearby, she led them a ways into the darkening forest.

They followed her to a moonlit waterfall that crashed down into a shallow pool—the same one Rowan had seen in her vision—following her lead as she slid along the rock wall, slipping between the water and the stony hill it cascaded down. It was impossible to escape being sprayed by the water, and by the time they entered the cave, Rowan was thoroughly soaked again.

I thought I was done with being wet all the time, she thought grumpily. Celine quickly got a fire going, and Rowan was able to dry off and warm her cold hands while Celine cleaned the rabbits.

The opening of the cave was completely covered by the waterfall, and Rowan had expected the cave itself to be damp and humid. But Celine had set up her fire a good distance from the opening. There must also have been some kind of hole for ventilation, for the smoke streamed up and disappeared instead of building up inside the cave.

Sure enough, when Rowan asked, Celine pointed up with her dagger. "There are holes—or tunnels, I suppose—all over the roof of the cave, and a very cramped back exit over there." She indicated a stretch of rock that looked impenetrable to Rowan. "I swear it's there," she said in response to the look Rowan gave her. "But I don't recommend it; it's a tight squeeze."

Remembering how her sister panicked in enclosed spaces, Rowan grimaced and changed the subject.

"How long have you been here? When did you..." She broke off, unsure of how to ask her sister what had happened to her. She glanced at Keziah. He met her eyes and nodded his understanding.

"I'll fetch some water," he said, grabbing the water skins. Rowan watched him go gratefully—it would be easier for her to talk to her sister without an audience.

Celine hadn't answered her first question, but she seemed to be thinking about it.

Rowan unstrapped the axe from her leg and set it down between them, the handle toward Celine. She crouched beside her sister.

"We found your camp, and your other axe. Did me a lot of good against some imps."

Celine glanced at her axe but didn't reach for it.

"Keep it," she said abruptly, averting her eyes. "He did something to it. I don't want it anymore."

She reached up and touched the handle of her larger axe, which was still strapped to her back. "This one has done me just fine. Besides, you need something to protect yourself with." She smiled, but it failed to reach her eyes.

Rowan wondered if she had taken the axe off her back since she'd escaped Oak. "How did you get away from him?" she asked.

"I don't know. I mean," Celine said quickly, to clarify. "He kept me in a cell of saplings that grew back if I tried to cut them, but one day he left, and I put my hand on one, and they all started growing. They broke through the ceiling and I climbed out. But I don't know *how* that happened, or why. It was really as if..." She fumbled for the right words. "As if the trees did it to help me get out."

"They probably did," Rowan said. "They've been doing a great deal to help keep the Oak King from finding me."

"How did you know he had taken me? Surely the axe alone wasn't enough of a clue," Celine asked, perplexed.

"Keziah figured it out. He's... dealt with Oak before, knows what he's like."

Celine said nothing, only drew her knees in and rested her chin on them. She looked so small, so willowy, curled up like that. Rowan wanted to say more, say something of comfort, to let her sister know she was safe, but the words wouldn't come.

"We weakened him," she finally offered, hoping it would improve Celine's spirits a little, "enough for us to get you home safely.

Celine's head snapped up.

"Get *me* home? What about you?"

Rowan fumbled stupidly. She hadn't meant to put it that way, but in truth, the thought of leaving the forest filled her with more and more dread. How could she go back to the life she'd known before all this had happened? No, she was growing more certain by the minute that she was meant to be here, helping Keziah and Holly in their battle against the Oak King.

"I'll go home, for a little while. I just have some things I need to do after I make sure the younglings are all right."

"Things to do *here*?" Celine asked in disbelief.

Rowan nodded. "I want to help, if I can."

Celine stared at her for a moment, then shook her head.

"I'm not going home, not to mother and father. I'm going for Irys, and the two of us will leave at once."

She made no mention of the cabin, but Rowan knew they were both thinking of it.

"But what about the younglings? What if mother and father have been…" She didn't know what she was trying to say. What if her parents had been cruel to them in their absence? And surely, without Celine bringing in regular money, they would have sent Ademun to find work. She only hoped it wasn't as bad as she expected it to be.

"Grandmother's nearby—she always looks out for the younglings," Celine said, sounding less sure than she probably had hoped to.

"Grandmother can't do anything to actually help them. She couldn't help *us*," Rowan reminded her.

"I love the younglings, but I'm not their parent; I can't save them from mother and father," Celine said, her voice rising. "And I shouldn't have to."

"But we could take them away with us, away from the village." It was an echo of the conversation they'd had before Celine had left on her woodcutting trip, and Rowan knew even before she finished her sentence that it would do her no good with Celine.

"And live where? Here? Bring a herd of children into an enchanted forest with a man determined to kidnap and kill intruders? I'd rather not have that on my conscience, thanks very much," Celine said hotly.

Rowan stared at her.

"Celine, did he hurt you?"

"He didn't get the chance, thanks the gods." But her voice still shook as she spoke. "He did these... *tests,* to try and find out what magic I had and how it worked. He had this plan for extracting it from me—it sounded horrible. But fortunately, he had to leave and I was able to get away." She closed her eyes, hugging her knees in tight to her chest. "It was terrifying. Knowing he had these plans for me and there was nothing I could do to stop him."

Rowan wanted to reach out, to hug her sister, but Celine looked very much like she didn't want to be touched.

"I'm sorry I couldn't get to you sooner. Oak's a monster. Keziah says he's been doing this kind of thing for years. Celine, *that's* why I want to come back; someone needs to stop him," Rowan said vehemently.

Celine didn't say anything, but she opened her eyes and looked at the fire.

"I'll help you get back to Irys. You deserve to feel safe again," Rowan promised.

Celine snorted. "I don't think I'll ever feel completely safe again. But some distance would help," she acknowledged.

Still, she said nothing about Irys, nothing about what Rowan so obviously knew. Rowan's heart sank. This was supposed to have been a happy reunion, where Celine realized just how much her sister cared about her and finally decided to share what she had been hiding for so long. But clearly what Rowan had gone through to find her was not enough. It would never be enough.

Footsteps behind Rowan made her turn and look up. Keziah set down the two filled waterskins—the actual filling had probably only taken a few minutes, so he had most likely waited outside as long as he could before coming back, to give them time to speak to each other.

Rowan was grateful he'd returned now—Celine seemed to have nothing more to say to her.

"I can cook those rabbits, if you like," he offered to Celine, holding up a handful of herbs he had gathered.

Rowan caught a whiff of wild thyme and spring onion when he began to strip off the tiny leaves and tear the onions with his hands. Her stomach growled loudly. He rooted in his pack and pulled out a tiny parcel Rowan hadn't managed to find when she'd looked for food.

"Oh, good, there's still walnut bread left," he said, frowning at Rowan when she burst into laughter.

"What on earth is wrong with you?" Celine asked, just as puzzled.

"We just—oh, Holly and I just got so tired of it, we couldn't eat anymore," she explained. Seeing Celine's blank look, she realized she hadn't yet mentioned the time she'd spent with Holly.

Celine's look turned dark. "Holly?" she echoed, her tone implying she hoped Rowan wasn't referring to who she thought she was referring to.

"I guess I have a lot to tell you, too," Rowan said sheepishly. She'd forgotten that what she'd experienced, while certainly less traumatizing than being kept in a cell by an insane immortal forest god, might be worth mentioning.

"Tell us both," Keziah said, spitting the rabbits and suspending them over the fire on the iron rack. "There are a good many pieces to the story that I'm missing, too."

So she briefly went over the events that had first led her across Keziah's path before delving into her dealings with the King of Winter. She made a point of leaving out any mention of Keziah's past, including that Oak was his father. When she got to her narrow escape from the bone creature in the black lake, Keziah looked aghast. Celine only grew perplexed again.

"It was made of *bone*?" she asked, as though that was her only take-away from Rowan's brush with death, "How did it even stay put together? Without any muscle or meat, it should have been a soggy pile in the bottom of the lake."

"Well, it wasn't," Rowan snapped, disappointed that her chilling tale hadn't managed to impress her sister. She supposed it didn't show much valiance on her part; after all, the trees had had to rescue her.

"Anyway, I met the Bear Maiden, and then I found Keziah and that's when *you* found *us*—"

"And the two of you fought off Oak's tree-beasts like they were nothing," Keziah finished. "Quite a formidable pair of sisters, I must say."

Rowan flushed, pleased at the pride in his voice. "But I knew where you were—after I found Keziah, I was coming to find you. The power the Bear Maiden gave me let me see right where we needed to go—I saw *you*, here in this cave."

"Handy," Celine remarked, giving the rabbits another turn over the fire. "Don't suppose she also pointed out the fastest way home?"

"No, but I know where home is." She pointed, knowing which was west even in the dark of the cave. Celine shrugged, as though this was nothing new to her. Rowan realized she must have that same innate sense of direction that Rowan had. "That won't be a problem. The trees will help hide us."

Keziah began pulling the rabbits off the spits, laying them on a flat stone to carve off pieces.

"Don't count on that too much; he can amass quite a bit of strength from his groves. This is his season—he'll always have *some* power. Not like Holly."

He passed out chunks of tender rabbit meat, and they spent the next few minutes in silence, the three of them scarfing down the badly needed meal. After she finished, Rowan went and washed her face and hands in the water rushing over the cave entrance. When she came back, Celine was stretching out on the bare rock, her head laying on the small sack of supplies she'd had with her.

"What are you doing?" she asked her pointedly.

"I'm going to sleep," Celine said, rolling her eyes. "What does it look like I'm doing?"

Wordlessly, Rowan went to her pack and pulled out her bedroll. She unrolled it and pointed at it, daring her sister to refuse.

She could see the smallest hesitation cross Celine's face. Then she crawled over and lay down on the bedroll, pulling the blanket up over her shoulder.

"Thanks," she said gruffly.

"For what? It's one of yours. I don't even have one of my own," Rowan said loftily, taking Celine's place next to the fire. "Besides, you look like you haven't slept once since you left home, and if you've been sleeping on bare rock this whole time, it's no wonder. Good night."

"Good night," Celine mumbled, already sounding sleepy. A few seconds later, she was snoring faintly.

CHAPTER 41

Rowan

Rowan stirred the fire for a while, then looked up at Keziah in time to catch the smile playing around his lips.

"What?" she whispered, hoping she wasn't disturbing Celine.

He shrugged. "Siblings," he whispered back, nodding his head at Celine. "I can tell you missed each other."

She rolled her eyes and poked at the fire unnecessarily. "Of course I missed her. My earliest memory is of her dangling a toy bunny into my crib. I *adored* her as a child."

Keziah only chuckled and didn't say anything.

Rowan prodded at some coals until her stirring stick started burning, and she had to take it out and whack it on the stones to put out the tiny fire. Then she sighed.

"She needs to get out of this forest," she whispered, glancing at Celine. She seemed fast asleep.

Keziah nodded. "And what about you?"

Rowan looked at the water rushing over the cave entrance. She missed the younglings badly. More than anything else, she wanted to know that her absence hadn't made life worse for them. It wasn't that she thought they'd go hungry or lose their home; she was worried their parents would start treating them the way they treated Celine and

Rowan. They didn't deserve that. But she had such a certainty in her stomach; her work in the forest was not done, not with the power of Autumn whirring beneath her skin. Again, the image of Holly and the terror that filled his face seared through her mind—she needed to make amends for what had happened to him because of her. Oak would never have found them if Sphagnum hadn't found her. She hadn't meant to give away where Holly was, but that didn't make what had happened any better.

"I don't know. I don't want to go back—to my parents, I mean. But Ademun and Kestrel and Danica... I need to make sure they're all right. What will you do?" she asked hesitantly. He might not even know yet himself.

But obviously he had been thinking of the same things she had. He squared his shoulders, his thoughts on the future.

"Soon Oak will realize he can leave the Forest again." He spoke quietly, gazing into the fire, but his eyes glimmered with purpose. "And my debt to the Bear Maiden is fulfilled. I swore to serve her as long as Oak was bound to the forest, and technically I've done that. Though I can't say I feel good about it. I'd like to go home, if I can," he confessed, the longing deepening in his voice, "see if it's still how I remember it. See if I fit there anymore, or if this place has changed me too much. And see my mother. I have a great deal to apologize for."

What could Rowan say to that? The thought of Keziah leaving the Forest, leaving the *country*, made her deeply sad, but Rowan couldn't fault him for it.

And I've only been gone for a matter of days, not years, she thought bitterly.

"Though I do worry about leaving while Holly is so vulnerable," Keziah added with a sigh. "Hopefully you bought him enough time to fortify himself against Oak's next attack."

Rowan's brow furrowed. "How did he cast Winter all these years, if he's been on the run from Oak nearly every waking minute?"

Keziah shrugged. "His people always helped him bring on the seasons—Wither, Frost, Decay, and the others. They can make the plants go dormant and call down the right kinds of weather. But they aren't strong enough to fight Oak. The lot of them went into hiding when Holly fell. Oak does get bored of the chase sometimes. He works on his 'experiments' or tests the boundaries of the forest. I think when that happens, Holly builds up a little strength and uses it to help his season along. That would explain why Oak finds him so easily in Spring—he's got no reserves left."

Speaking of Holly and his plight made Rowan feel deeply sad. She hugged her knees to her chest, clenching her hands together around them.

"I wish there was something I could do," she said finally. "He doesn't deserve to live like this, year after year."

"You have done something already, Rowan," Keziah pointed out. "You gave him time to rest, time with one of his trees. You kept Oak from... from getting to him again, and he got back home because of it. Now he'll have months to recover before Winter. That might be all he needs to keep Oak from driving him out again."

But Rowan shook her head.

"You didn't see his face, when Oak was talking to him. *Taunting* him, telling him he was going to do it again and there was nothing he could do to stop him. As long as he lives, Oak won't stop trying to hurt him in some way. And he doesn't even have to *be* there to hurt him. Any time Holly thought of him, any time something even reminded him of what happened, he shut down. I don't think he'll ever get better if there's always the chance Oak is going to come for him."

Keziah didn't say anything for a long time. He ran a hand over his face, pushing his hair out of his eyes. There was dirt smudged across his cheeks. He needed a bath. They all desperately needed a bath, but unless they were willing to freeze under the waterfall, the best they could do was splash cold water over themselves and wait.

"I'll see what I can do for him," he said finally, looking upset that that was all he could offer. "I've kept Oak off his trail a handful of times, but it's hard because Oak can't trace me the way he traces mortals, and if I don't leave a convincing enough trail, he loses interest. This was the first time he's caught me, since I made my wish." He smiled ruefully. "I'm shocked at how little he's changed."

An immortal boy, speaking of his hateful immortal father, discussing ways to help the immortal King of Winter keep his enemy from hurting him again. *Not much like any fairy tale I've ever heard of before*, she thought as Keziah lay back in his own bedroll. He hadn't closed his eyes yet, and she watched him lying there, staring up at the shadows cast over the cave ceiling by the fire.

A thought occurred to her.

"Didn't you see Holly? After... after it happened?" she asked.

He shook his head without looking at her.

"Not for more than a moment. I should have gone to see him. I know I should have. But... It was my fault. All of it happened because he helped me, with something so entirely selfish. No, it was selfish," he said when Rowan made a noise of dissent, "and it cost Holly nearly everything. I didn't think he'd want to see me. He still probably doesn't want to. But I should have gone anyway. By the time I *was* ready to see him, Oak had learned he was still alive and had started after him."

"I think he would like to see you," Rowan said gently. "He talked about you—he was relieved to hear you were still alive. Truly, Oak is the only person to blame for what happened to both of you."

Another question was bothering her.

"Won't Oak just go to the mountains to get to Holly?"

Keziah shook his head. "Even before they bound him to the forest, the mountains were dangerous for Oak. Everything there hates him. That doesn't stop him from sending Narra after Holly, of course, but she does far less damage than he could do. She is, unfortunately, very good at driving Holly out of the mountains and back into the Forest."

"It almost seems like Holly should just leave, get away from Oak once and for all," Rowan muttered.

Keziah sat up, leaning his elbows on his bent knees. "He could never do that. Holly couldn't leave here even if he was strong enough. This place *is* him. He's too closely tied to the magic, animals, the plants, the land. It would pull him back eventually, just as it pulled Oak."

Rowan studied him for a moment, thinking about what the Bear Maiden had told her about Oak and Holly losing their powers someday.

"What about you?" she asked. "Will it pull you back, too?"

Keziah's face flickered, unreadable.

"I don't think so. After all, I have another kind of magic from a completely different place, and I only inherited Oak's power. No one charged me with ruling over the forest. The only thing binding me here was my debt to the Bear Maiden, and now that Oak is free to leave… so am I."

Rowan hadn't thought of it that way.

Keziah gave the fire a final stir, then turned and lay down on his side, his face turned to the shadows.

"Should one of us keep watch?" Rowan asked, oddly chilled despite the fire.

"You and I will both wake up, if anything comes near us. Try to get some sleep, Rowan."

Well, I suppose that's that. Rowan wished they could have stayed up longer talking. There were things she wanted to say to Keziah—things she might not even have the courage to actually say—but the past few days seemed to have taken a severe toll on him.

Rowan leaned against her pack and dozed through the night, jerking awake from time to time and adding more wood to the fire when it burned low.

The next morning, they broke their fast on cold rabbit, the last of the dreaded walnut bread, and some dried fruit. Keziah shook his head at Rowan as she passed over her piece of bread.

"I don't think any of us are in a position to waste food," he chided her, wrapping the piece back up in cloth.

"I'm not *wasting* it; I just can't face eating it yet." Rowan was much more excited about coffee. Keziah made enough for all three of them to have two cups, and even Celine looked brightened at the prospect of drinking hot coffee for the first time in weeks.

She took a sip and a dreamy look went over her face. "Oh, I have missed this," she muttered into her cup, savoring the hot brew.

"We can stop by my cabin on our way to Gramylka," Keziah said as he packed away his little grinder and the almost empty bag of coffee beans, "We can resupply the packs and maybe even wash up. I haven't managed to add to my stores yet this Spring, but I'm due for a purchase in your village, so I can restock there."

Rowan looked guiltily into her coffee cup. Keziah had already used up a great amount of his own supplies *and* his time, thanks to her, and he would have fewer pelts to sell and less time to make up for it now. But he didn't seem bothered by it. He whistled as he packed up his bedroll and helped Rowan put away the cooking things. She realized he must have been happy to be on the move again, headed home.

They left the cave soon after breakfast, with Rowan and Keziah keeping their ears and eyes peeled for any sound of a patrol approaching. Celine and Rowan both carried their axes at the ready, while Keziah kept his hands free. She heard Celine offer the use of her hunting knife and Keziah's polite refusal.

Rowan wondered if Celine would believe that Keziah could shoot fire from his fingertips.

When they started out, they came across a path of moss or a ring of white mushrooms nearly every minute. Whenever they caught sight of one or the other, they quietly skirted it, not speaking until it was out of sight. A few times, they hid in the trees as a winged stag or a herd of giant spindlebugs—spiderlike creatures with minuscule bodies and disturbingly long legs--stalked by. But the further west they moved, the sparser Oak's sentinels became.

It took them three days to reach Keziah's cabin. As soon as he opened the door, Keziah went and pulled a squat tub from a closet. He set water to heat on the stove, pointed out where the soap and wash rags were, and left. "You two can fight over who gets the first bath; just let me know when you're both done so I can come take one. Clothes are in that chest over there."

Then he went outside to check his garden, which looked horribly overgrown with weeds and vegetables alike.

Rowan waved Celine toward the bath. "I had one more recently than you did, and I've had clean clothes to change into, too. Go ahead."

She laid out a fresh change of clothes for Celine and another for herself. Then she brewed a pot of tea on the stove, using herbs from the labeled jars on a shelf lining the kitchen wall. She hoped Keziah wouldn't mind. She left a mug on the kitchen counter for Celine, then went outside holding two mugs, one for her, one for Keziah.

CHAPTER 42

Rowan

Rowan found him hacking at brambles that had wrapped themselves up the trunk of a young apple tree.

"I swear these blackberries *knew* I was gone," he said, huffing and puffing. Then he saw the mug in Rowan's extended hand. "Oh. Thank you." He set down the knife he'd been using and took the mug from her, inhaling the scent of the tea with a peaceful look on his face. He sat down on a wide stump at the edge of the garden and waved for Rowan to sit next to him.

"You know, I can't remember the last time someone else made me a cup of tea," he said, looking down into his cup as he swirled it.

"Really? No one in town has invited you to supper?" Rowan was surprised. Trappers and hunters, especially good ones, were usually welcome guests at any household. And a young, handsome one like Keziah would surely appeal to any number of parents as a suitable guest to dine beside their unwed daughters.

He grinned and shook his head. "I'd be lying if I said I hadn't gotten any invitations, but I thought it best if folk don't get to know me too well. I cycle through the villages every few years, so they don't get suspicious about who I am. I spend a few months trading and selling my furs at one market, then move on to another. I *have* made the acquaintance of a village girl or two in that time," he said with a devious grin at

Rowan. "But that's usually at the tavern, where no one will remember me the next day."

Rowan tried to imagine Keziah leering at the village girls in the pub the way the Gramylka men leered at her, but she just couldn't picture it. It didn't seem to be his style. Still, her heart fell a little at the thought of him flirting with other village girls. She'd had it in her head that he stayed away from other people, isolated in the forest. But of course that wasn't true.

Keziah held out a closed hand to her.

"Here," he said, dropping something small and warm into her palm. "I may not be an expert on the powers of Autumn, but I can teach you how to use them at least a little."

Rowan looked at her palm. There sat a red, wizened berry.

"Hawthorn," she and Keziah said at the same time. She flushed.

"Try to think about its seeds," Keziah told her. "Try to sense the life within it, just as you do with the full-grown trees that you've commanded."

Rowan stared hard at the dry old berry. When that didn't seem to work, she closed her eyes, listening, *reaching* for something akin to the buzzing she felt in the woods around her.

And there it was, faint but present, in her own palm.

"Very good," Keziah murmured. "Now, tell it to grow."

Rowan's brow wrinkled.

"Tell it that it has everything it needs—from you. From your magic."

You have all you need.

She sent out that intention, and to her surprise, the berry in her palm shifted. Her eyes flew open. A little leaf burst from the berry, and tiny tendrils of roots spread from its base. As Rowan watched, the leaf stretched even higher, and the roots sprawled across her palm, reaching for the ground.

"But that's incredible!" she gasped.

Keziah grinned. "It is. You're a quick learner, Rowan. Much faster than I was."

She flushed again. "Well, it helps to have such an excellent teacher."

She bent down and dug a little hole beside the stump, nestling the sprouted berry in the dirt. She covered the roots with dirt and left the little leaves free, hoping it would get enough sunlight here at the edge of the garden.

Keziah seemed to be thinking about something. Rowan gently bumped his shoulder with her own. "What's on your mind?"

"Rowan," he began, his voice soft, "I hope you know you've been incredibly brave. I didn't want you getting mixed up in all of this, but it turns out you've managed to turn the tide. The Bear Maiden and I have been waiting for years, hoping to find something that will help diminish Oak's powers, but he keeps finding little ways to grow stronger. Then suddenly you show up and stop him in his tracks." He shook his head, setting his cup down on the stump beside him. "What I'm trying to say, Rowan, is thank you."

The lump in Rowan's throat made speaking very difficult.

"Most of that thanks is due to you, Keziah. I certainly wouldn't have done anything at all if it hadn't been for you. No." She held up a hand as he started to protest. "Let's not go back and forth saying who matters more. We helped each other, and that's that." She slipped her hand into his and gave it a squeeze. A bemused grin spread across his face, and he squeezed back.

They fell silent and sat there looking at his garden, drinking their tea and breathing in the scent of the apple blossoms, until Celine called from the front door of the cottage. Keziah jerked his head at the cabin.

"Go on—you finally get the bath I promised you. And come show me your hair afterward—I can't really remember what color it was when I first met you."

Rowan made a face at him and took his empty mug inside with her. She helped Celine dump the tub outside. Then she went and boiled fresh water before stripping off her filthy clothing and sinking into the bath. Celine, dressed in a fresh pair of Keziah's trousers and one of his shirts, sat on the edge of the trundle bed and chatted with Rowan as she washed.

Celine started telling her about the cabin she had built in the *las graniczny*, how she'd gotten the materials and the furniture. Little by little, without directly acknowledging it, Celine began to talk about Irys, too. Rowan found she was enjoying envisioning the home her sister was creating for herself and her wife-to-be.

"Are you going to have a ceremony?" she asked tentatively, wringing out her hair after a final rinse. "Once you move in, I mean?"

Celine nodded. "Just a small one between the two of us, since we can't invite the family."

"Could I come? I'll make you bread, or maybe a cake, if I can get ahold of the ingredients."

Celine stared at her. She looked shocked.

"What? Did you really think I'd miss your wedding?" Rowan tried to sound joking, though there was a tightness in her throat. "The younglings would love to come, too—they'd fill up your house with willow boughs and lilacs. But it would be hard to get them away without mother and father knowing." She sighed.

"Maybe someday," was all Celine would say. Rowan thought her eyes looked a little red and watery, but she didn't comment on it. Maybe she was just thinking about how much she missed Irys and wanted to get back.

Rowan dressed in another of Keziah's shirt and another pair of his trousers.

"I really ought to sew him some replacements—the trousers I was wearing earlier are full of holes, and that shirt is stained beyond belief," she told Celine, who only gave her a pointed look and said nothing.

"What?" Rowan asked defensively. "He's done so much for both of us, and gods know he didn't have to."

"Oh, of course. And will you have him come in for a fitting?" Celine asked with a knowing smirk. "Just so you get to spend some time together while he's not quite dressed?"

Rowan turned beet red and spluttered at her sister. "It's not like that at all!" she insisted, knowing full well that it very much was like that.

"Of course it's not," Celine said sweetly, though her eyes glinted with mischief. "Why don't you call him for his bath?"

Rowan didn't like her feelings being found out by other people—it made her worry that Keziah, too, might have noticed how she felt, and *that* put her in a foul mood. She dumped the tub just outside the door and set more water to boil. Then she tugged Celine out the door with her and told Keziah the bath was his.

She and her sister walked through the garden, which was possible now that Keziah had pulled up or cut away many of the brambles that had grown over the path. There were many peas growing up shoots against the fence. Though it was very early for peas, they looked ripe, so Rowan and Celine picked as many as they could find, storing them in the excess cloth of their shirts. Rowan pulled up a few weeds, tossing them into the forest.

"So. He lives *here*, in the middle of the forest?" Celine asked, gesturing to the cabin behind them.

"He built it all himself, and he trades in nearly all the villages along the Border," Rowan explained, wary of telling Celine too much about Keziah.

Celine looked displeased. "How does he get away with it? Surely patrols and the like would have come across this place at some point."

Rowan shifted guiltily. "Oak can't trace him, just like he can't find us."

"But *why*?" Celine wasn't going to let it drop. "Why can't he find him? And why can't he find us?"

Her eyes narrowed as she surveyed her sister. "You met with the Bear Maiden herself. I find it hard to believe you didn't get any answers from her."

Rowan fiddled with the hem of Keziah's shirt. "Grandmother," she said finally. "She told me that Grandmother is descended from her—from one of her cubs, that is. She didn't say how it worked," she said. It wasn't the whole story. She was quite intentionally *not* telling Celine that Keziah was the Oak King's son and that a good many in the forest considered him Oak's heir. She had the feeling Celine would *not* be comfortable keeping company with the Oak King's son, no matter how much Keziah hated his father. So she said nothing about Keziah, hoping her sister would draw some other conclusion about him.

Celine kicked at a clump of dirt. "I've done things I shouldn't have been able to do," she muttered, "things that don't just *happen* on their own. I suppose it would all make sense, if I have the Bear Maiden's blood. That would explain why the trees helped me, at least."

"I think," Rowan said tentatively, "that the trees are tired of Oak. They may be trying to help stop him."

Rowan expected Celine to tell her that trees couldn't feel tired of people or want to help anyone, but to her surprise, her sister shrugged and nodded.

"Maybe so. But it's like something out of one of Grandmother's stories—when I needed to escape the cell, all I did was hold the tree and wish for something to help me, and then it happened. I guess all I'm saying is..." She gave up trying to put words to her thoughts and ended up shaking her head. "I just don't understand it."

Keziah called them into the cabin for lunch, and they ate dried meat, cheese, bitter spring greens, and fresh strawberries from his garden. It was no great feast, but to Rowan it all tasted wonderful.

When they finished eating, they sat before the fireplace—unlit, as it was Summer—and talked of what they would do next.

"We could stay here a night or two, and rest up," Keziah offered, "or we could leave now, once we pack."

Rowan looked to Celine for an answer. She was the main reason they were going back at all, and she knew how eager Celine was to get Irys out of the village and go to her new home.

"In the morning," she said finally, after a few moments' thought. "I'm dead-tired after three days of trekking through this forest, and I could use a good night's sleep before going the rest of the way."

Relief spilled over Rowan. She hadn't realized how apprehensive she was about seeing home again. And she didn't want to say goodbye to Keziah yet. She had the awful feeling that, once they parted ways, she would never see him again, and even though she had no expectations of anything happening between them, she just wasn't ready to say goodbye.

She liked his cabin, too; homely but comfortable.

It's a nice place, well cared for, she thought, but that wasn't the only reason she liked it. The place was wholly Keziah, with everything he had lived with and used for the last five years. She could see his hand in the stitches on the blanket over the back of the chair, the handmade chest at the foot of the bed, the carefully labeled jars and pots of herbs and medicines lining the little shelves tacked up above the stove. He had done all of it himself, too, with no one to help or inform him. She wondered, not for the first time, if his life had been lonely here, or if, from time to time, he'd had visitors or friends from the forest.

Then she remembered what he'd said about spending time with village girls in the pub, and she flushed. Clearly he wasn't hard up for company, when he wanted it. She was silly for thinking he needed *her* to keep from feeling lonely; he could seek out other people whenever he liked.

Keziah nudged her with his foot and she jerked back to the conversation, realizing she'd been asked something.

"Where were you? You looked all sad for a moment there," he said with some concern.

"Just thinking," she said, mortified that she'd been sad thinking of *him,* and that he'd noticed.

"I asked if you were sure you wanted to go home," Celine repeated. "Mother and father will probably be very angry, especially since, for all they know, you came home without me after weeks of looking."

Rowan sighed. "I need to make sure the younglings are all right. That's all I really care about."

"But what about after? Once you know they're all right and mother and father have locked you up in your room as punishment, what then?" Celine looked truly worried about it, too.

Why do you care? You're leaving all of us anyway, Rowan wanted to say, but she didn't. Celine caring about what happened to her was new, and she appreciated it.

"I don't know," she admitted. "I don't really want to *stay,* but if they do lock me up..." She rubbed her face with her hands. All she wanted to do was see her little brother and sisters. She didn't even feel guilty about not wanting to see her parents—the memory of her last argument with her mother, her mother striking Celine in the face, her father sternly ordering her not to defy her mother—those were all so fresh in her mind still.

Celine was clearly thinking of it, too. But though her face was troubled, all she said was, "It will be all right," sounding very much as though she *didn't* think it would be all right.

The three of them spent the evening playing a game with dice before the fire in Keziah's cabin. Full of peas and strawberries from the garden and fish stewed with spring onions, Rowan felt as close to normal as she had in a long time. *Which is odd, because* this *isn't normal,* she thought, glancing at Keziah as he crowed for rolling higher than her.

She knew what her parents would think of her keeping company with a man she wasn't married to, even though she'd only done it to find Celine. But she didn't care if they knew or not. More likely, if they found out, it would besmirch her marriageability in their eyes and they would rush to find her a forgiving suitor. It didn't matter anyway because she didn't intend to tell them much about her time in the forest.

Rowan

The next morning came far too soon, and after breakfast, Rowan found herself looking back at the little cabin with its tangle of a garden as they set off through the trees, following the same way she had come months ago. She half hoped something would jump at them from behind the trees and prolong their stay—foolishly, she knew; it wouldn't be good for any of them to get hurt—but nothing scathed them.

Keziah also noticed that they were passing through the forest without anything coming to meet them. He kept frowning and looking around them, as though expecting to see something.

"It's too *quiet* for this time of year," he murmured to Rowan, his voice troubled.

"Is that a bad thing?" she asked, wondering if he always got attacked by something when he went out by himself.

"It's just not normal. Even the birds are staying fairly quiet."

And the impish little redcaps were all tucked away, only poking out their heads to see who was passing. They saw no deer, no rabbits—none of the forest creatures she would have expected to see out on a day like this.

And that troubled Keziah.

"Creatures only hole up like this when they know danger is afoot. I don't like it."

Nevertheless, they reached the *las graniczny* without interruption. Keziah crossed the Border with them, saying, "I'll walk you as far as your house, Rowan," after Celine told them she intended to break off and go to Irys's.

Rowan was half grateful, half mortified as she waved goodbye to her grinning sister, promising she would come visit soon. She was being so silly—she'd been alone with Keziah so many times, but never with all the *awareness* of how she felt about him dancing around her head. Worse still, she thought she might cry as they went up the little hill with the holly tree she had gathered from late last year, which was always the marker that told her home wasn't too far away.

They walked quietly, neither of them finding anything to say. Rowan pointed out the red of her family's barn peeping through the trees, trying to sound at least a little bit happy about it, though her stomach was turning over itself in a truly terrible way.

They came to a stop. She looked up at Keziah, wondering what on earth she could say, how she could tell him she wanted to come see him again. But there was no way to say it, not without sounding like a dithering idiot, bent on rushing through an enchanted forest after some boy.

"Thank you," she said finally, thinking that at least she could sound sane saying that. "For everything."

"Even the walnut bread?" he asked, raising his eyebrows.

"Especially the walnut bread," she laughed, glad he had alleviated the awkwardness.

"Thank *you*," he said, reaching out and squeezing her hand. "For saving my life, and Holly's life."

"*You* wouldn't have been in any danger if it hadn't been for me, and I think it undid all the help I gave Holly when Oak found him again," Rowan said, unable to help herself. She couldn't stop thinking about it —Keziah could have escaped capture if he hadn't been out traveling with her when the fire started, and Holly... Well, she should have known better than to speak to Sphagnum. She should have kept her eyes peeled for the moss patches. Holly could have recovered so much more.

"I *would* have been in danger aplenty, because as soon as Oak attacked Holly, I would have been out there doing the exact same thing, only with no Rowan to save my skin," he said, very seriously. "And the only reason Holly is safe now is because of you. He's stronger now that he's had a chance to commune with one of his trees. Don't forget that."

Rowan didn't trust herself to speak without her voice quavering, and so she only nodded.

Keziah looked as though he had something more to say, and hope pricked in Rowan's stomach as he looked down at her, his face looking as though he was trying to work up what to say. But he closed his mouth, obviously deciding against it.

Instead, he pulled her close to him and pressed his lips gently to hers.

Rowan was so surprised that she didn't even have time to move before he released her.

"Don't let those parents of yours be mean to you," he said softly, his face so close to hers that his hair brushed her cheek. "You've got magic of your own—remember that."

He pressed something into her hand; she looked down and saw the hilt of his dagger sitting in her palm. And he stepped back, waiting for her to walk away.

And walk away she did. Every bit of her knew that this was not what she wanted to do. All she wanted was to walk back with Keziah to his cabin and sleep in the trundle bed and help him tend his garden. But there had been no talk of that, so it wasn't an option. She did look back, because of course she did, and Keziah was still standing there at the top of the little hill. She raised her hand and waved to him, and he waved back. Then she made herself turn and keep going. She tucked the dagger into her belt. Now the tears flowed down her face, with no one to see them. She didn't know what she would do with the way she felt about him. But there wasn't anything she could do at the moment.

Rowan gazed up at the trees swaying gently with the warm Spring breeze. Keziah was somewhere behind her, walking alone along the path leading back to his cabin. She hoped she'd see it again soon—in Summer when his garden flourished, in Autumn, when the quaking aspens had turned brilliant yellow and cascaded their leaves over the roof of his home. She looked back over her shoulder again, hoping she might still be able to see him walking back through the forest, but all she saw was the mountains looming dark over the new Spring green. Holly was up there, somewhere, still tormented with nightmares about Oak.

She'd see him again, too, she hoped. But her family needed taking care of first.

Acknowledgments

It takes a village to raise a child, and it takes a community to write a book. I know I could never in a million years thank each specific person who helped contribute to the creation of this book in some way, but gosh darn it, I'm gonna try!

First and foremost, I would like to thank Meagan Friedman and Quills and Cosmos Press for believing in this book and giving it a home. Under your guidance, the story has grown so strong. This press truly is the perfect place for Rowan, Celine, and Keziah's story.

Next, I'd like to thank each and every person who ever laid eyes on any of the drafts of Beyond the Border Forest or its query package and offered their feedback. A HUGE thank-you to Caitlin, Molly R., Yaba, Sam, Emily O., Jennifer, and everyone else who suggested edits and/or advice.

I'd also like to thank the family members who took the time to read the manuscript and provide edits—Mom, Dad, Ethan, Krystyna, and Emily (I can't wait for YOUR book to be published, too!).

And thank you to Audrey, Robin, Nick, Kala, Beka, and all the other the friends and family who cheered me on and celebrated with me every step of the way.

A special thank-you to Jeni Chapelle from RevPit—your #10queries feedback helped me rework the manuscript into the version that got me my book deal.

To the writing professors at Whitworth University—I didn't know what I was doing or where I was going at the time, but you helped me learn to love writing again after academia and burnout had destroyed my confidence. Eternal gratitude to Laurie, Vic, Thom, and Nicole for everything you taught me.

And thanks to every teacher who saw potential in my writing and encouraged me. I'm sorry for reading under my desk during class time, but if I could do it over again, I wouldn't change a thing.

A GIANT thank-you to the bookstagram community. Thank you for cheering for my book and for being such a welcoming, positive group of friends. Special thanks to Jess, Jasmine, Krista, Emily B., Tri, Mana, Angela, Madi, Hannah, Meli, Rae, Leah, and Lauren. And to the author community on Threads and Instagram—you helped demystify publishing and the query trenches for this AuDHDer. Thank you for your support and your friendship. Special shoutouts to G.W. Prouse, Arlo Z. Graves, and Sarah Goehrke.

Another thank-you to my parents and my grandparents for instilling in me a love of books and words. You are the reason I fell in love with reading to begin with.

Billy—you were my first reader. You were the one who made me believe I hadn't just vomited a bunch of fairytale nonsense into a word document. You gave the first—and frankly, best—feedback, and you made sure I had time to write between parenting and work. You let me babble about writing, work through plot points, and spout nonsense about social media and querying, even though it's not your wheelhouse. Thank you for supporting and encouraging me. I never could have finished the book without your help.

And Alva. You may not have read the book yet, or even been aware that it existed, but I only became a writer after I became your mom. You became the center of my world and taught me who I am. You are already the most incredible main character in your own story, and I can't wait to see where your story takes you.

About the Author

Molly Haniszewski is a queer, non-binary person with ADHD and autism. She is an avid baker who loves to forage for ingredients in the mountains near her home. Hiking and camping trips offer her lots of opportunities to identify wildflowers and teach her daughter about the natural world. She has a bachelor's degree in creative writing from Whitworth University. She has had poetry and creative nonfiction published in Montana Woman Magazine, Into the Beautiful: Daring, and several other literary journals and magazines.

Find Molly online at www.mollyhaniszewski.com.

instagram.com/into_the_bookish_wild

threads.com/@molly_should_be_writing

bsky.app/profile/mollyhaniszewski.bsky.social

Content Warnings

Queerphobia
Transphobia
Child abuse (emotional & light physical of adult child)
Fantasy violence

* * *

AUTHOR'S NOTE

In chapter 14, a character is compared to an owl. I recognize that owls can be a distressing symbol for people of certain cultures. The inclusion of an owl here is not meant to be part of any specific belief system or real-world culture; it is simply meant to evoke forest imagery. Owls have many different meanings in different cultures. Out of respect, I want to ensure that people who may find their mention alarming are forewarned about their inclusion in this book.
-Molly Haniszewski